IN MEMORY OF SHARON REED DAYTON, A HOLY MAN.

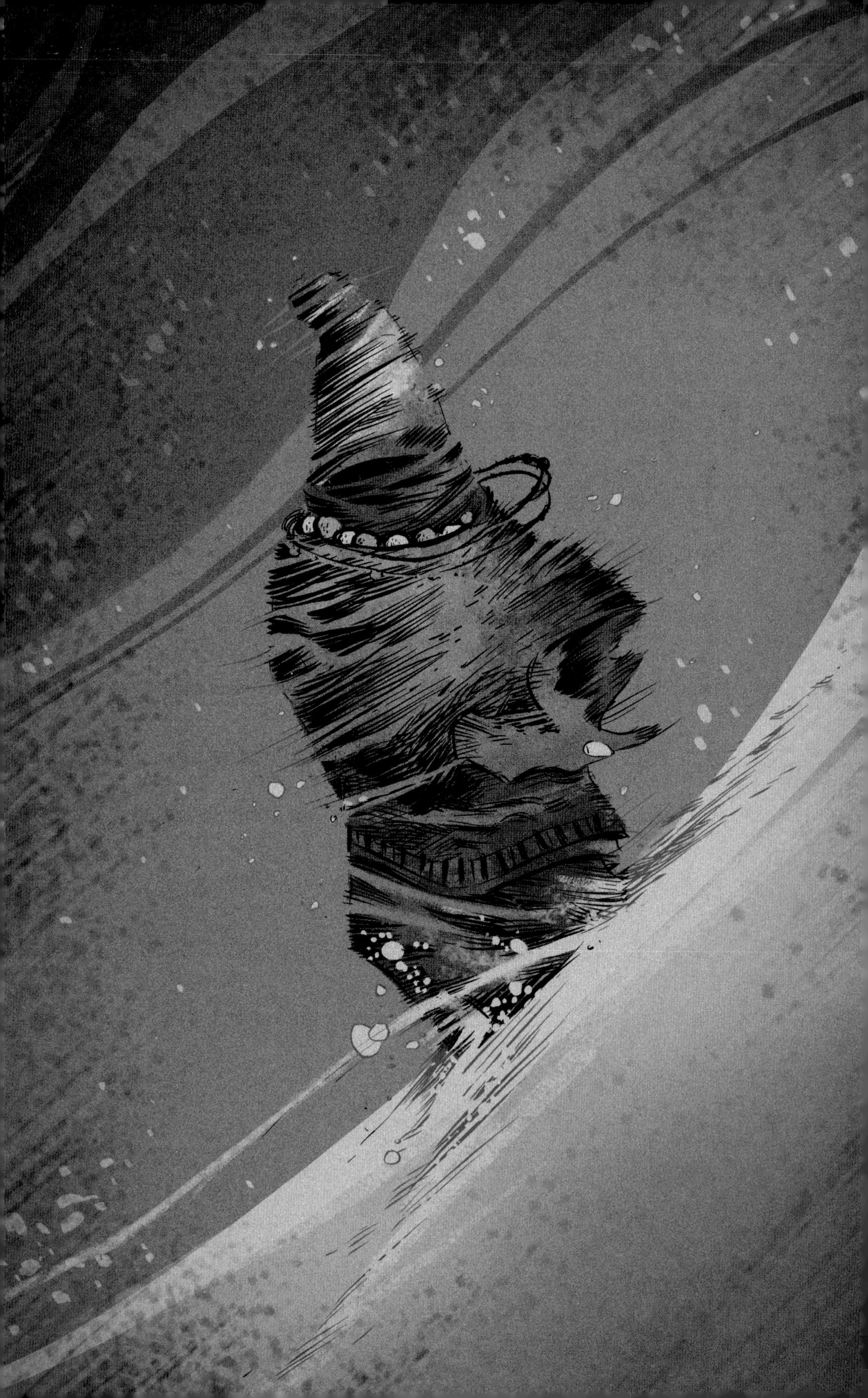

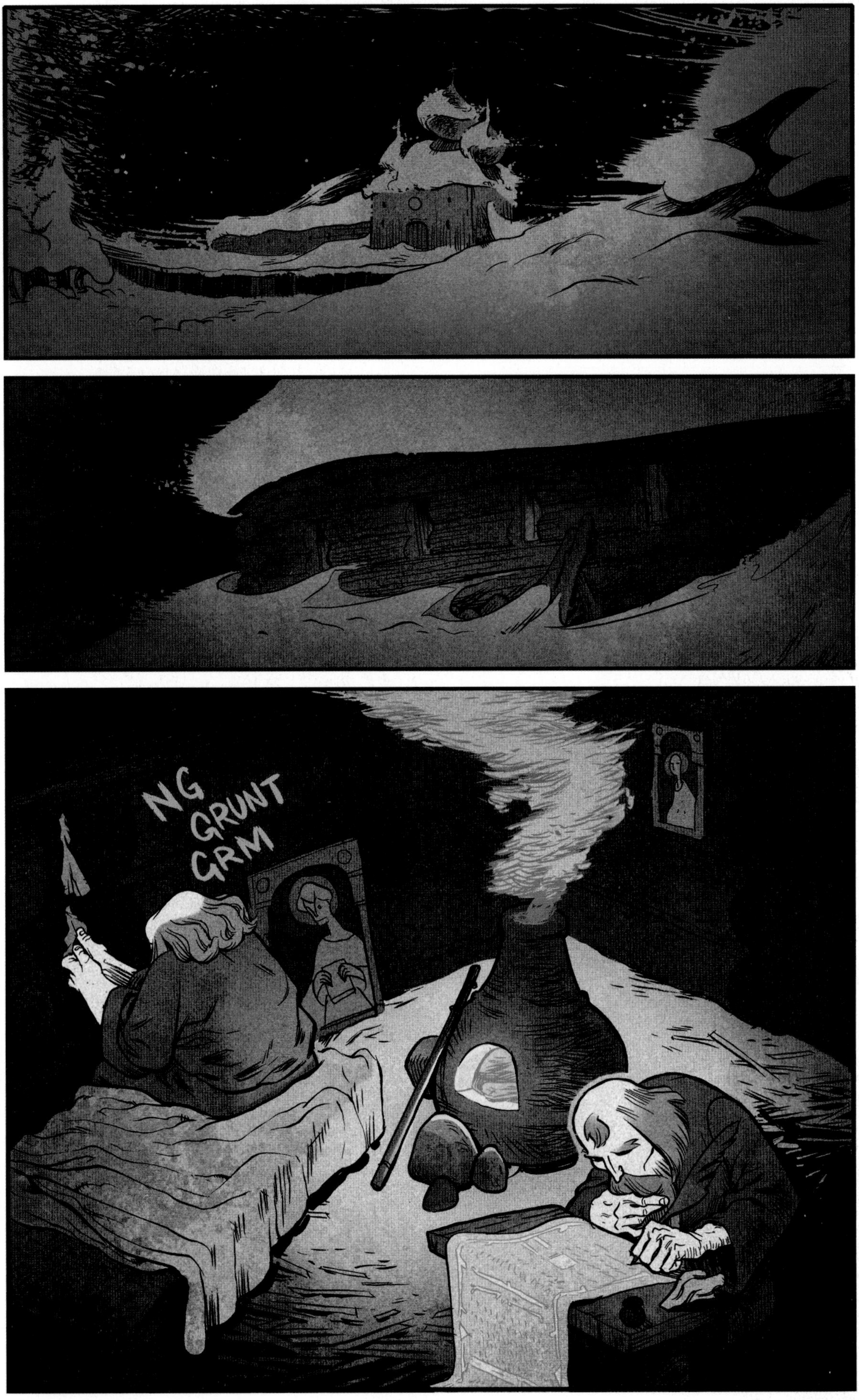
NG
GRUNT
GRM

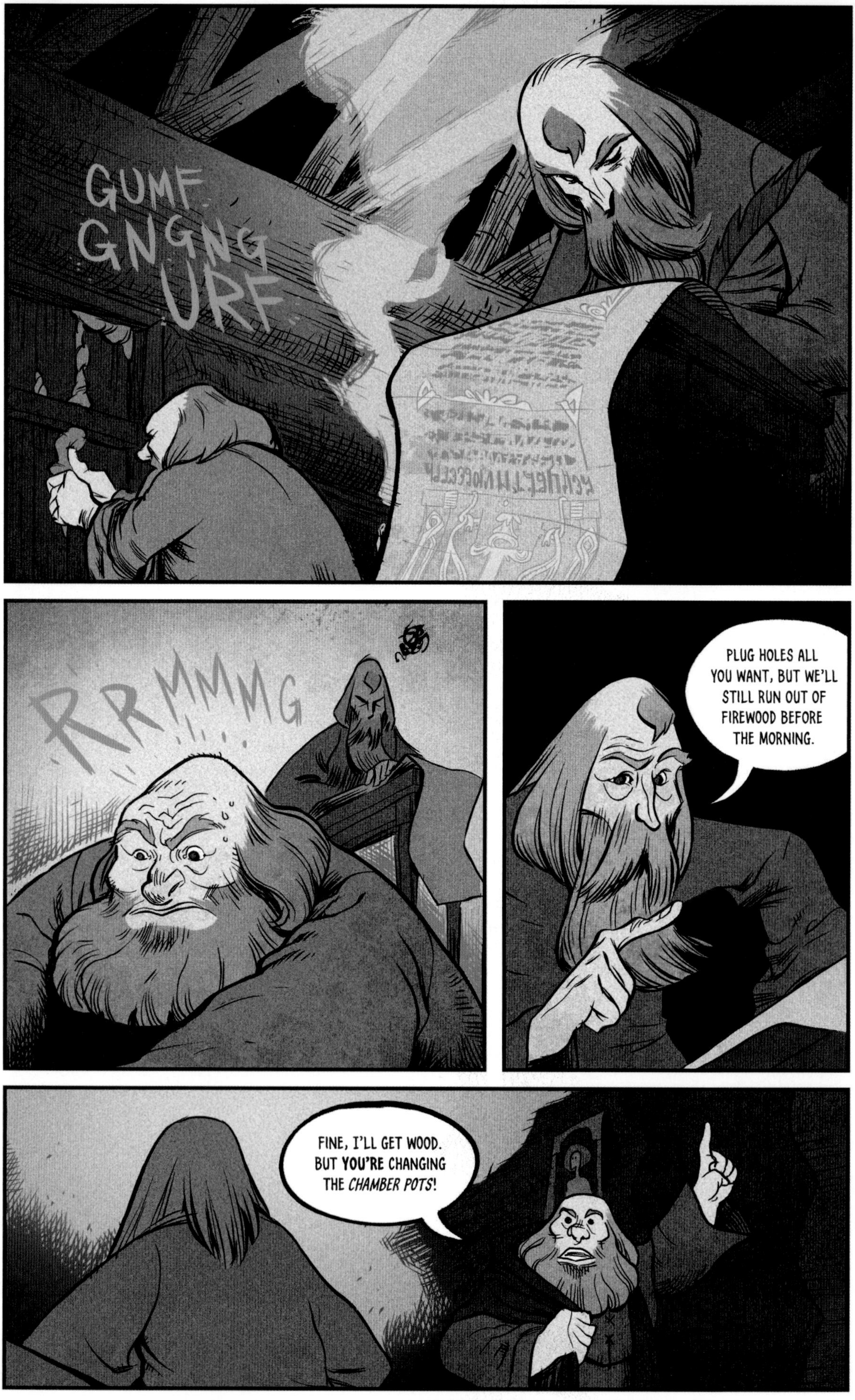
GUMF GNGNG URF
RRMMMG
PLUG HOLES ALL YOU WANT, BUT WE'LL STILL RUN OUT OF FIREWOOD BEFORE THE MORNING.
FINE, I'LL GET WOOD. BUT **YOU'RE** CHANGING THE *CHAMBER POTS*!

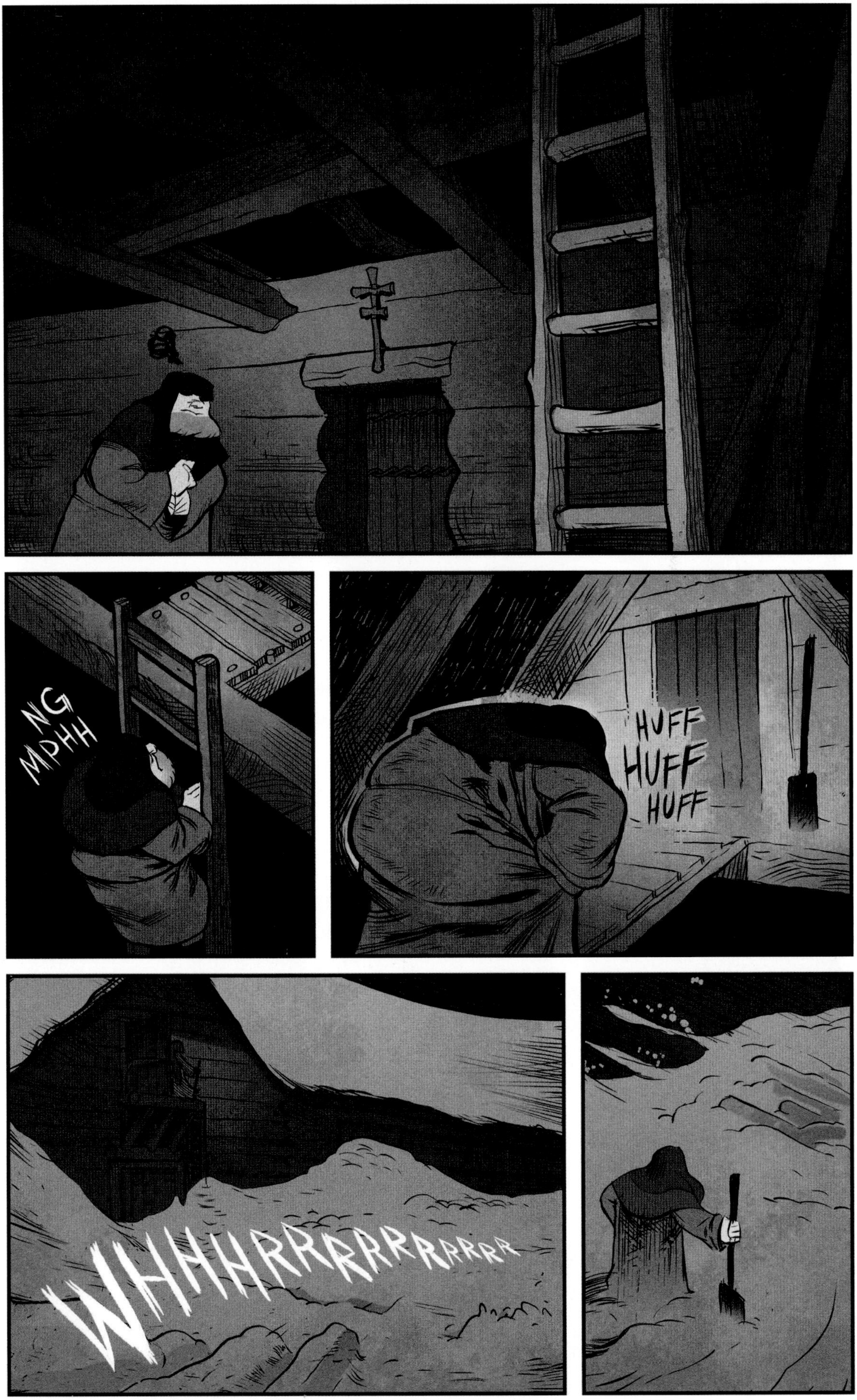
NG MPHH
HUFF
HUFF
HUFF
WHHHRRRRRRRRRR

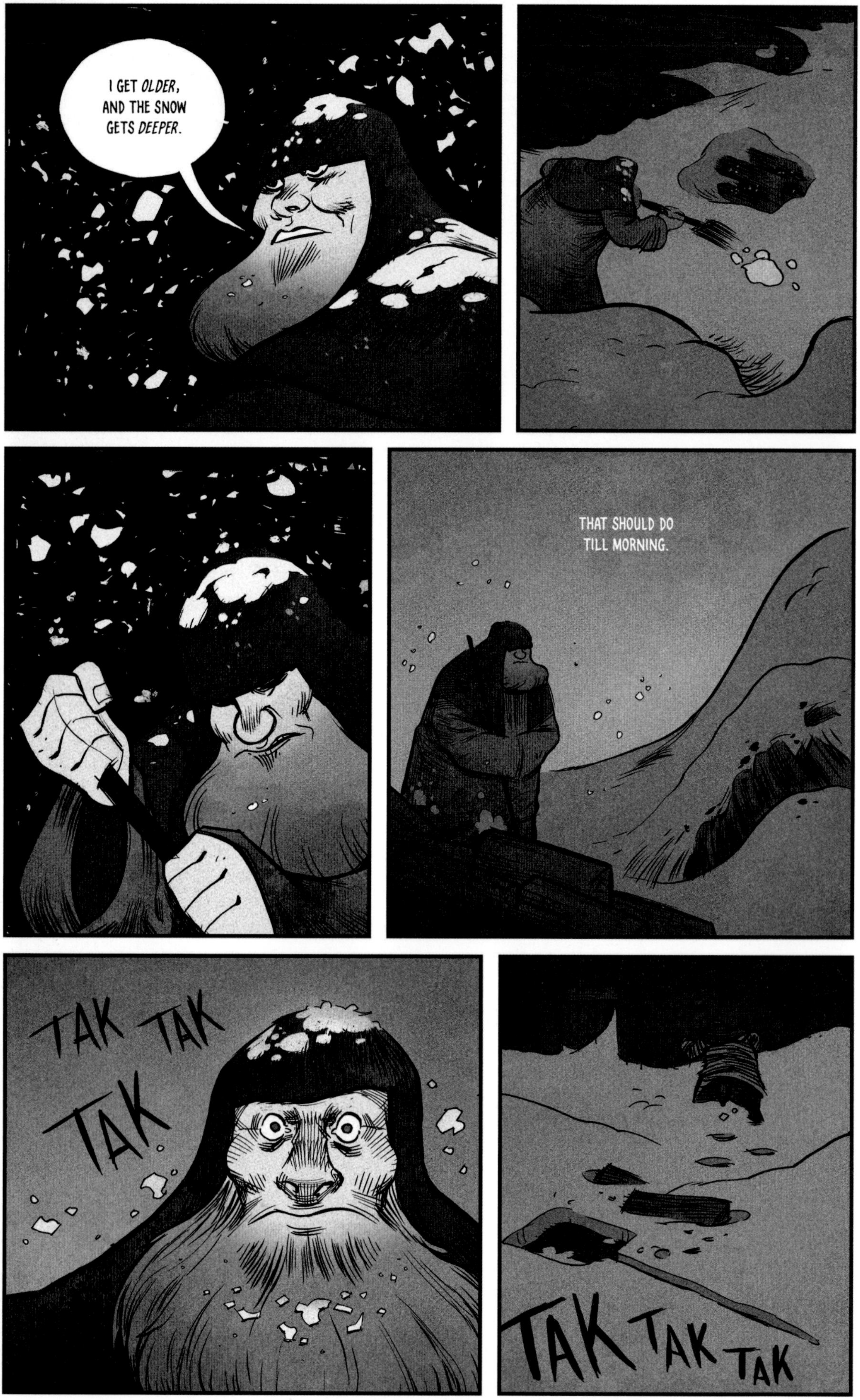
I GET *OLDER*, AND THE SNOW GETS *DEEPER*.
THAT SHOULD DO TILL MORNING.
TAK TAK
TAK
TAK TAK TAK

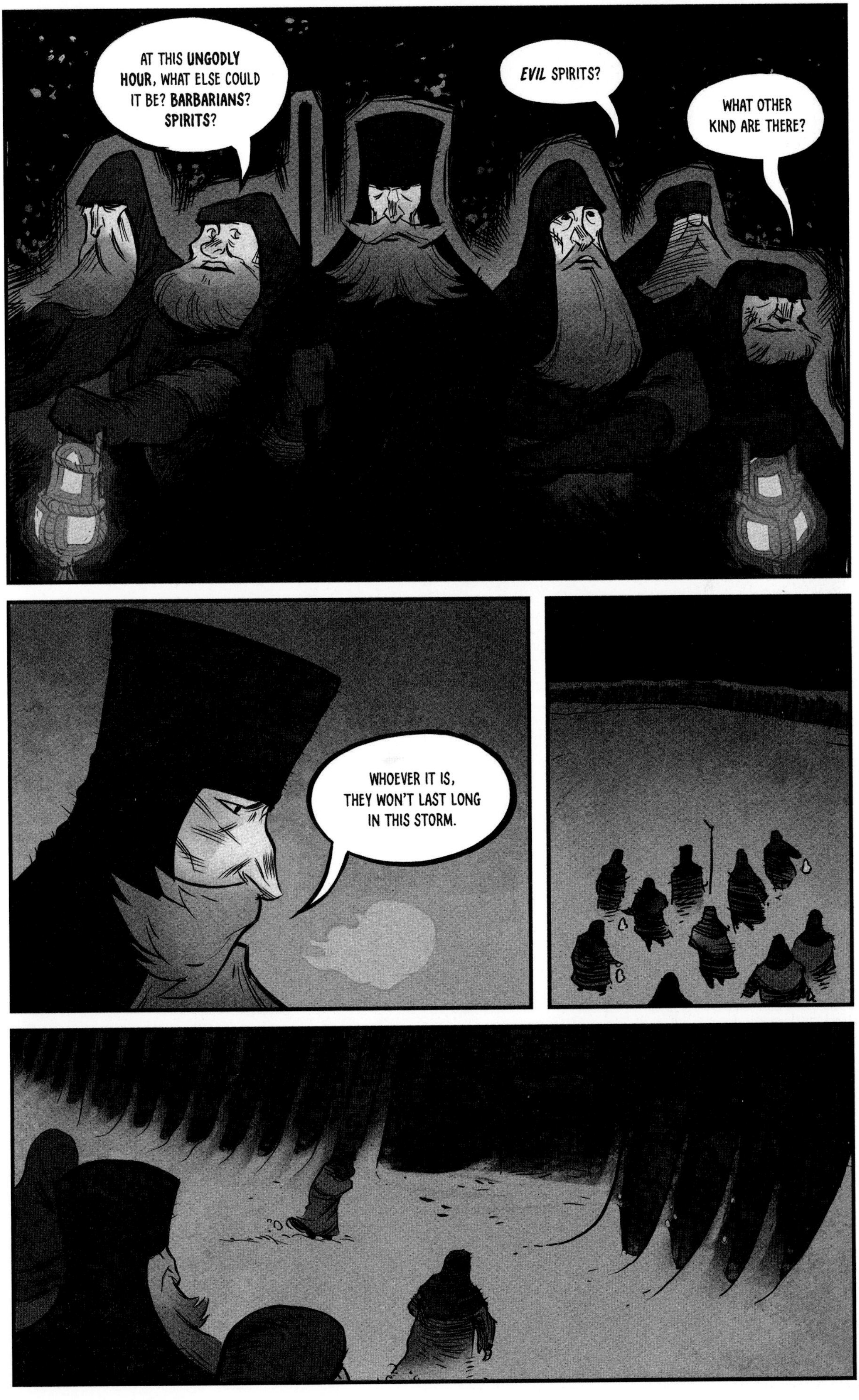
AT THIS UNGODLY HOUR, WHAT ELSE COULD IT BE? BARBARIANS? SPIRITS?
EVIL SPIRITS?
WHAT OTHER KIND ARE THERE?
WHOEVER IT IS, THEY WON'T LAST LONG IN THIS STORM.

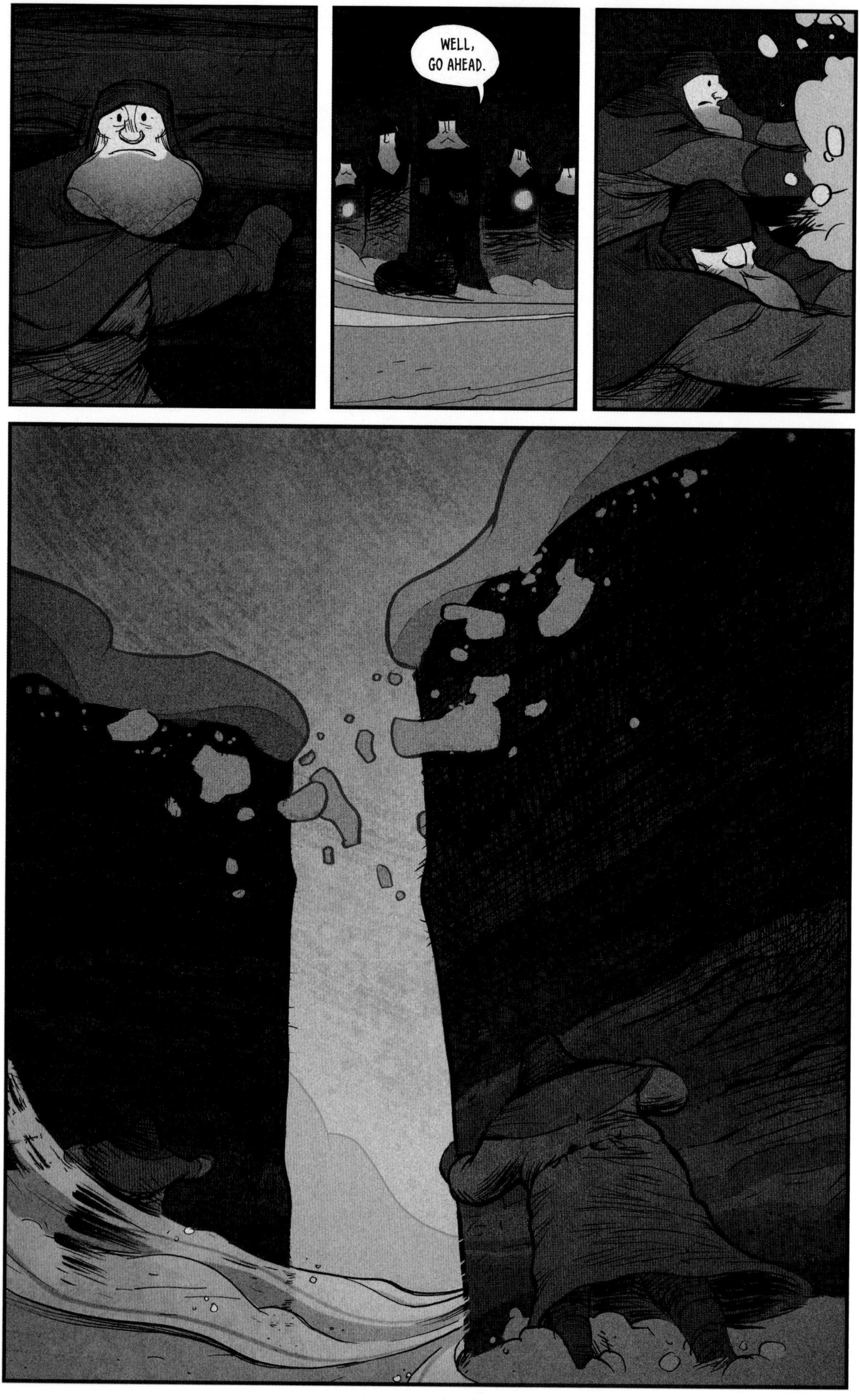
WELL, GO AHEAD.

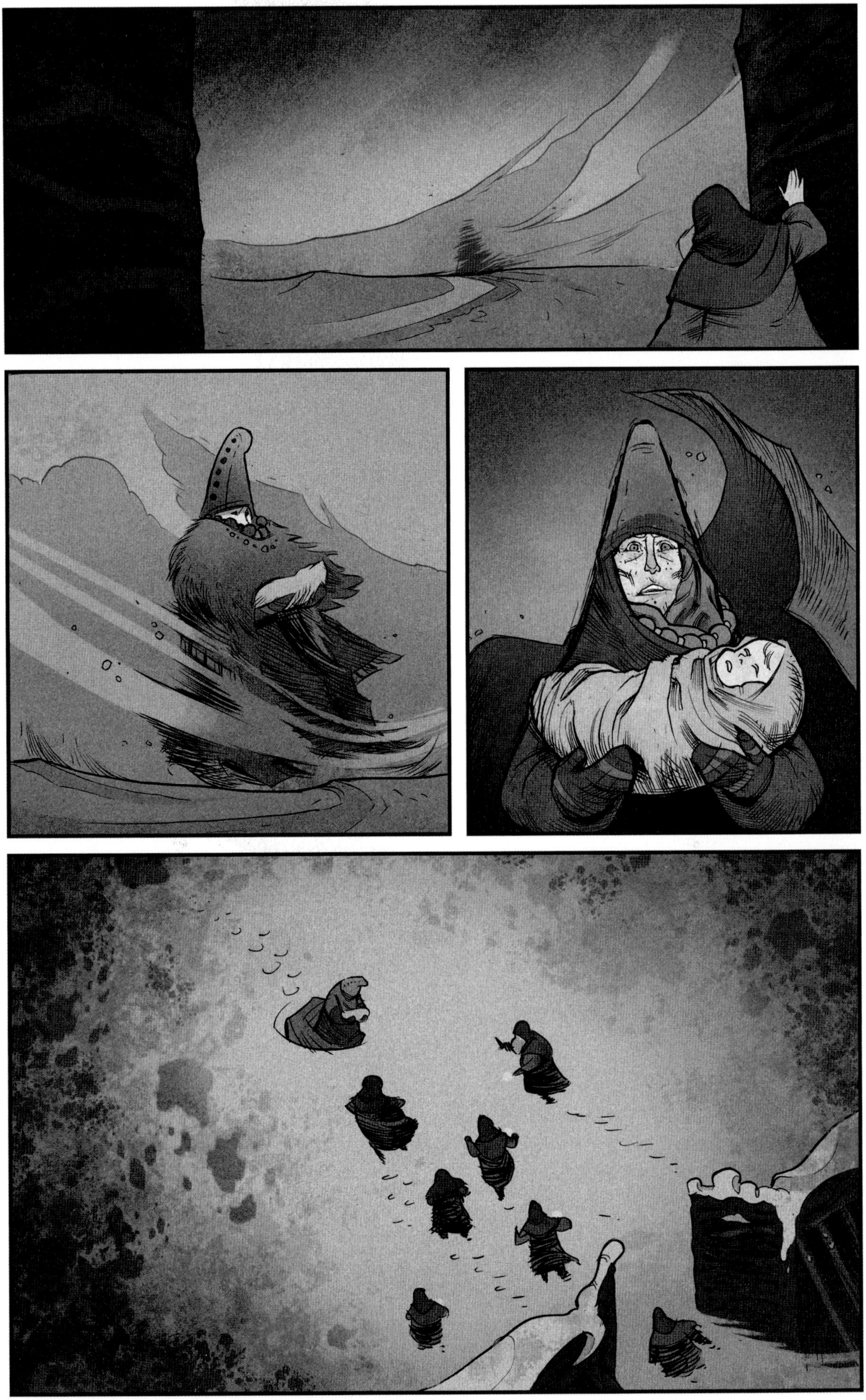

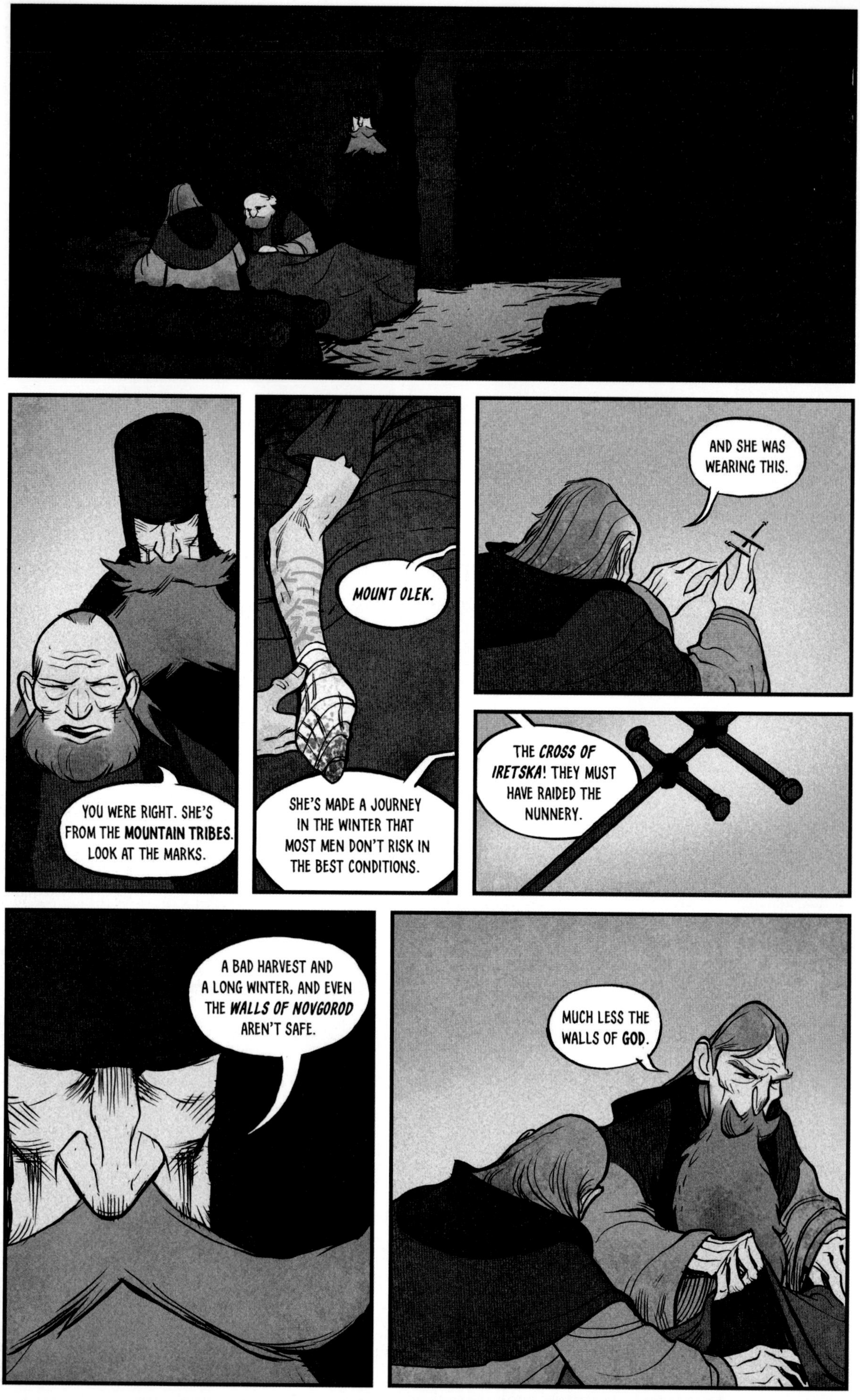
YOU WERE RIGHT. SHE'S FROM THE **MOUNTAIN TRIBES**. LOOK AT THE MARKS.
MOUNT OLEK.
SHE'S MADE A JOURNEY IN THE WINTER THAT MOST MEN DON'T RISK IN THE BEST CONDITIONS.
AND SHE WAS WEARING THIS.
THE ***CROSS OF IRETSKA***! THEY MUST HAVE RAIDED THE NUNNERY.
A BAD HARVEST AND A LONG WINTER, AND EVEN THE ***WALLS OF NOVGOROD*** AREN'T SAFE.
MUCH LESS THE WALLS OF **GOD**.

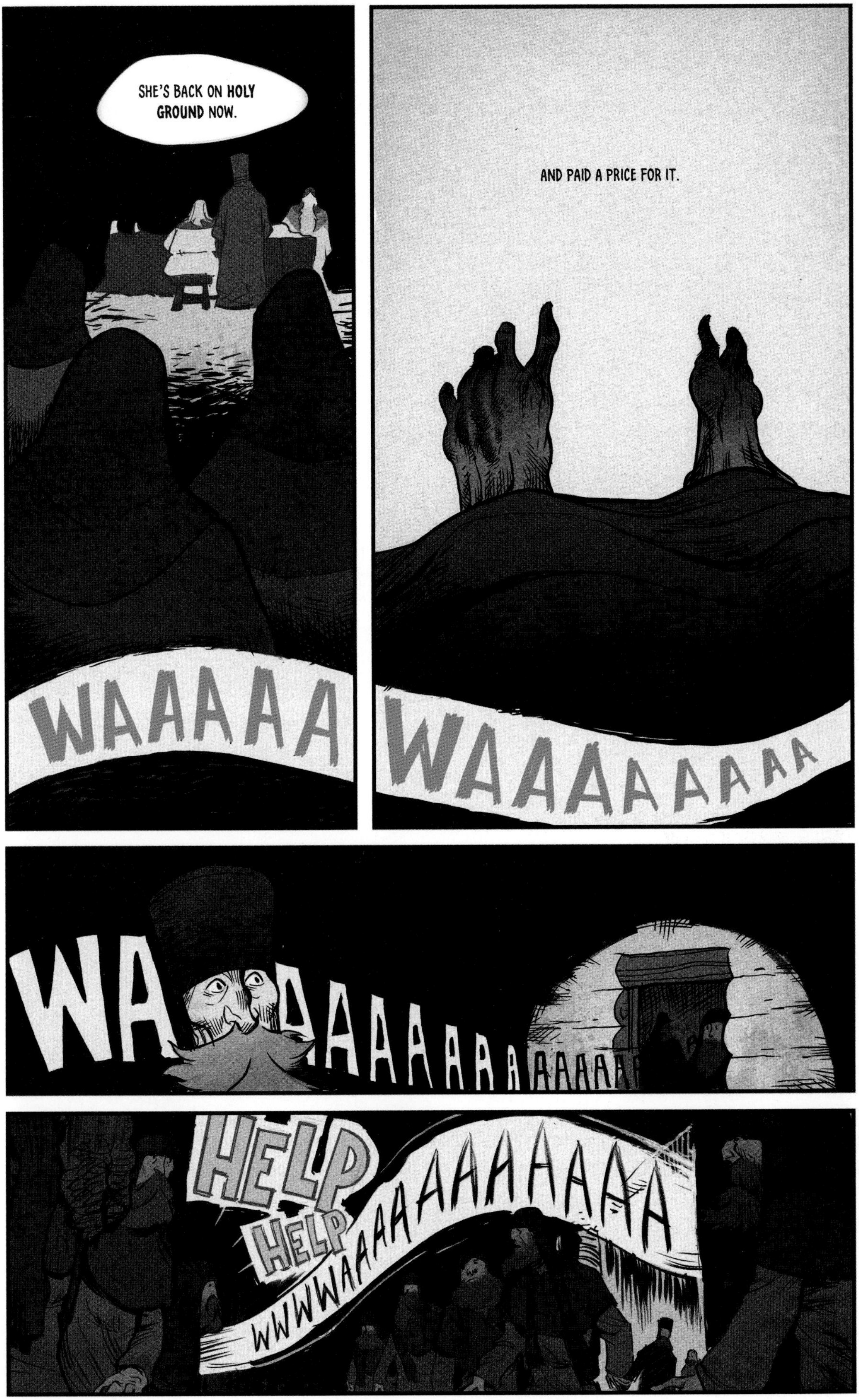
SHE'S BACK ON HOLY GROUND NOW.
WAAAAA
AND PAID A PRICE FOR IT.
WAAAAAAAAA
WAAAAAAAAAAAAAA
HELP
HELP
WWWWAAAAAAAAAAAAA

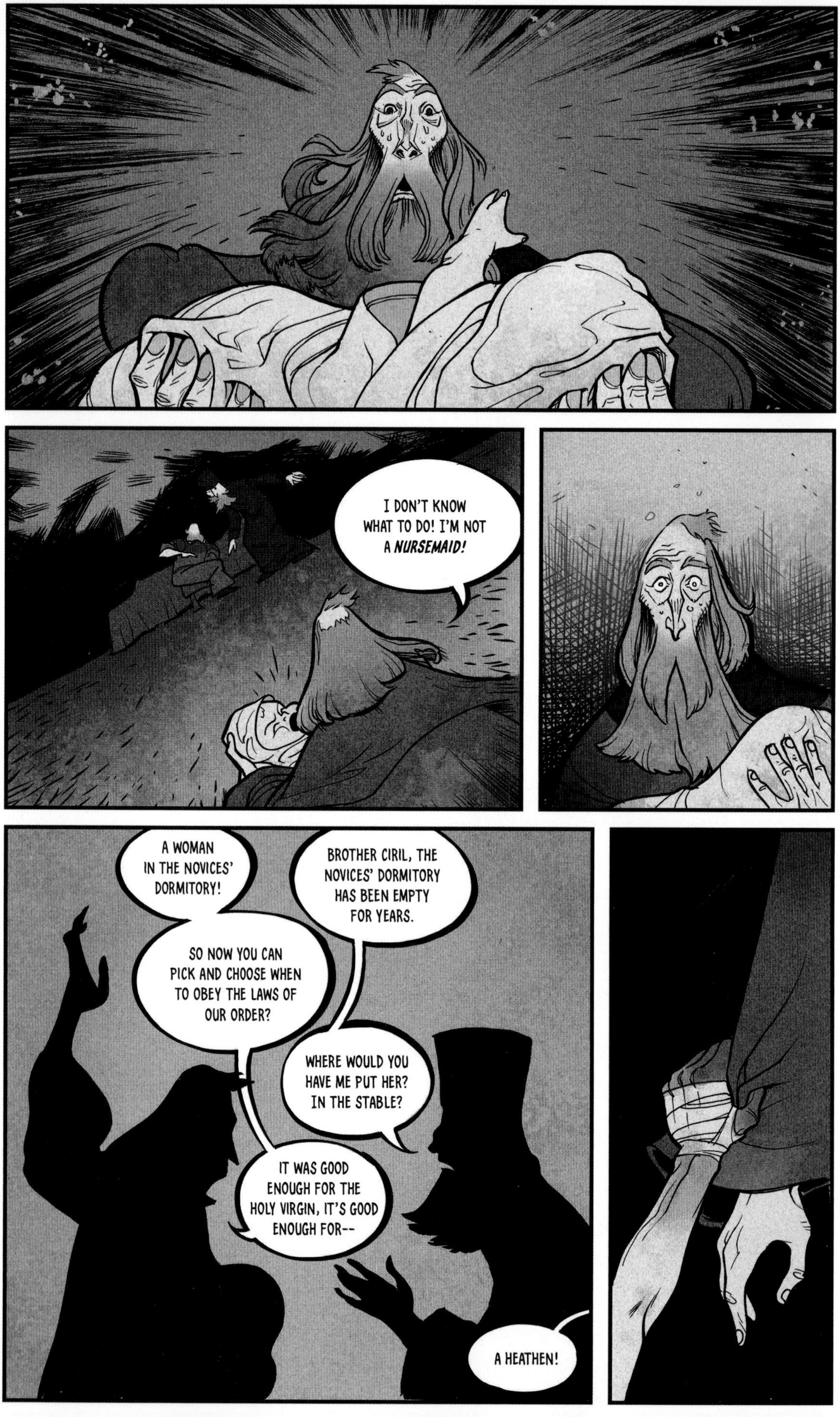
I DON'T KNOW WHAT TO DO! I'M NOT A *NURSEMAID!*
A WOMAN IN THE NOVICES' DORMITORY!
BROTHER CIRIL, THE NOVICES' DORMITORY HAS BEEN EMPTY FOR YEARS.
SO NOW YOU CAN PICK AND CHOOSE WHEN TO OBEY THE LAWS OF OUR ORDER?
WHERE WOULD YOU HAVE ME PUT HER? IN THE STABLE?
IT WAS GOOD ENOUGH FOR THE HOLY VIRGIN, IT'S GOOD ENOUGH FOR--
A HEATHEN!

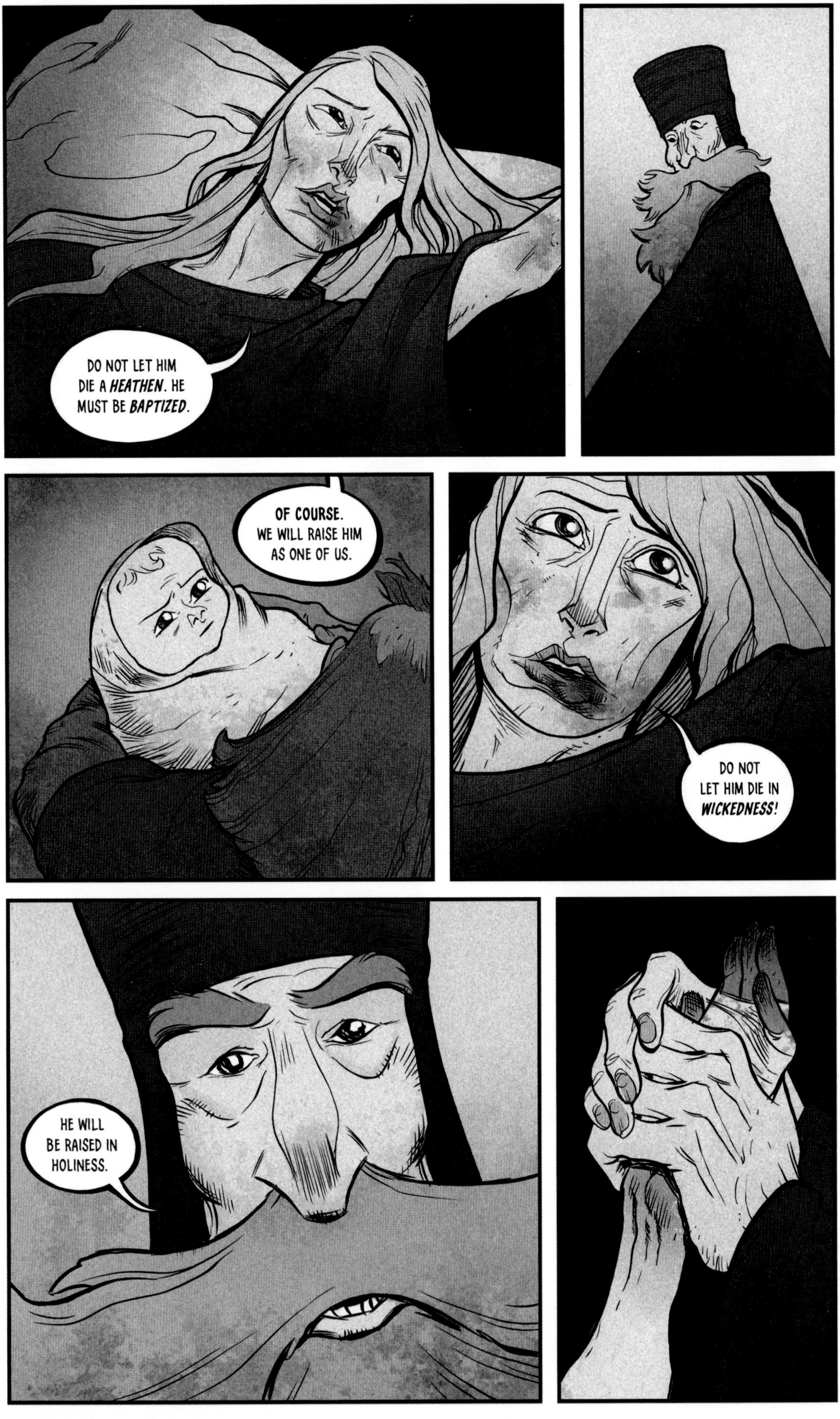
DO NOT LET HIM DIE A HEATHEN. HE MUST BE BAPTIZED.
OF COURSE. WE WILL RAISE HIM AS ONE OF US.
DO NOT LET HIM DIE IN WICKEDNESS!
HE WILL BE RAISED IN HOLINESS.

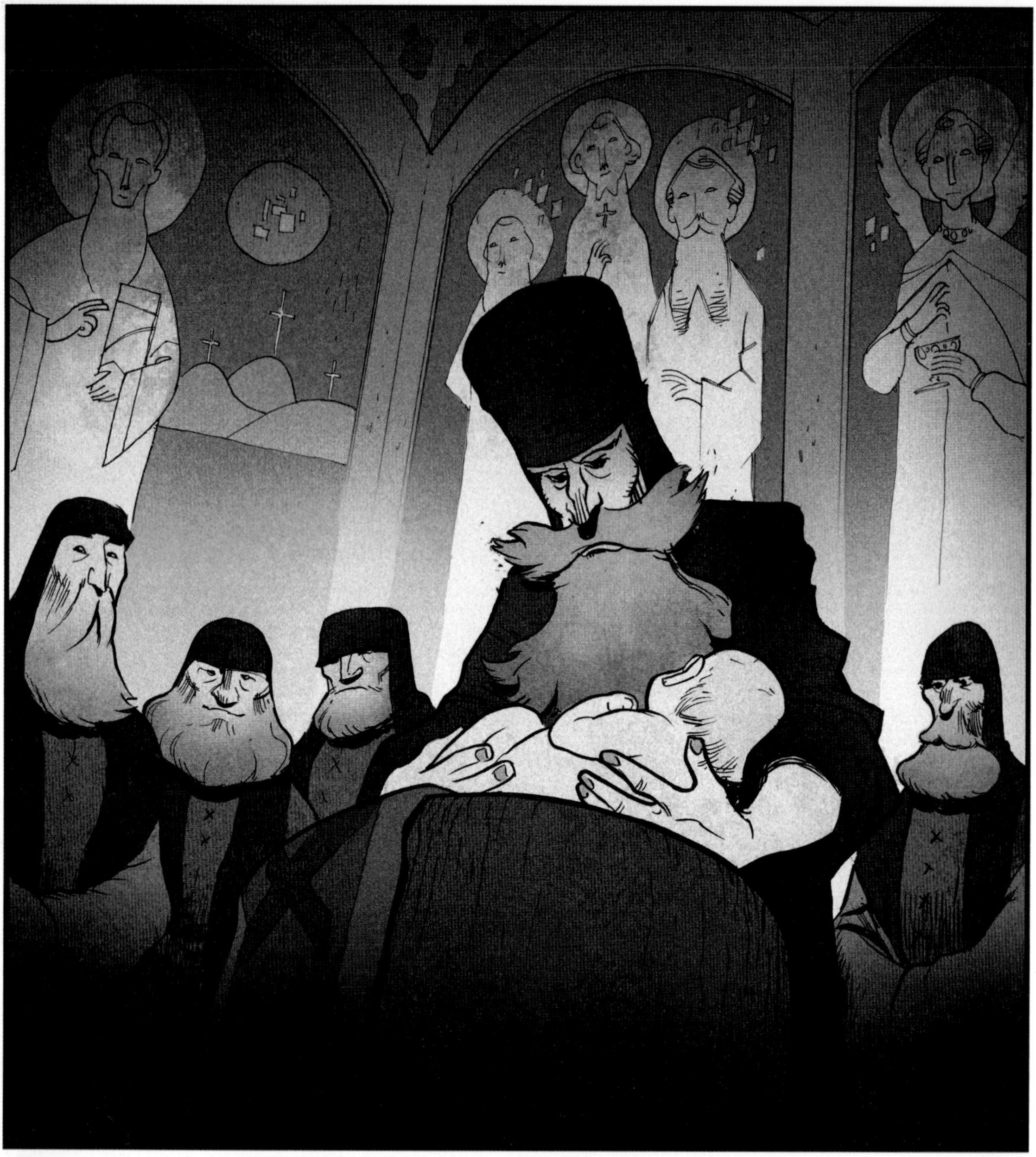

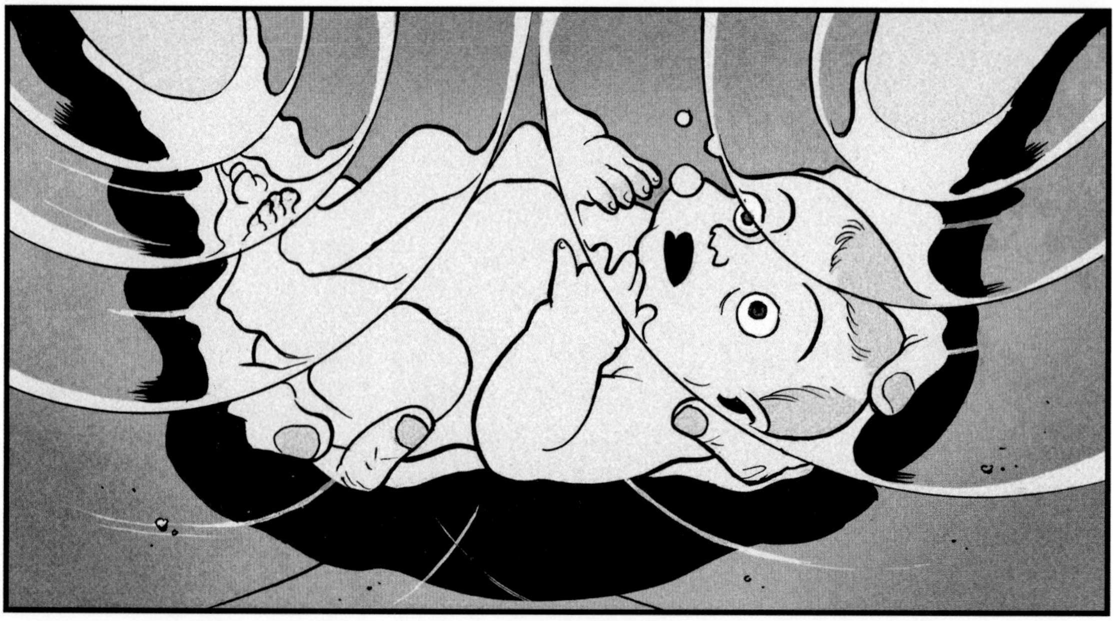

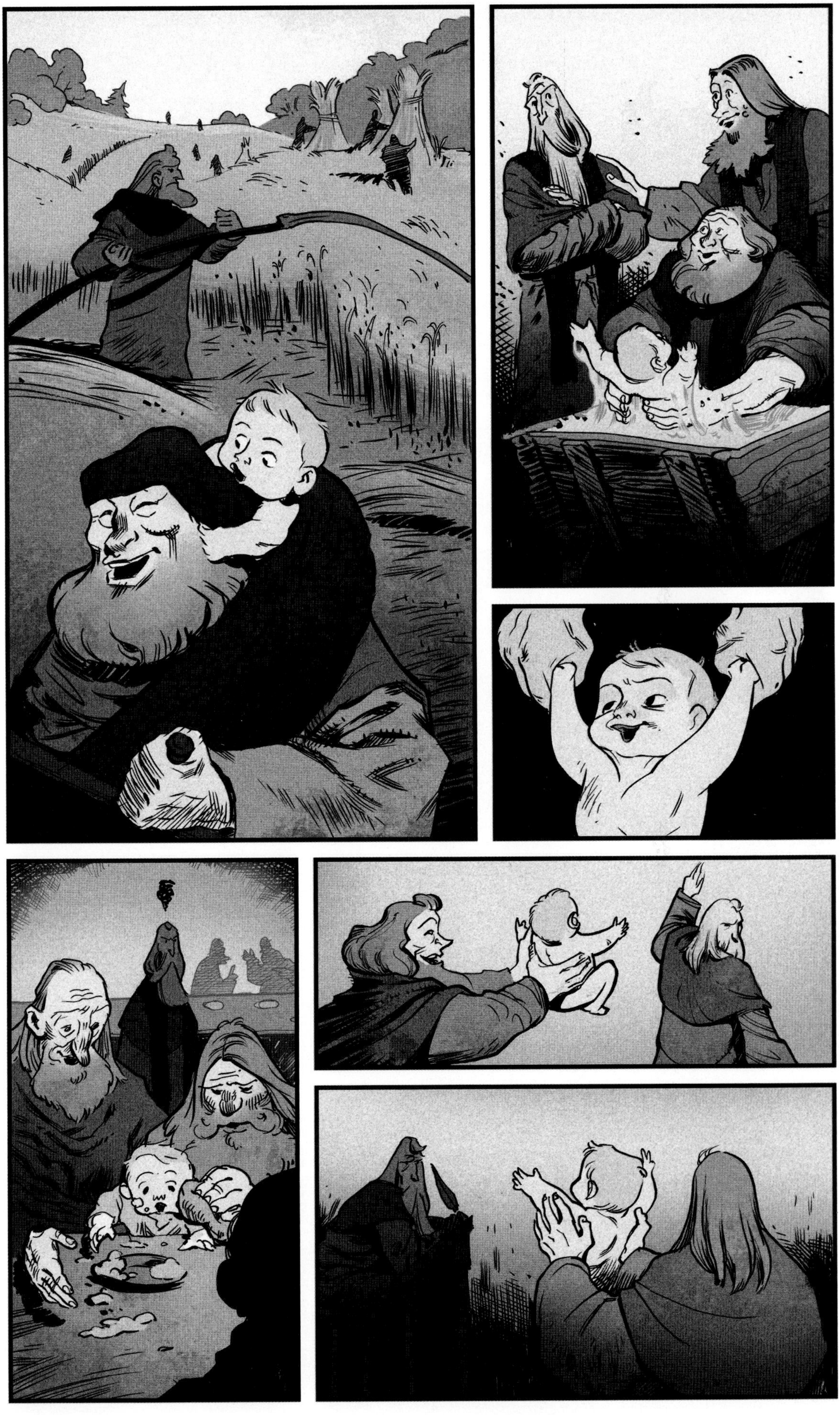

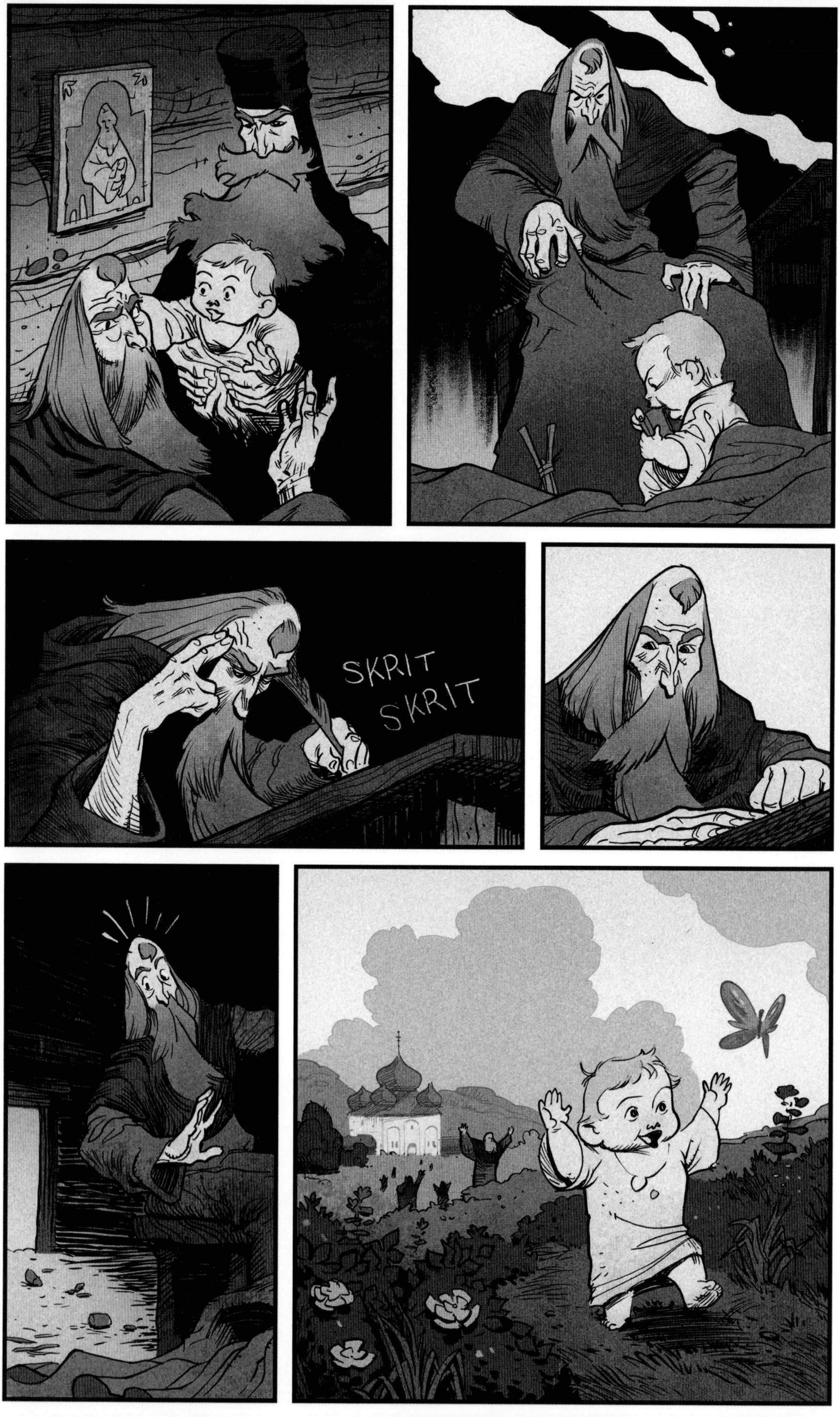
SKRIT
SKRIT

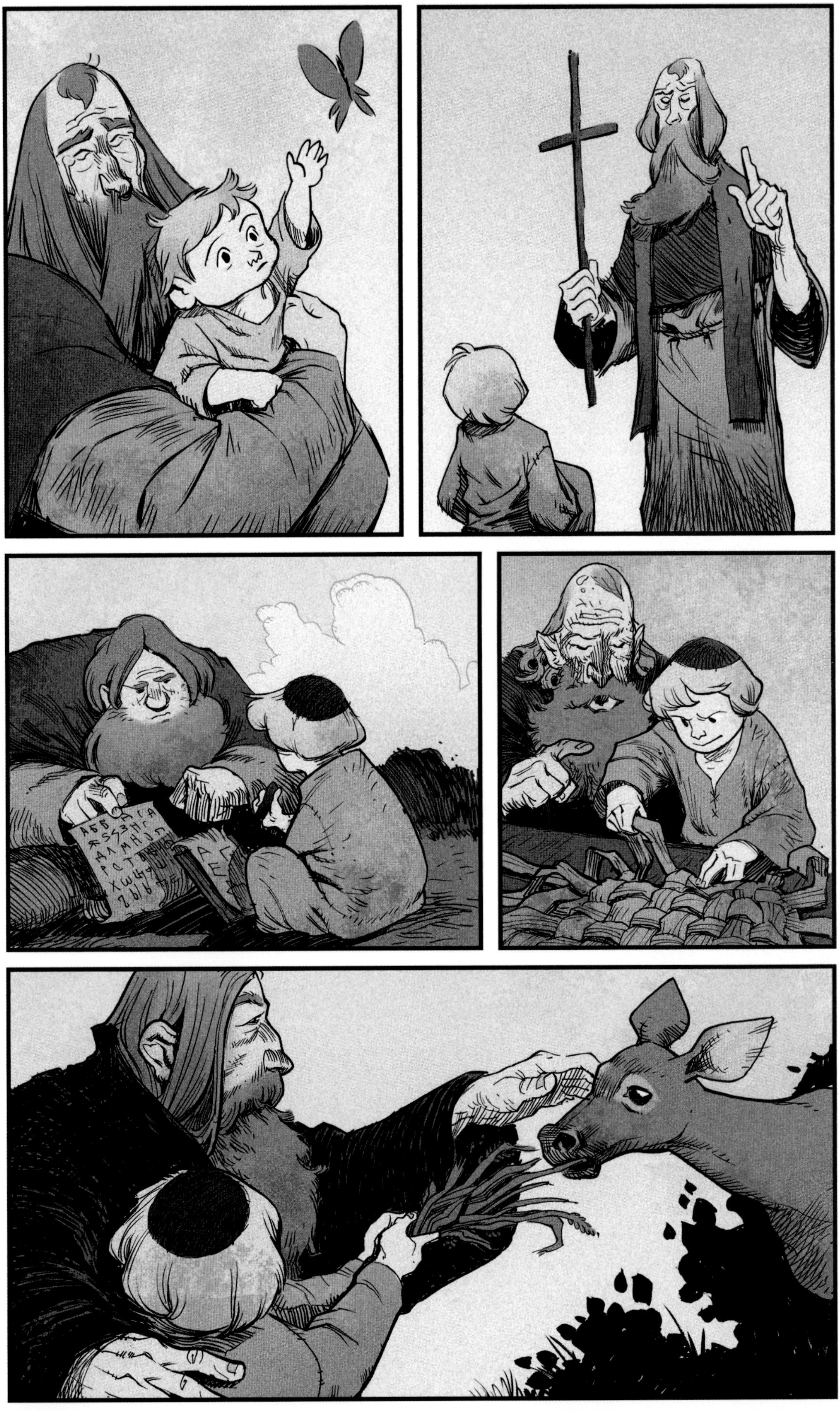

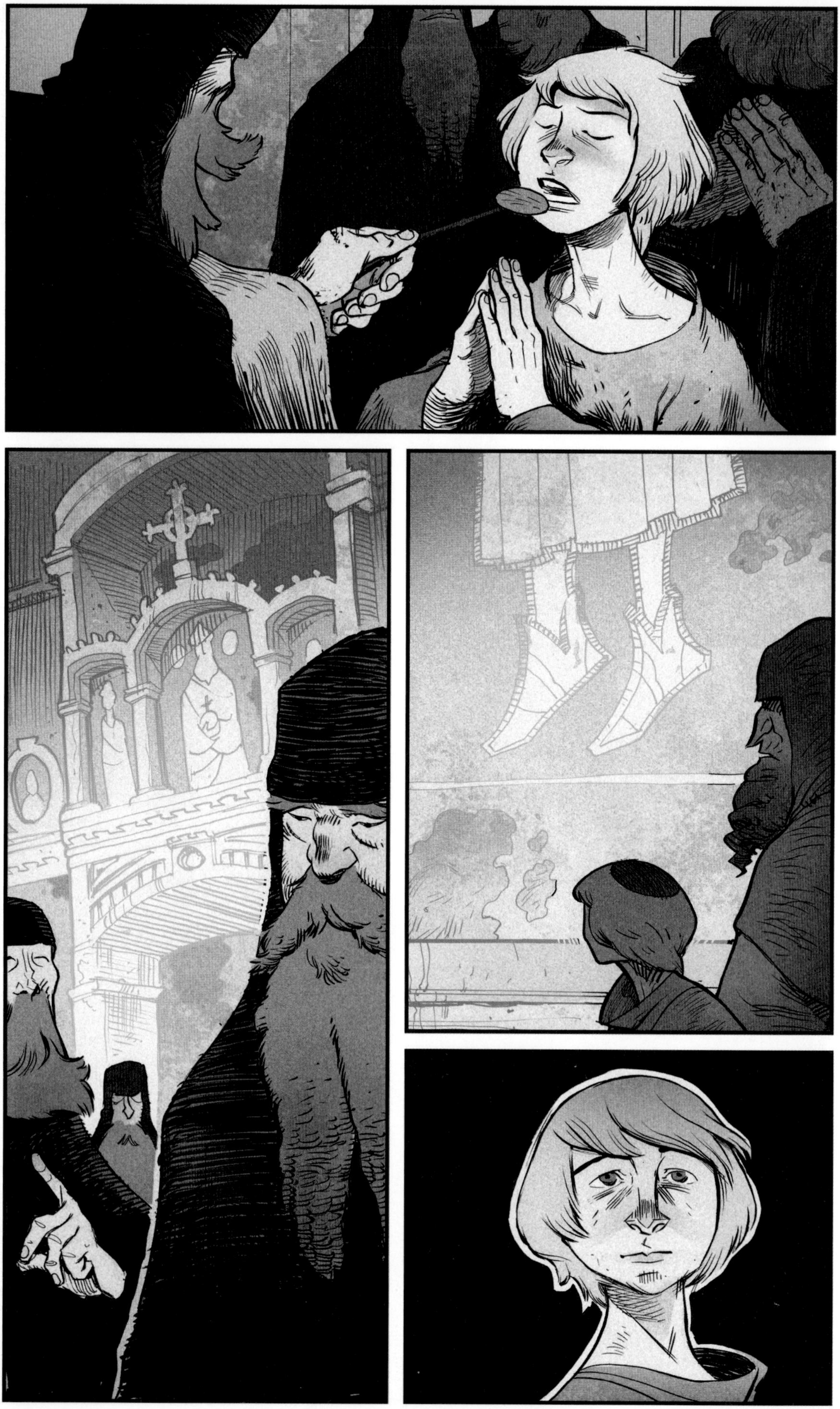

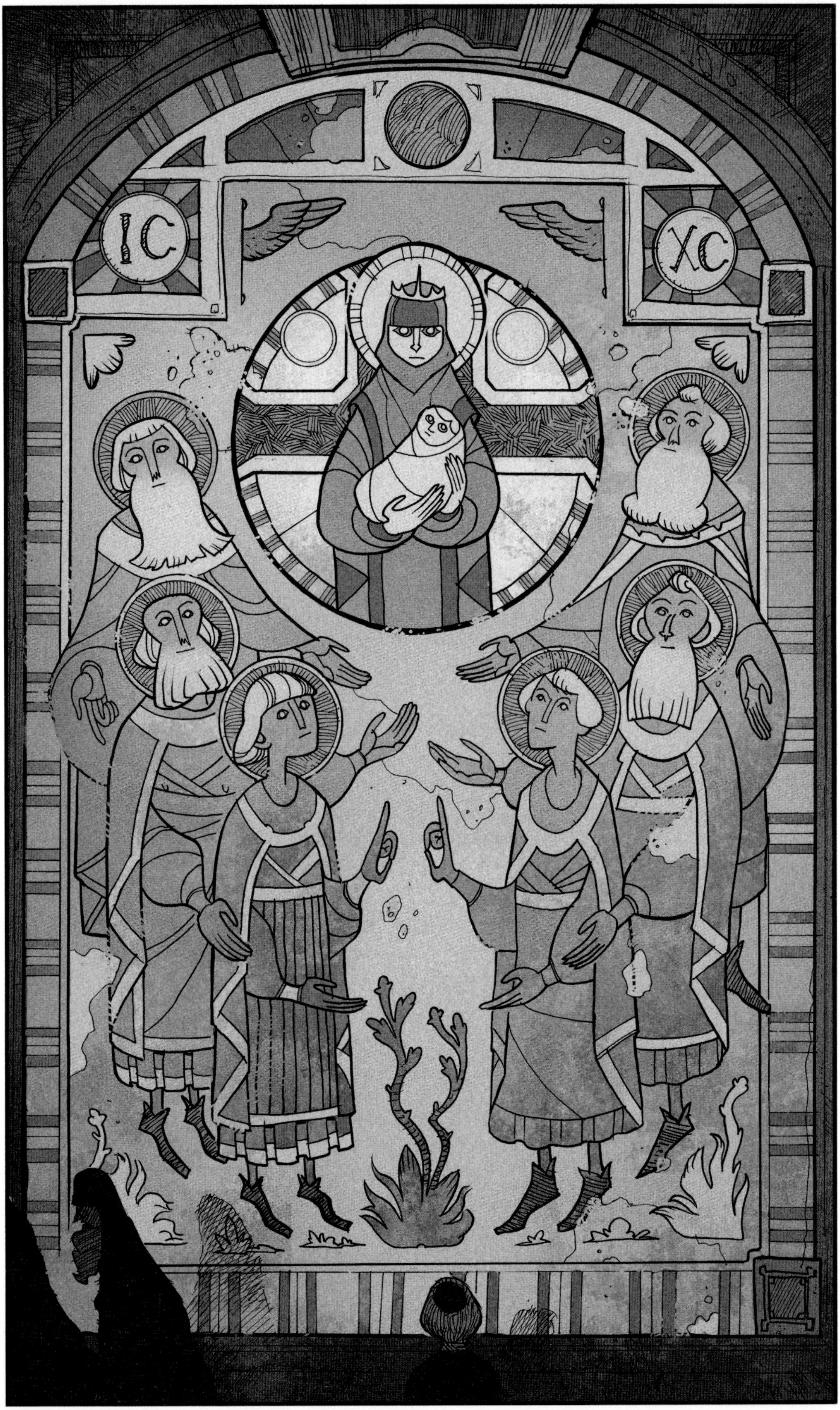
IC
XC

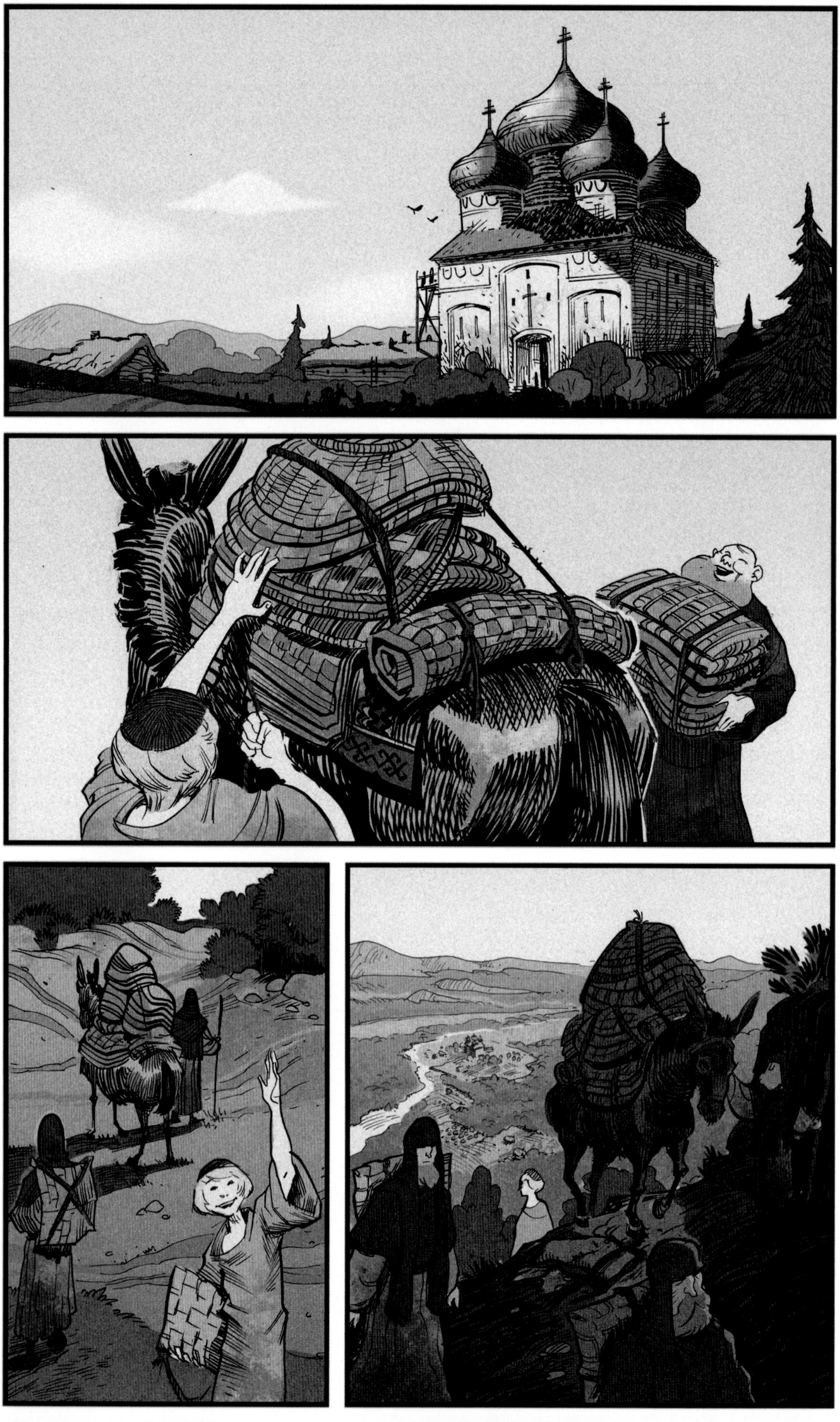

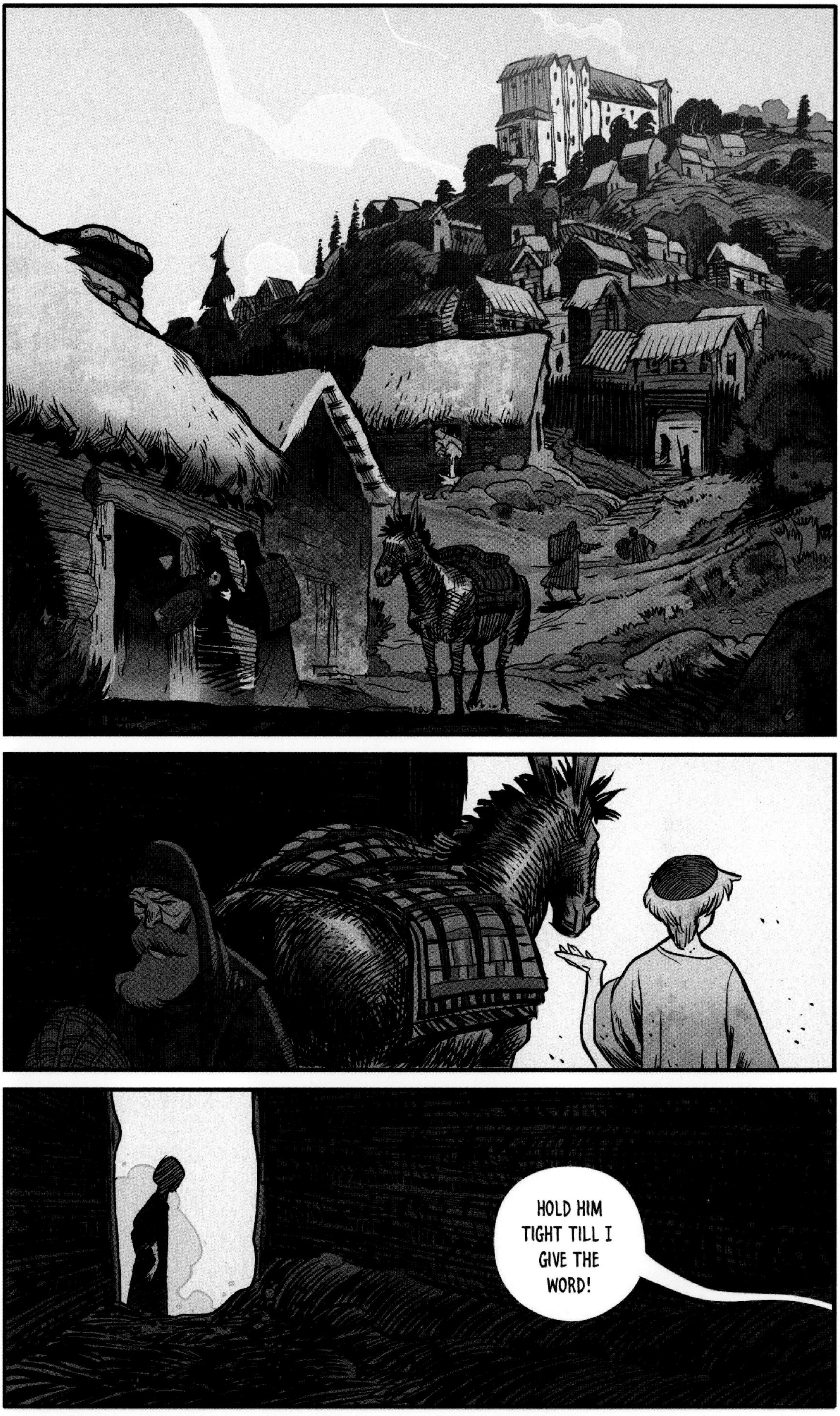
HOLD HIM TIGHT TILL I GIVE THE WORD!

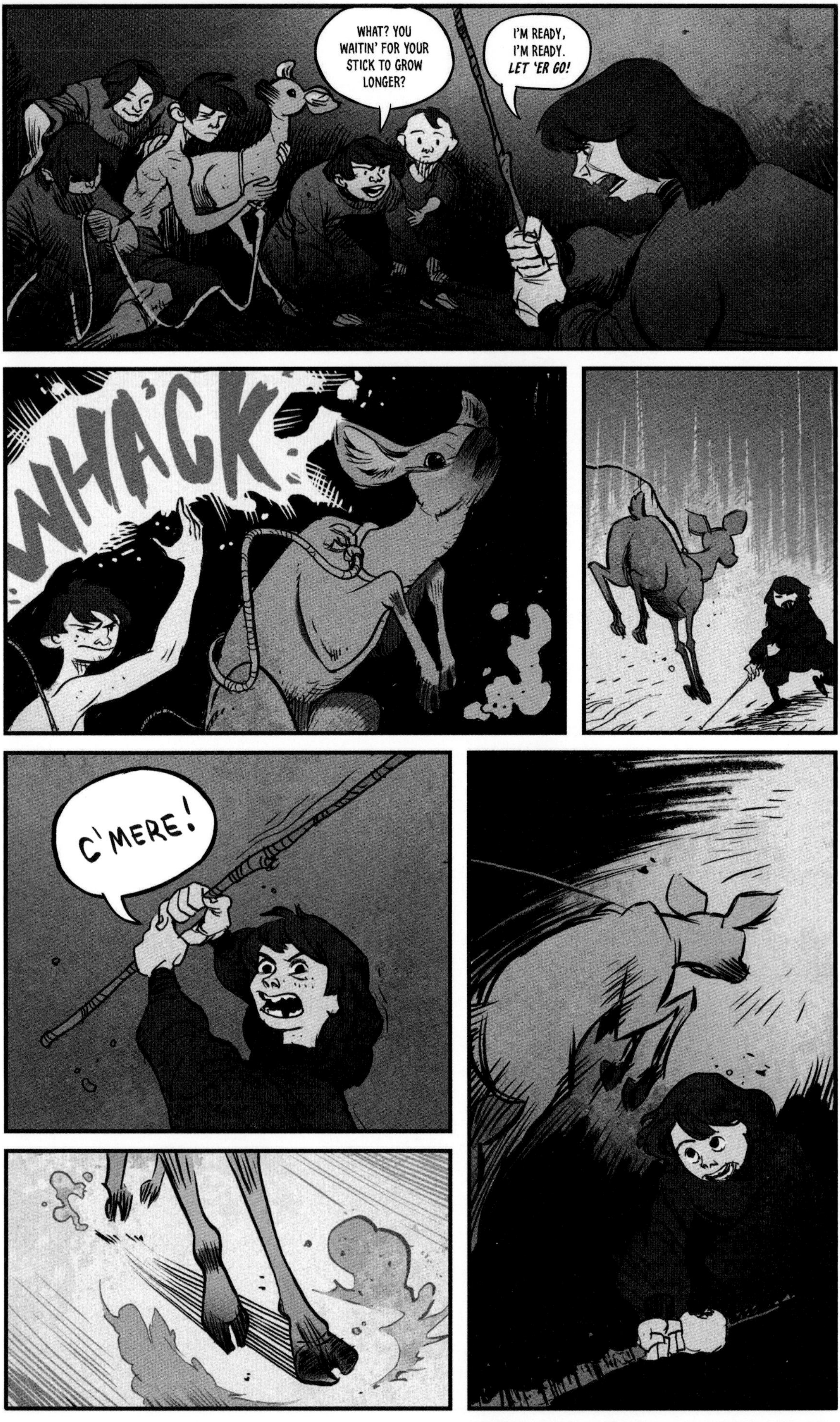
WHAT? YOU WAITIN' FOR YOUR STICK TO GROW LONGER?
I'M READY, I'M READY. *LET 'ER GO!*
WHACK
C'MERE!

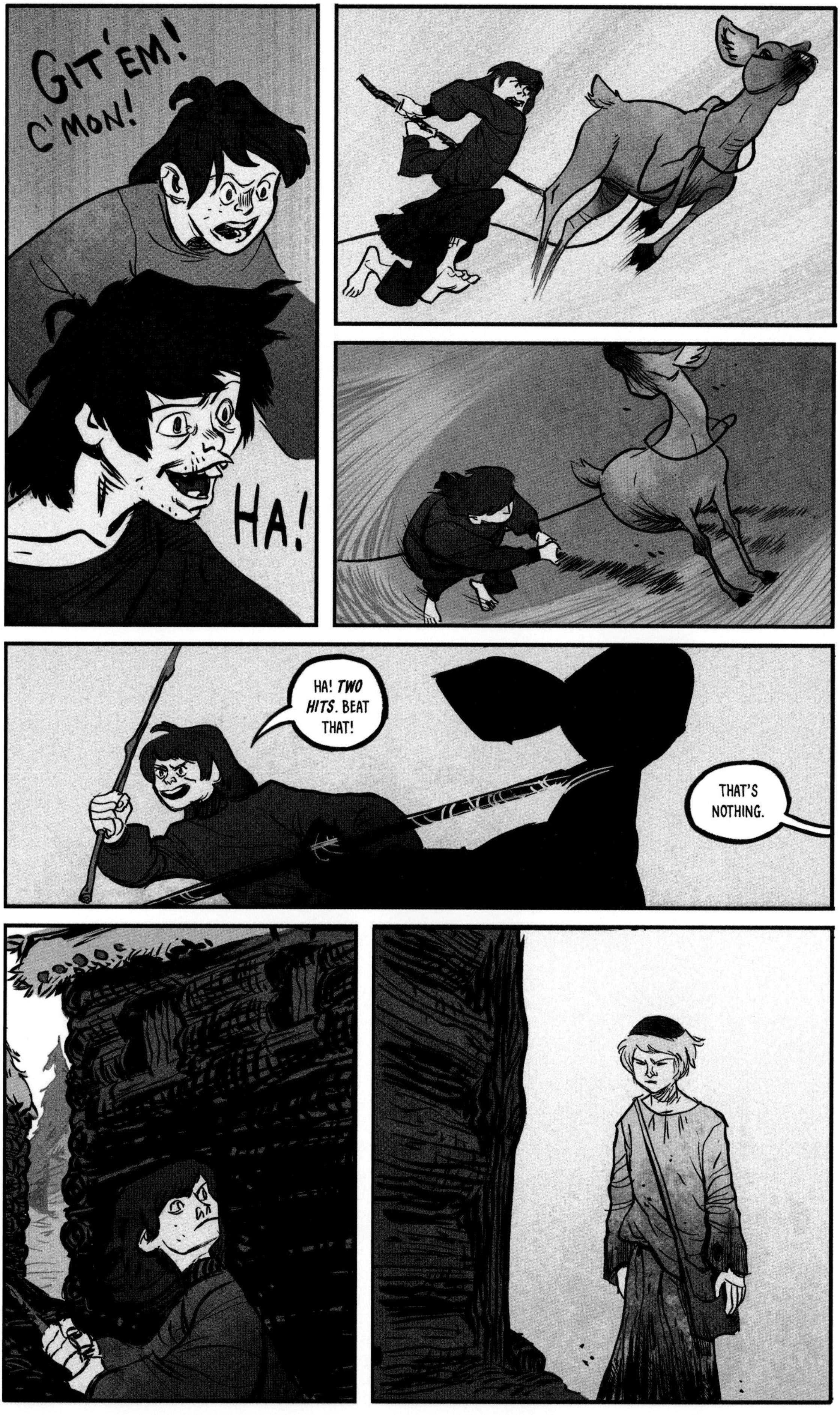
GIT 'EM! C'MON!
HA!
HA! TWO HITS. BEAT THAT!
THAT'S NOTHING.

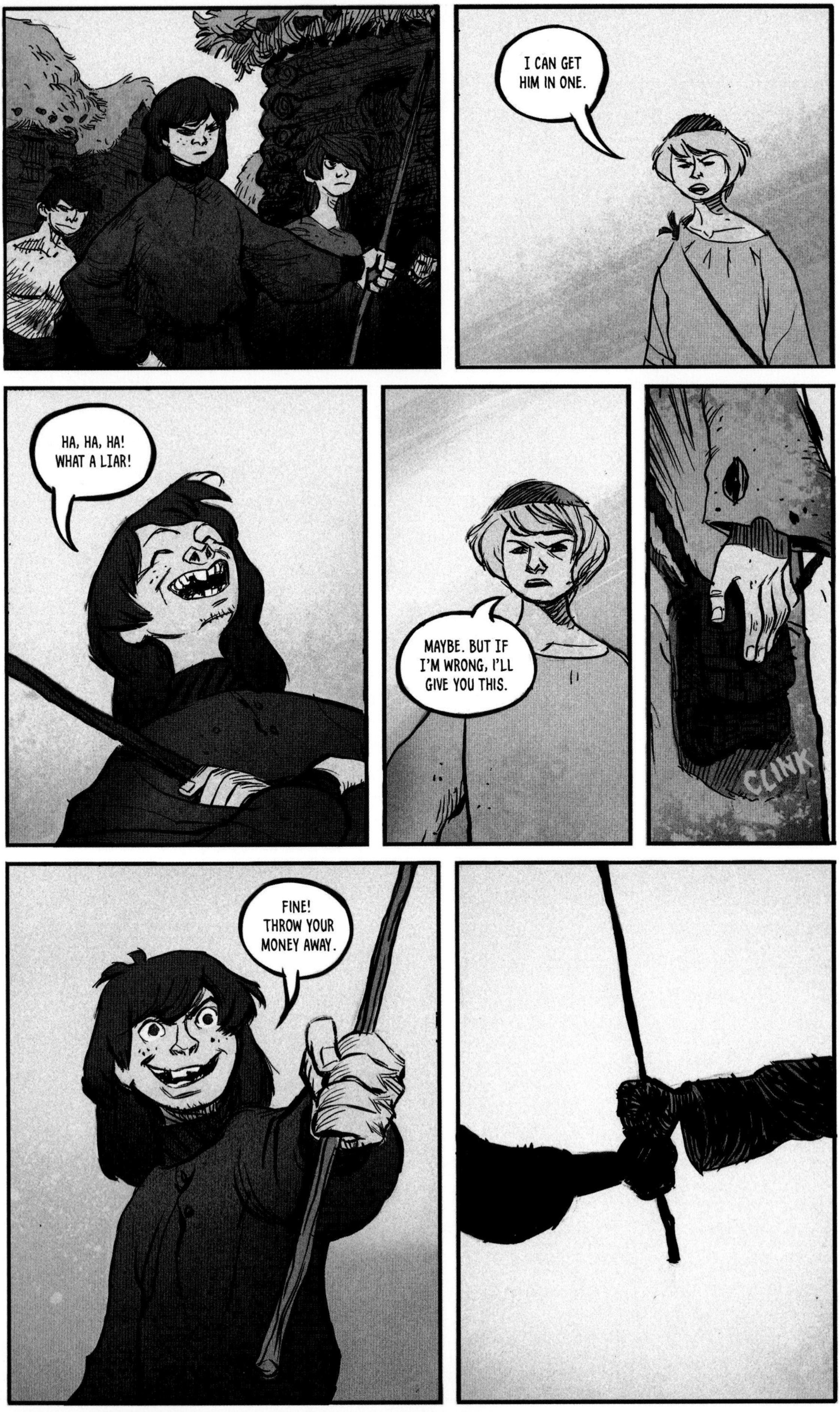
I CAN GET HIM IN ONE.
HA, HA, HA! WHAT A LIAR!
MAYBE. BUT IF I'M WRONG, I'LL GIVE YOU THIS.
CLINK
FINE! THROW YOUR MONEY AWAY.

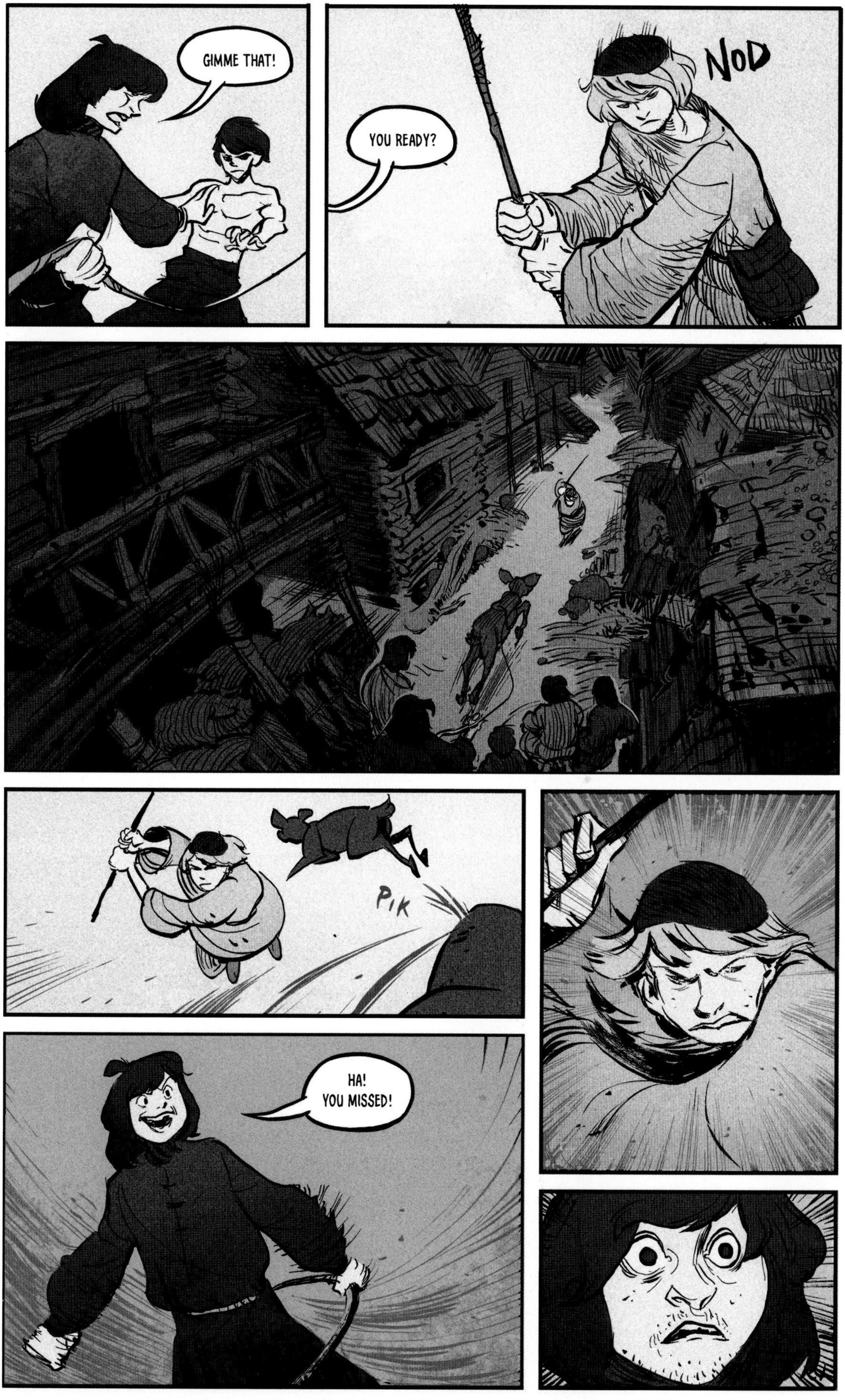
GIMME THAT!
YOU READY?
NOD
PIK
HA! YOU MISSED!

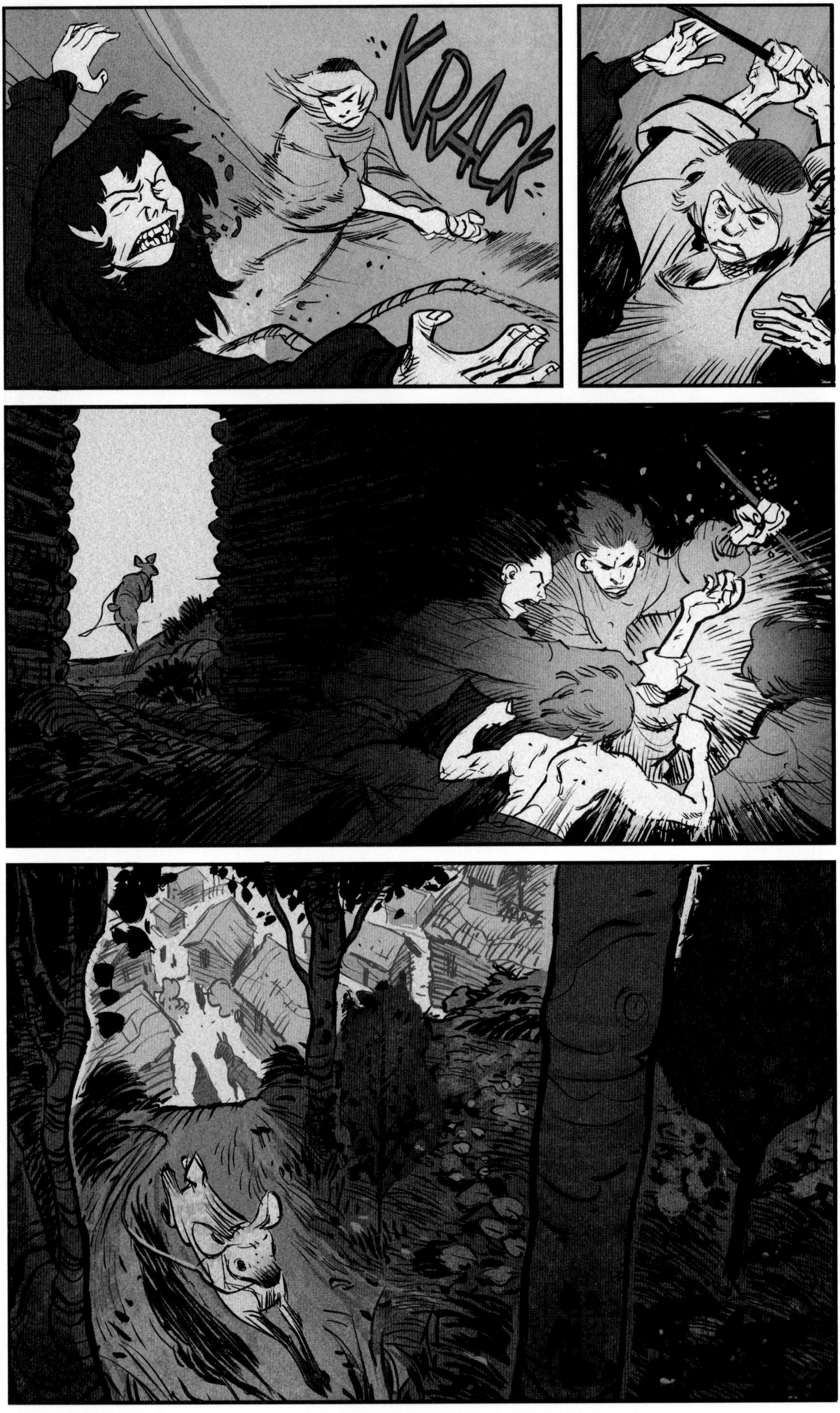
KRACK

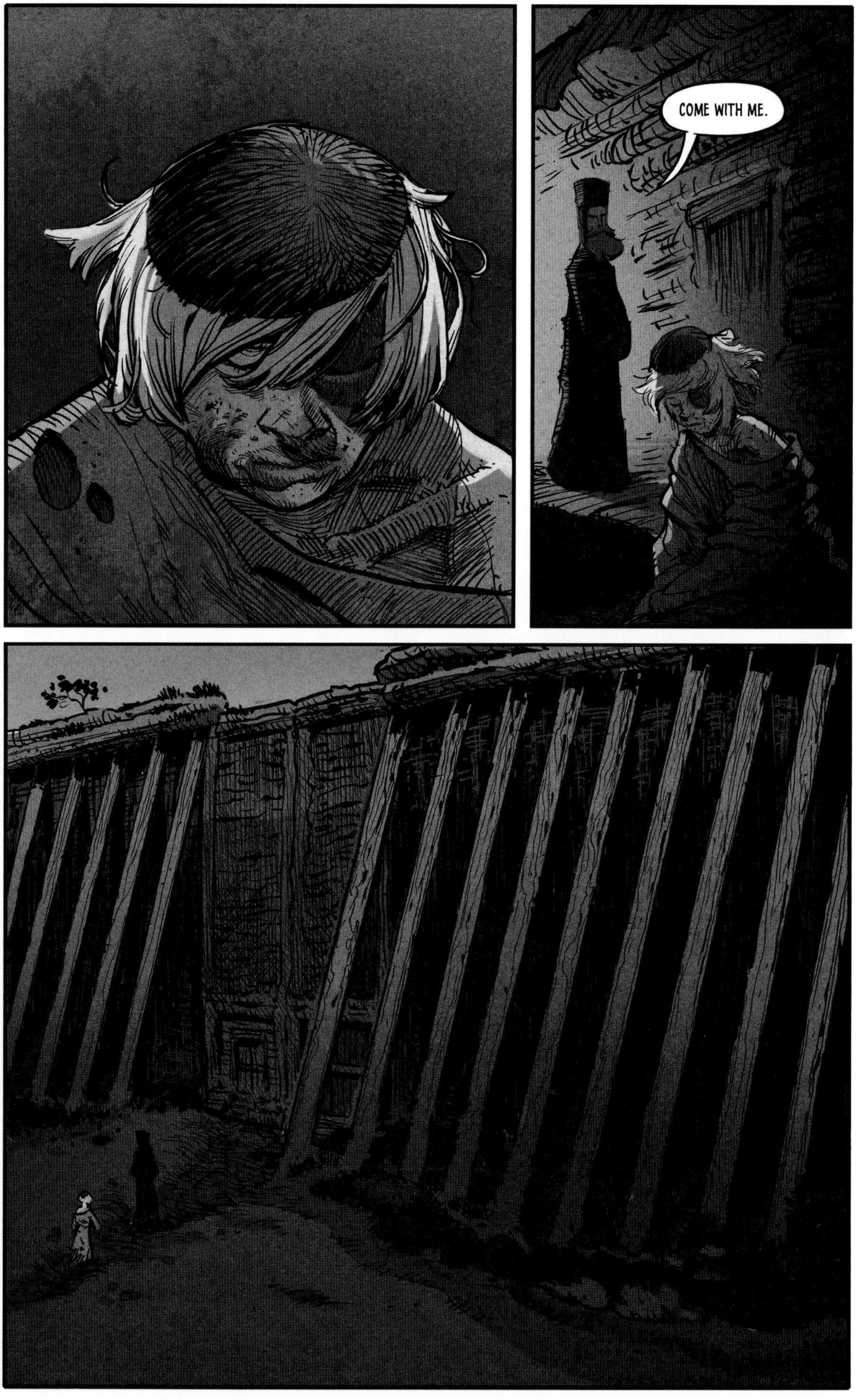
COME WITH ME.

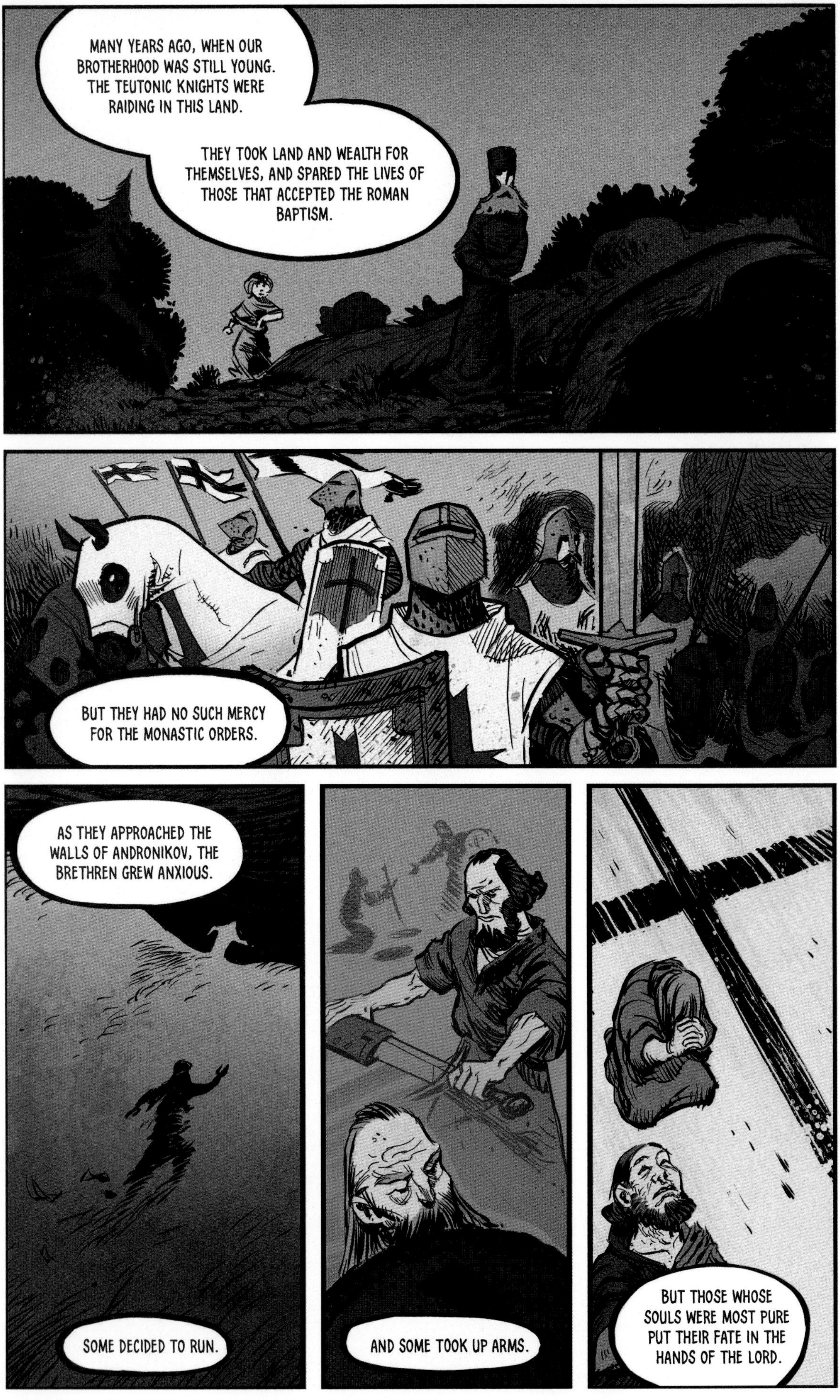
MANY YEARS AGO, WHEN OUR BROTHERHOOD WAS STILL YOUNG. THE TEUTONIC KNIGHTS WERE RAIDING IN THIS LAND.
THEY TOOK LAND AND WEALTH FOR THEMSELVES, AND SPARED THE LIVES OF THOSE THAT ACCEPTED THE ROMAN BAPTISM.
BUT THEY HAD NO SUCH MERCY FOR THE MONASTIC ORDERS.
AS THEY APPROACHED THE WALLS OF ANDRONIKOV, THE BRETHREN GREW ANXIOUS.
SOME DECIDED TO RUN.
AND SOME TOOK UP ARMS.
BUT THOSE WHOSE SOULS WERE MOST PURE PUT THEIR FATE IN THE HANDS OF THE LORD.

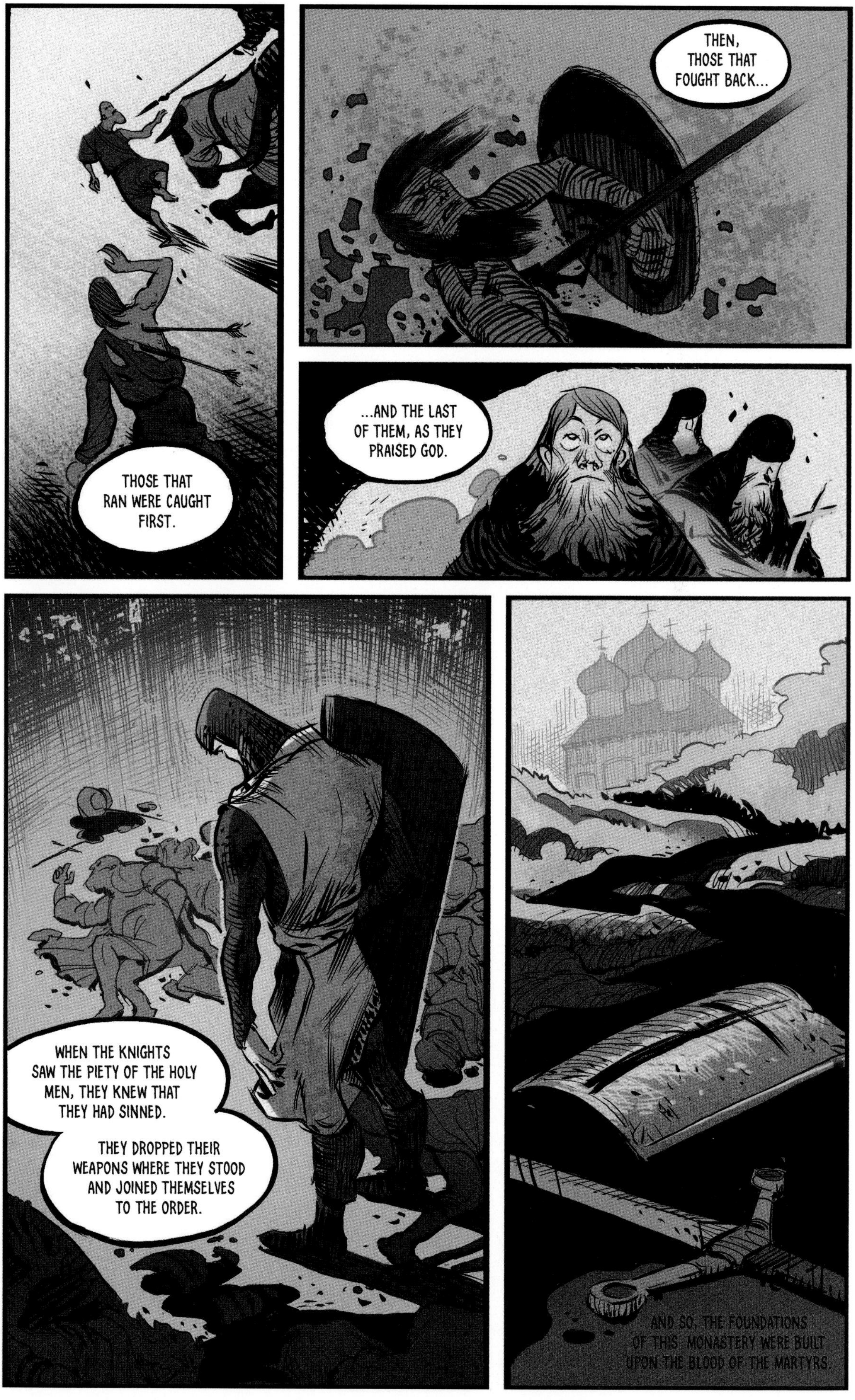
THOSE THAT RAN WERE CAUGHT FIRST.
THEN, THOSE THAT FOUGHT BACK...
...AND THE LAST OF THEM, AS THEY PRAISED GOD.
WHEN THE KNIGHTS SAW THE PIETY OF THE HOLY MEN, THEY KNEW THAT THEY HAD SINNED.
THEY DROPPED THEIR WEAPONS WHERE THEY STOOD AND JOINED THEMSELVES TO THE ORDER.
AND SO, THE FOUNDATIONS OF THIS MONASTERY WERE BUILT UPON THE BLOOD OF THE MARTYRS.

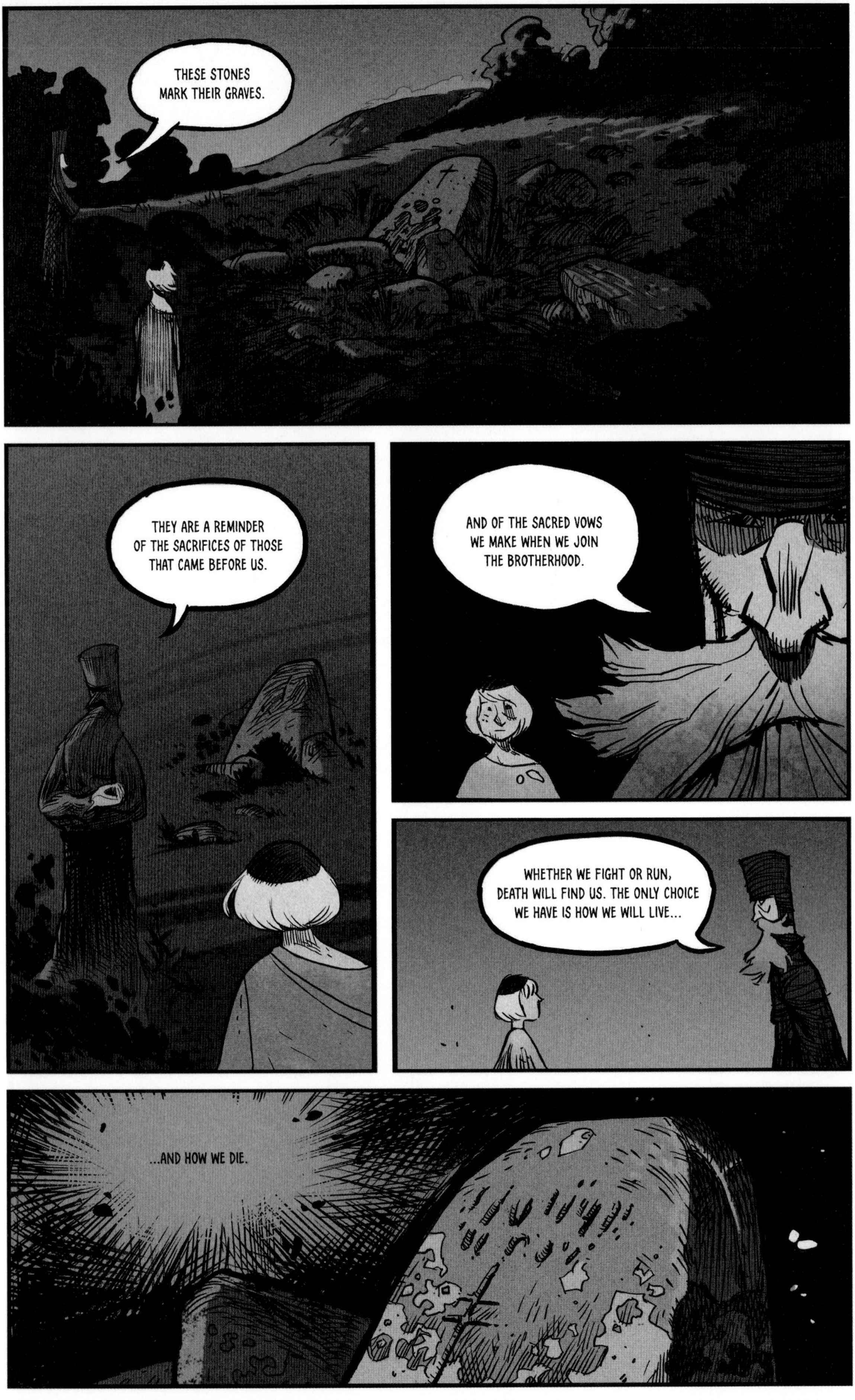
THESE STONES MARK THEIR GRAVES.
THEY ARE A REMINDER OF THE SACRIFICES OF THOSE THAT CAME BEFORE US.
AND OF THE SACRED VOWS WE MAKE WHEN WE JOIN THE BROTHERHOOD.
WHETHER WE FIGHT OR RUN, DEATH WILL FIND US. THE ONLY CHOICE WE HAVE IS HOW WE WILL LIVE...
...AND HOW WE DIE.

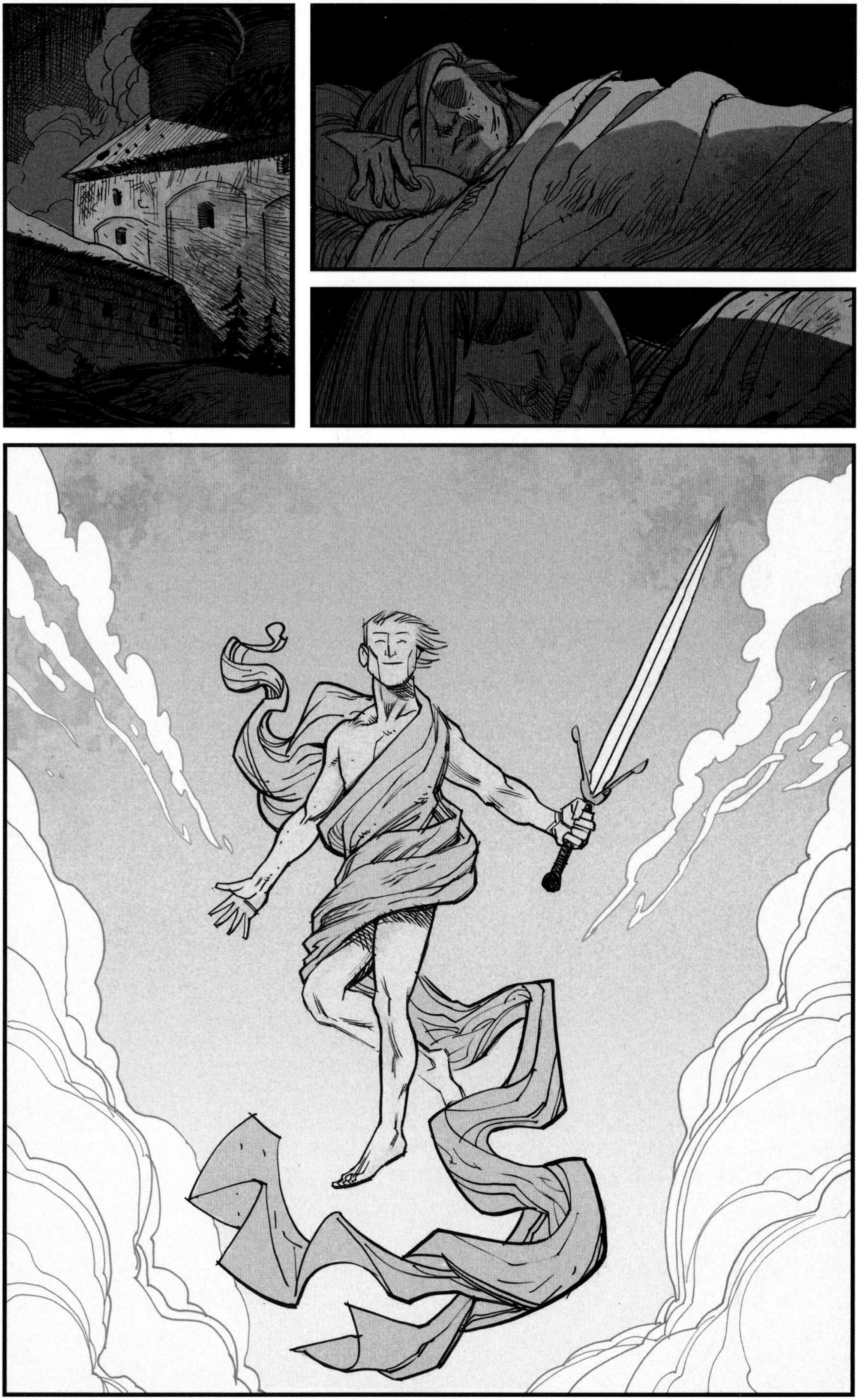

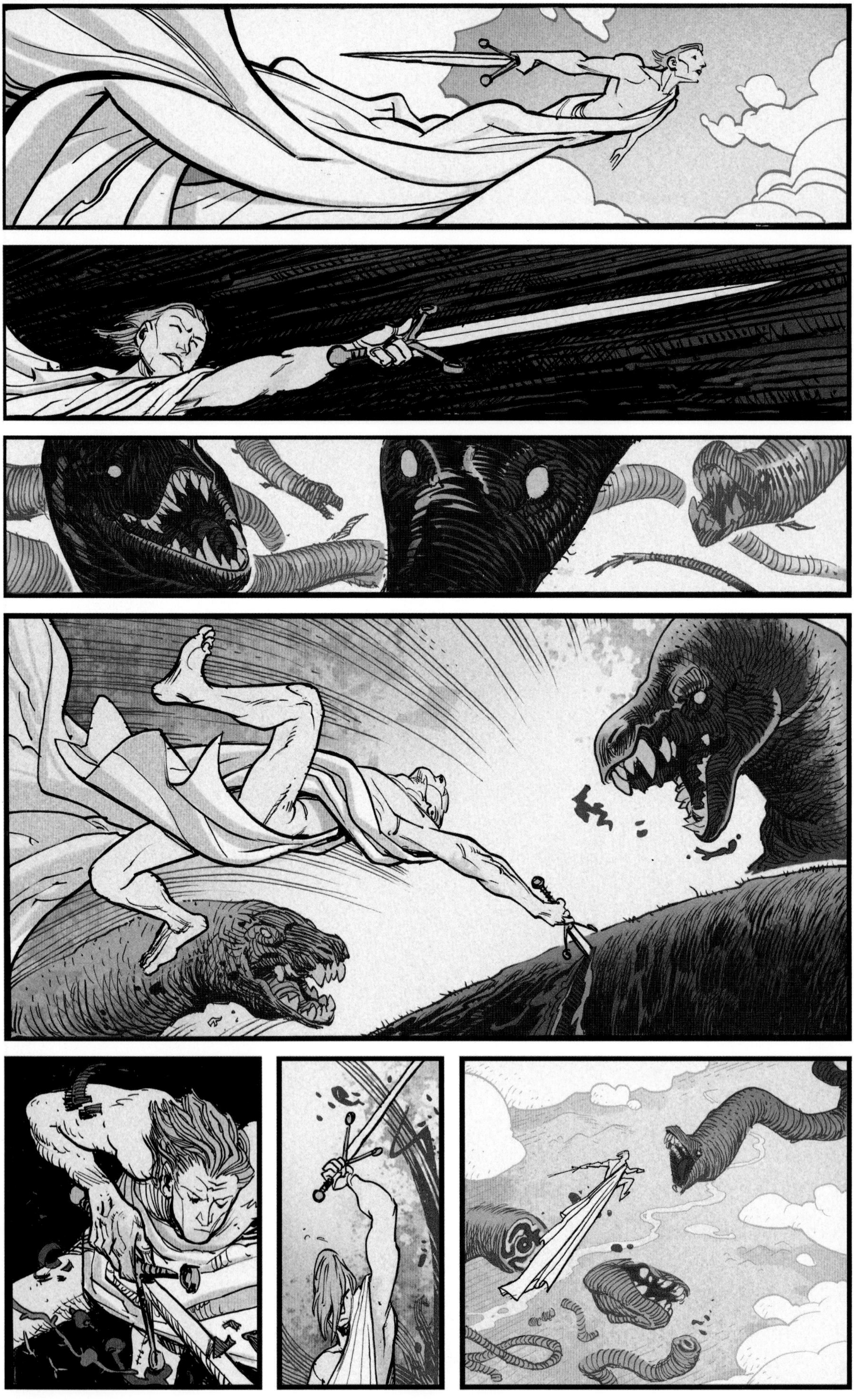

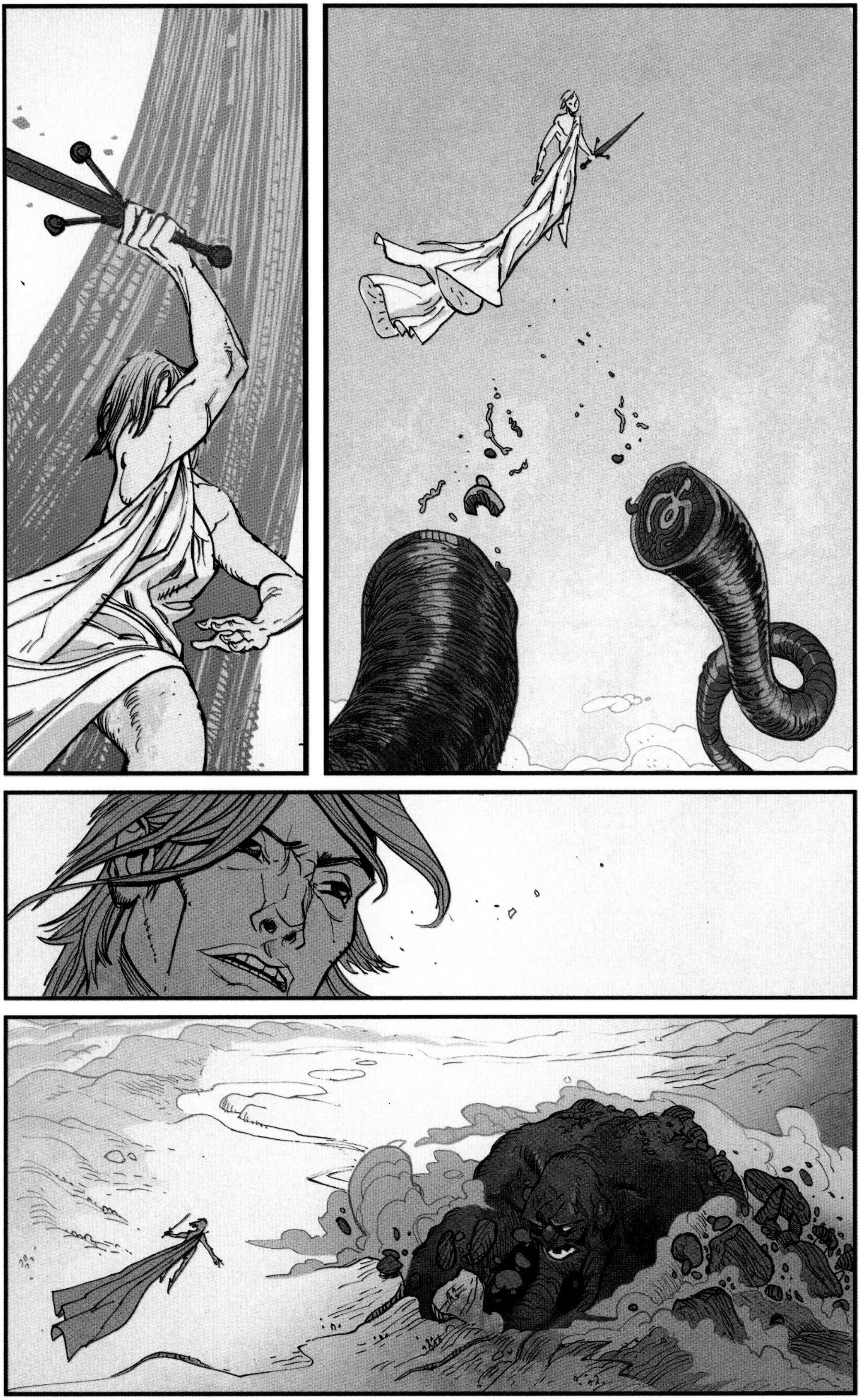

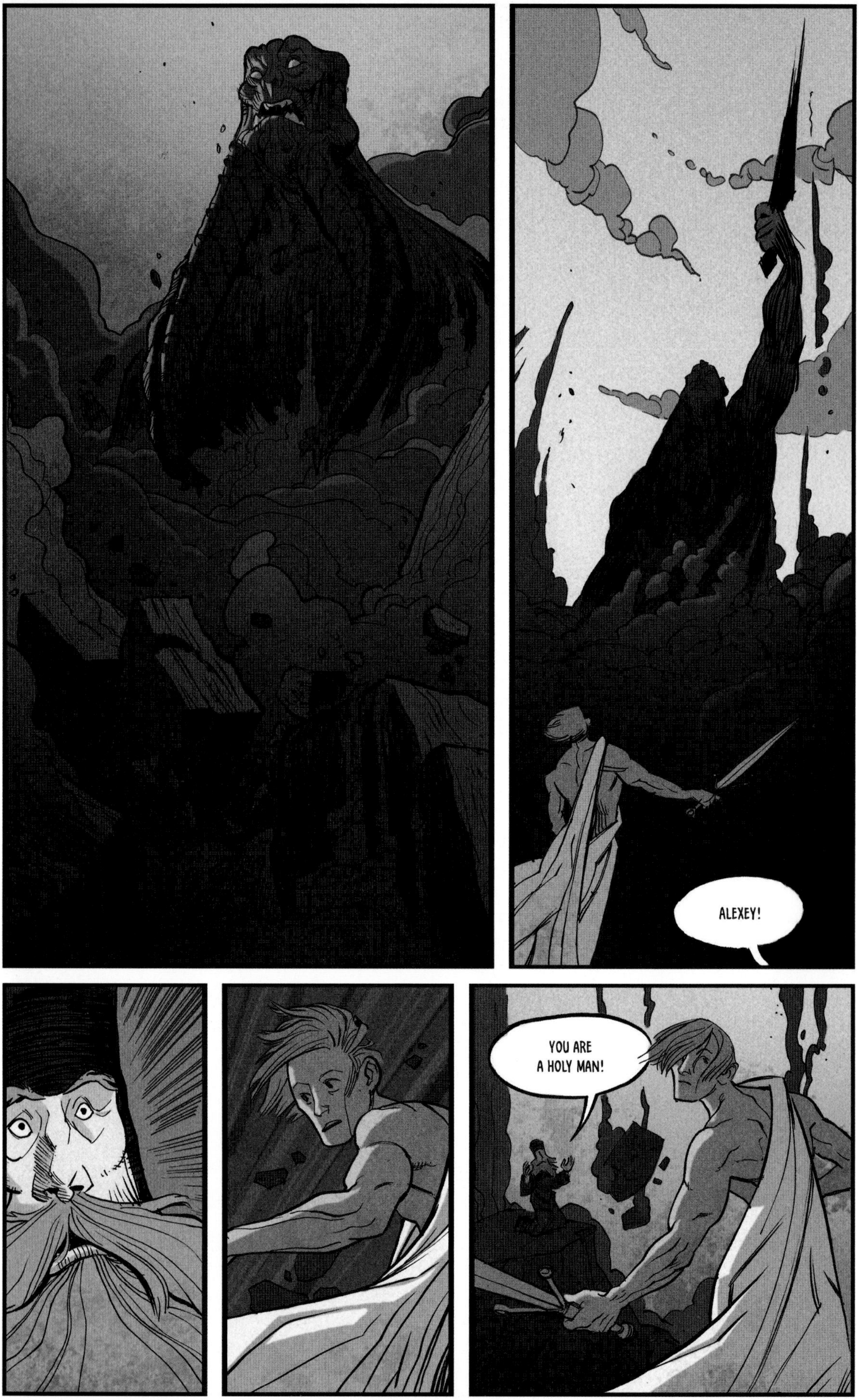
ALEXEY!
YOU ARE A HOLY MAN!

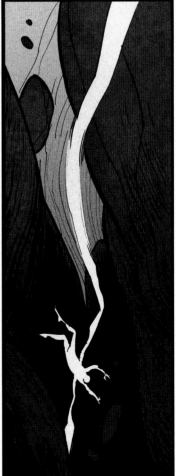

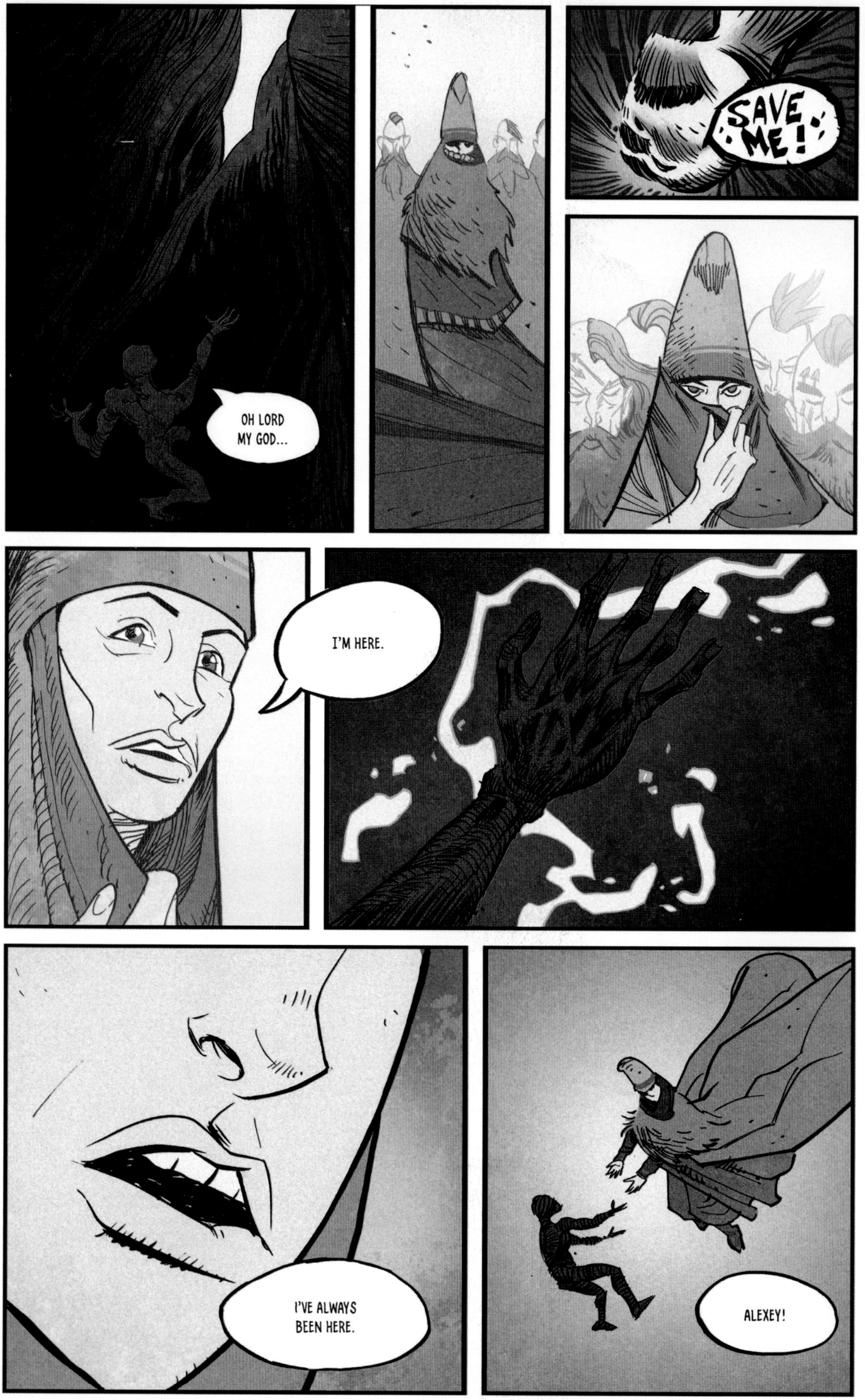
OH LORD MY GOD...
SAVE ME!
I'M HERE.
I'VE ALWAYS BEEN HERE.
ALEXEY!

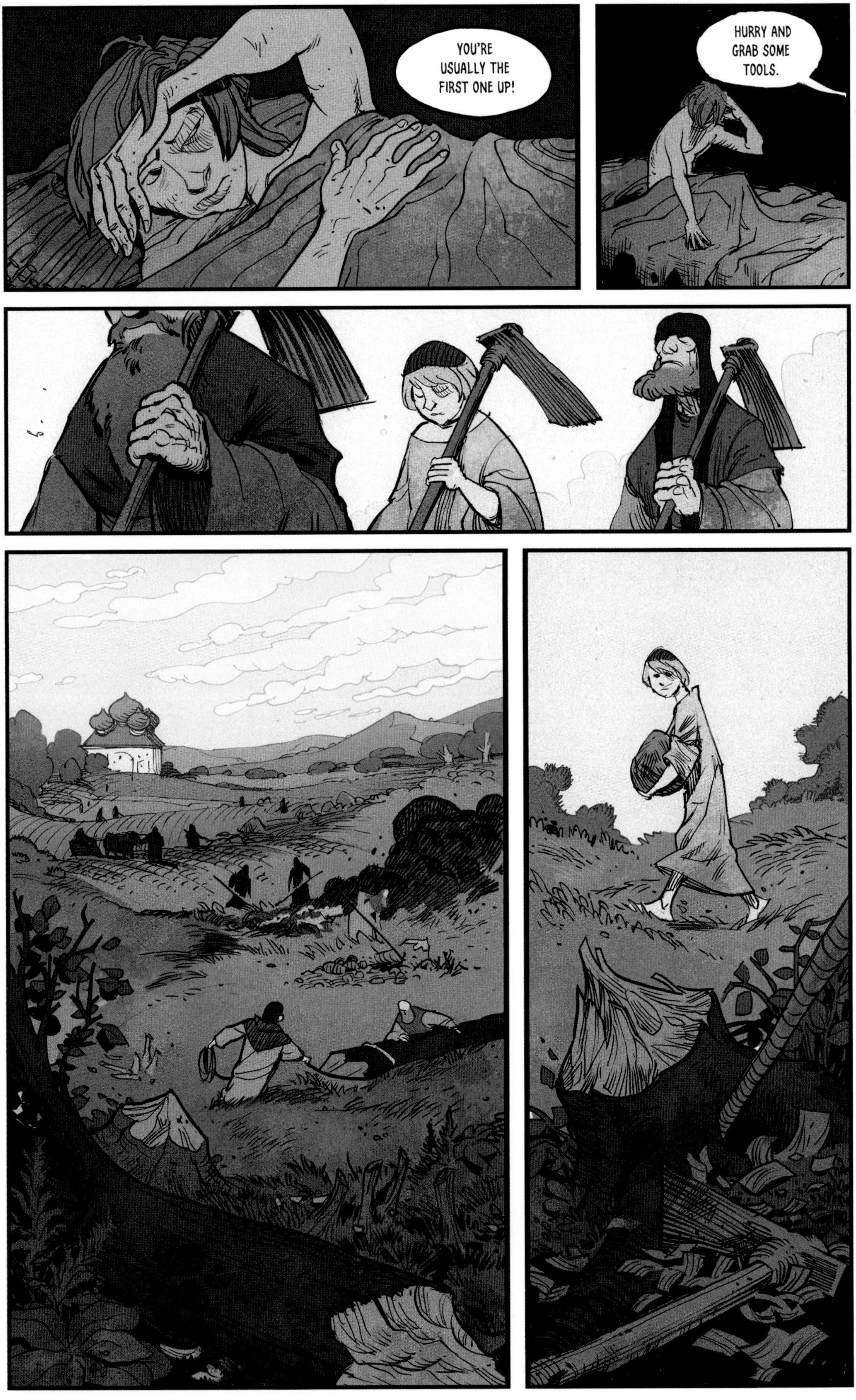
YOU'RE USUALLY THE FIRST ONE UP!
HURRY AND GRAB SOME TOOLS.

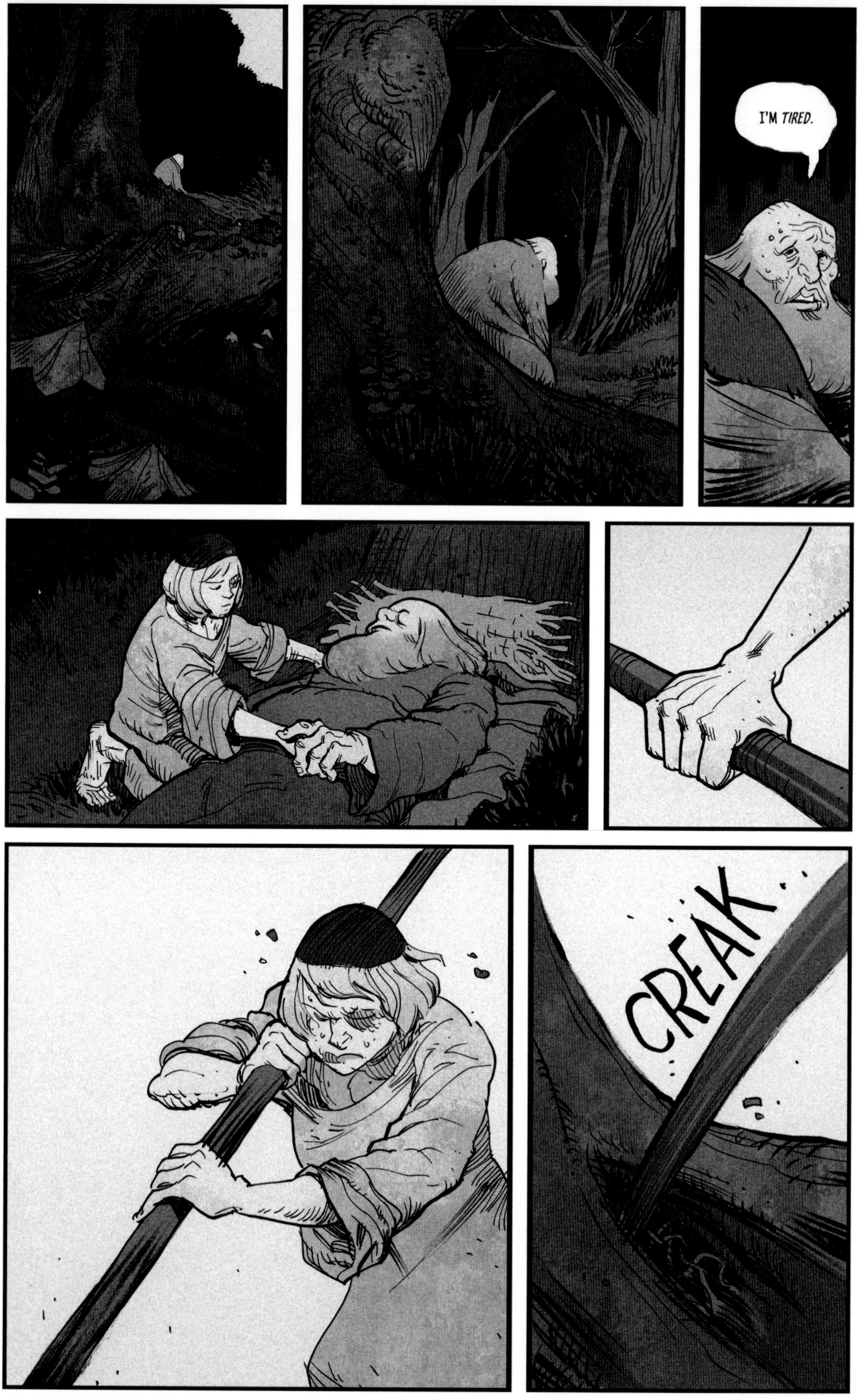
I'M *TIRED.*
CREAK

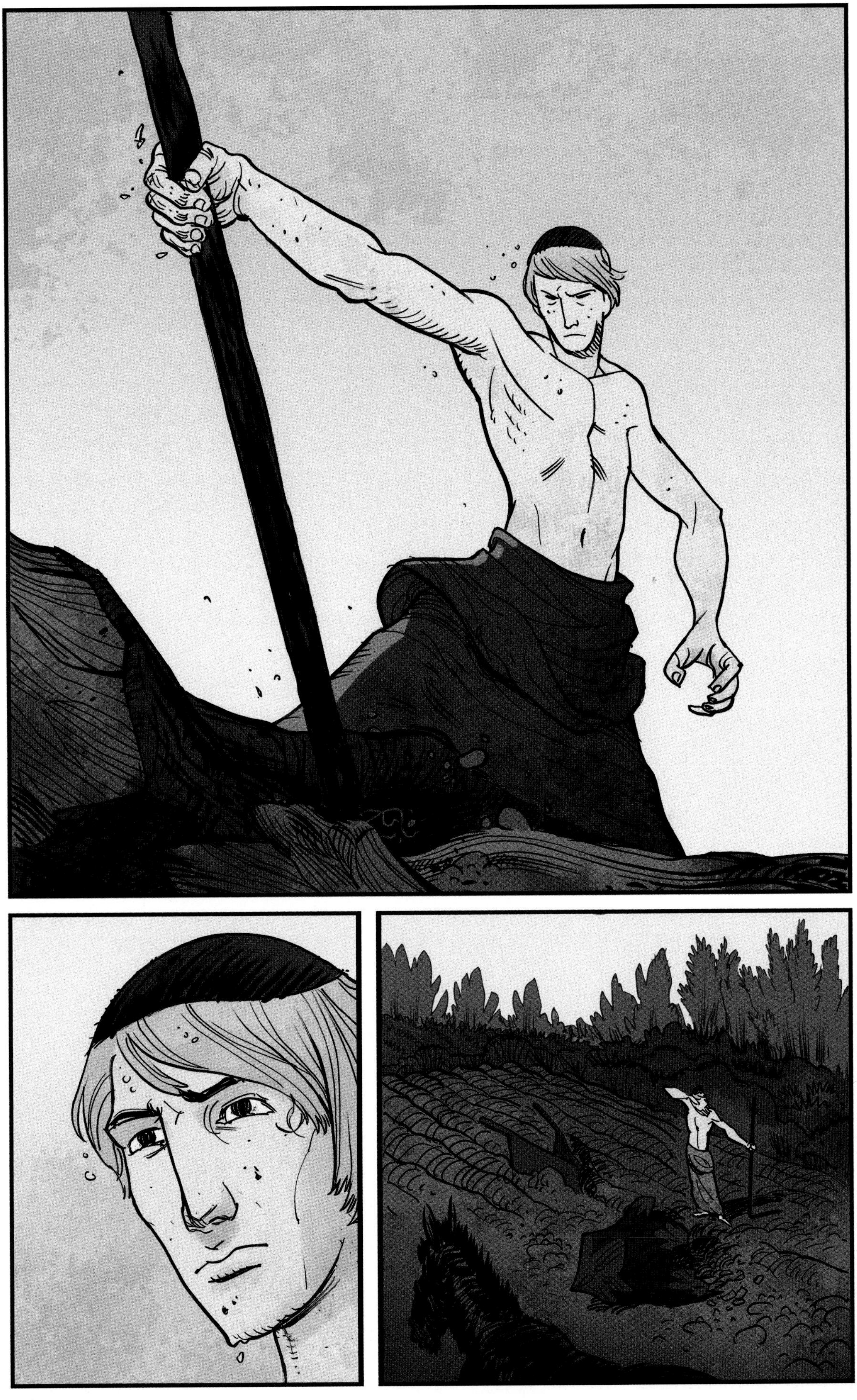

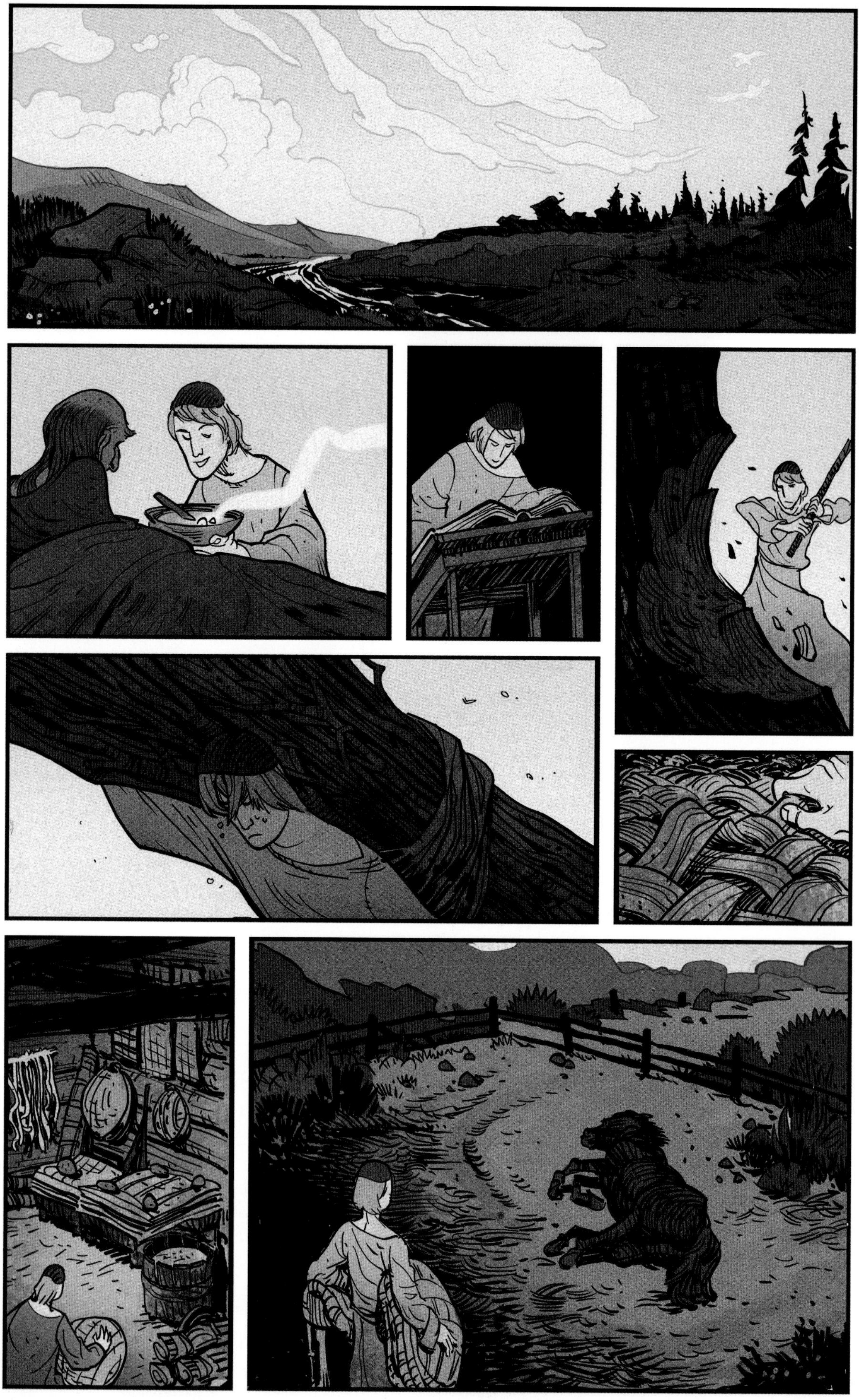

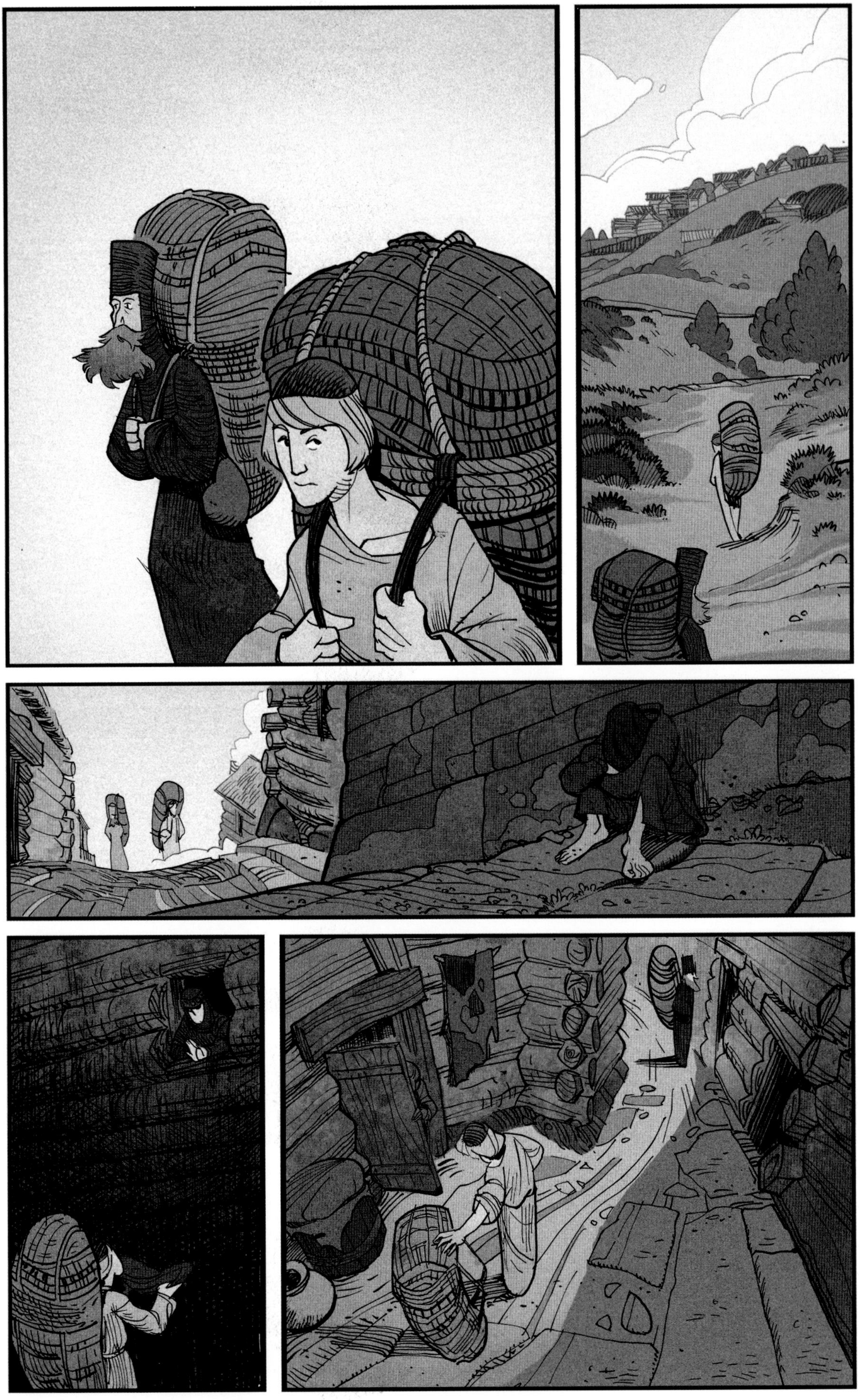

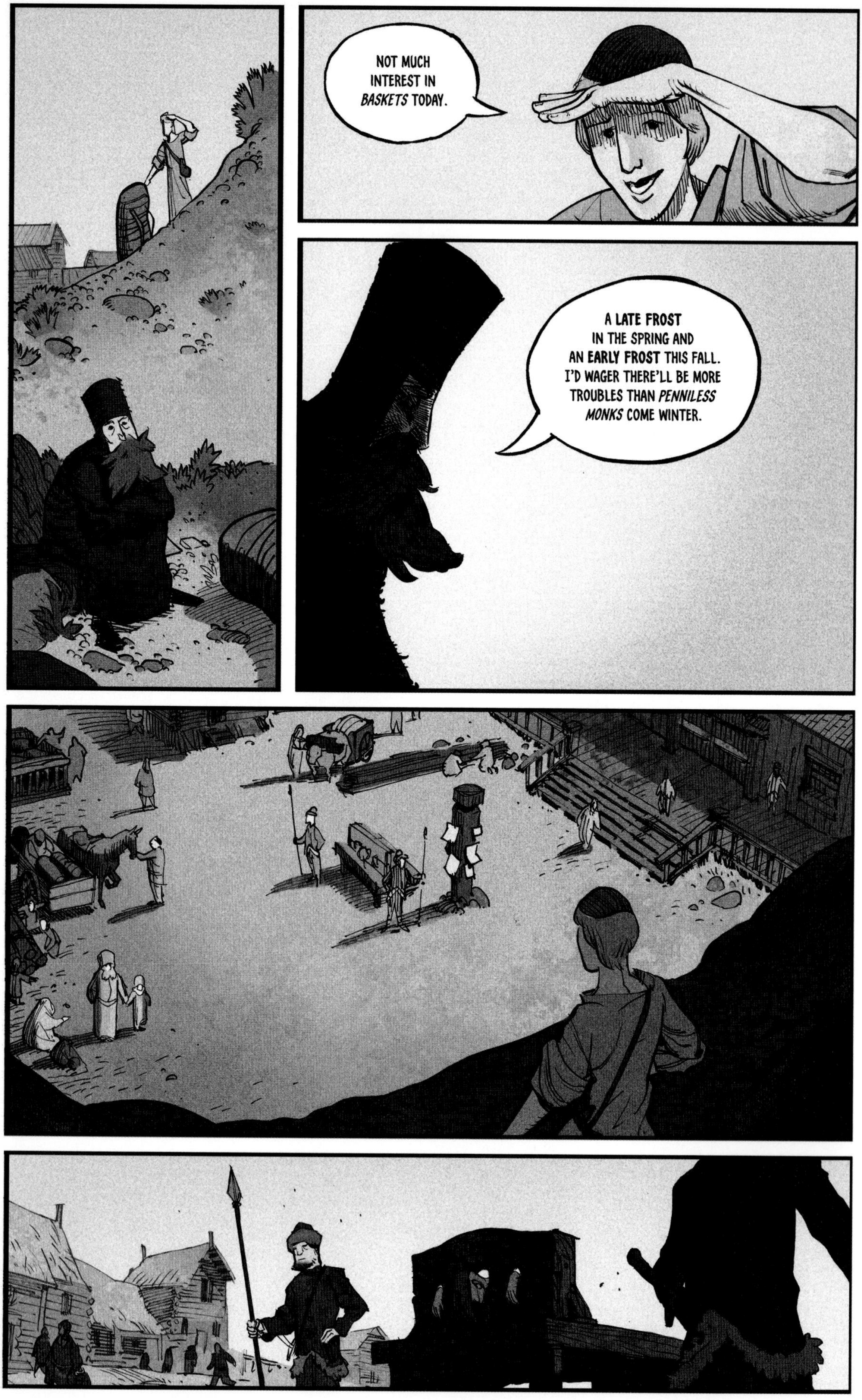
NOT MUCH INTEREST IN *BASKETS* TODAY.
A **LATE FROST** IN THE SPRING AND AN **EARLY FROST** THIS FALL. I'D WAGER THERE'LL BE MORE TROUBLES THAN *PENNILESS MONKS* COME WINTER.

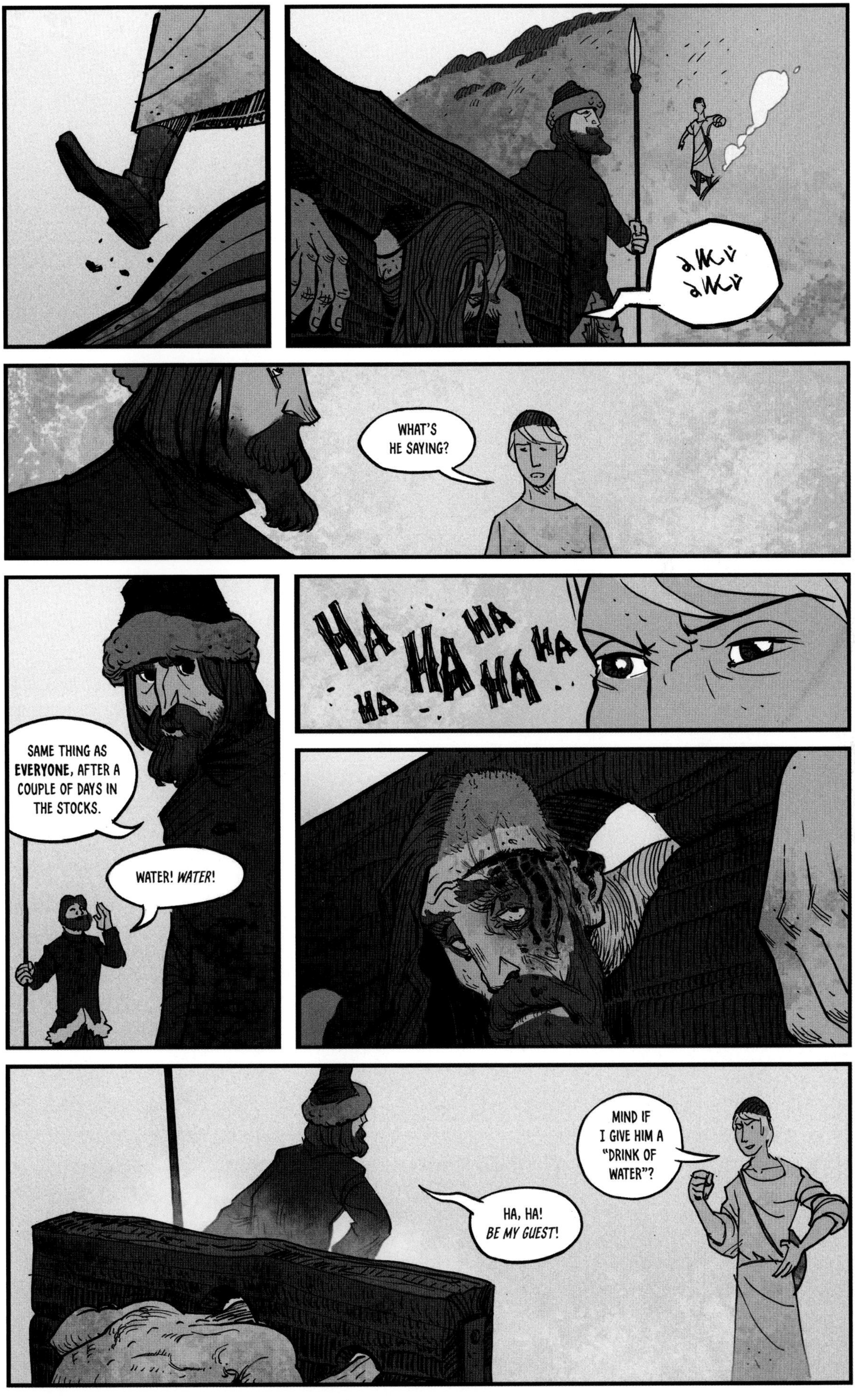
WHAT'S HE SAYING?
SAME THING AS EVERYONE, AFTER A COUPLE OF DAYS IN THE STOCKS.
WATER! WATER!
HA HA HA HA HA HA HA HA
MIND IF I GIVE HIM A "DRINK OF WATER"?
HA, HA! BE MY GUEST!

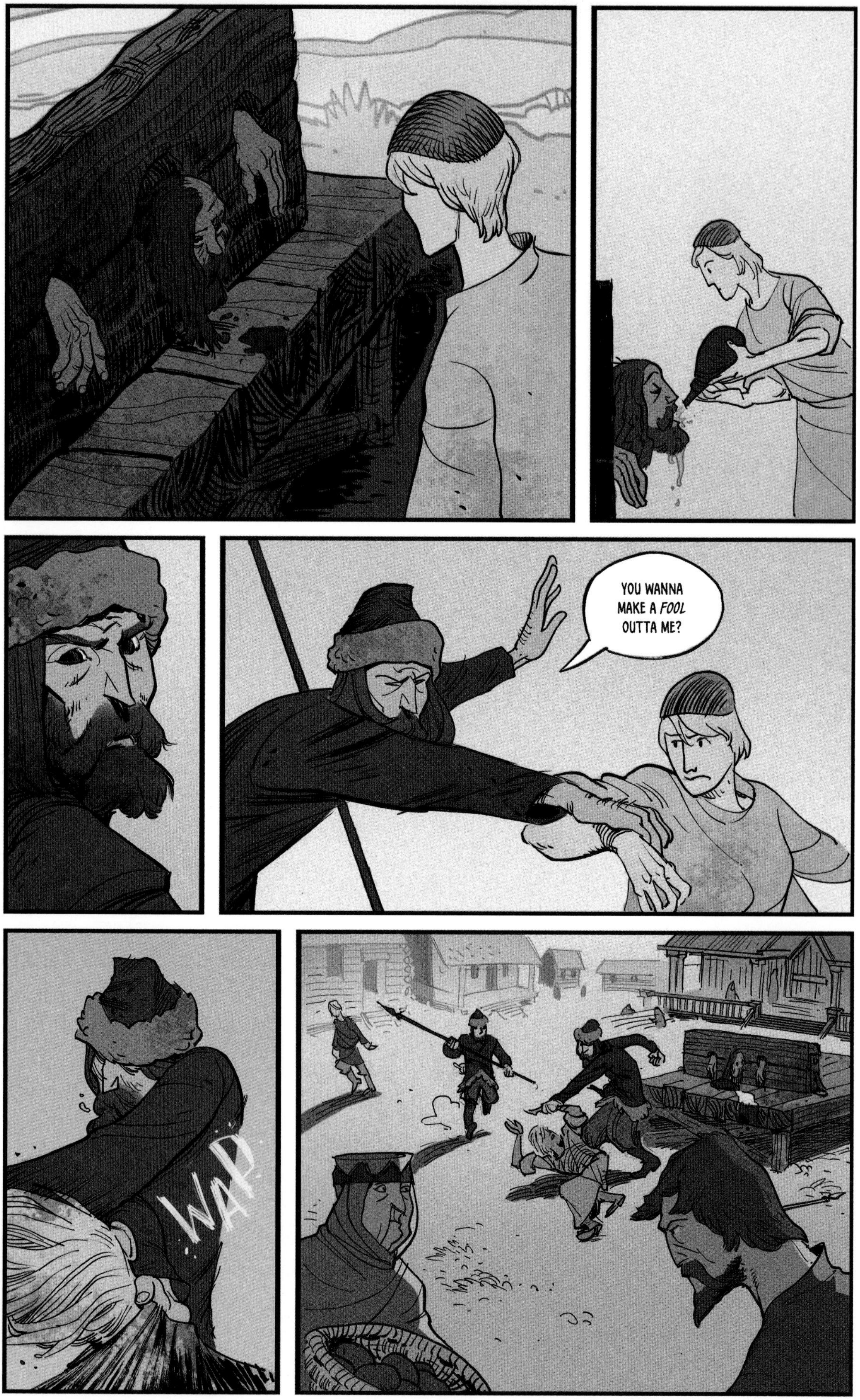
YOU WANNA MAKE A *FOOL* OUTTA ME?
WAP

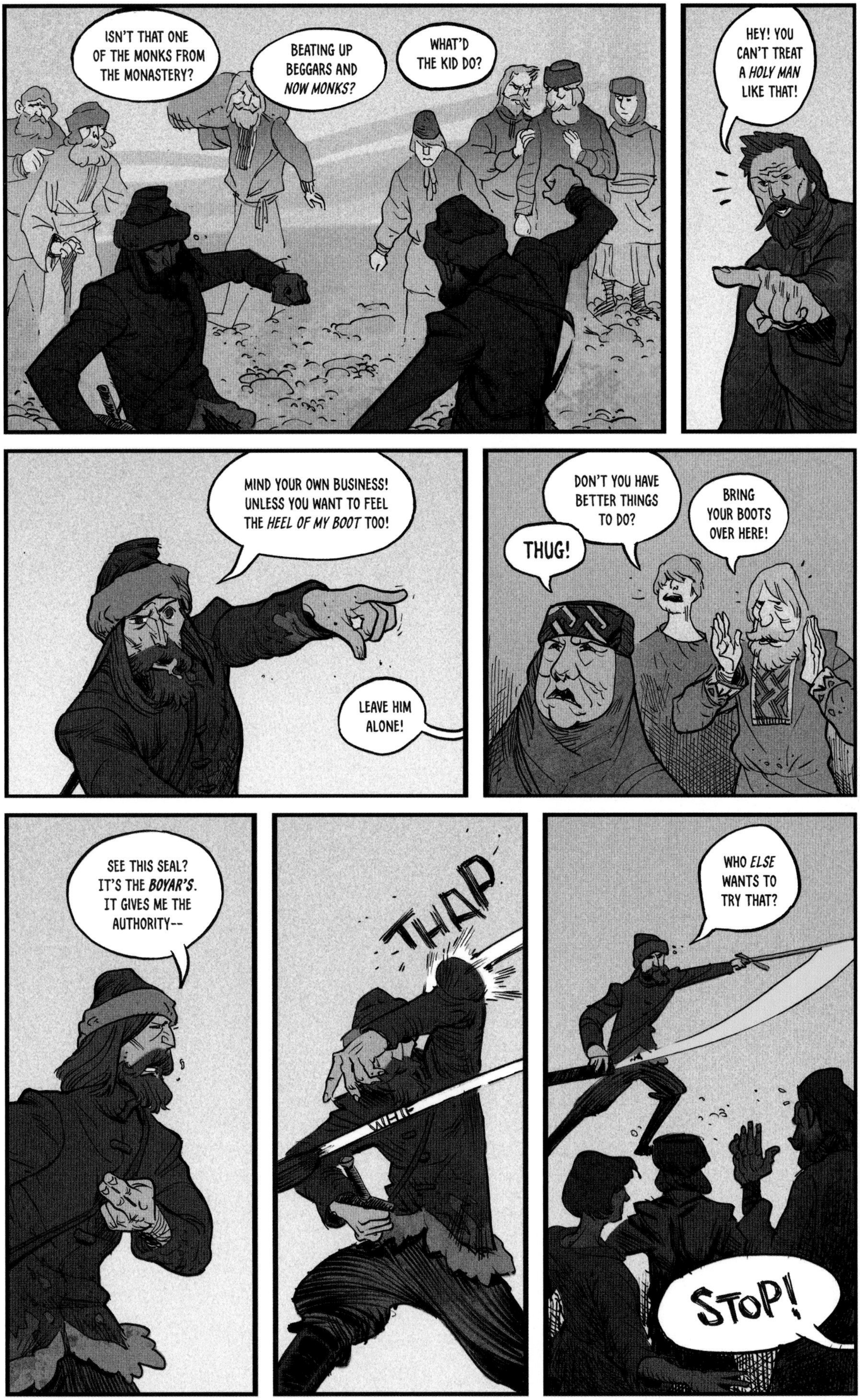
ISN'T THAT ONE OF THE MONKS FROM THE MONASTERY?
BEATING UP BEGGARS AND *NOW MONKS?*
WHAT'D THE KID DO?
HEY! YOU CAN'T TREAT A *HOLY MAN* LIKE THAT!
MIND YOUR OWN BUSINESS! UNLESS YOU WANT TO FEEL THE *HEEL OF MY BOOT* TOO!
LEAVE HIM ALONE!
THUG!
DON'T YOU HAVE BETTER THINGS TO DO?
BRING YOUR BOOTS OVER HERE!
SEE THIS SEAL? IT'S THE *BOYAR'S*. IT GIVES ME THE AUTHORITY--
THAP
WHO *ELSE* WANTS TO TRY THAT?
STOP!

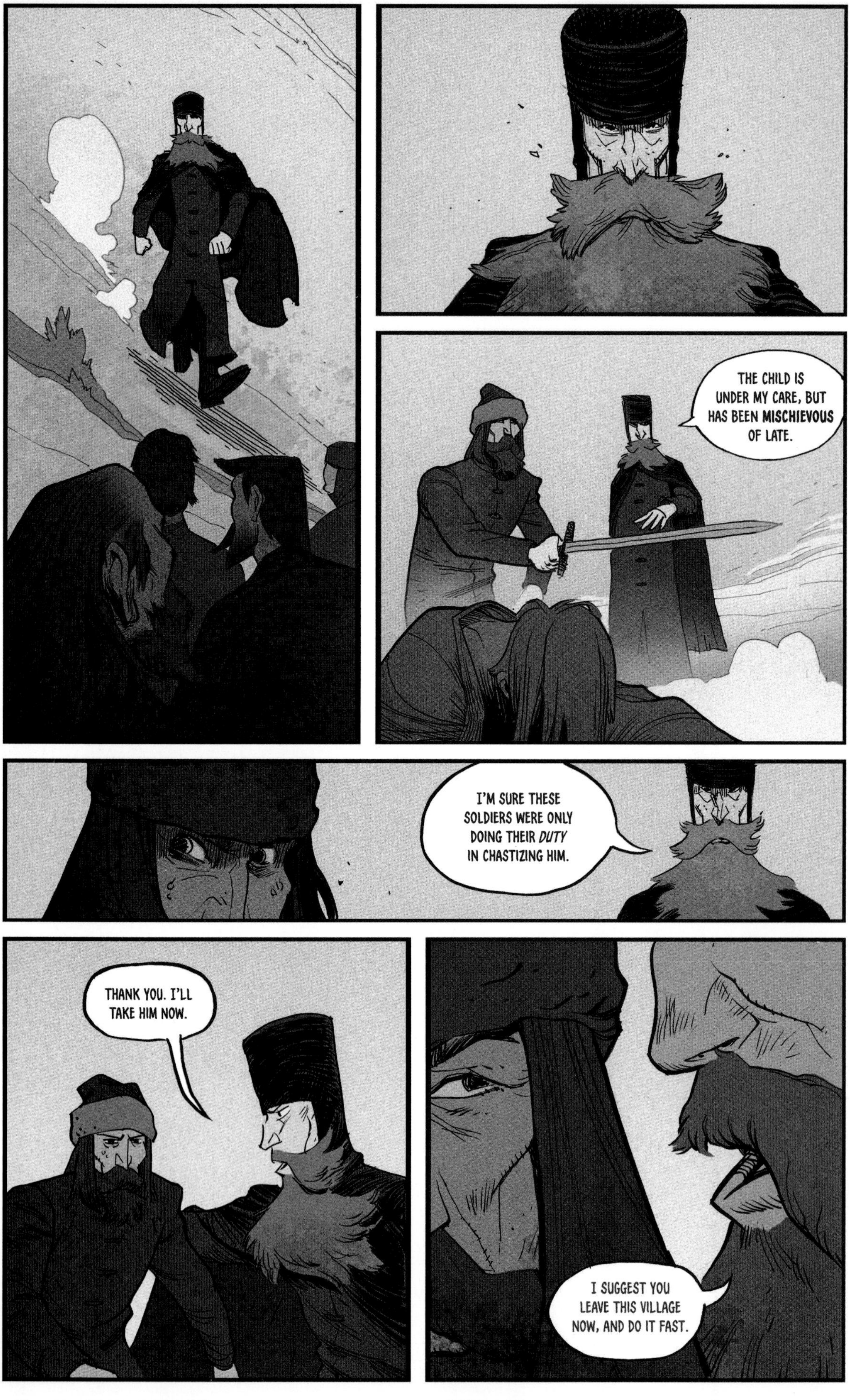
THE CHILD IS UNDER MY CARE, BUT HAS BEEN **MISCHIEVOUS** OF LATE.
I'M SURE THESE SOLDIERS WERE ONLY DOING THEIR *DUTY* IN CHASTIZING HIM.
THANK YOU. I'LL TAKE HIM NOW.
I SUGGEST YOU LEAVE THIS VILLAGE NOW, AND DO IT FAST.

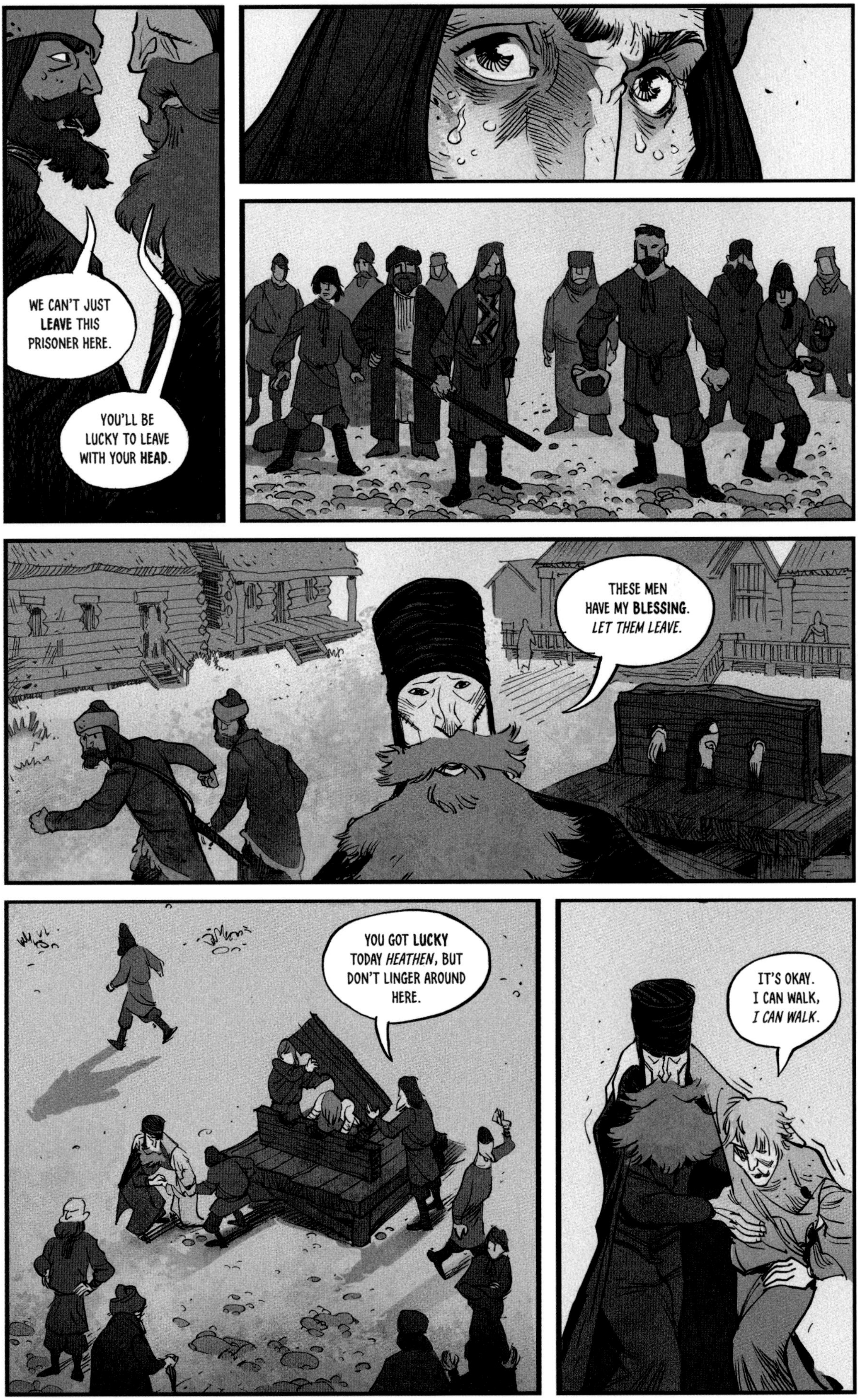
WE CAN'T JUST **LEAVE** THIS PRISONER HERE.
YOU'LL BE LUCKY TO LEAVE WITH YOUR **HEAD**.
THESE MEN HAVE MY **BLESSING**. *LET THEM LEAVE.*
YOU GOT **LUCKY** TODAY *HEATHEN*, BUT DON'T LINGER AROUND HERE.
IT'S OKAY. I CAN WALK, *I CAN WALK*.

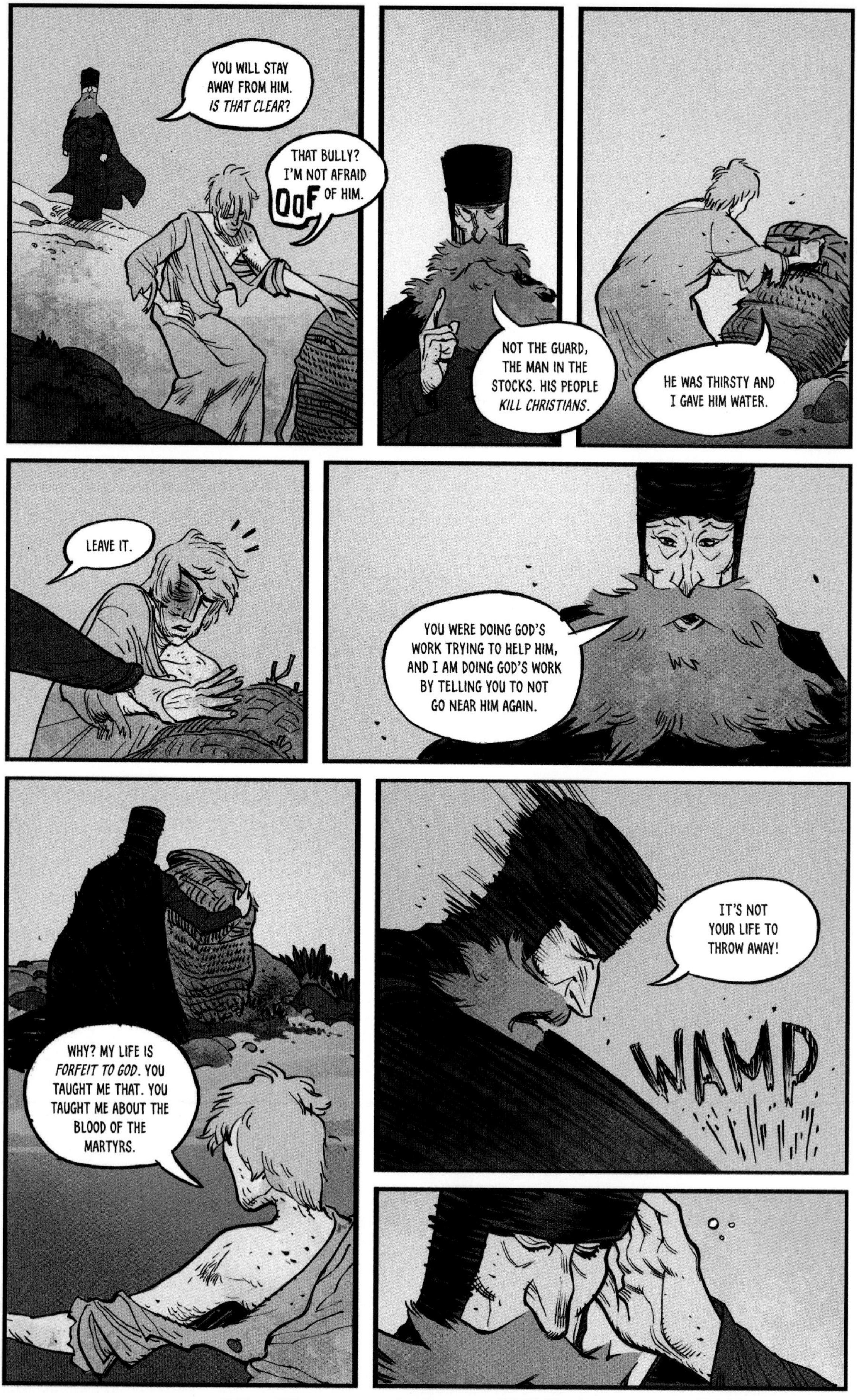
YOU WILL STAY AWAY FROM HIM. *IS THAT CLEAR?*
THAT BULLY? I'M NOT AFRAID OF HIM.
OOF
NOT THE GUARD, THE MAN IN THE STOCKS. HIS PEOPLE *KILL CHRISTIANS*.
HE WAS THIRSTY AND I GAVE HIM WATER.
LEAVE IT.
YOU WERE DOING GOD'S WORK TRYING TO HELP HIM, AND I AM DOING GOD'S WORK BY TELLING YOU TO NOT GO NEAR HIM AGAIN.
WHY? MY LIFE IS *FORFEIT TO GOD*. YOU TAUGHT ME THAT. YOU TAUGHT ME ABOUT THE BLOOD OF THE MARTYRS.
IT'S NOT YOUR LIFE TO THROW AWAY!
WAMP

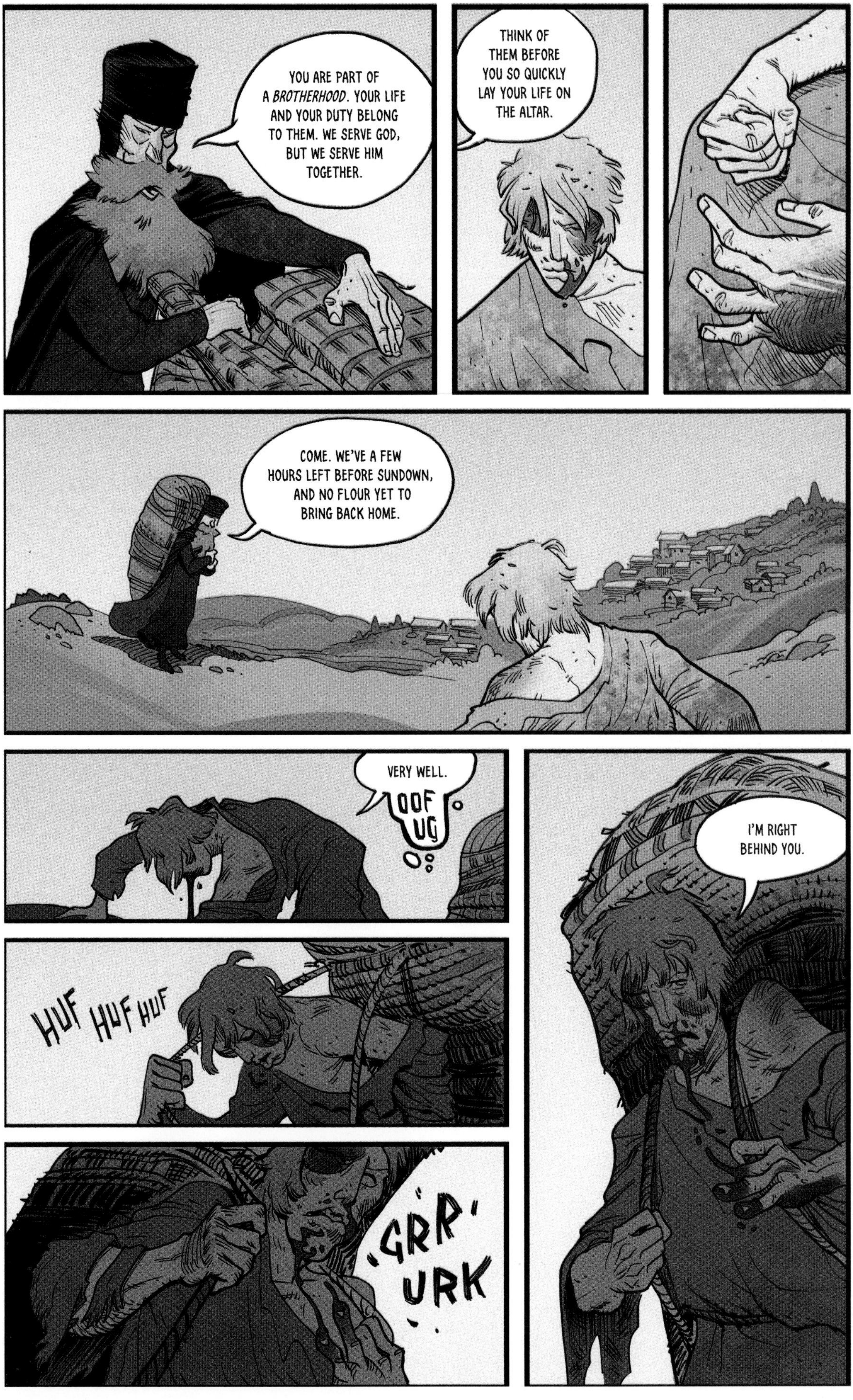
YOU ARE PART OF A *BROTHERHOOD*. YOUR LIFE AND YOUR DUTY BELONG TO THEM. WE SERVE GOD, BUT WE SERVE HIM TOGETHER.
THINK OF THEM BEFORE YOU SO QUICKLY LAY YOUR LIFE ON THE ALTAR.
COME. WE'VE A FEW HOURS LEFT BEFORE SUNDOWN, AND NO FLOUR YET TO BRING BACK HOME.
VERY WELL.
OOF UG
HUF HUF HUF
GRR URK
I'M RIGHT BEHIND YOU.

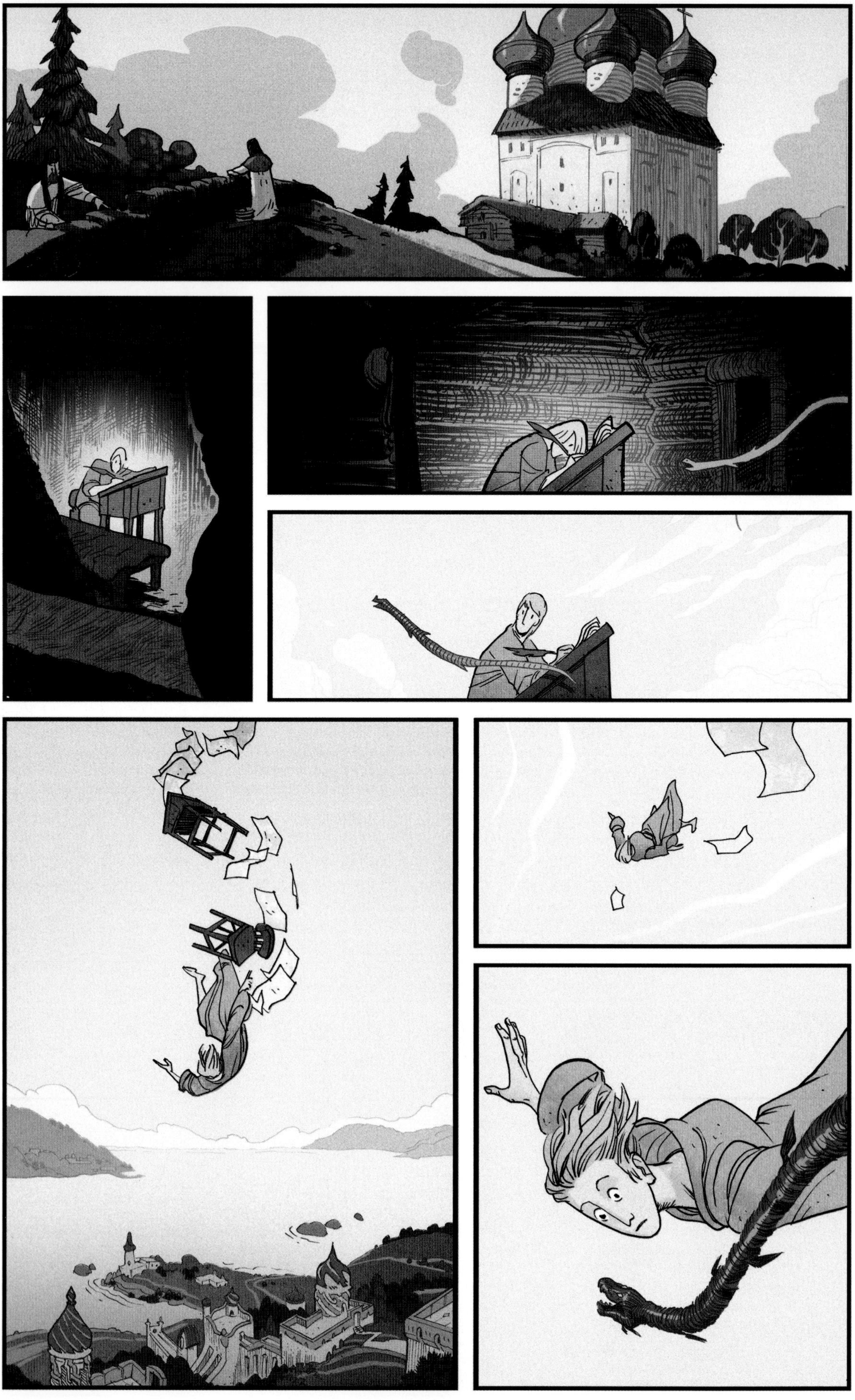

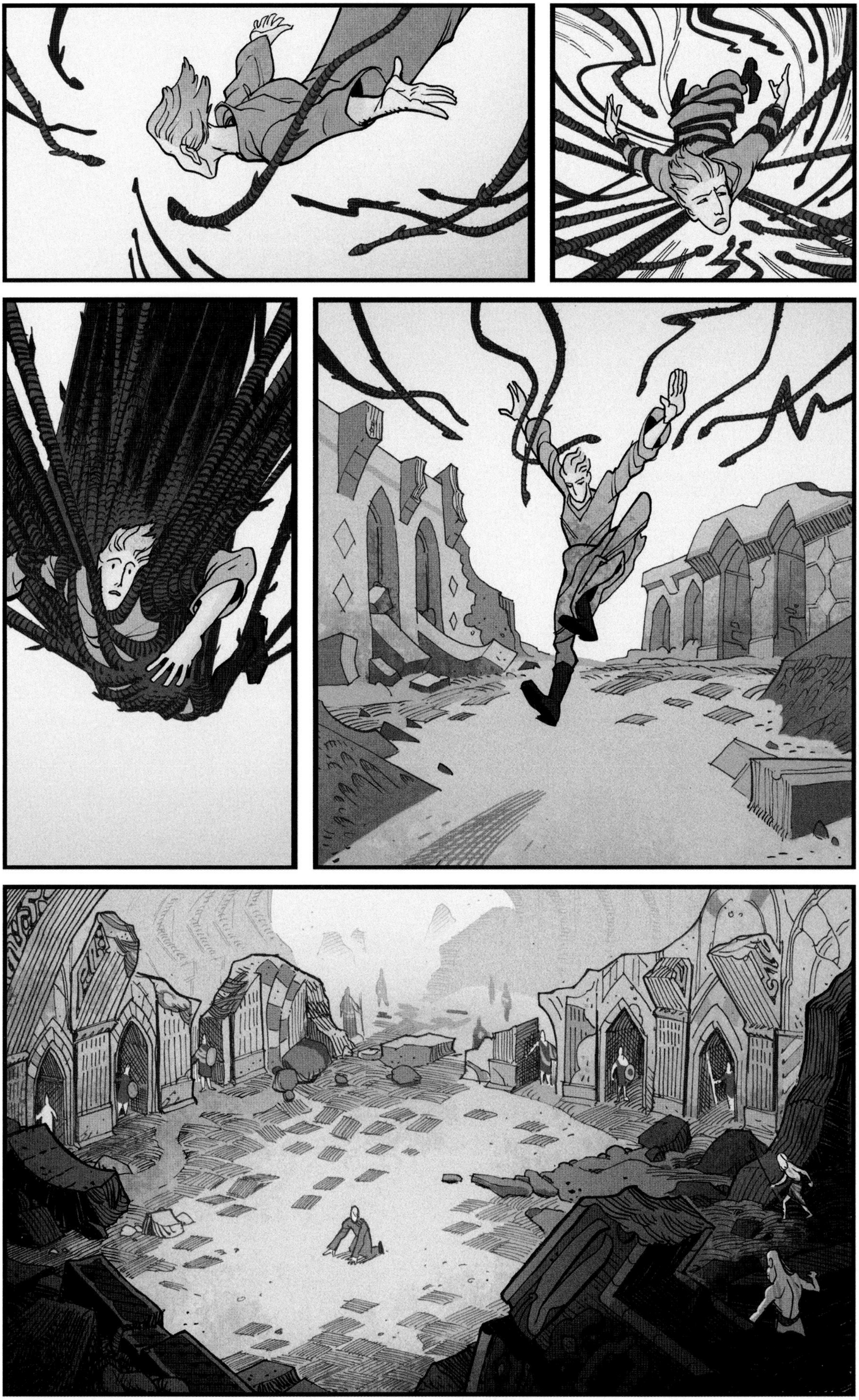

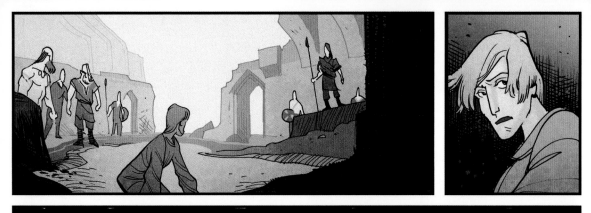

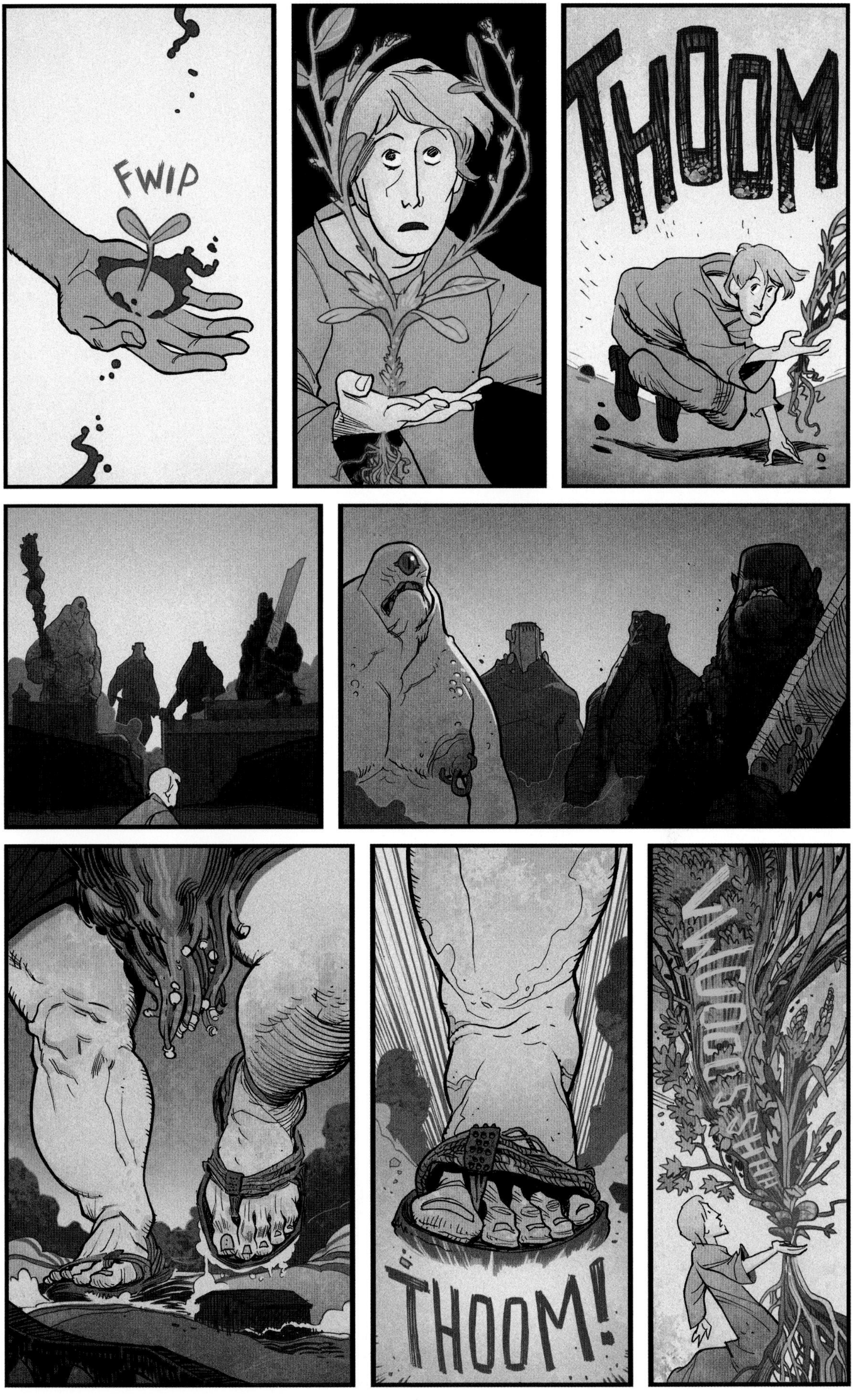
FWIP
THOOM
THOOM!
WOOOOSSHHH

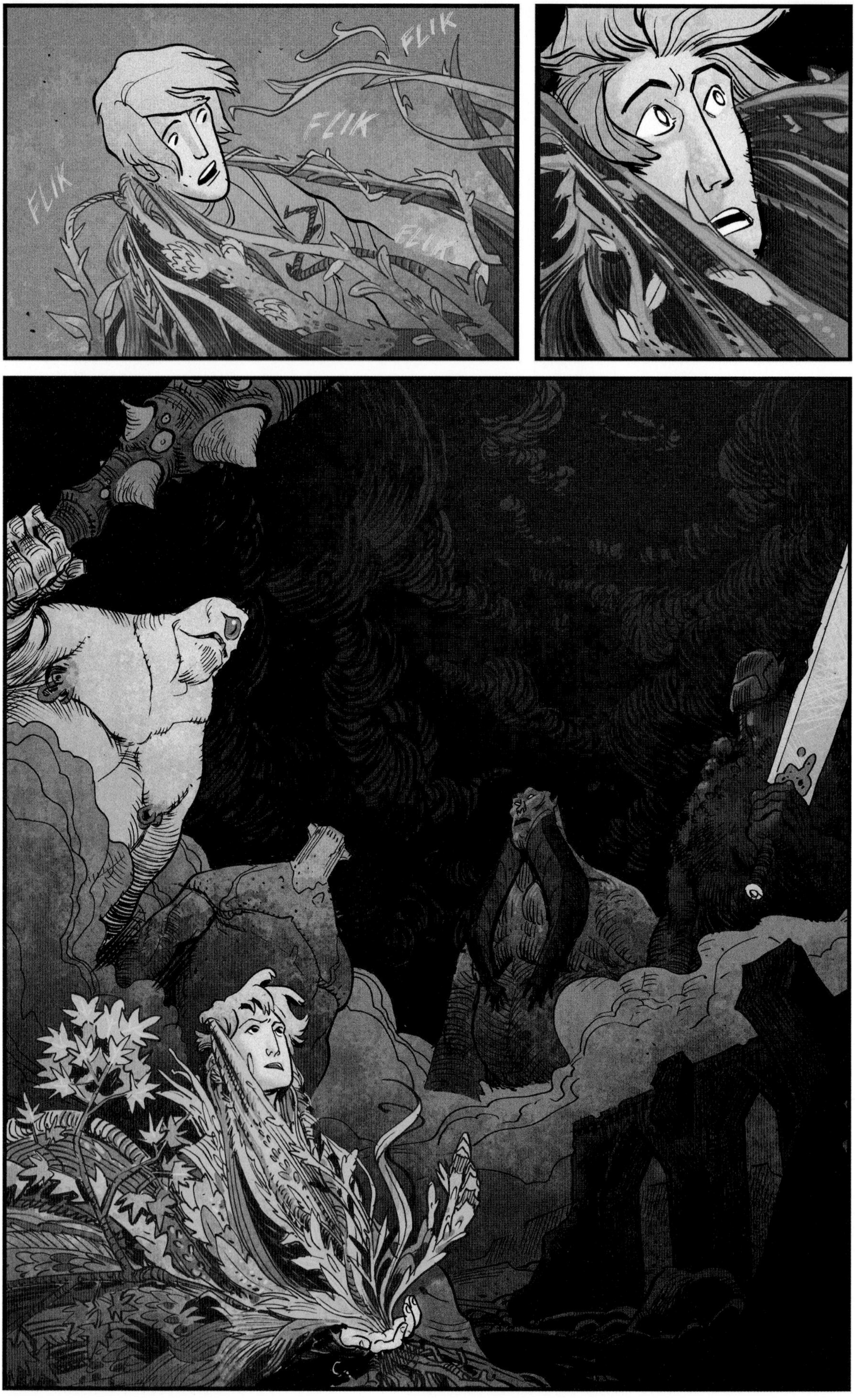
FLIK
FLIK
FLIK
FLIK

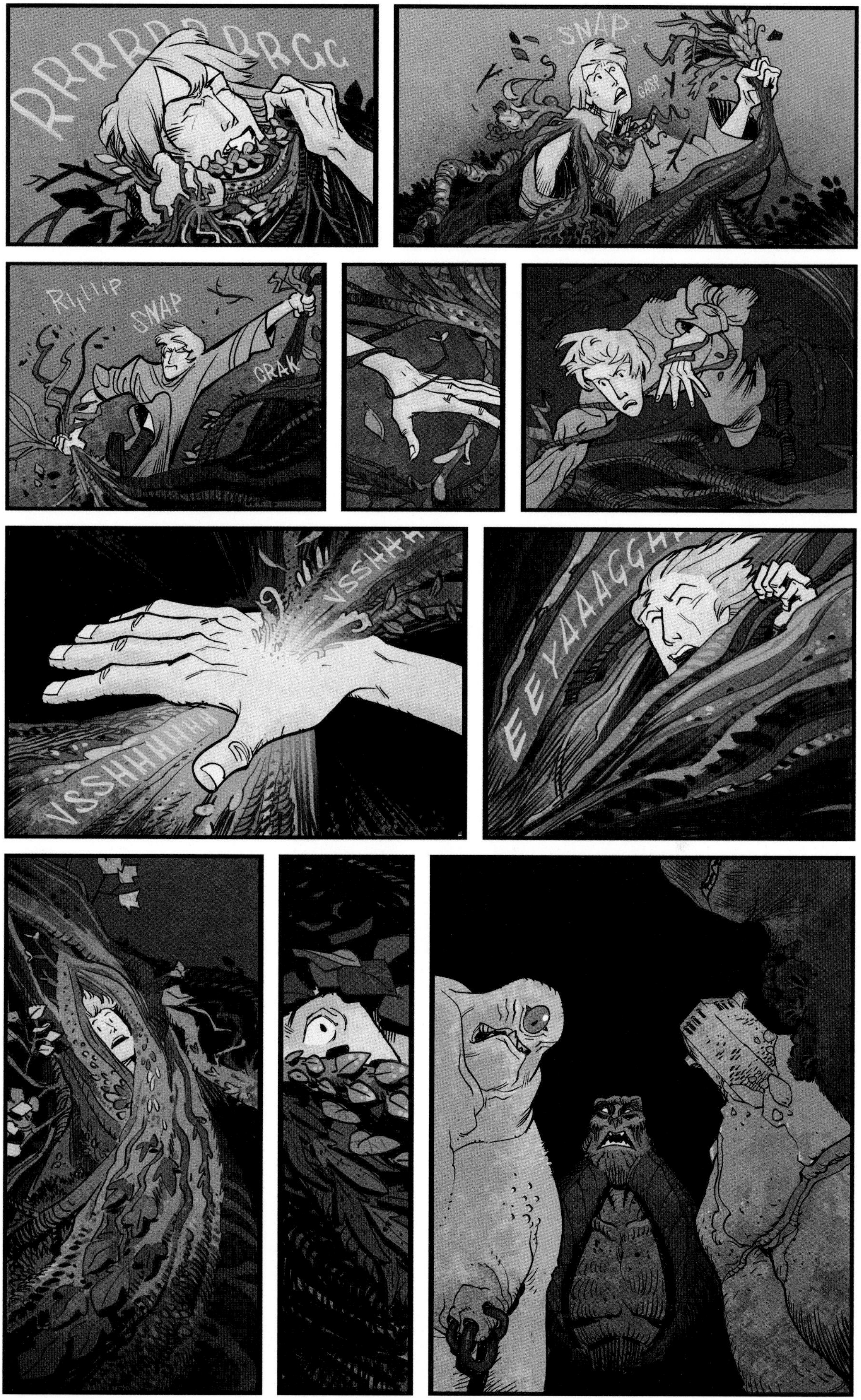
RRRRRRRRGC
SNAP
GASP
RIIIIP
SNAP
GRAK
VSSHHH
VSSHHHHHH
EEYAAAGGH

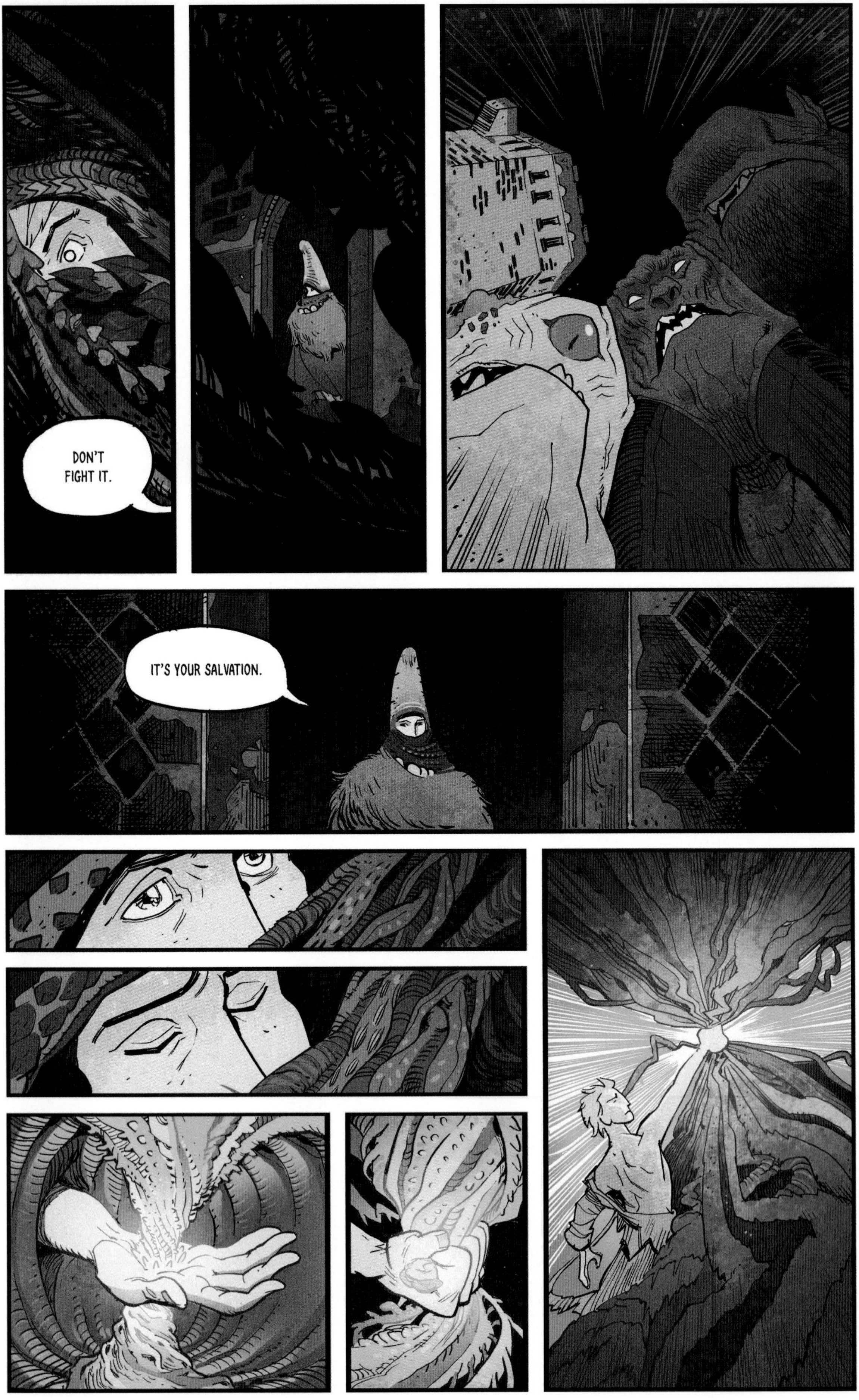
DON'T FIGHT IT.
IT'S YOUR SALVATION.

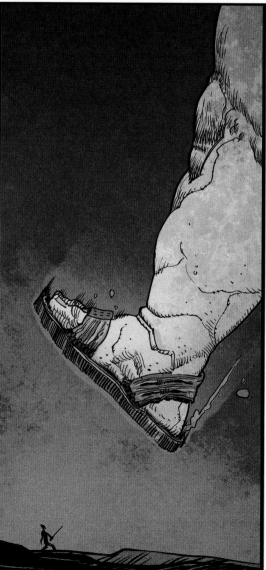

BRAAAM

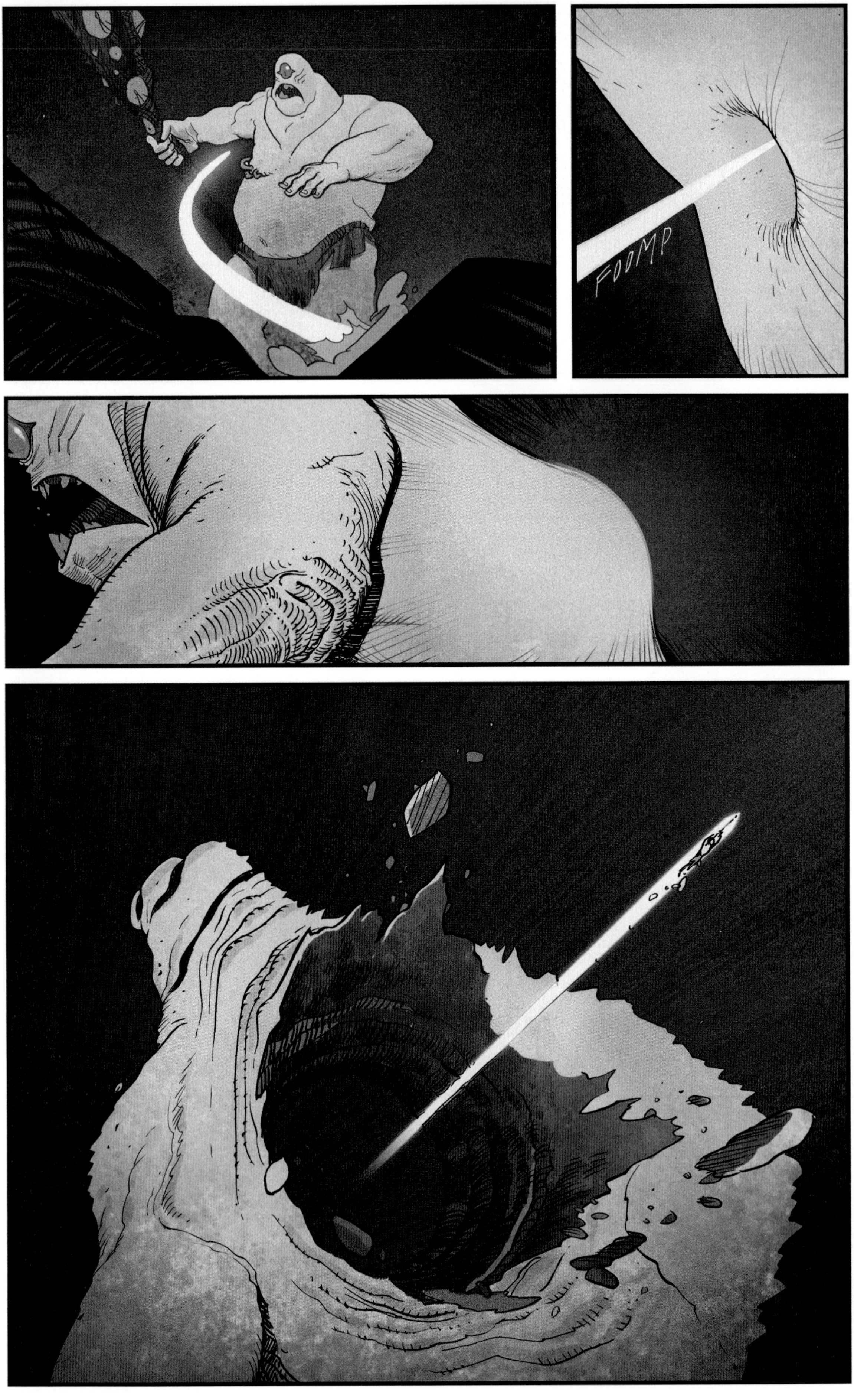
FOOMP

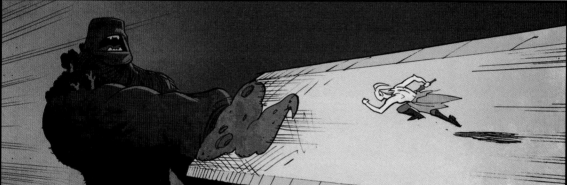

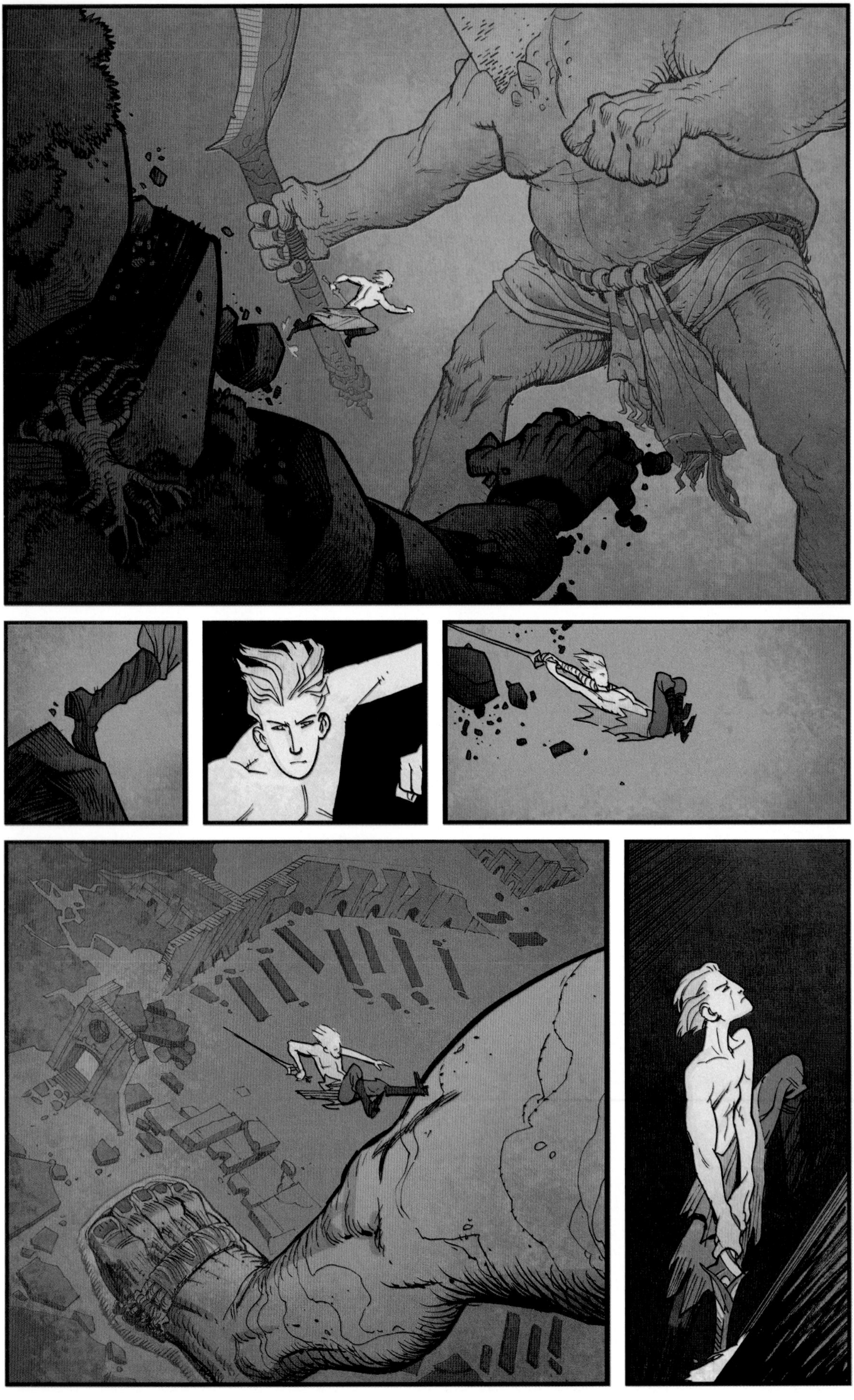

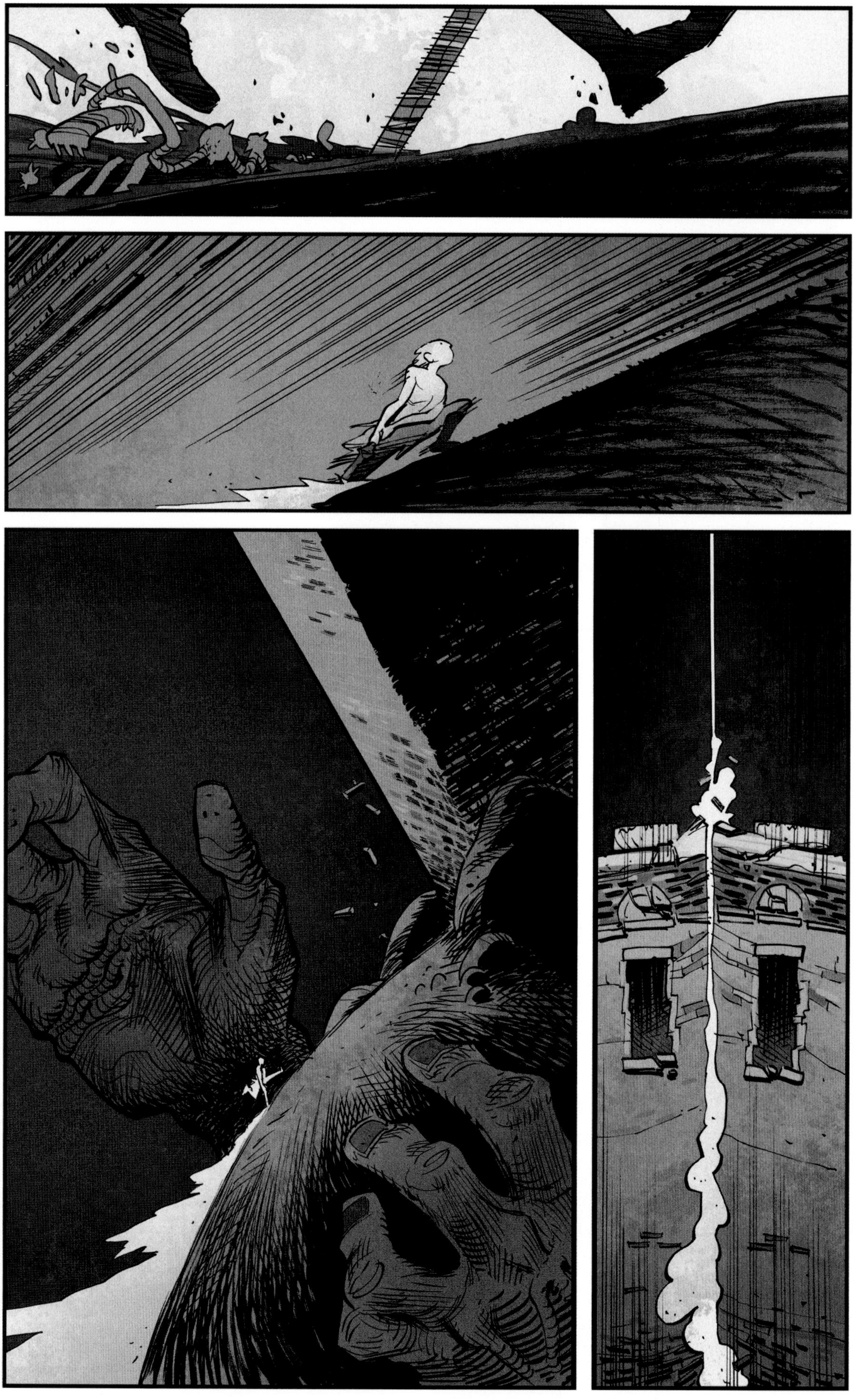

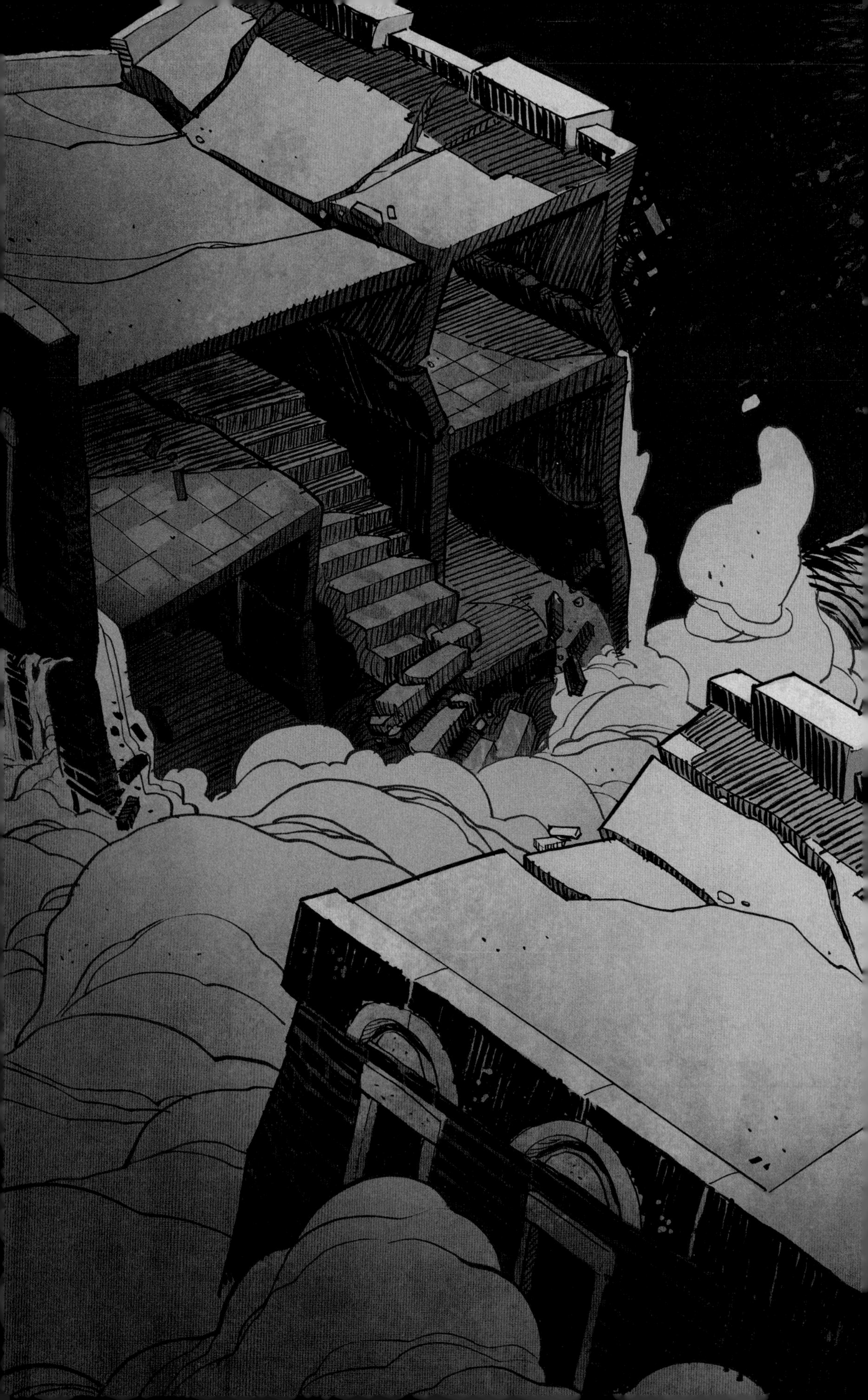

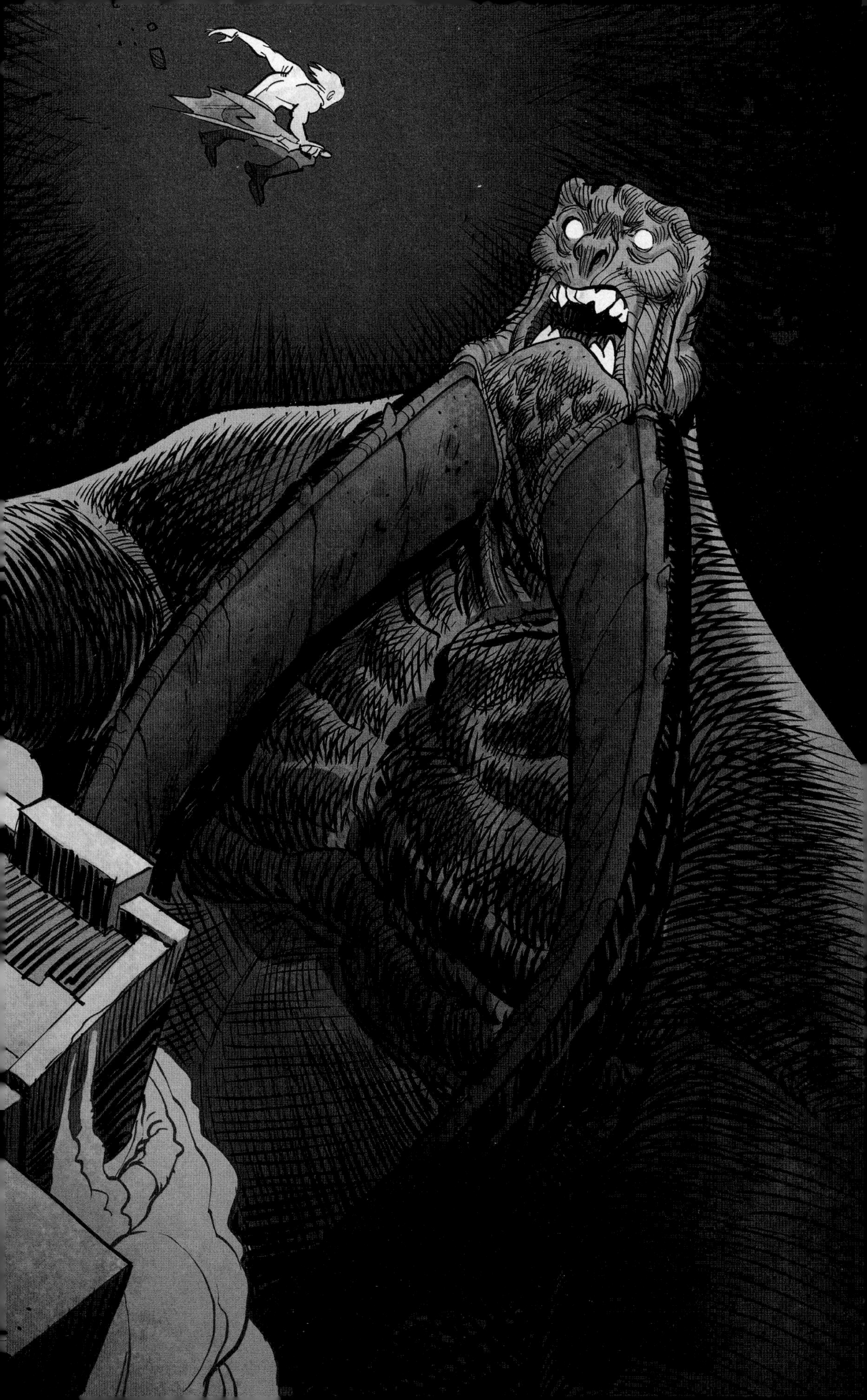

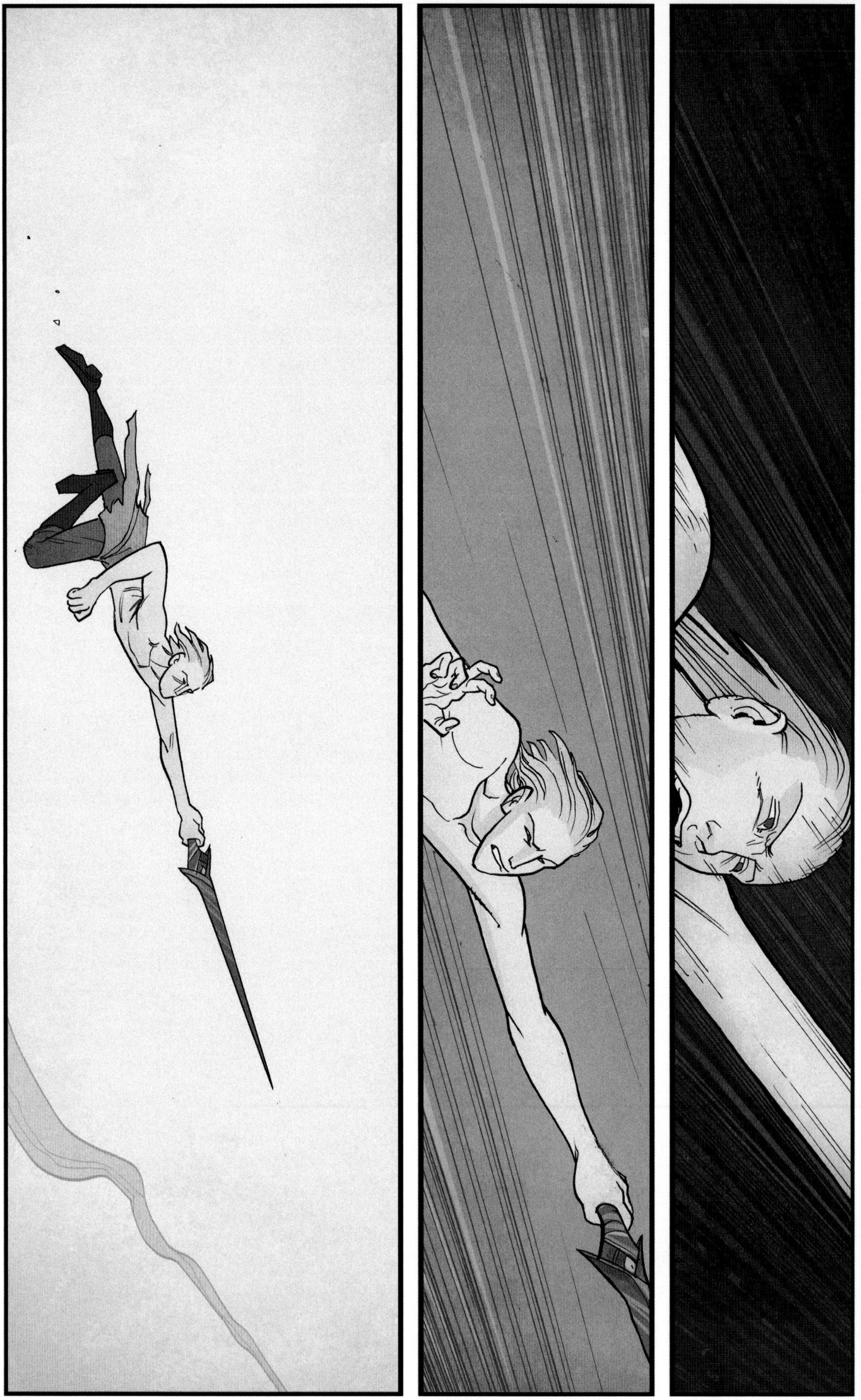

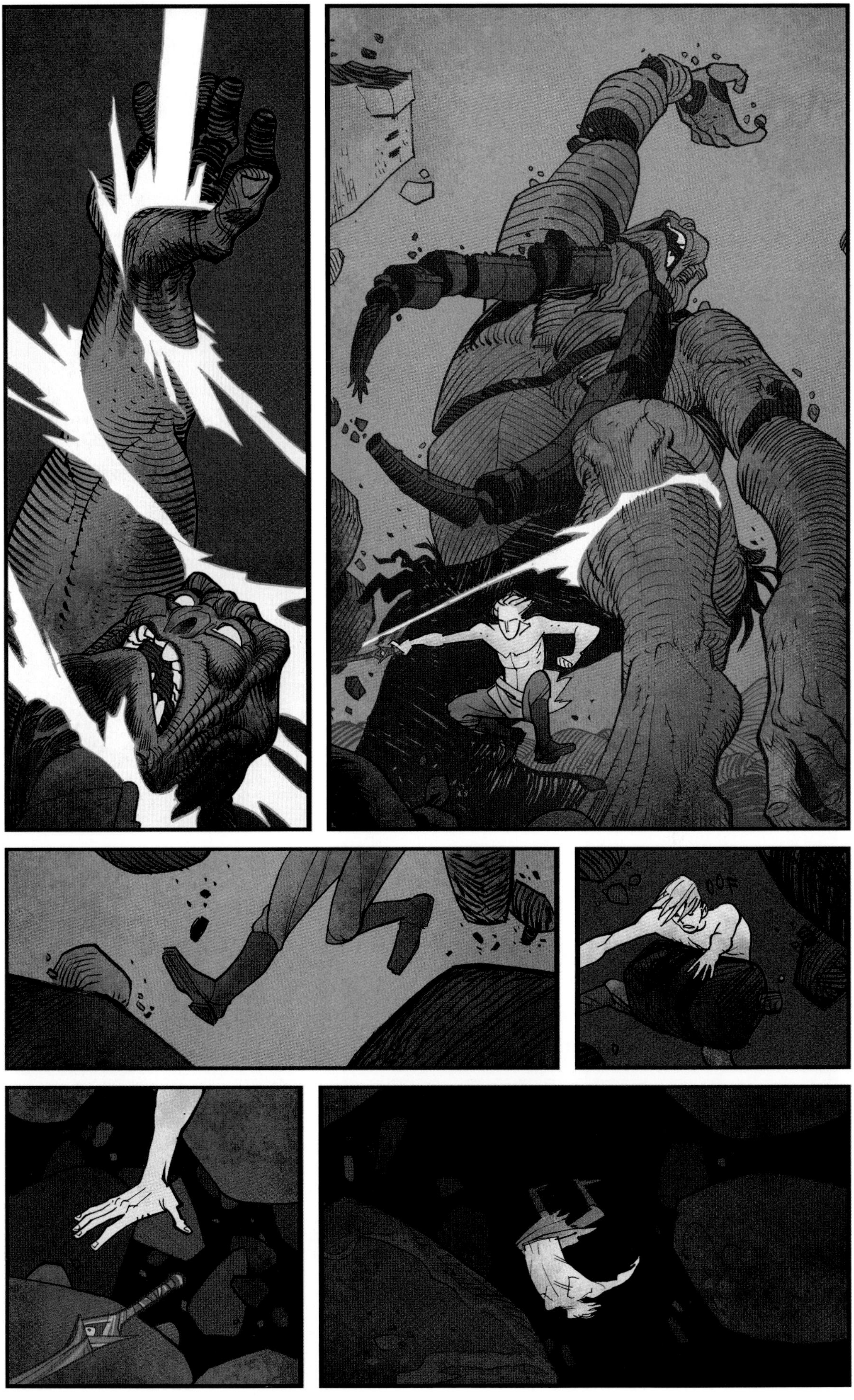
OOF

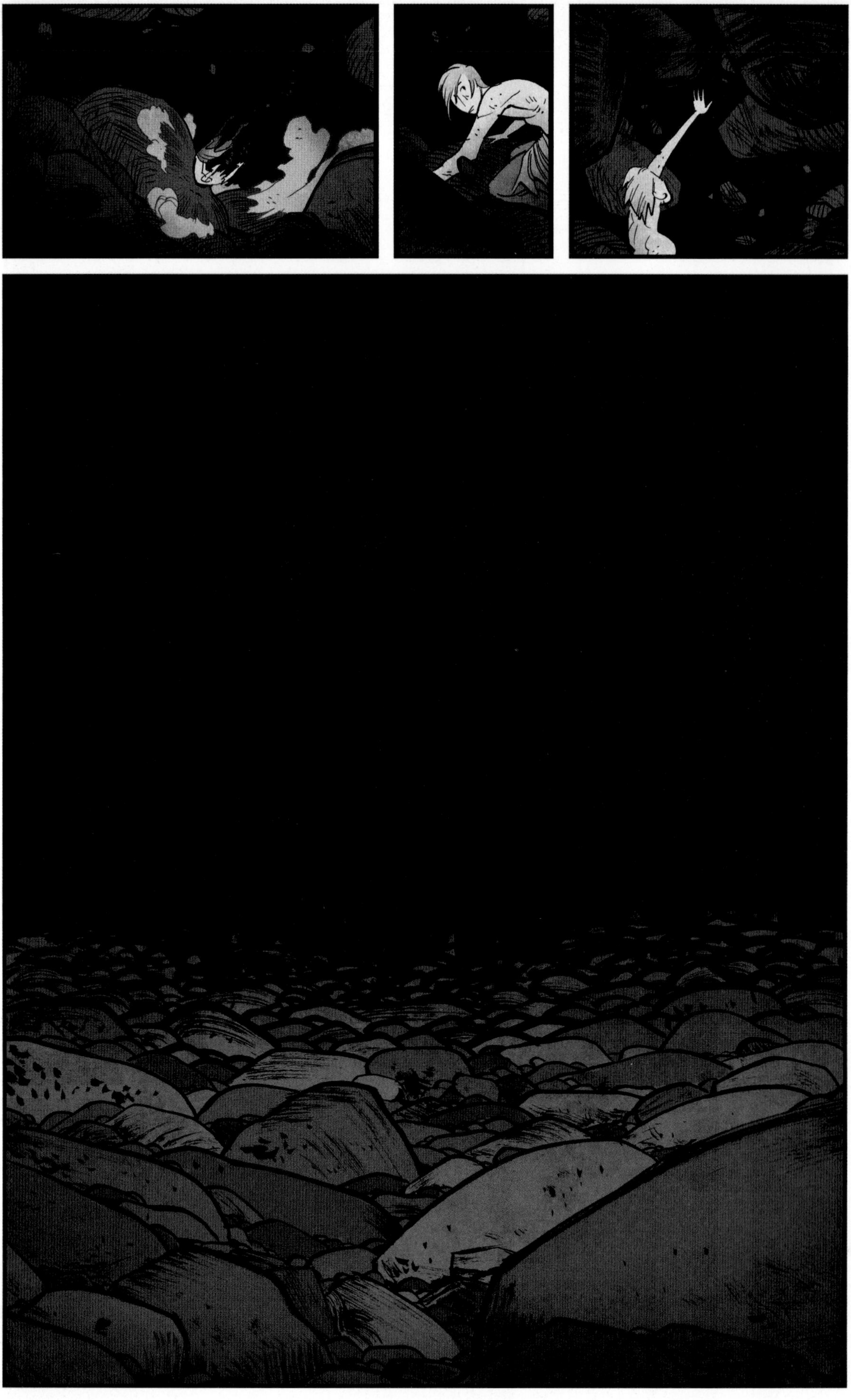

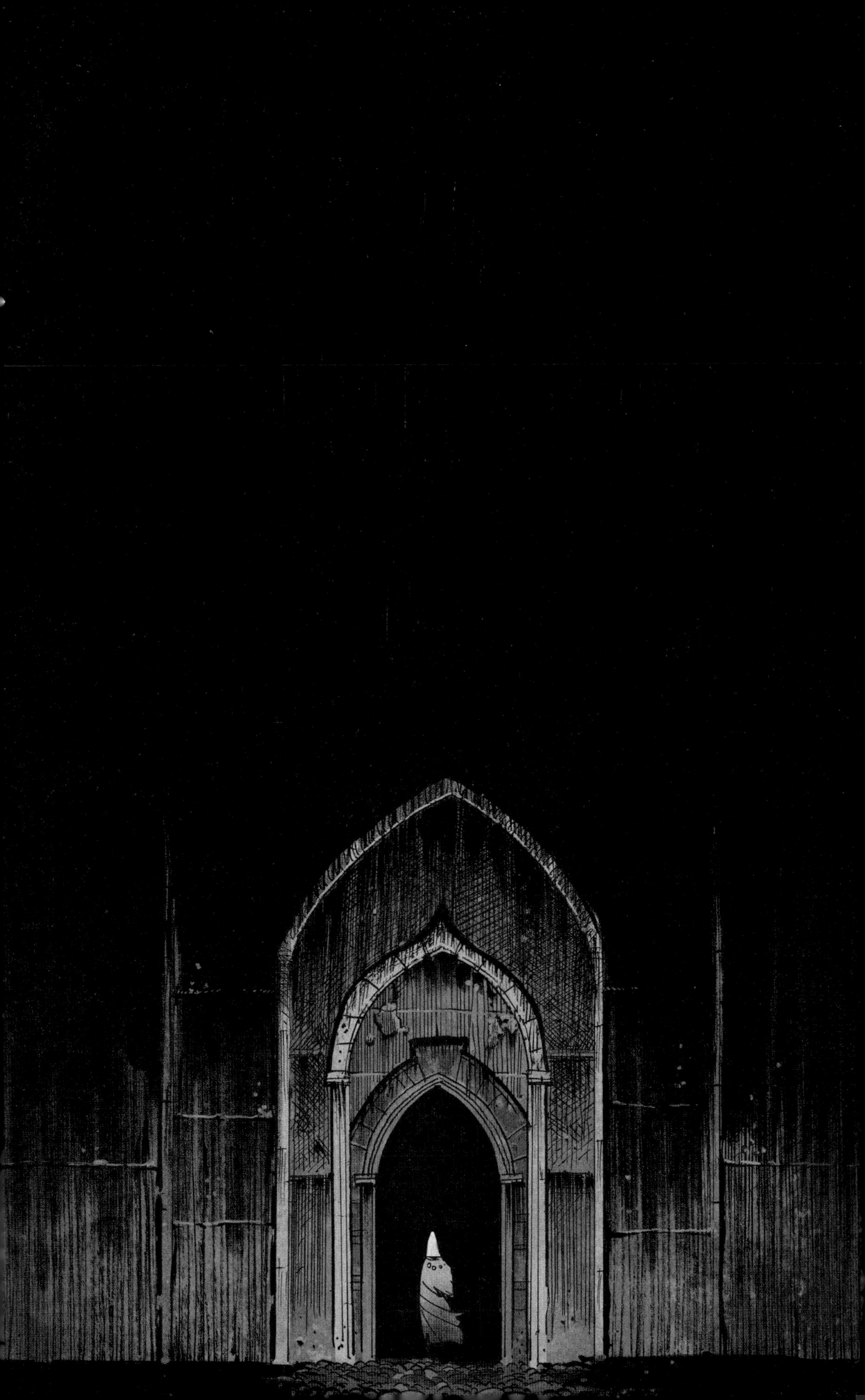

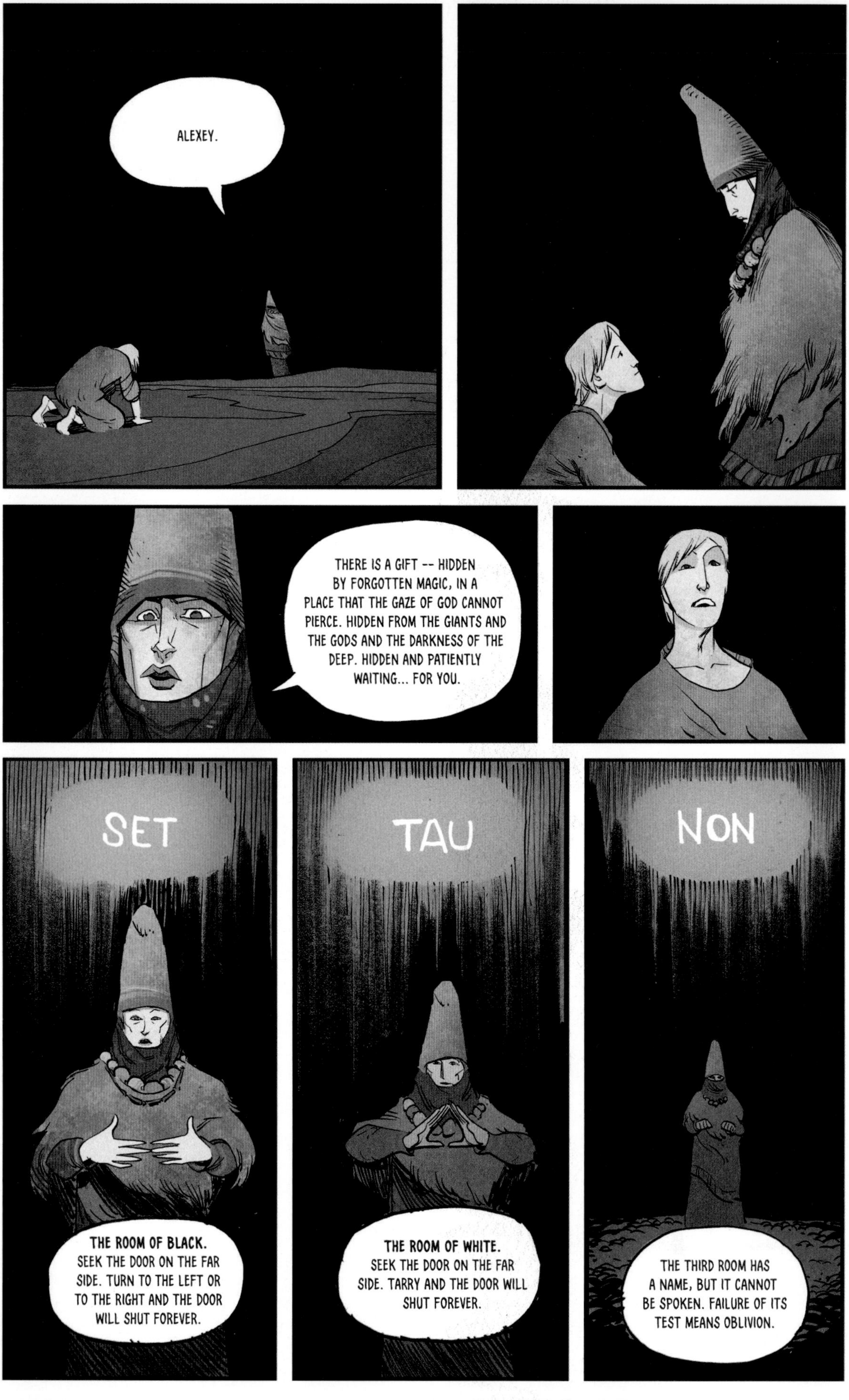
ALEXEY.
THERE IS A GIFT -- HIDDEN BY FORGOTTEN MAGIC, IN A PLACE THAT THE GAZE OF GOD CANNOT PIERCE. HIDDEN FROM THE GIANTS AND THE GODS AND THE DARKNESS OF THE DEEP. HIDDEN AND PATIENTLY WAITING... FOR YOU.
SET
THE ROOM OF BLACK. SEEK THE DOOR ON THE FAR SIDE. TURN TO THE LEFT OR TO THE RIGHT AND THE DOOR WILL SHUT FOREVER.
TAU
THE ROOM OF WHITE. SEEK THE DOOR ON THE FAR SIDE. TARRY AND THE DOOR WILL SHUT FOREVER.
NON
THE THIRD ROOM HAS A NAME, BUT IT CANNOT BE SPOKEN. FAILURE OF ITS TEST MEANS OBLIVION.

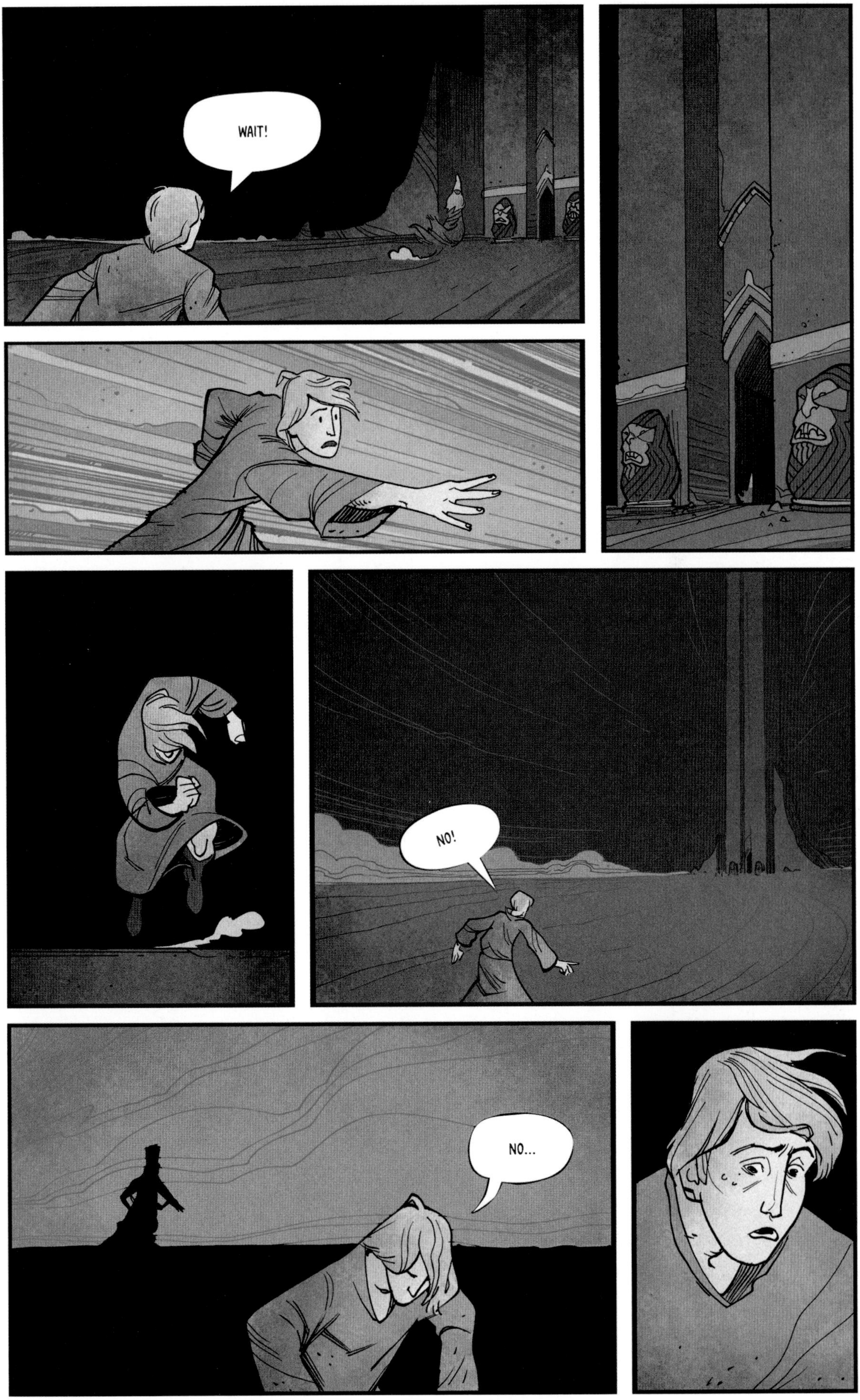
WAIT!
NO!
NO...

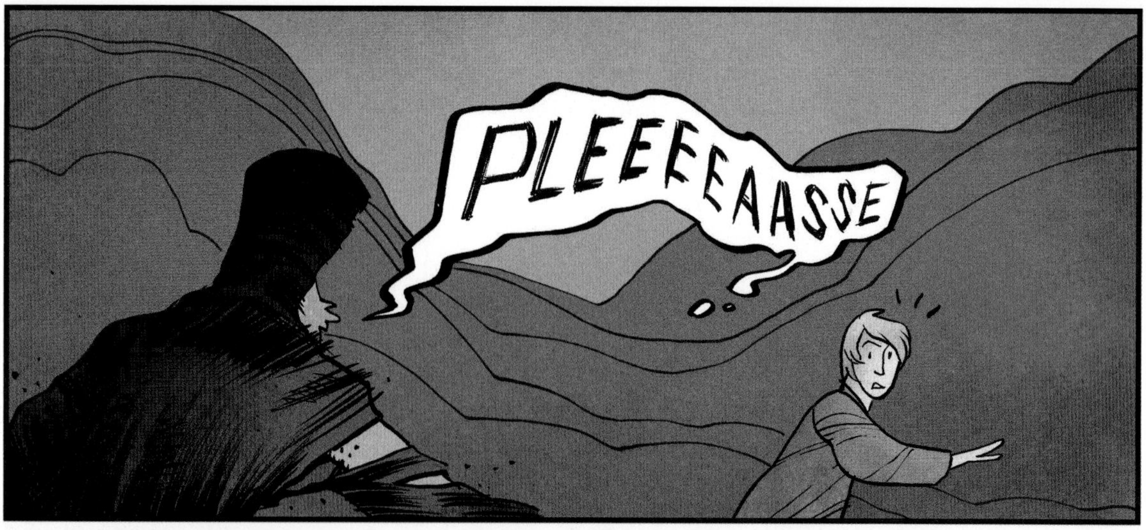
PLEEEEEAASSE

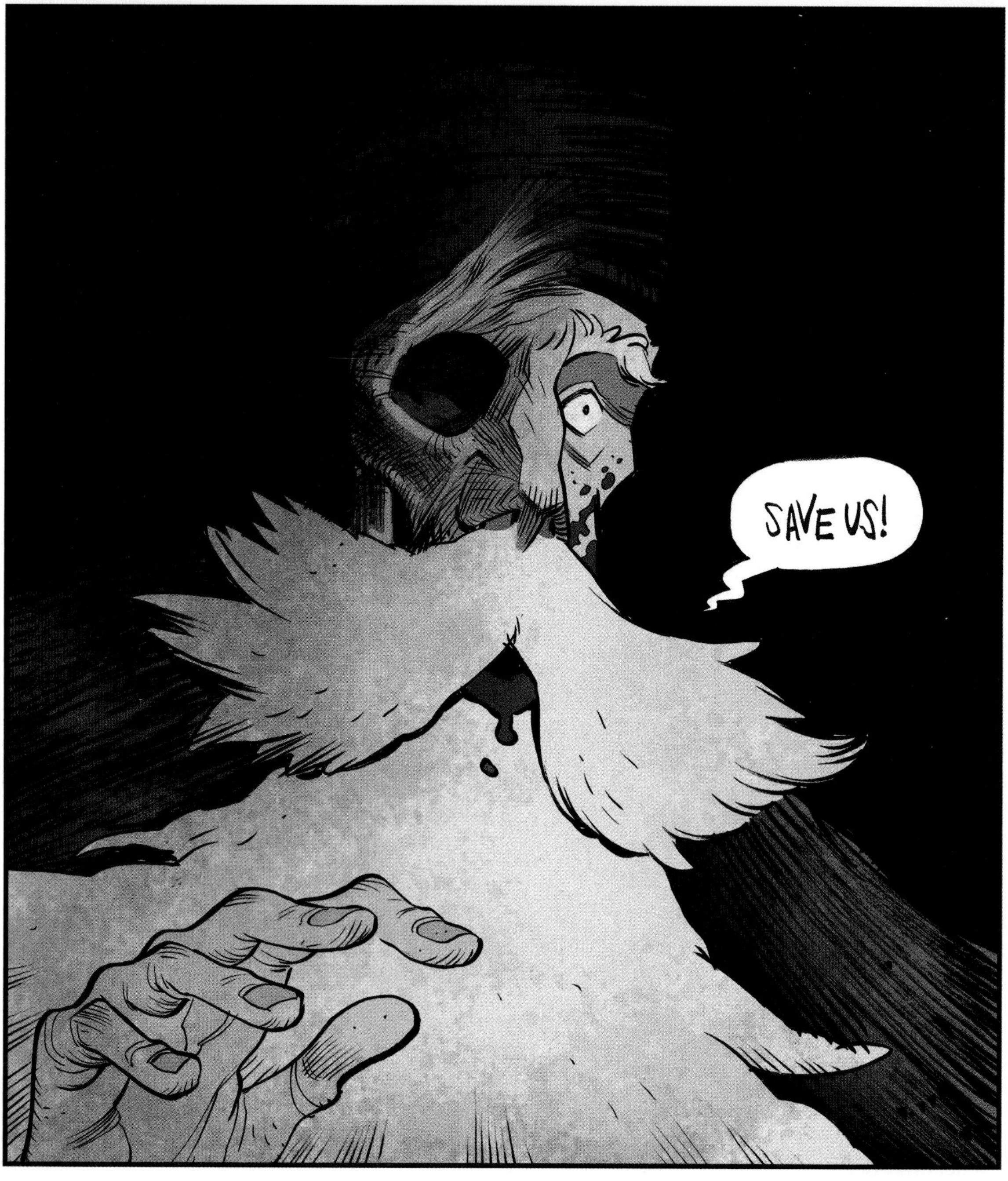
SAVE US!

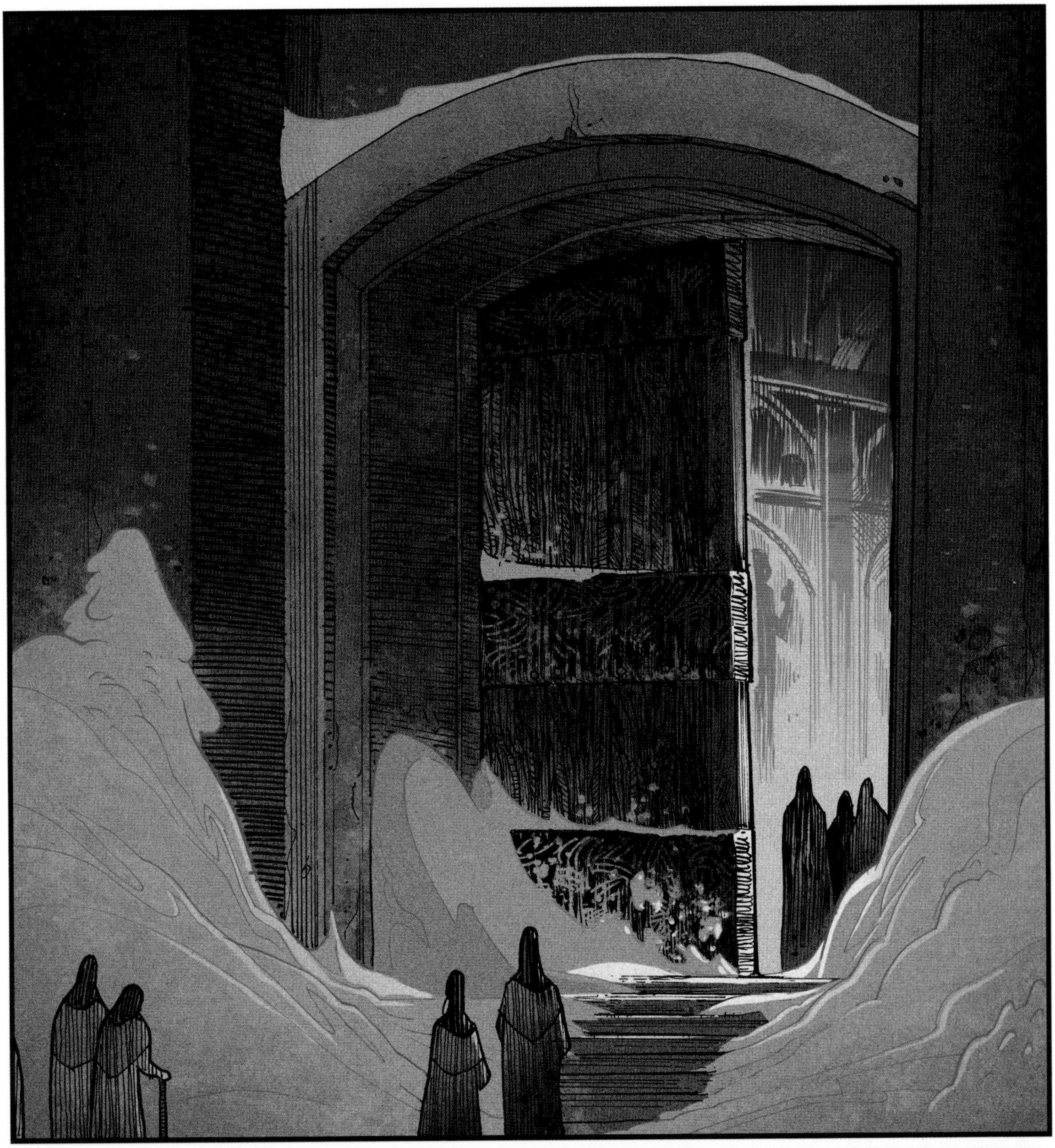

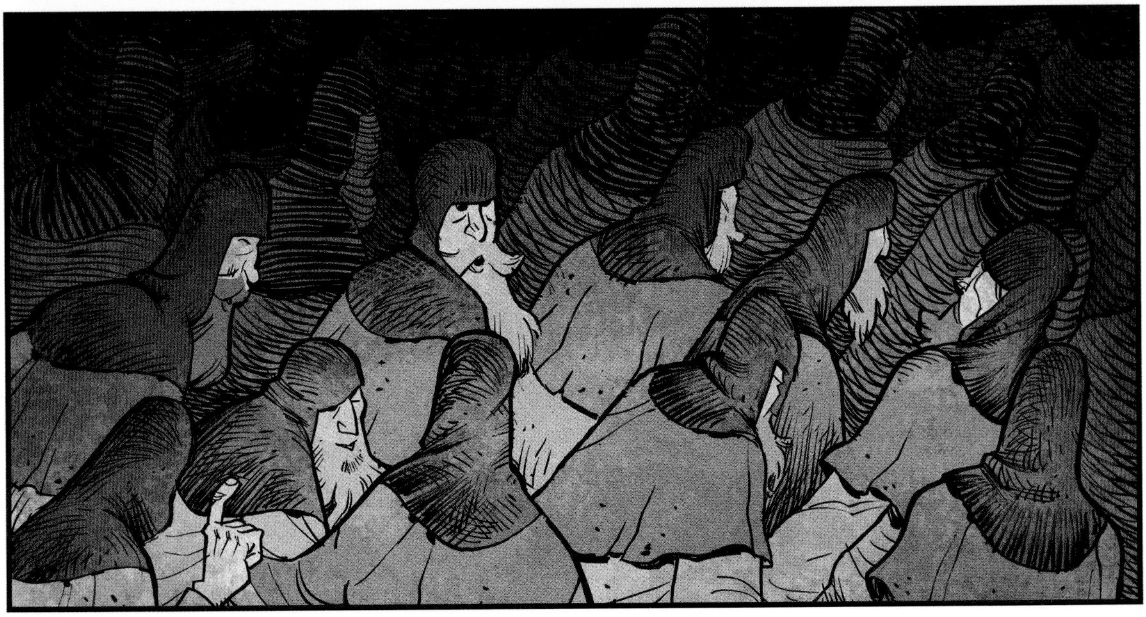

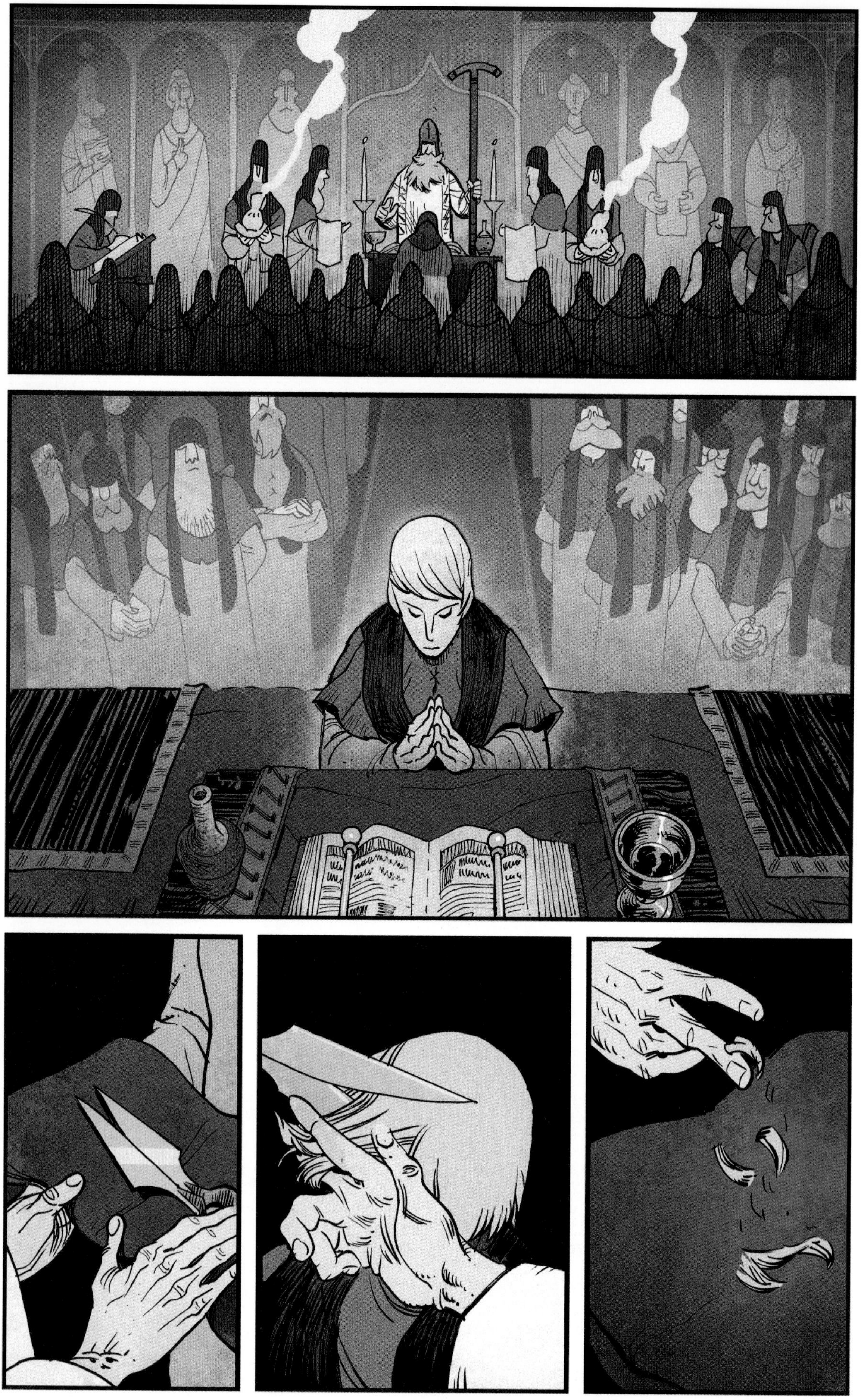

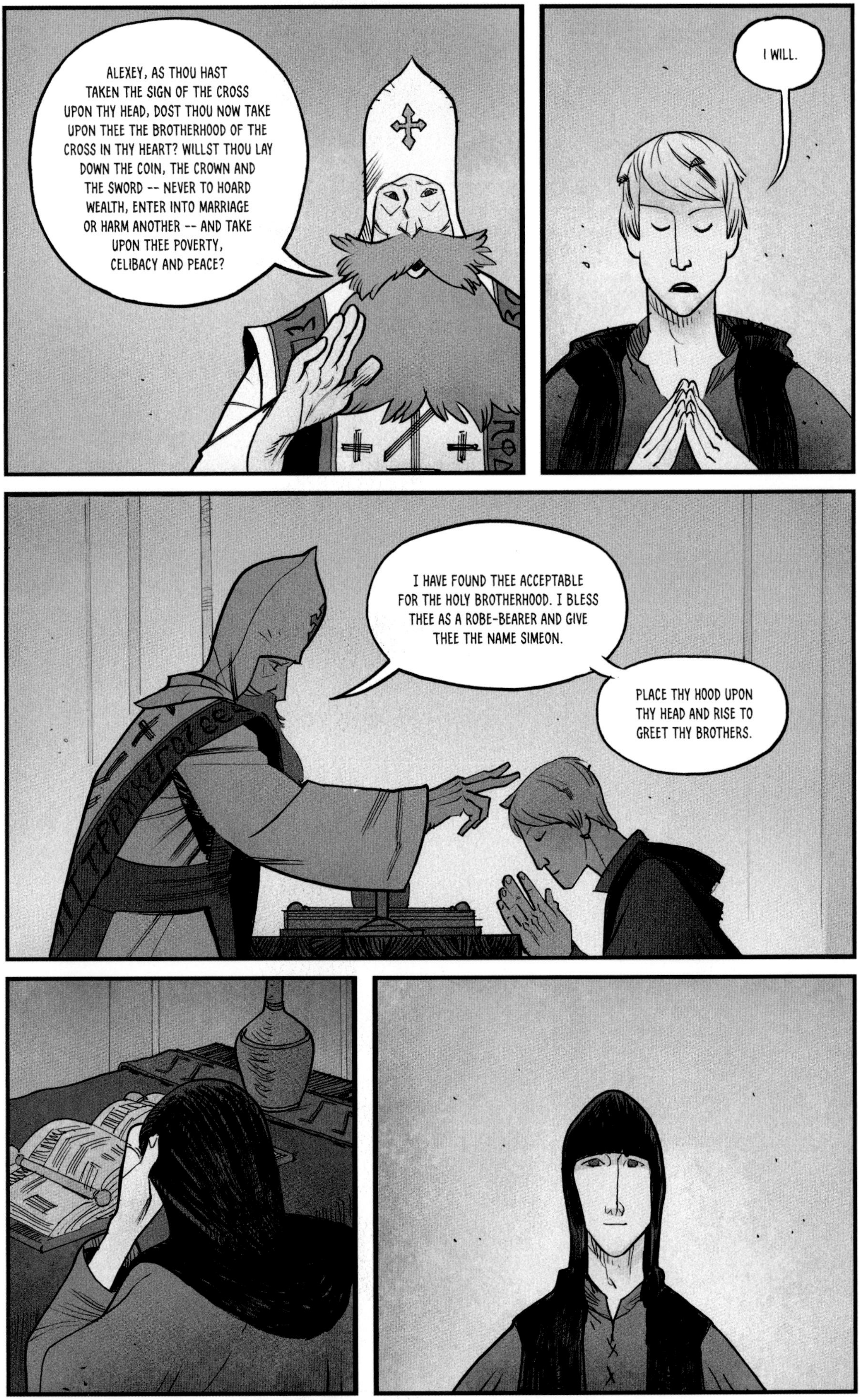
ALEXEY, AS THOU HAST TAKEN THE SIGN OF THE CROSS UPON THY HEAD, DOST THOU NOW TAKE UPON THEE THE BROTHERHOOD OF THE CROSS IN THY HEART? WILLST THOU LAY DOWN THE COIN, THE CROWN AND THE SWORD -- NEVER TO HOARD WEALTH, ENTER INTO MARRIAGE OR HARM ANOTHER -- AND TAKE UPON THEE POVERTY, CELIBACY AND PEACE?
I WILL.
I HAVE FOUND THEE ACCEPTABLE FOR THE HOLY BROTHERHOOD. I BLESS THEE AS A ROBE-BEARER AND GIVE THEE THE NAME SIMEON.
PLACE THY HOOD UPON THY HEAD AND RISE TO GREET THY BROTHERS.

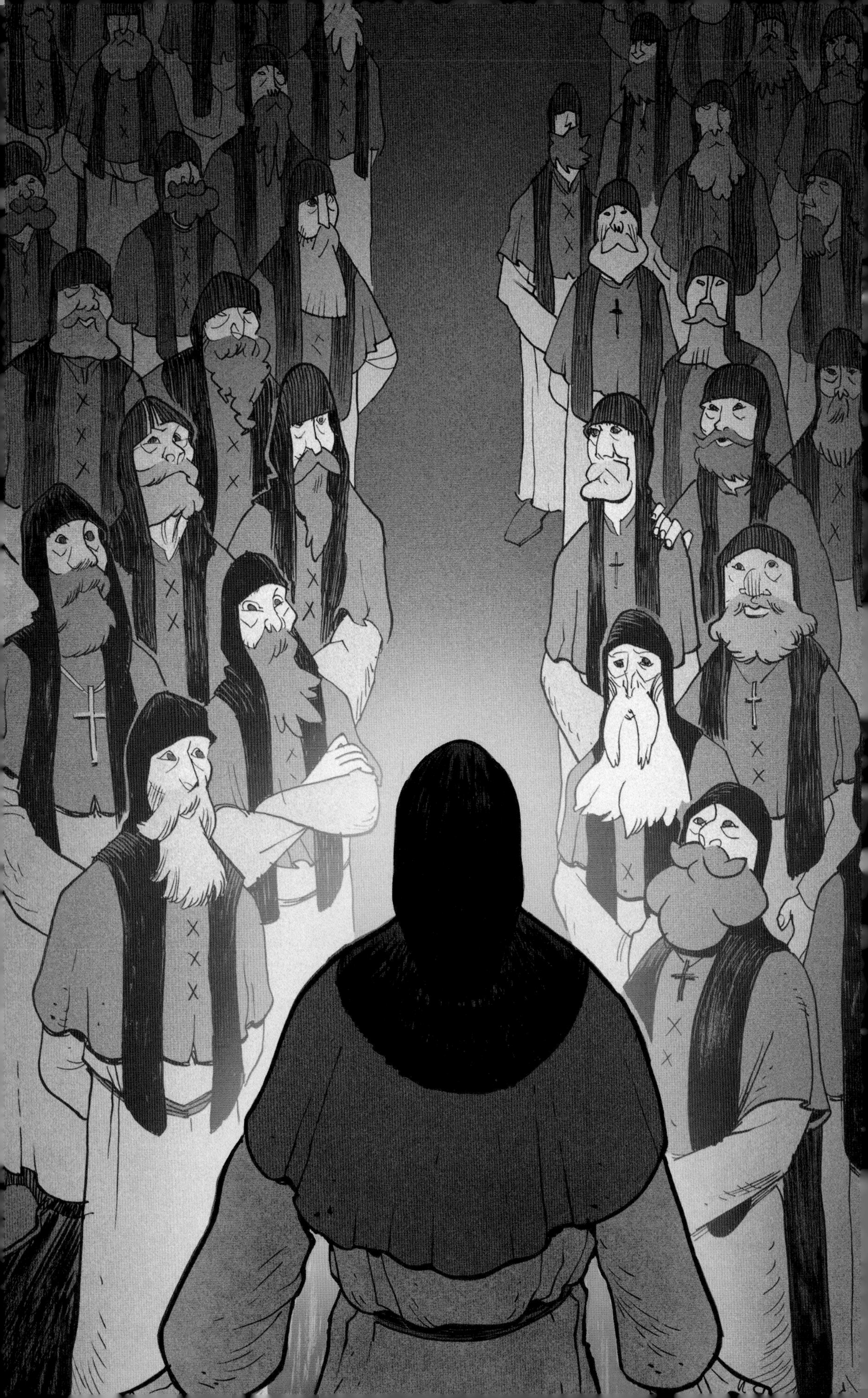

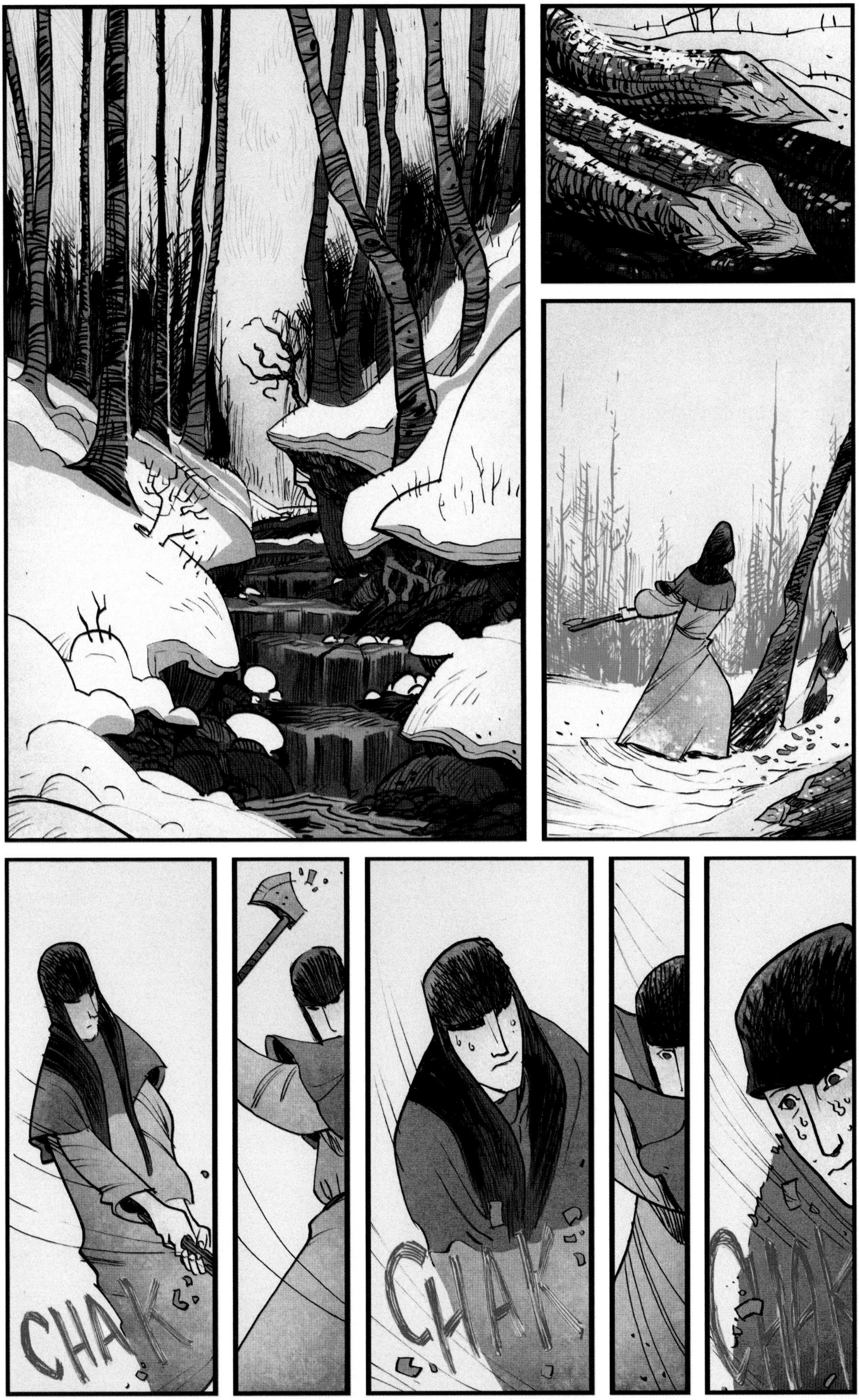
CHAK
CHAK
CHAK

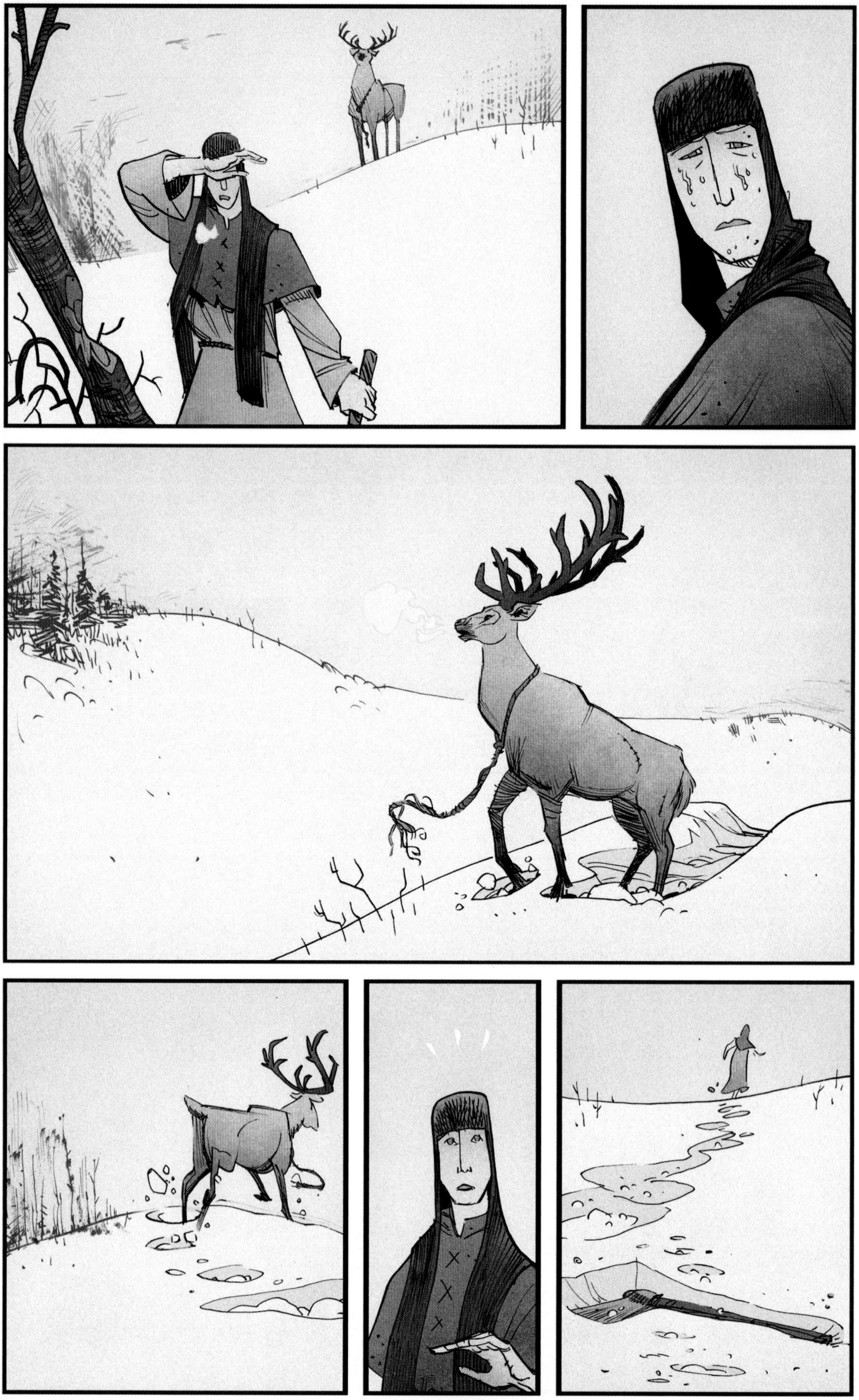

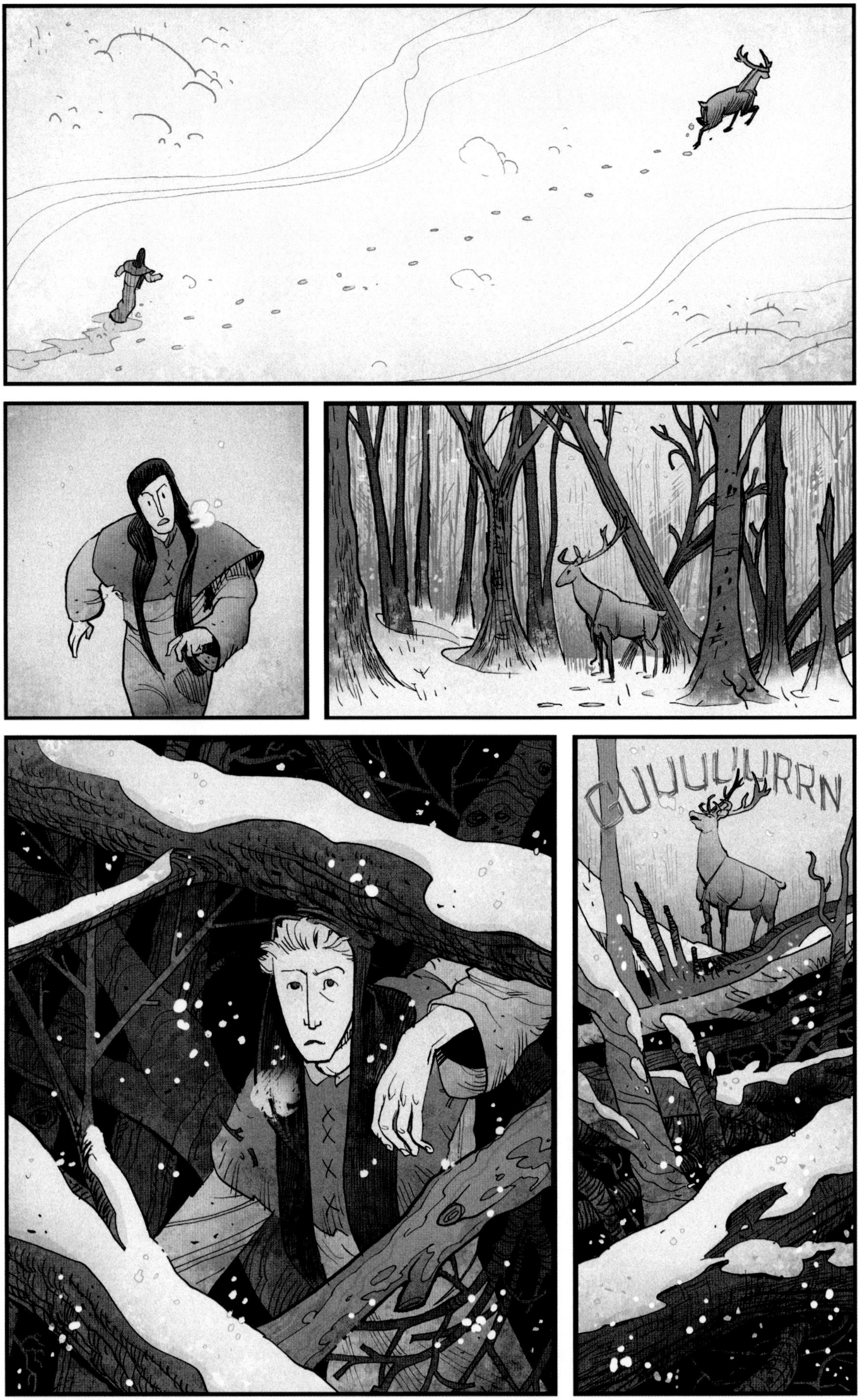
GUUULUURRN

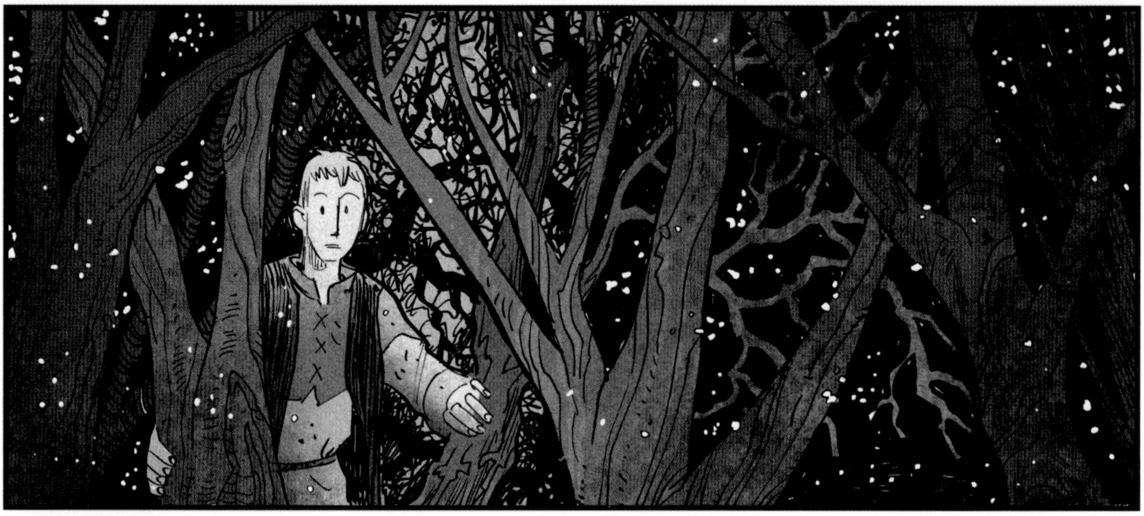

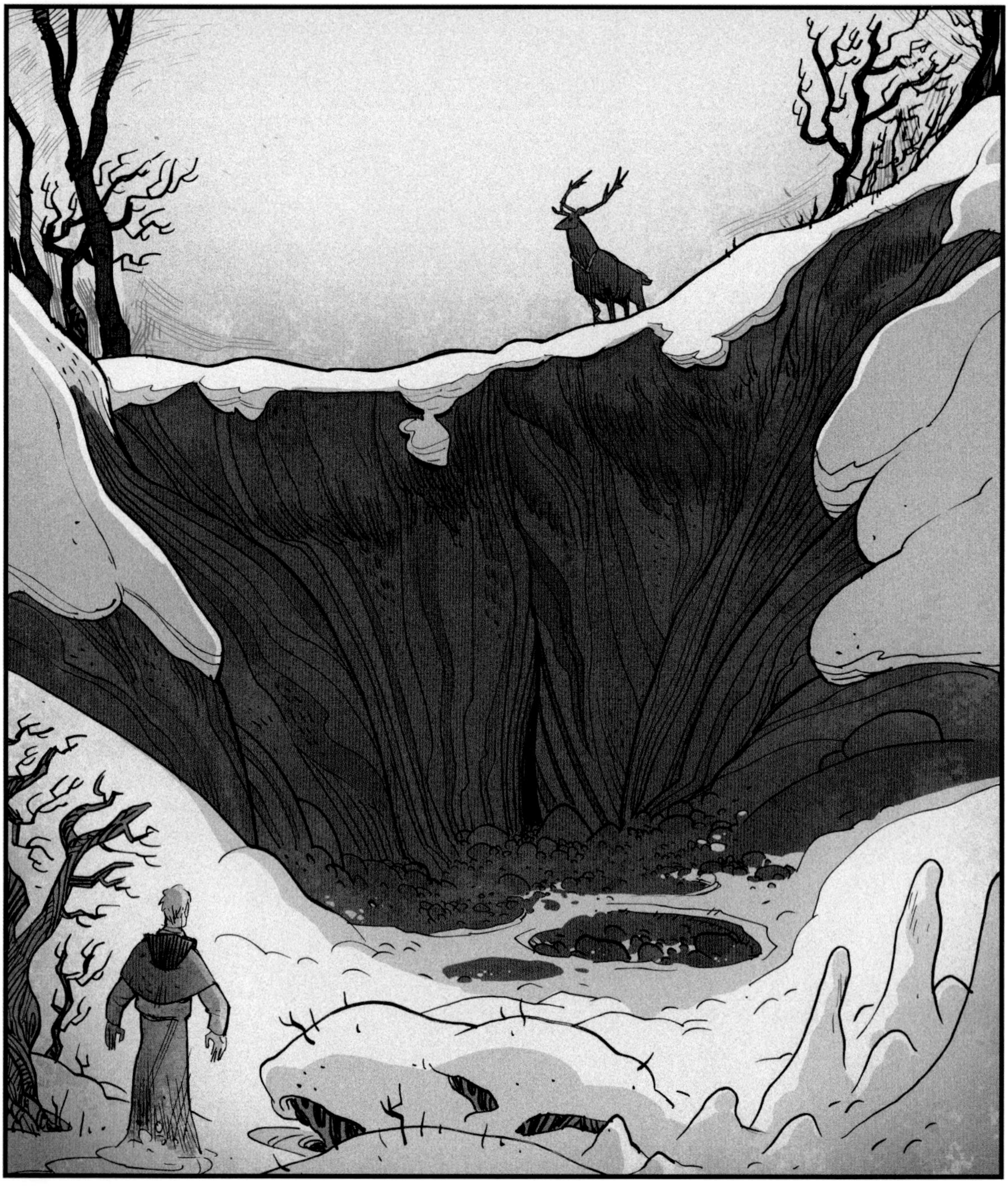

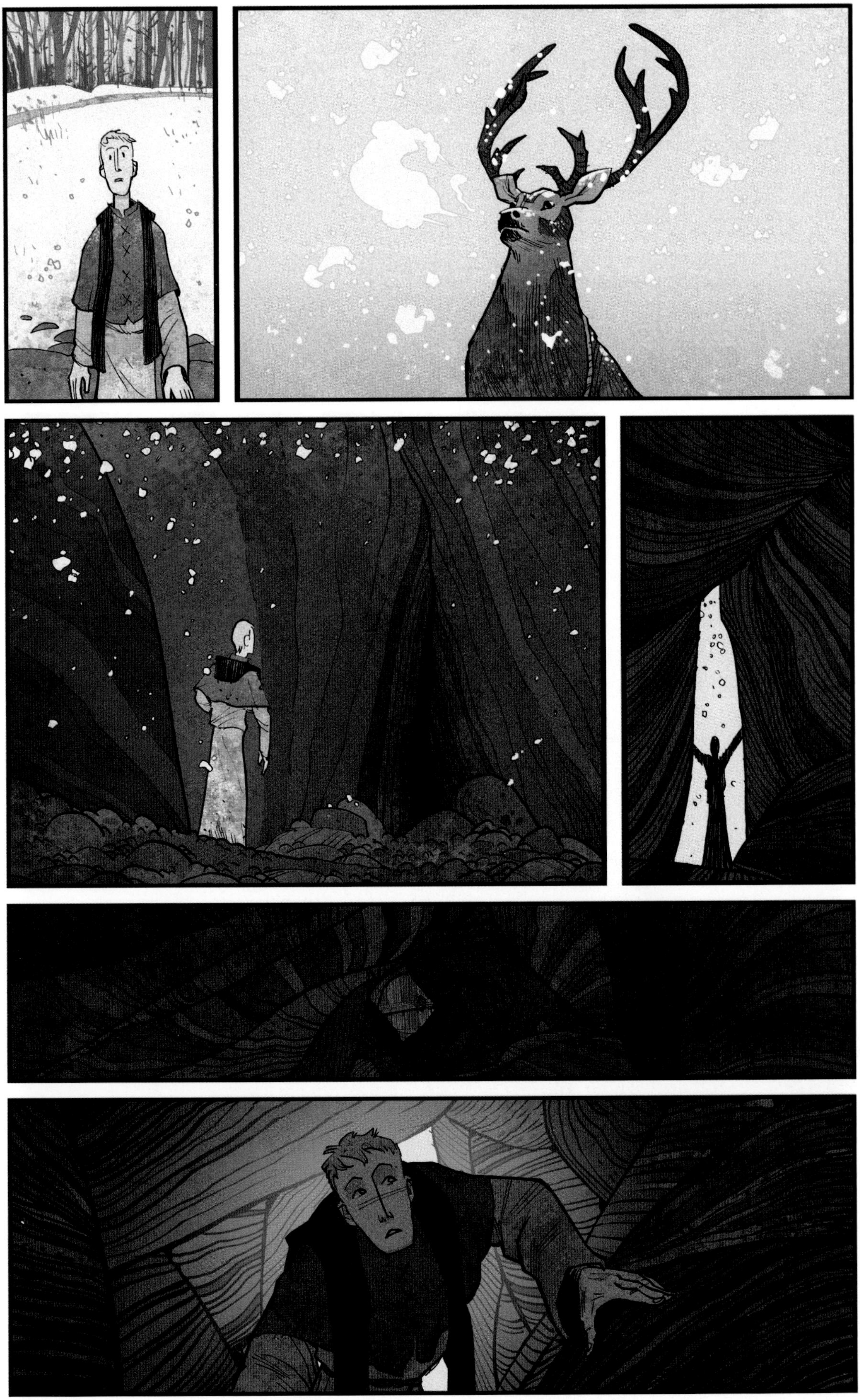

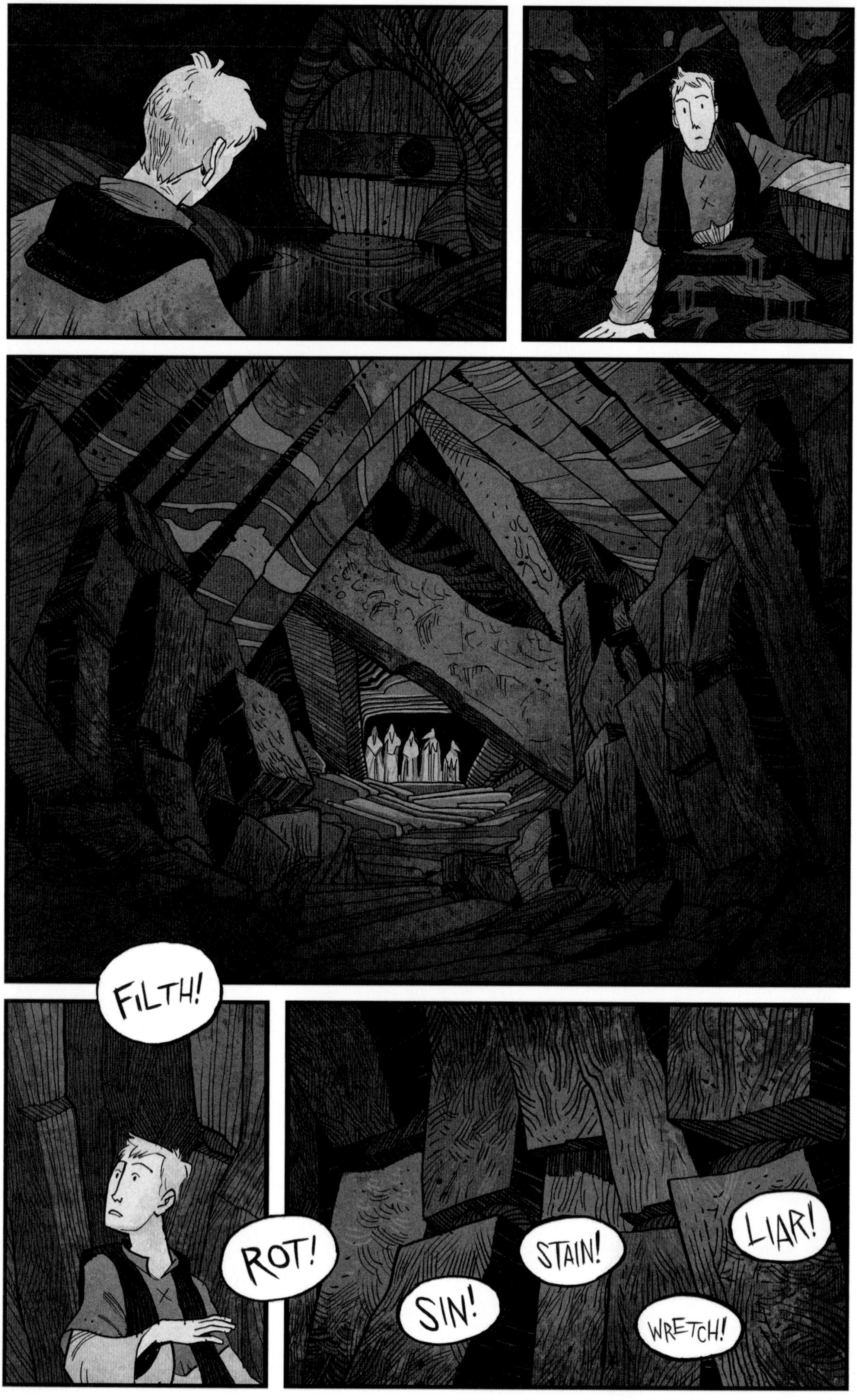
FILTH!
ROT!
SIN!
STAIN!
WRETCH!
LIAR!

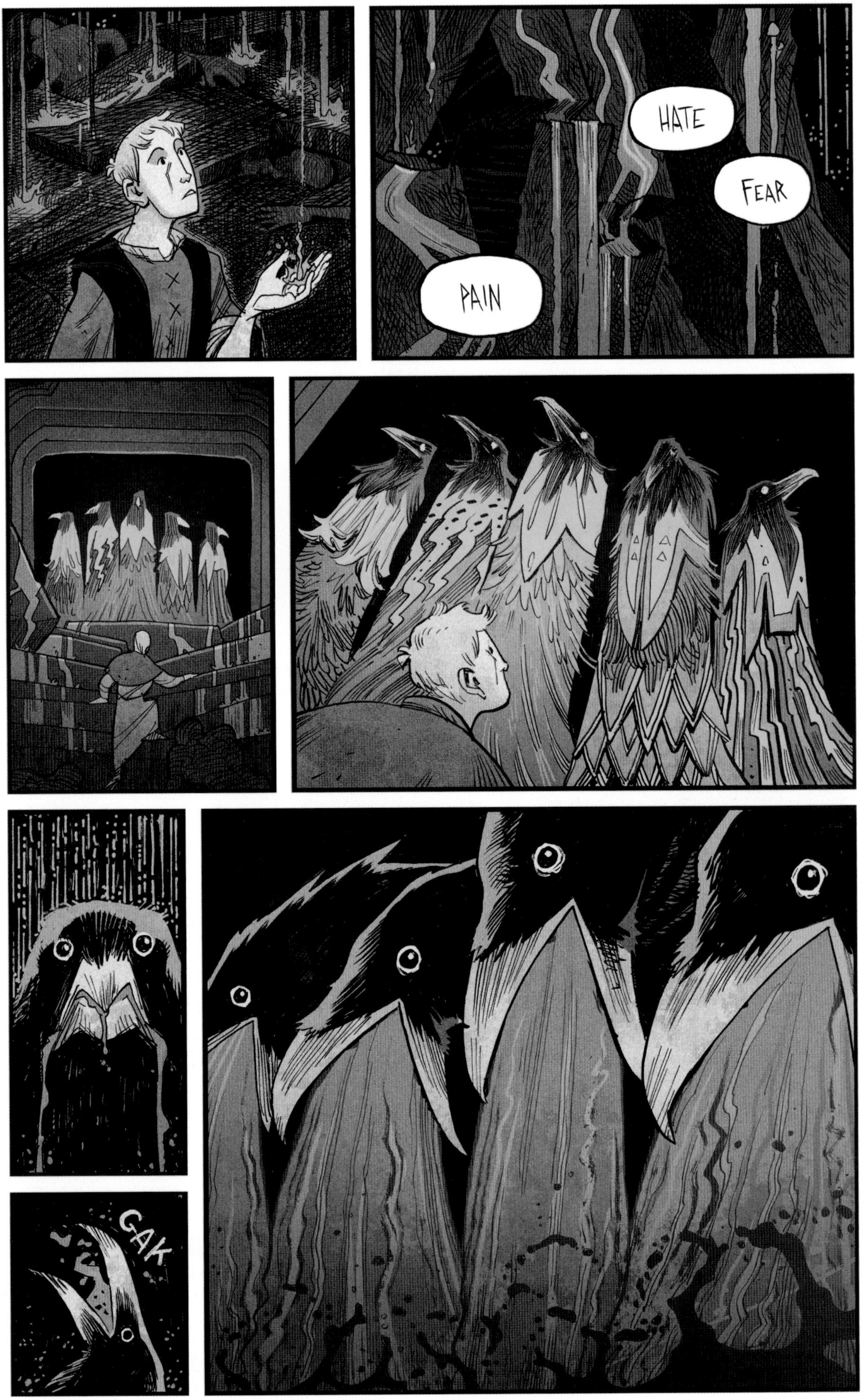
HATE
FEAR
PAIN
GAK

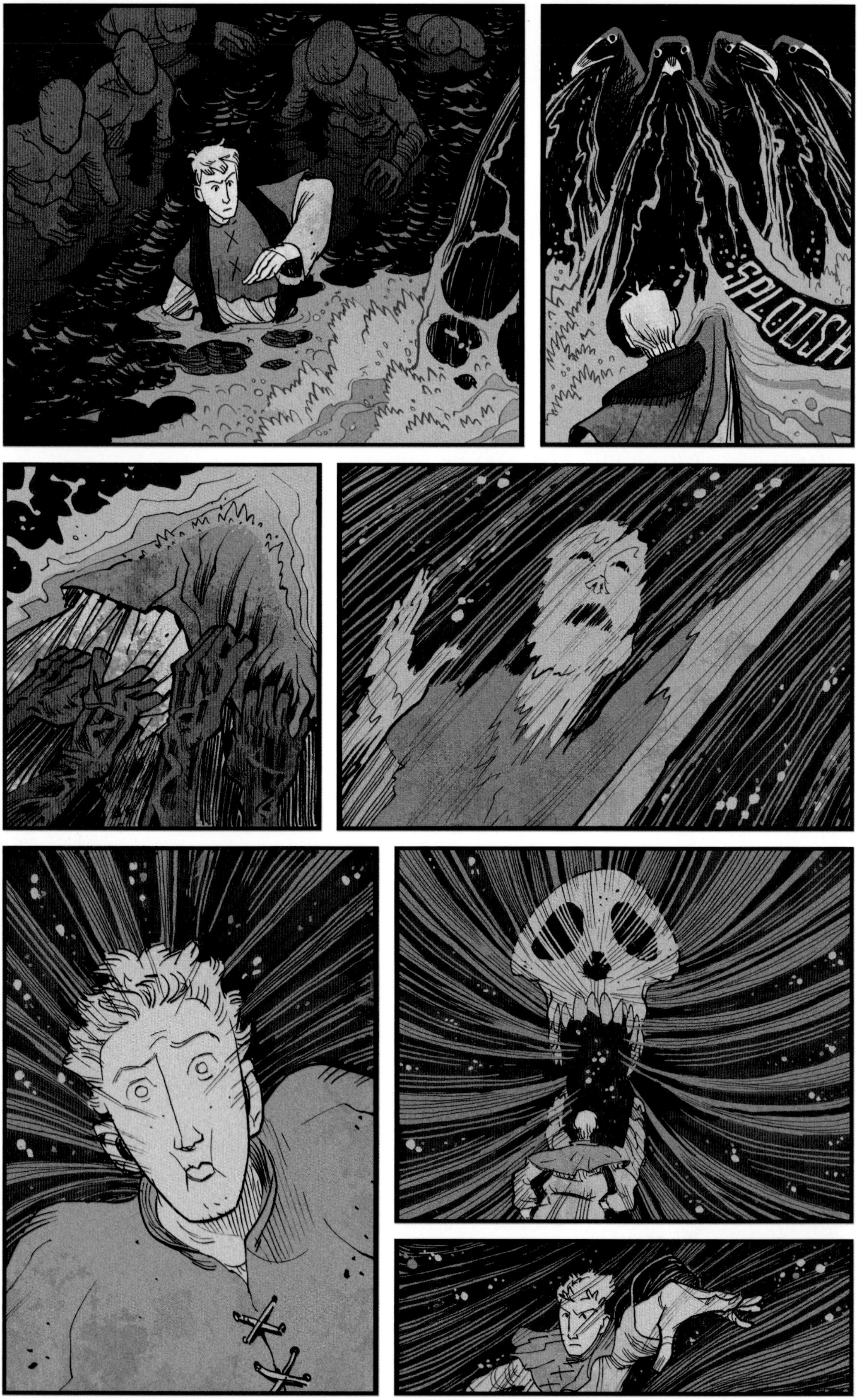
SPLOOSH

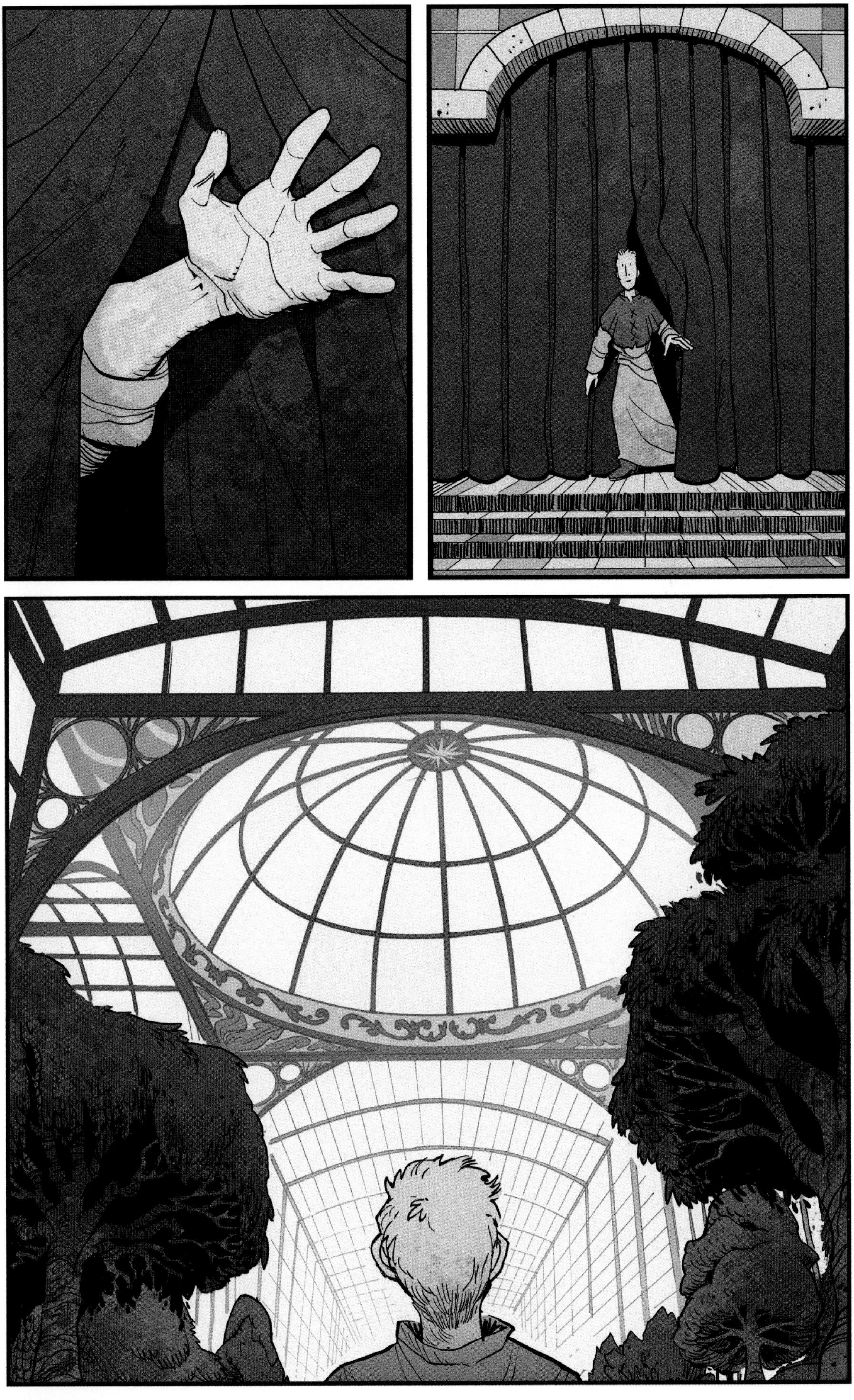

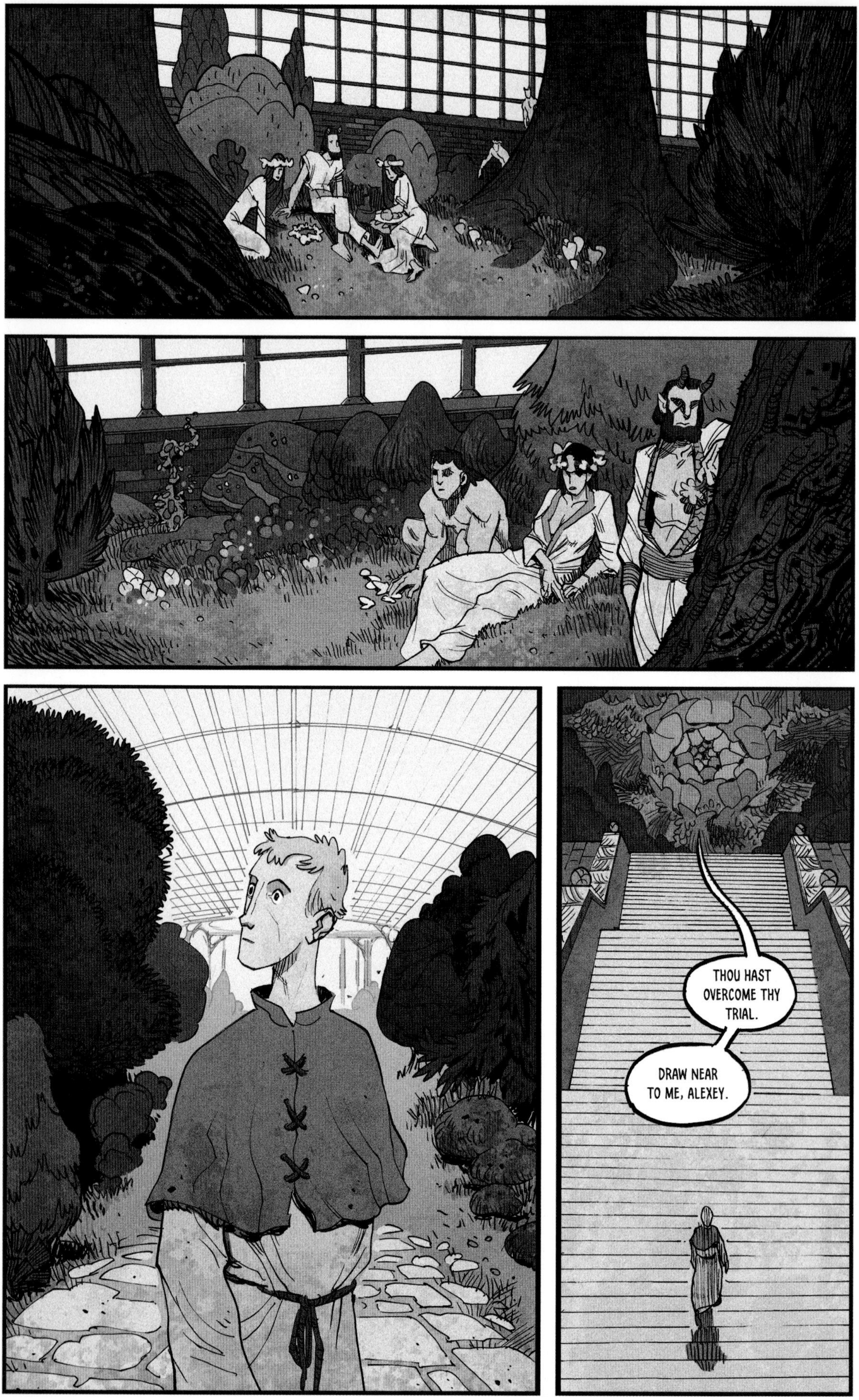
THOU HAST OVERCOME THY TRIAL.
DRAW NEAR TO ME, ALEXEY.

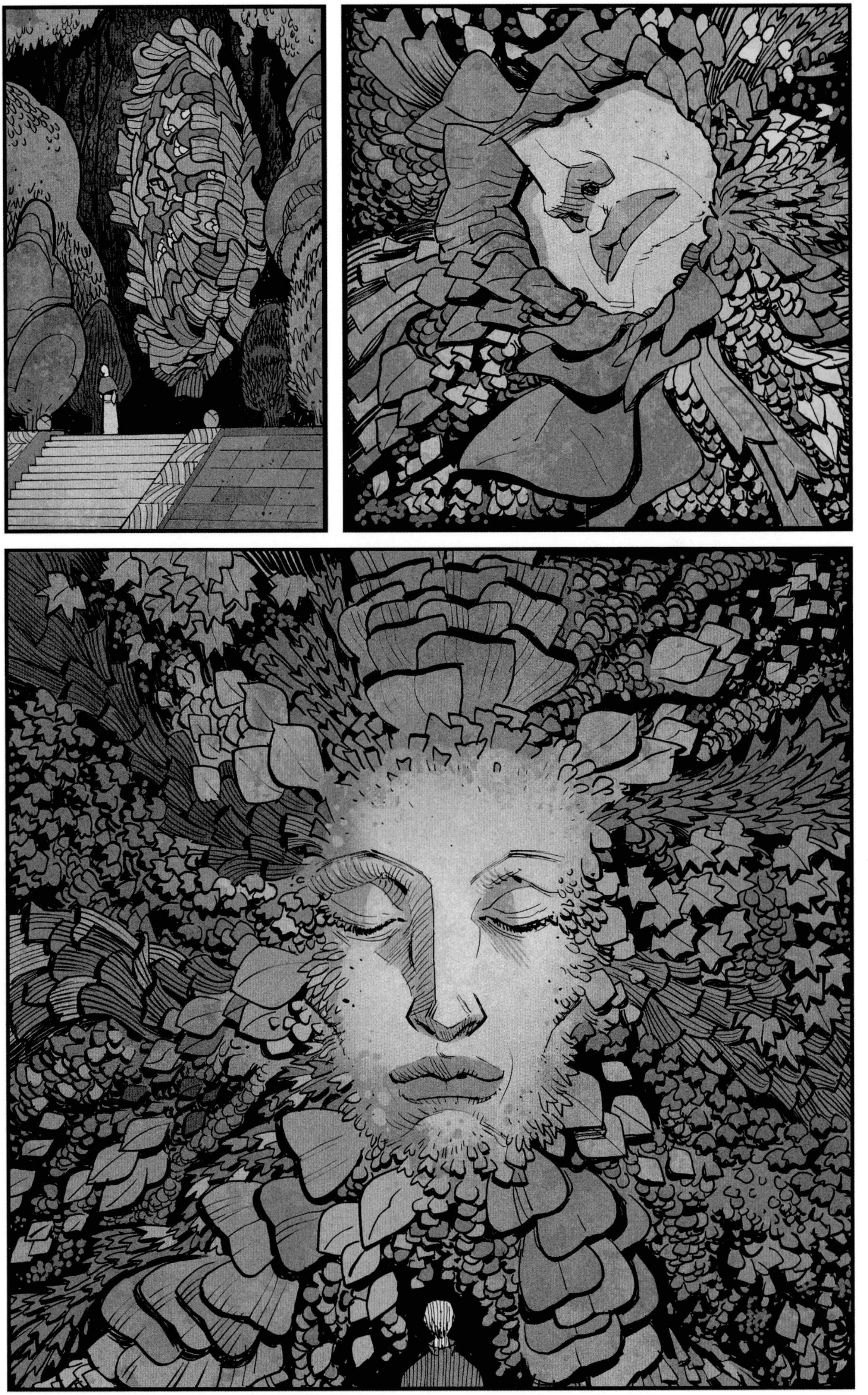

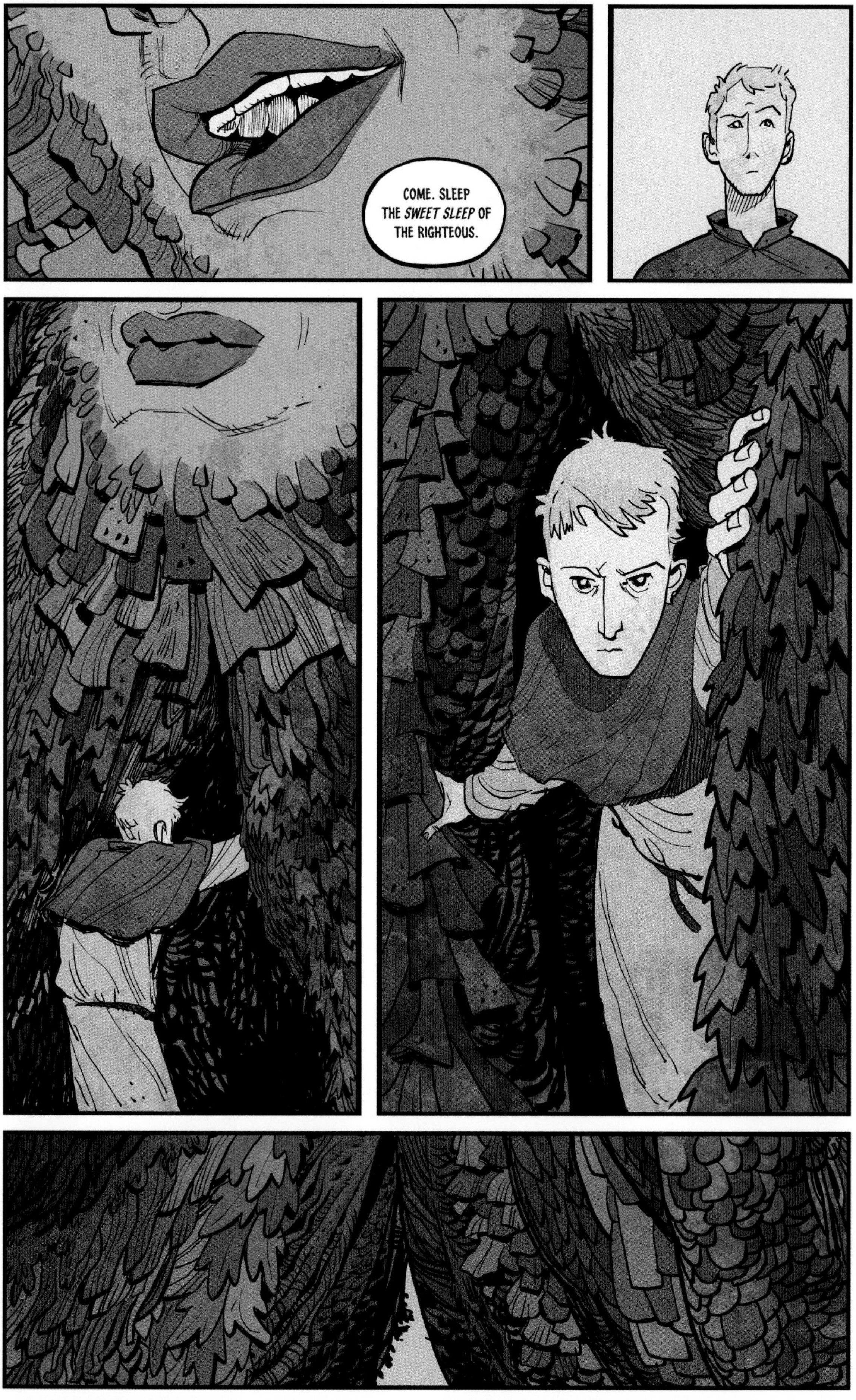
COME. SLEEP THE *SWEET SLEEP* OF THE RIGHTEOUS.

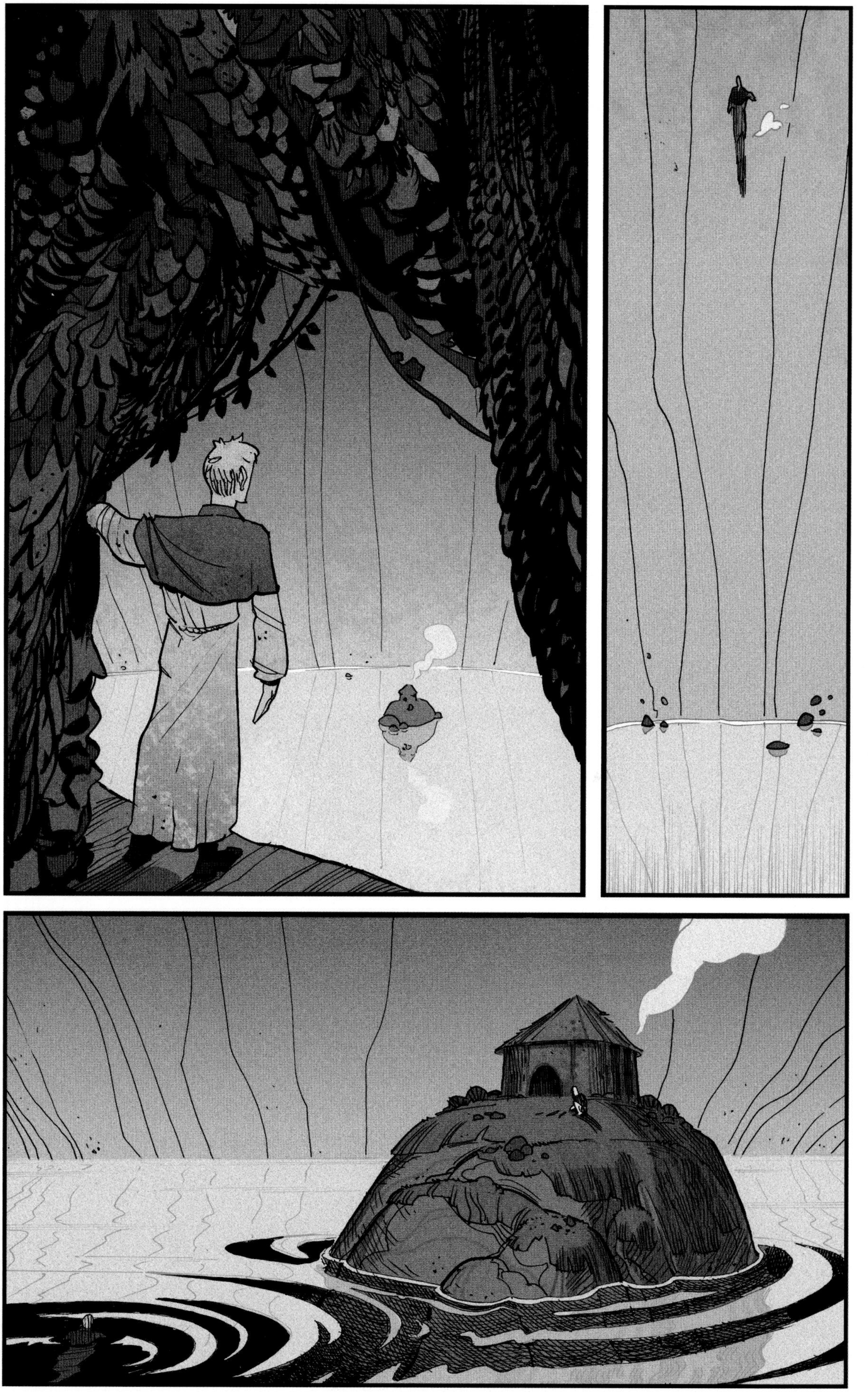

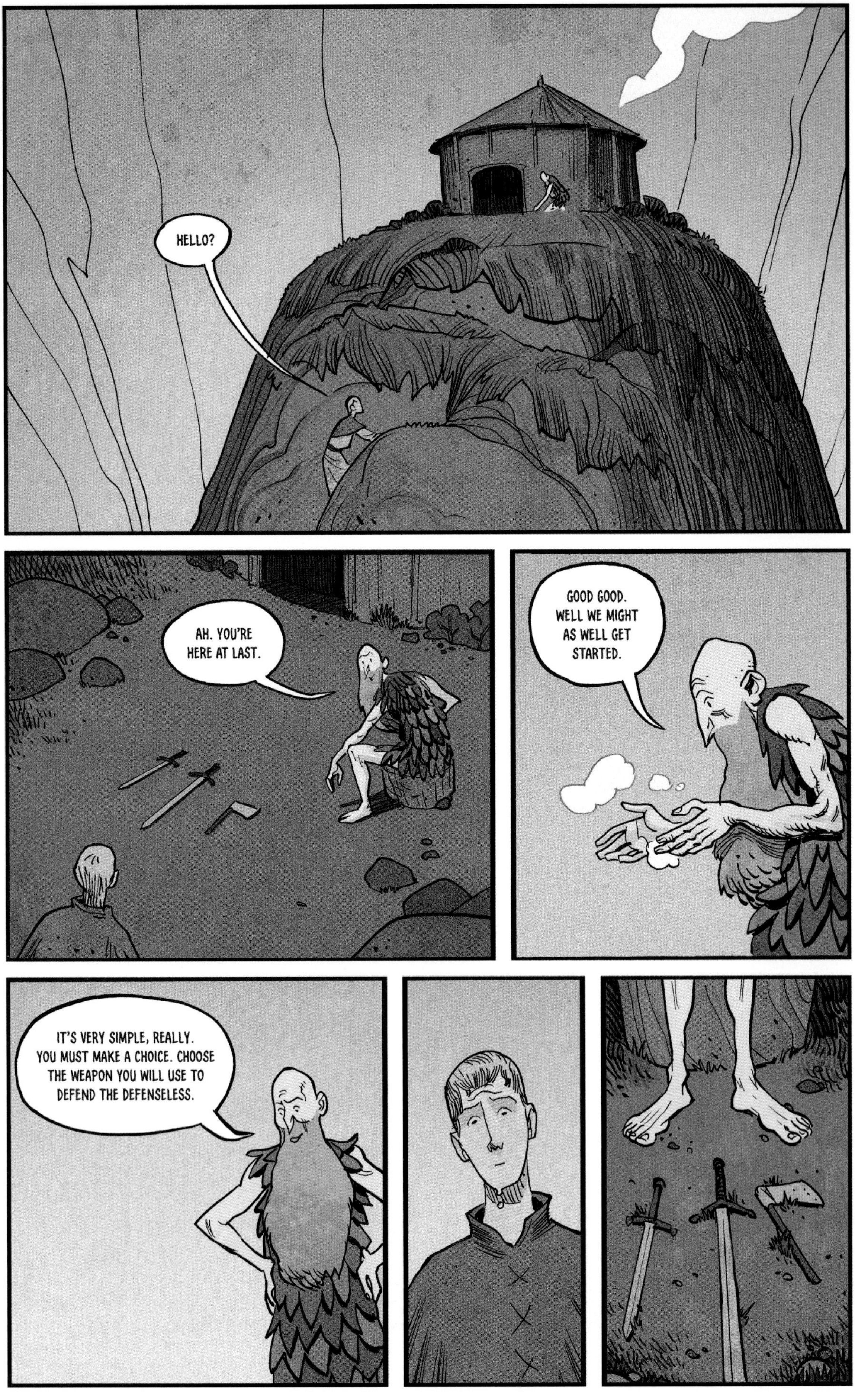
HELLO?
AH. YOU'RE HERE AT LAST.
GOOD GOOD. WELL WE MIGHT AS WELL GET STARTED.
IT'S VERY SIMPLE, REALLY. YOU MUST MAKE A CHOICE. CHOOSE THE WEAPON YOU WILL USE TO DEFEND THE DEFENSELESS.

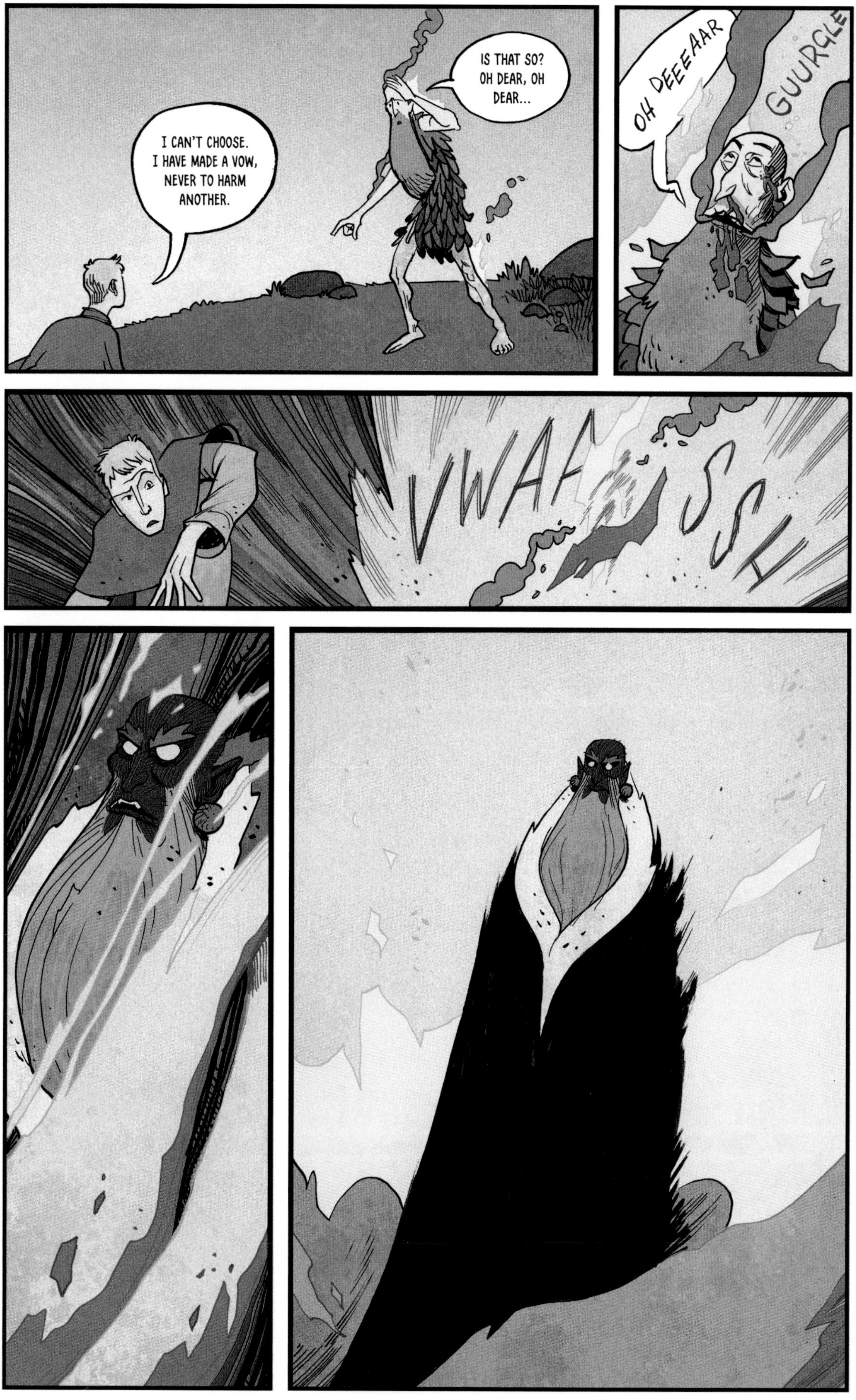
I CAN'T CHOOSE. I HAVE MADE A VOW, NEVER TO HARM ANOTHER.
IS THAT SO? OH DEAR, OH DEAR...
OH DEEEAAR
GUURGLE
VWAASSH

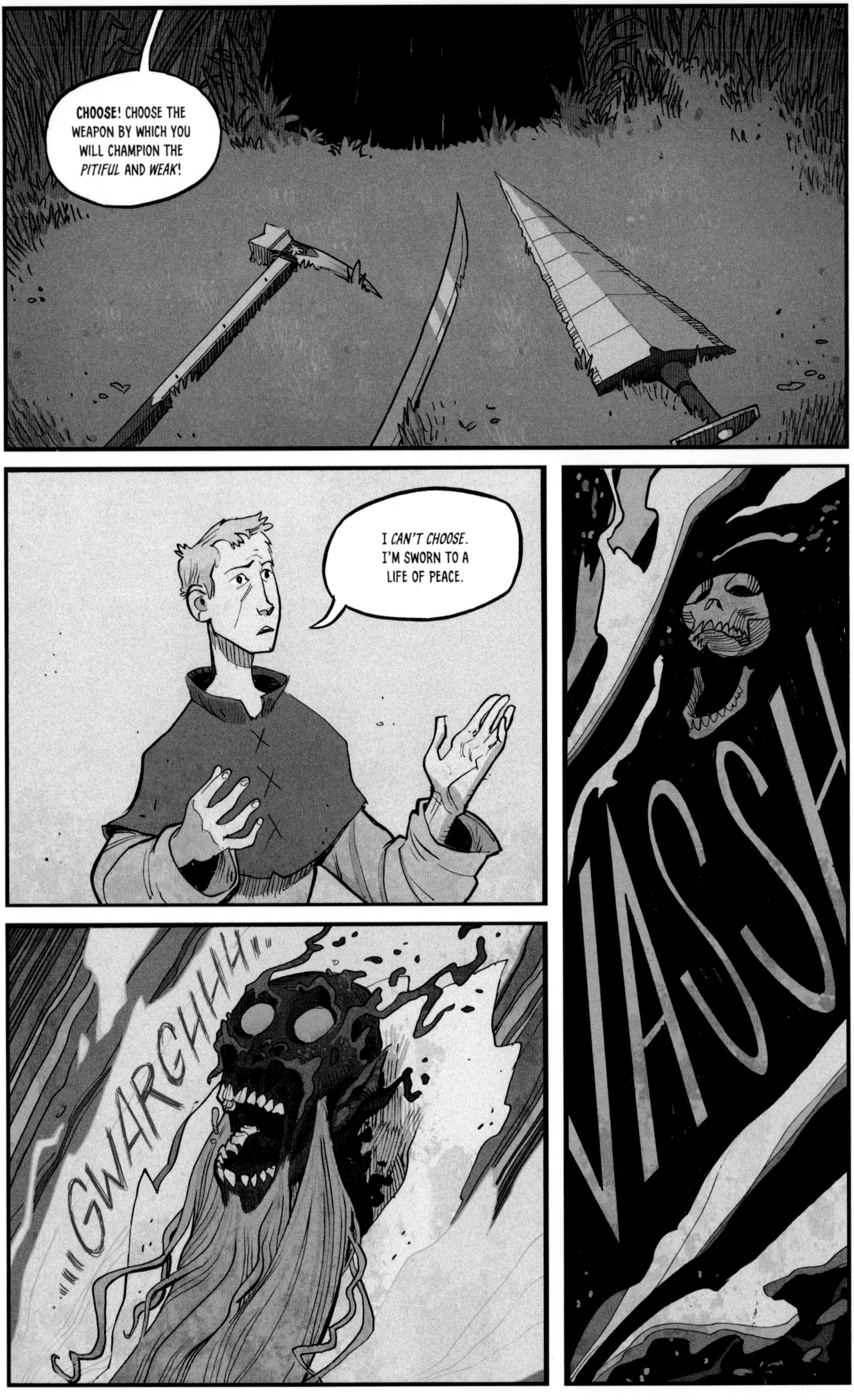
CHOOSE! CHOOSE THE WEAPON BY WHICH YOU WILL CHAMPION THE *PITIFUL* AND *WEAK*!
I *CAN'T CHOOSE*. I'M SWORN TO A LIFE OF PEACE.
VASCH
GWARGHHH

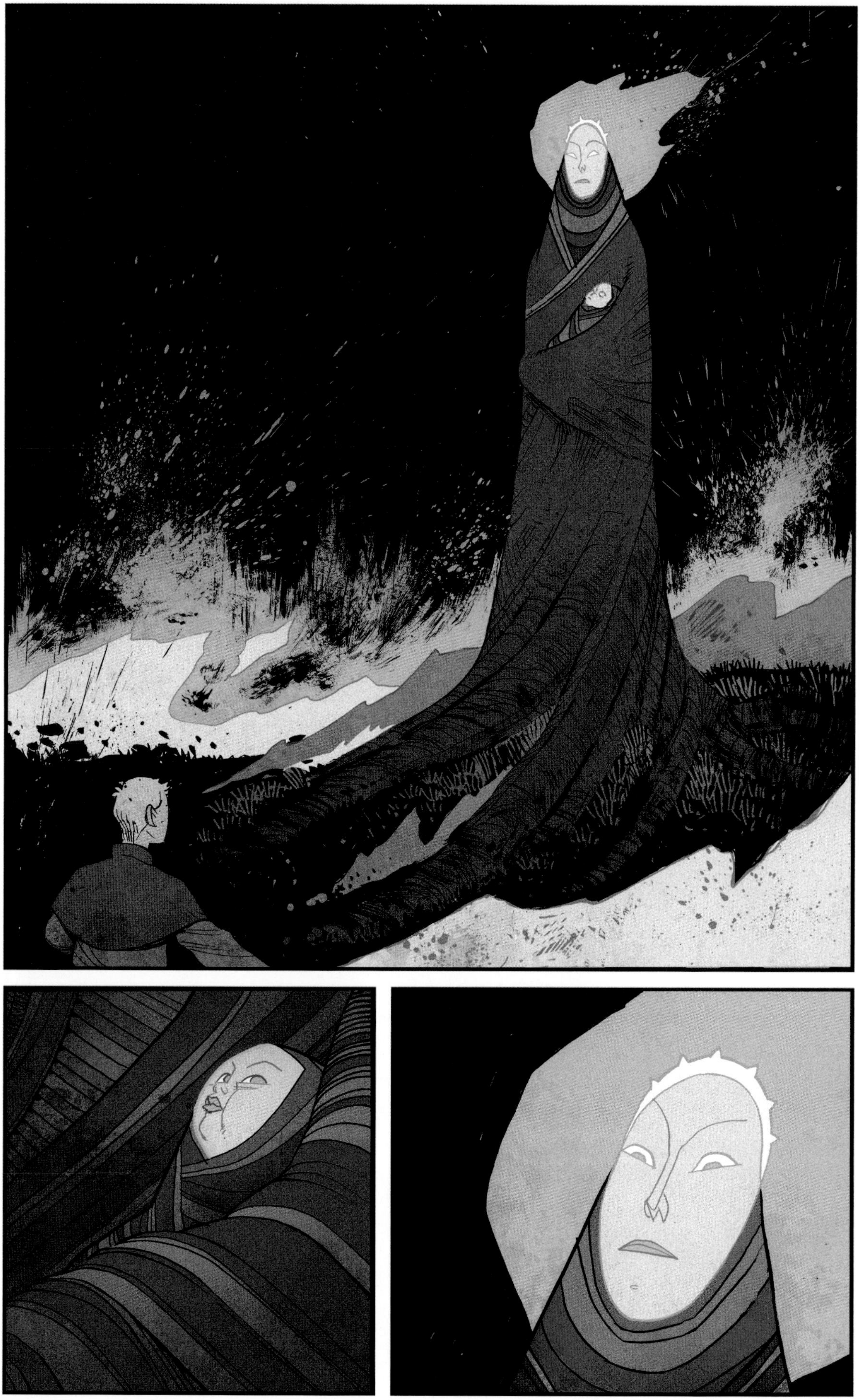

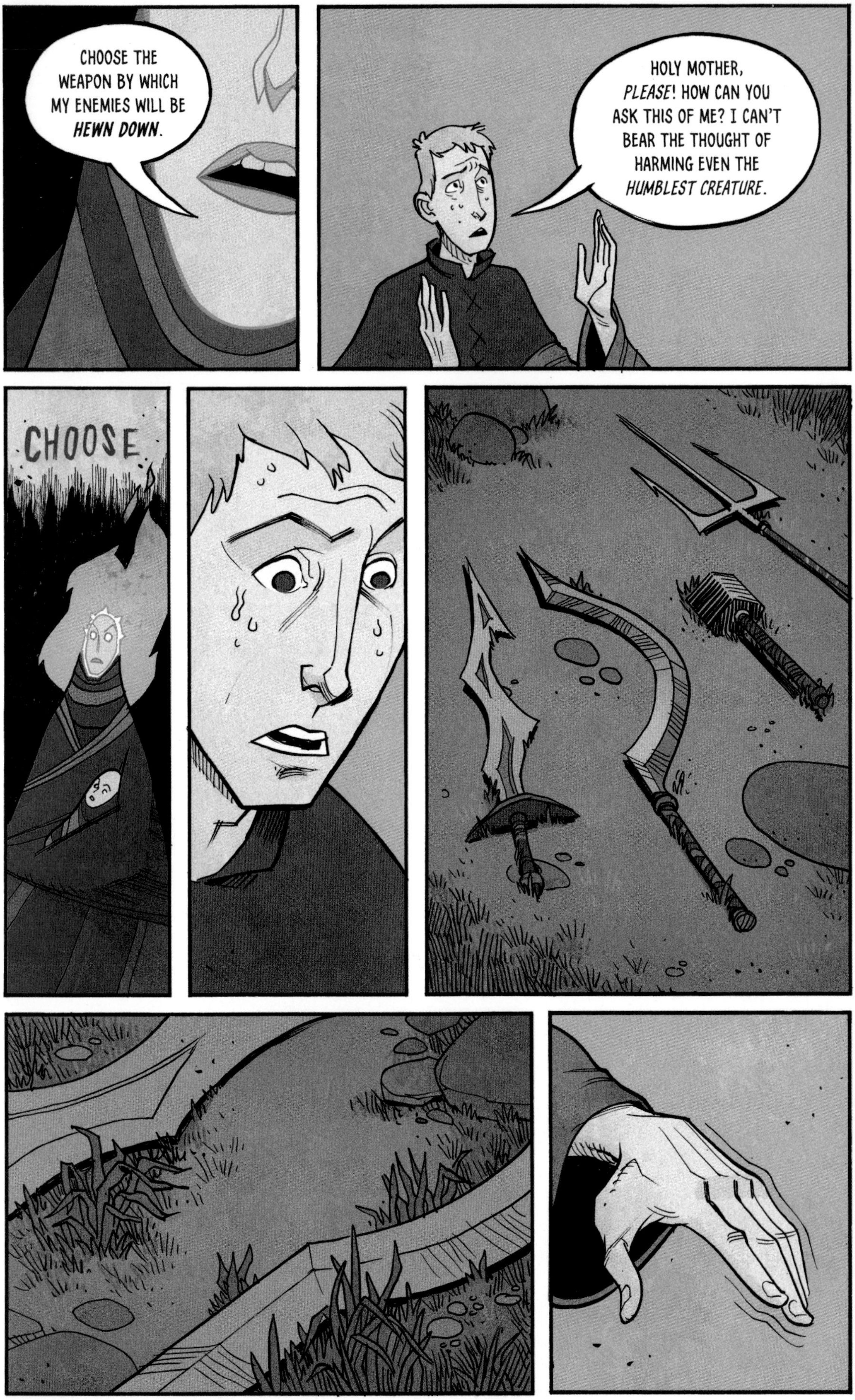
CHOOSE THE WEAPON BY WHICH MY ENEMIES WILL BE *HEWN DOWN*.
HOLY MOTHER, *PLEASE*! HOW CAN YOU ASK THIS OF ME? I CAN'T BEAR THE THOUGHT OF HARMING EVEN THE *HUMBLEST CREATURE*.
CHOOSE

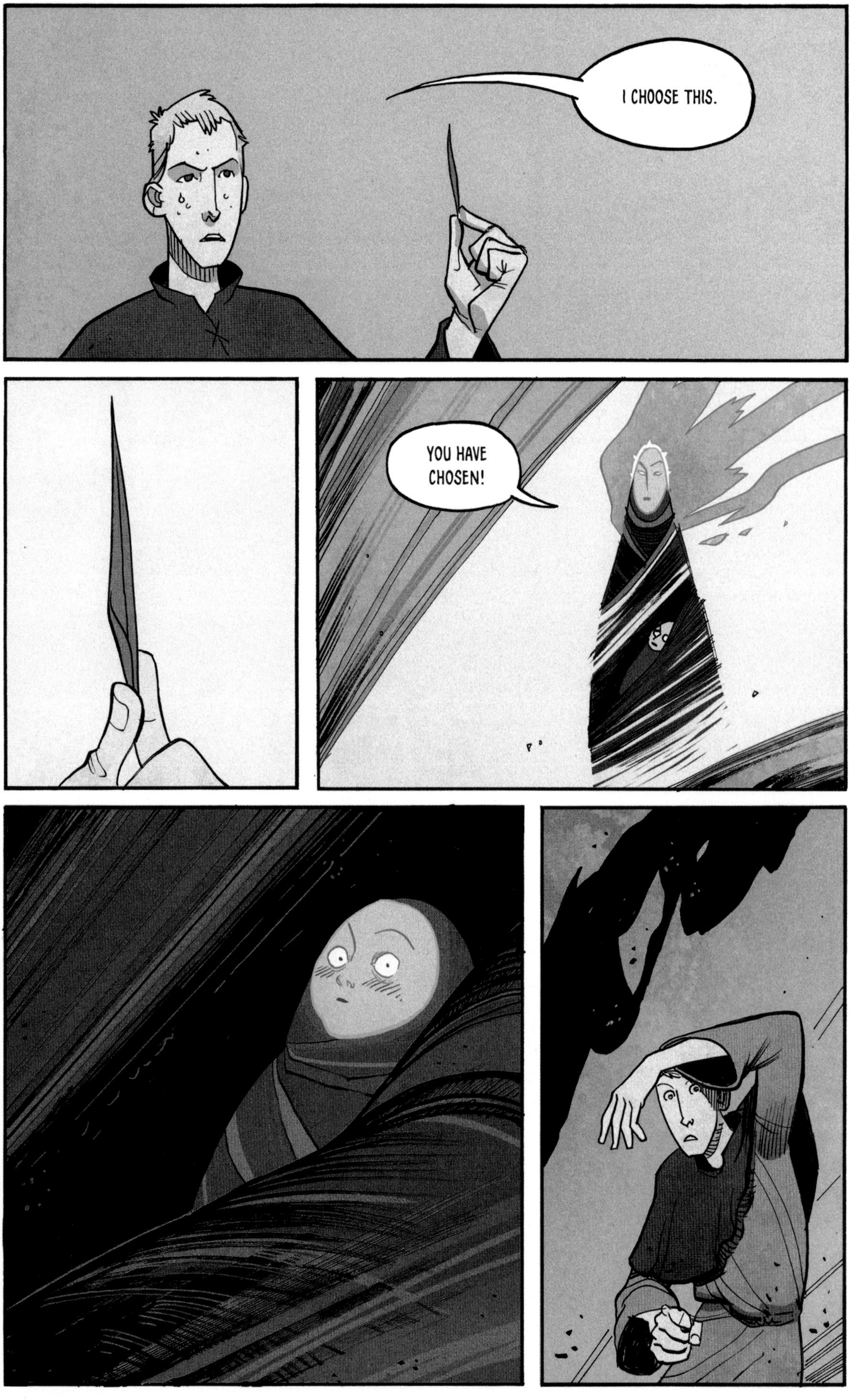
I CHOOSE THIS.
YOU HAVE CHOSEN!

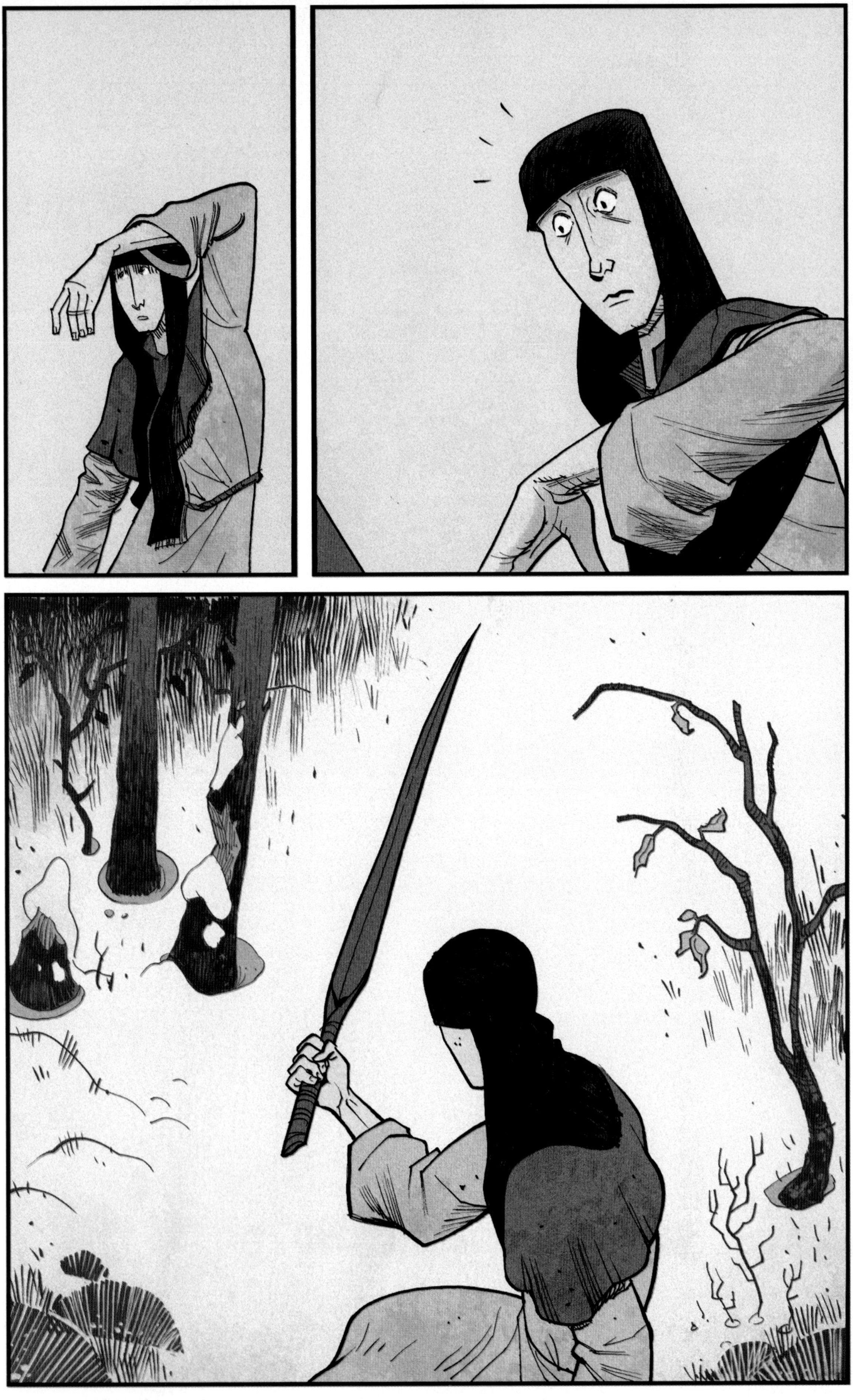

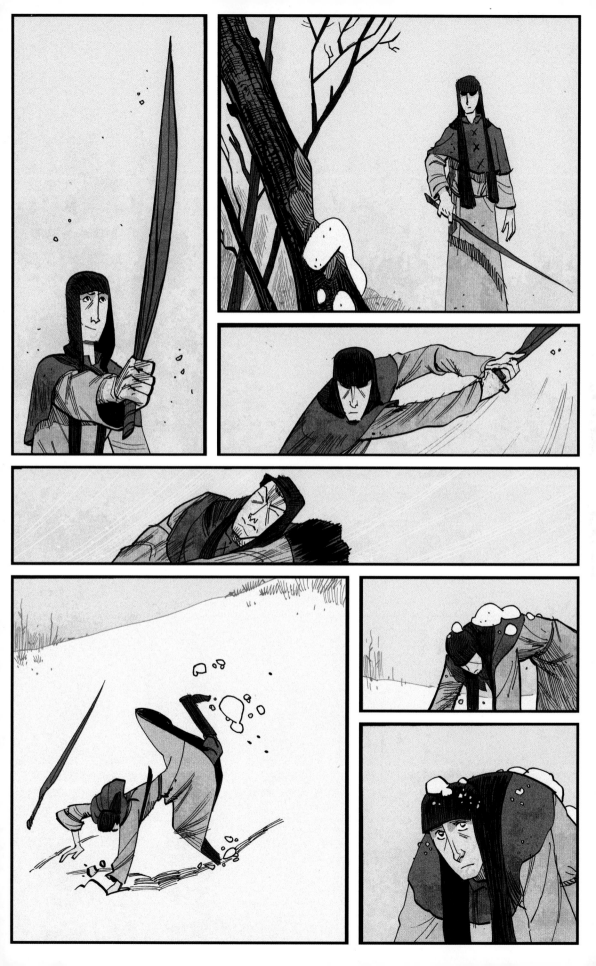

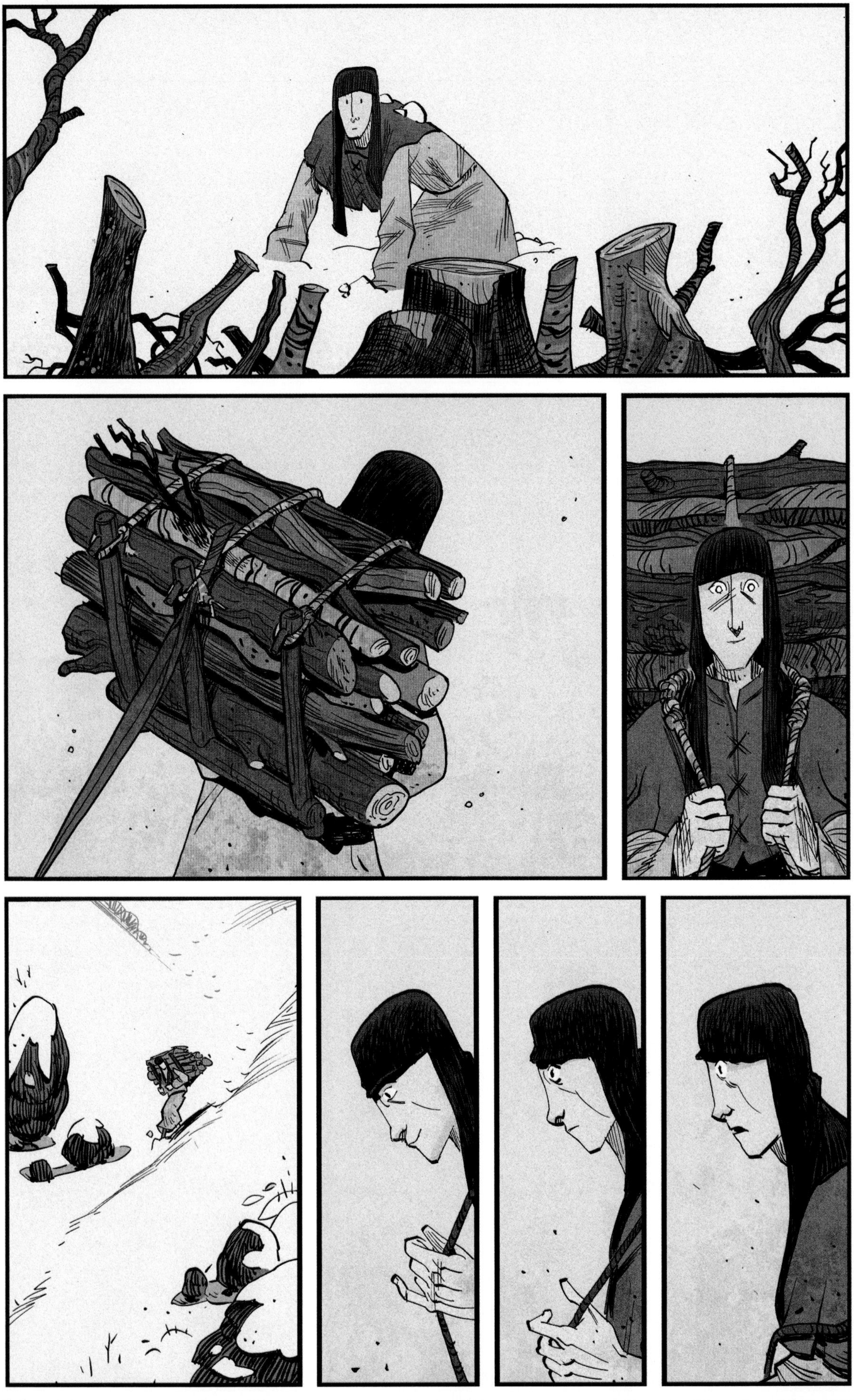

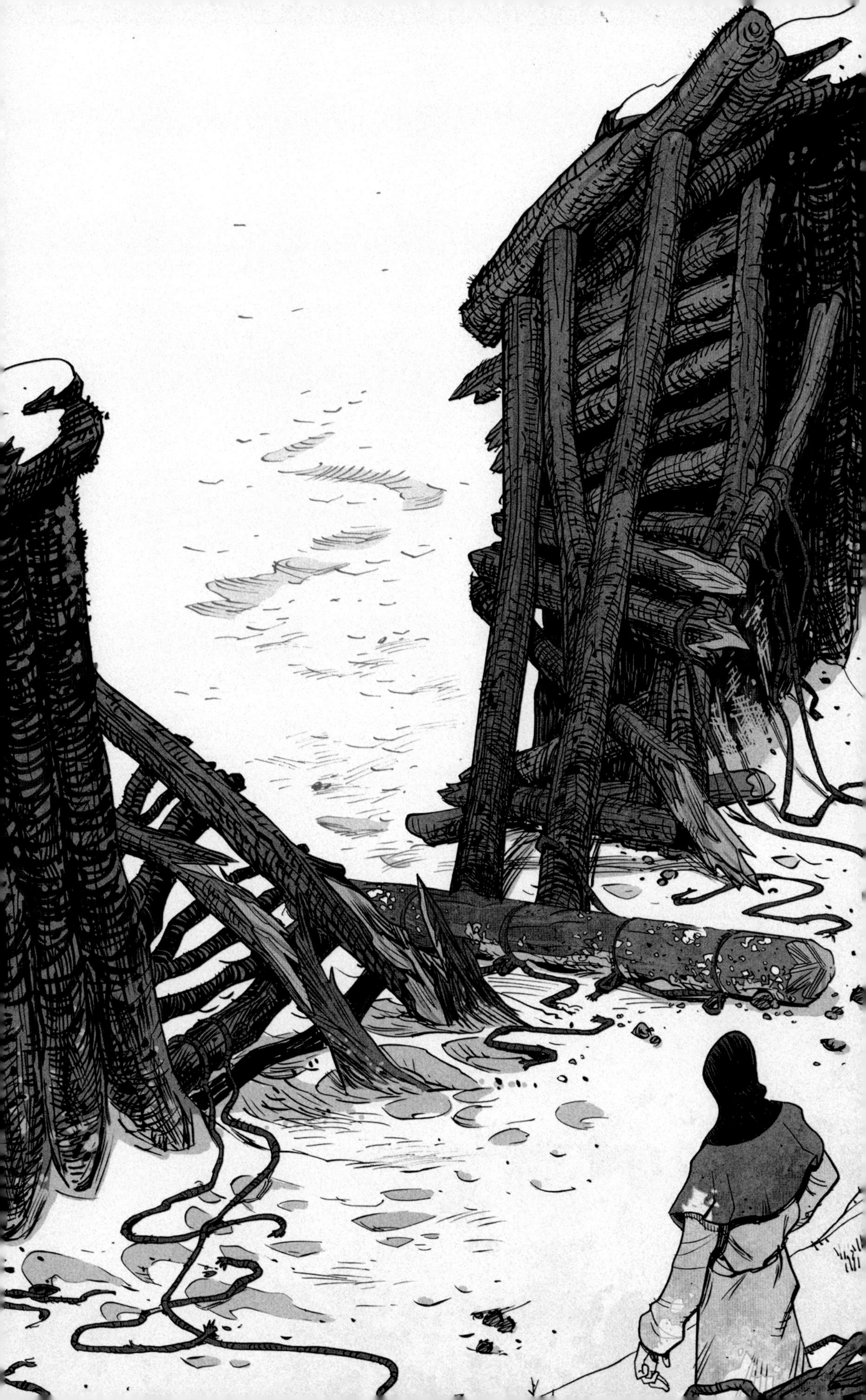

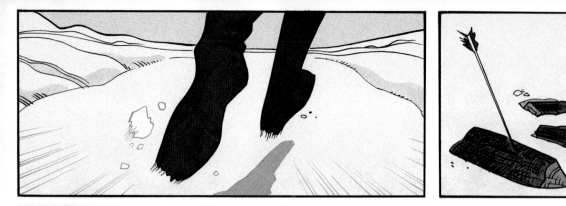

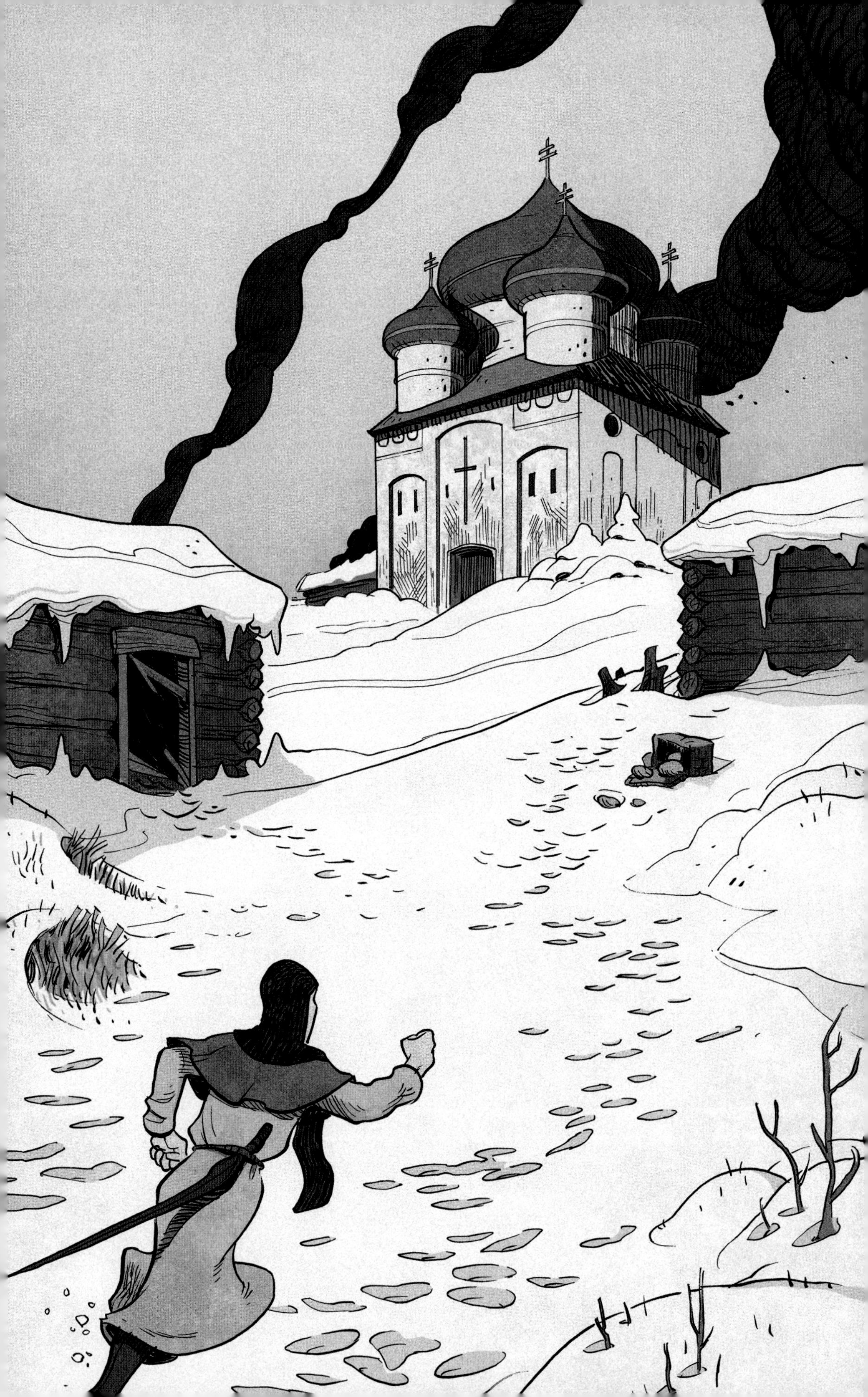

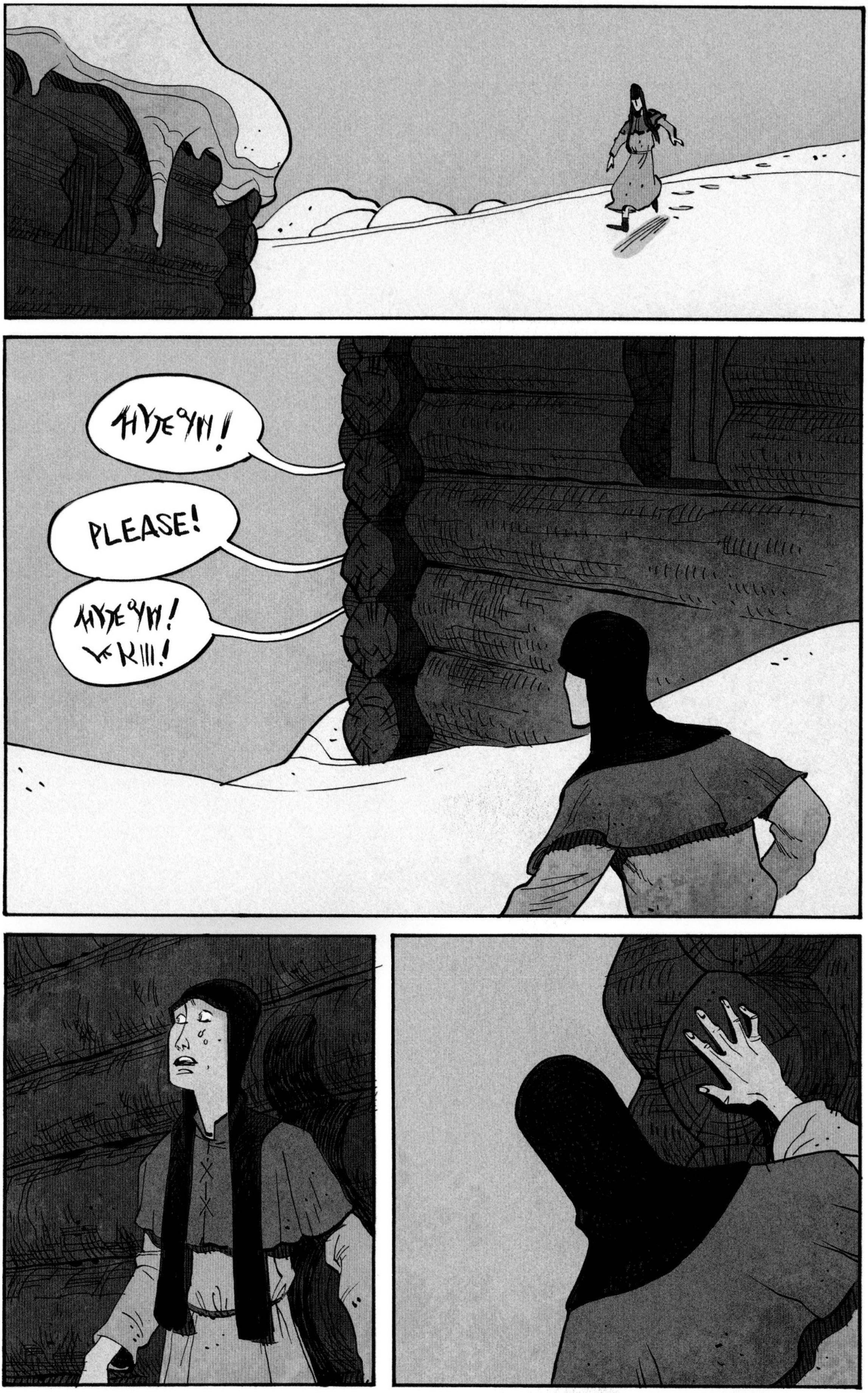
PLEASE!

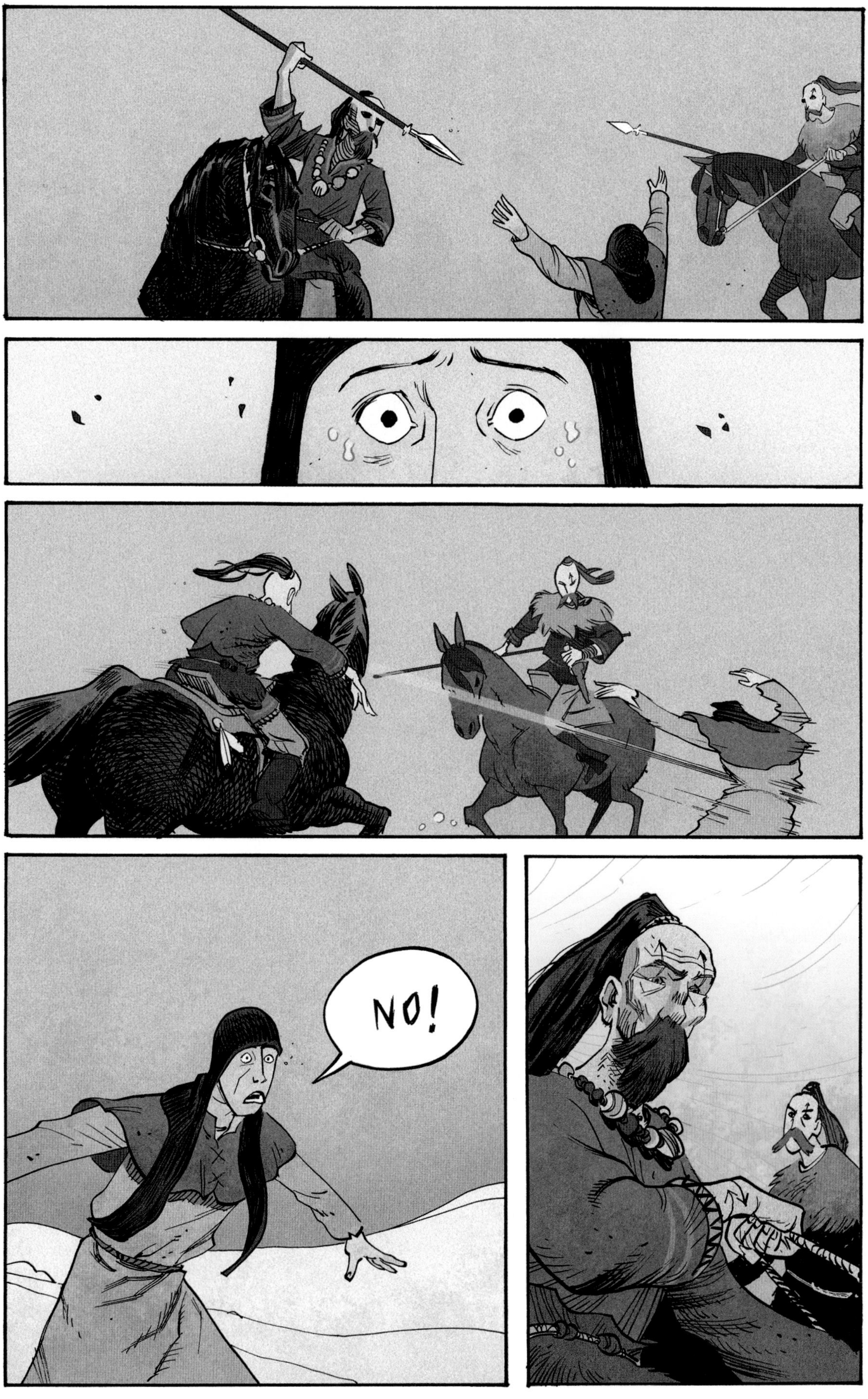
NO!

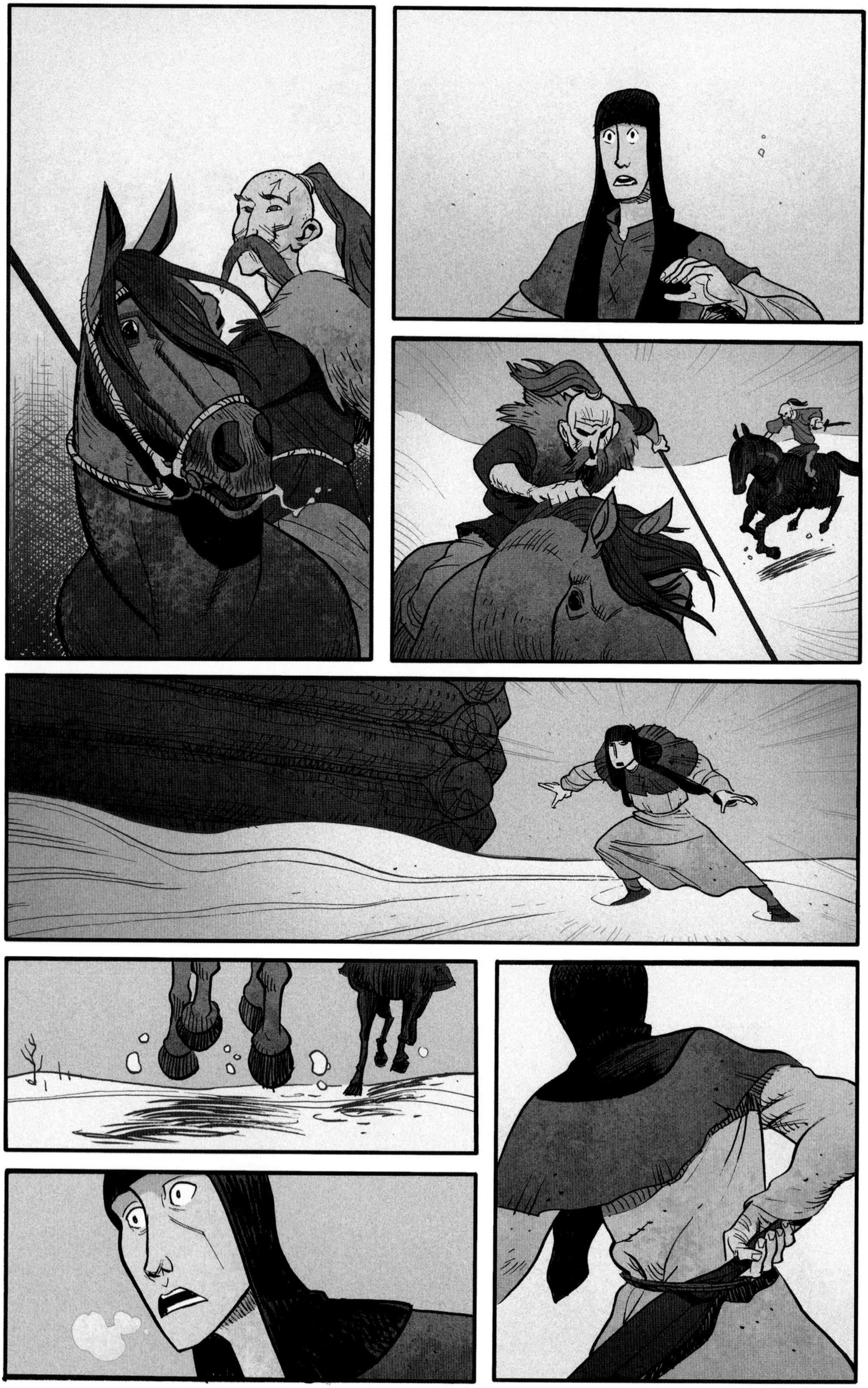

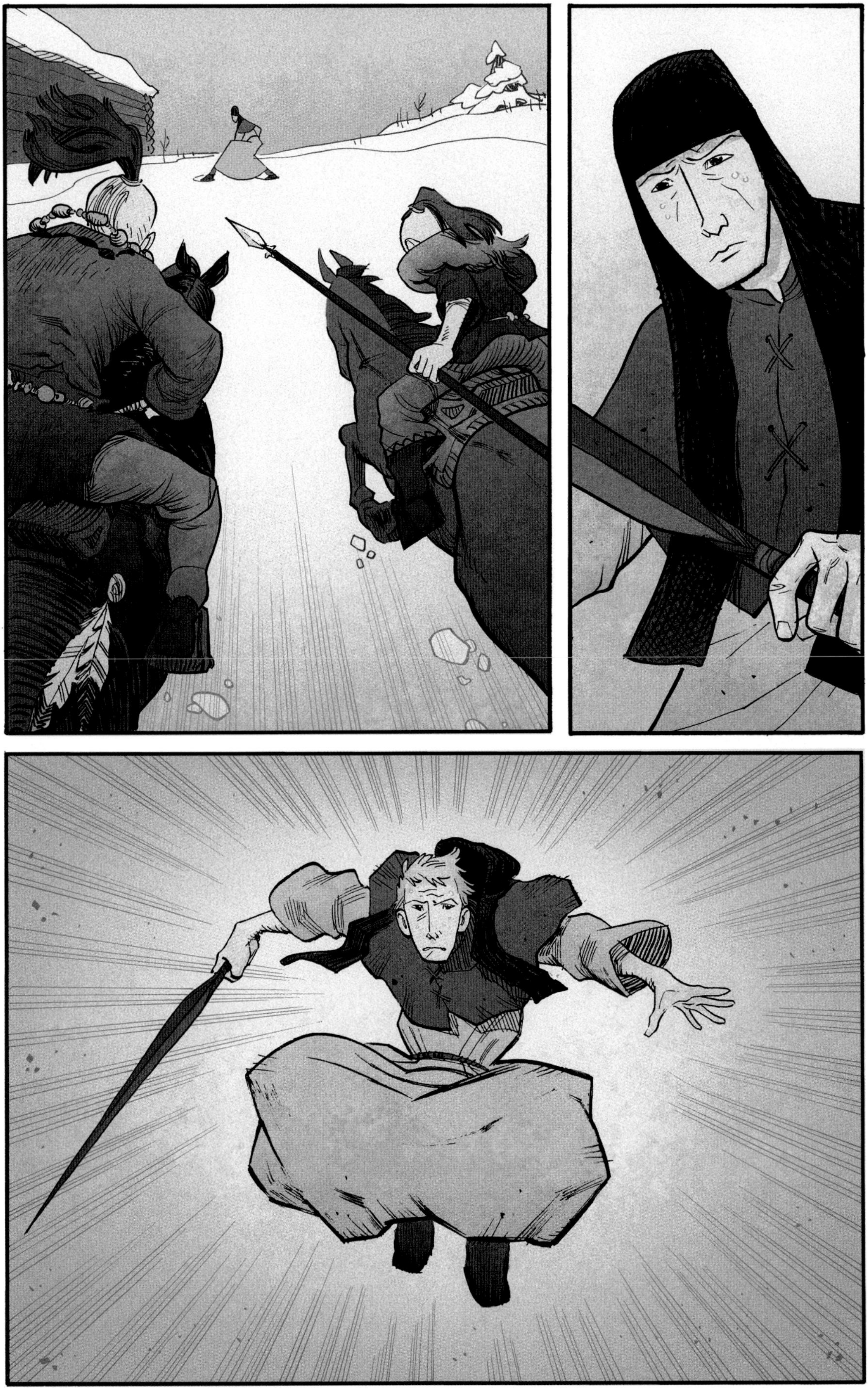

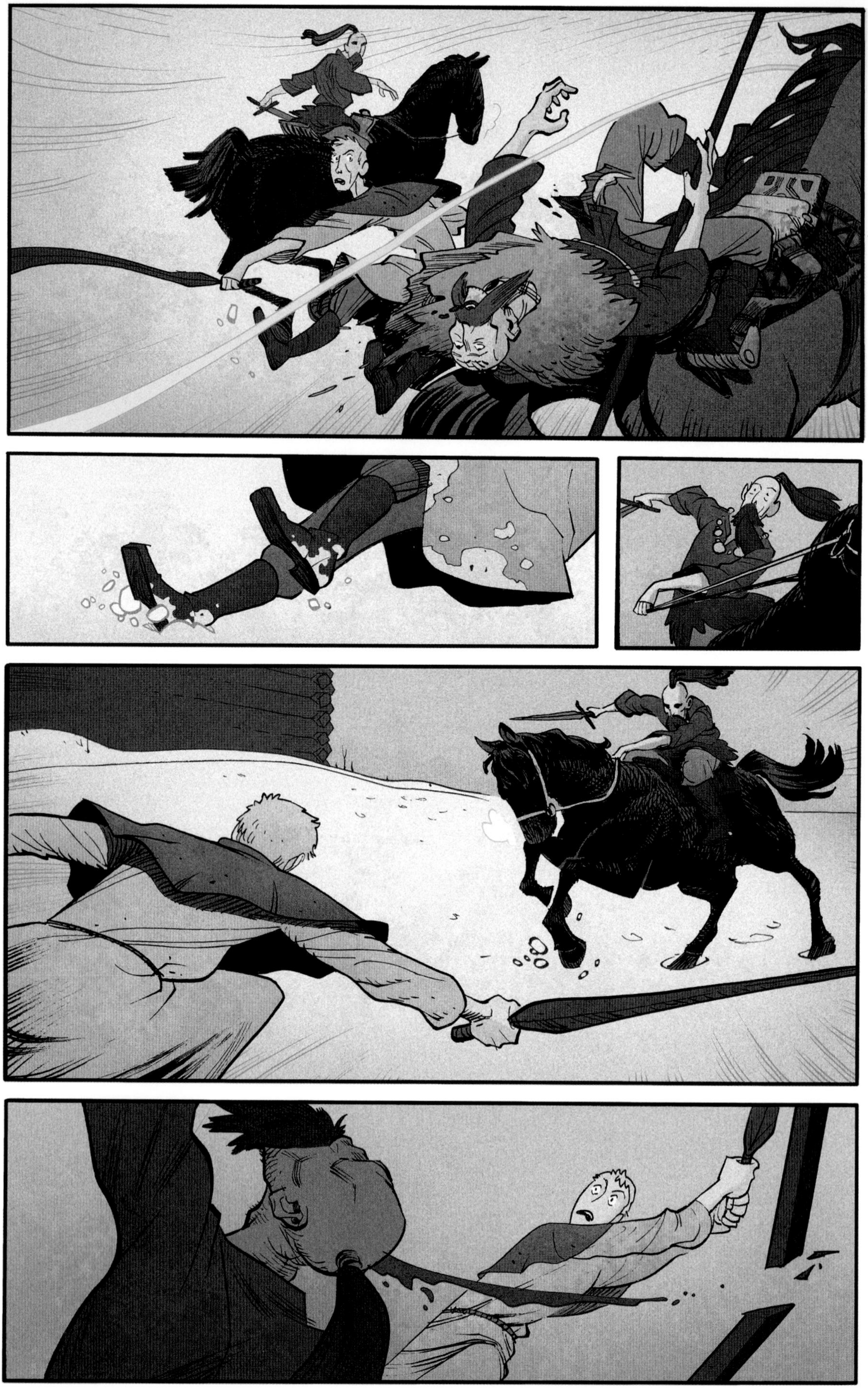

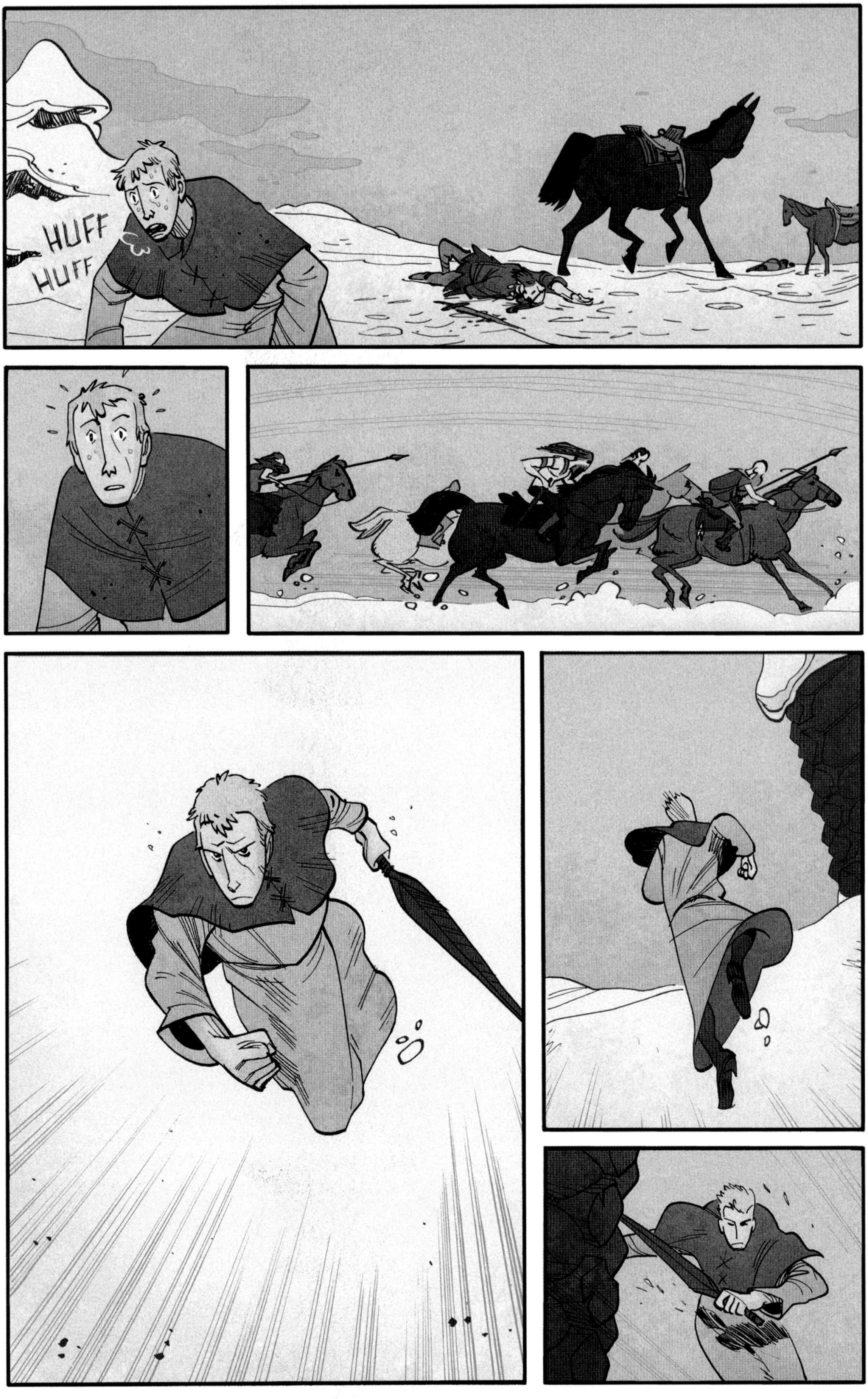
HUFF
HUFF

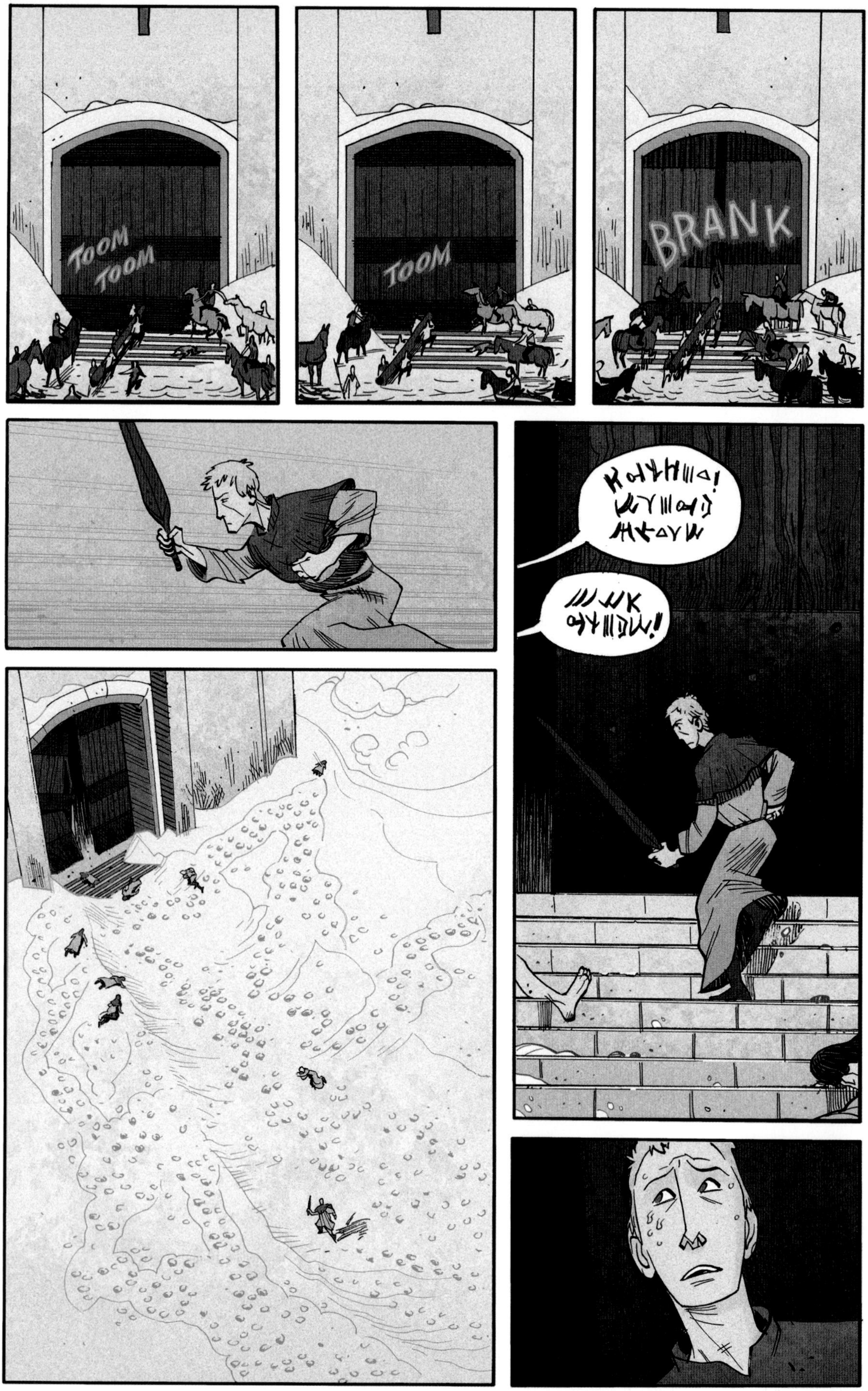
TOOM TOOM
TOOM
BRANK

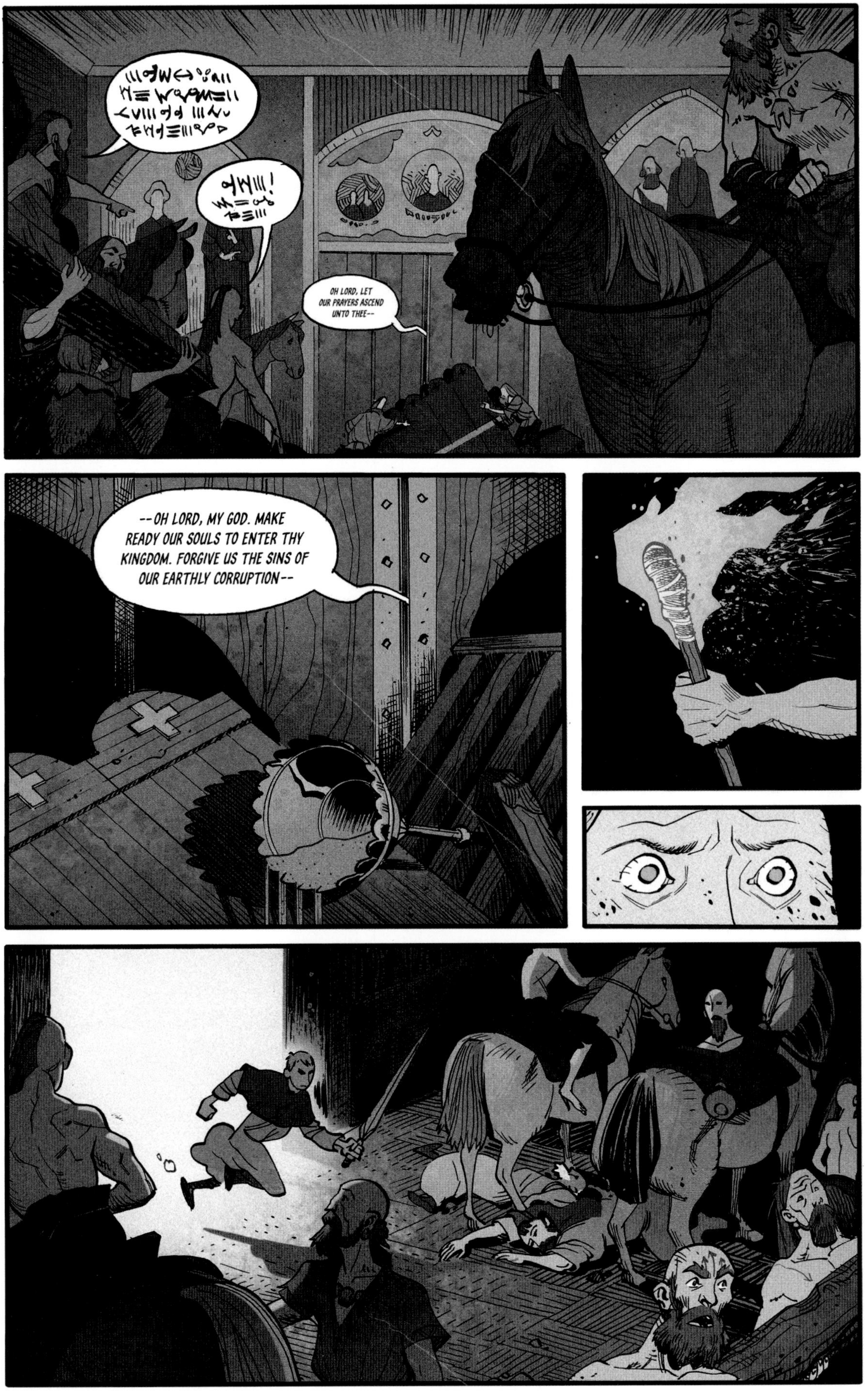
OH LORD, LET OUR PRAYERS ASCEND UNTO THEE--
--OH LORD, MY GOD. MAKE READY OUR SOULS TO ENTER THY KINGDOM. FORGIVE US THE SINS OF OUR EARTHLY CORRUPTION--

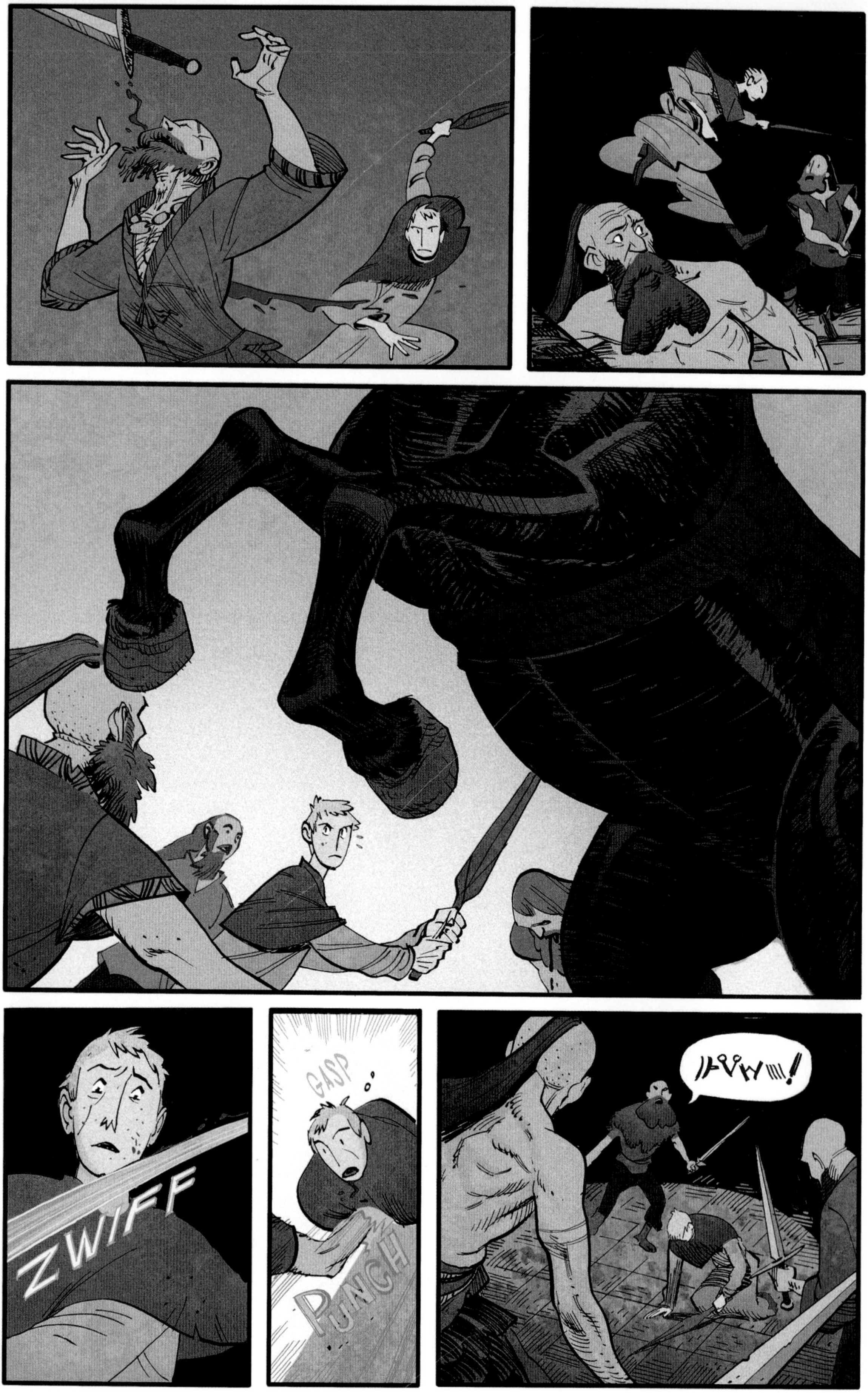
ZWIFF
GASP
PUNCH

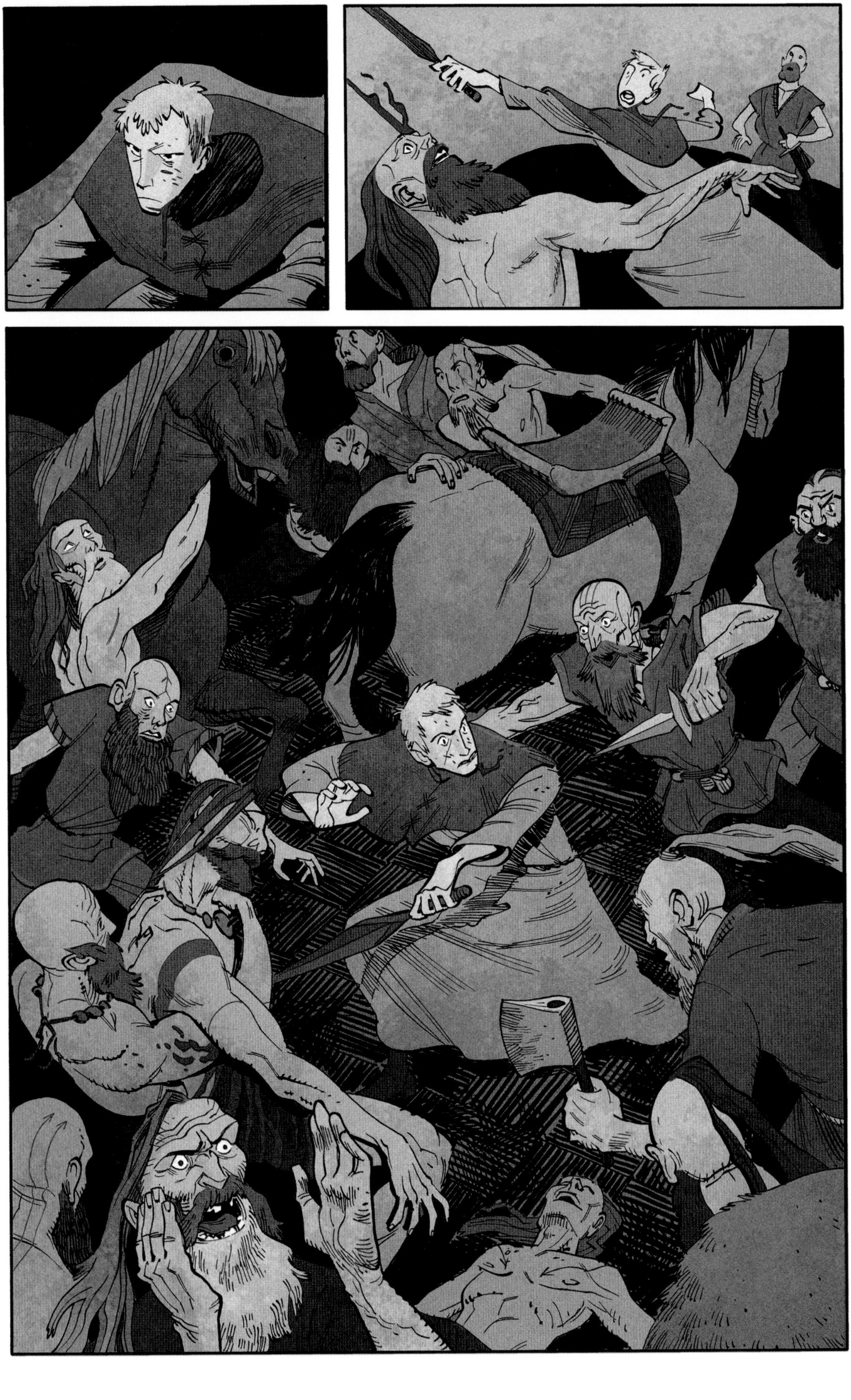

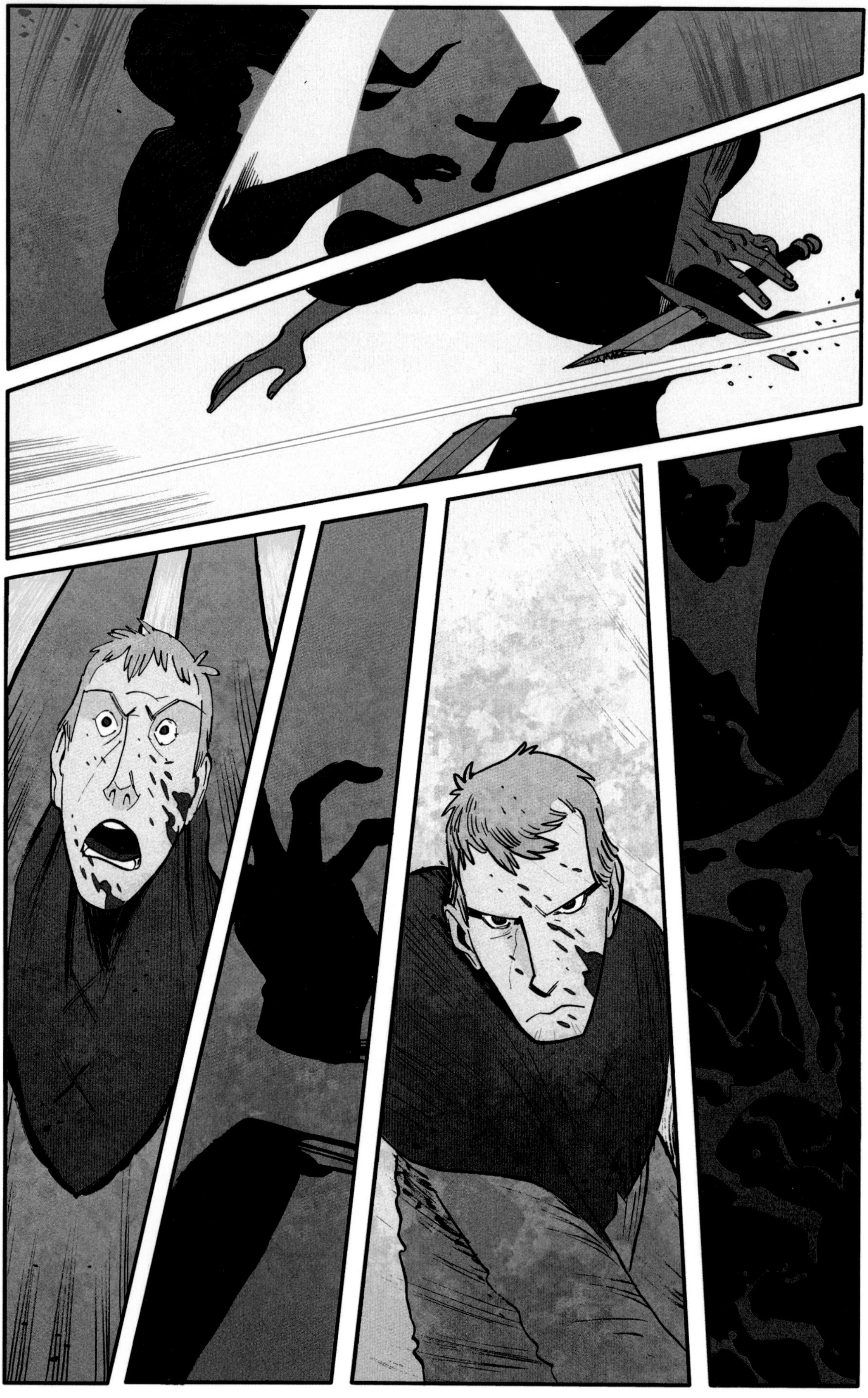

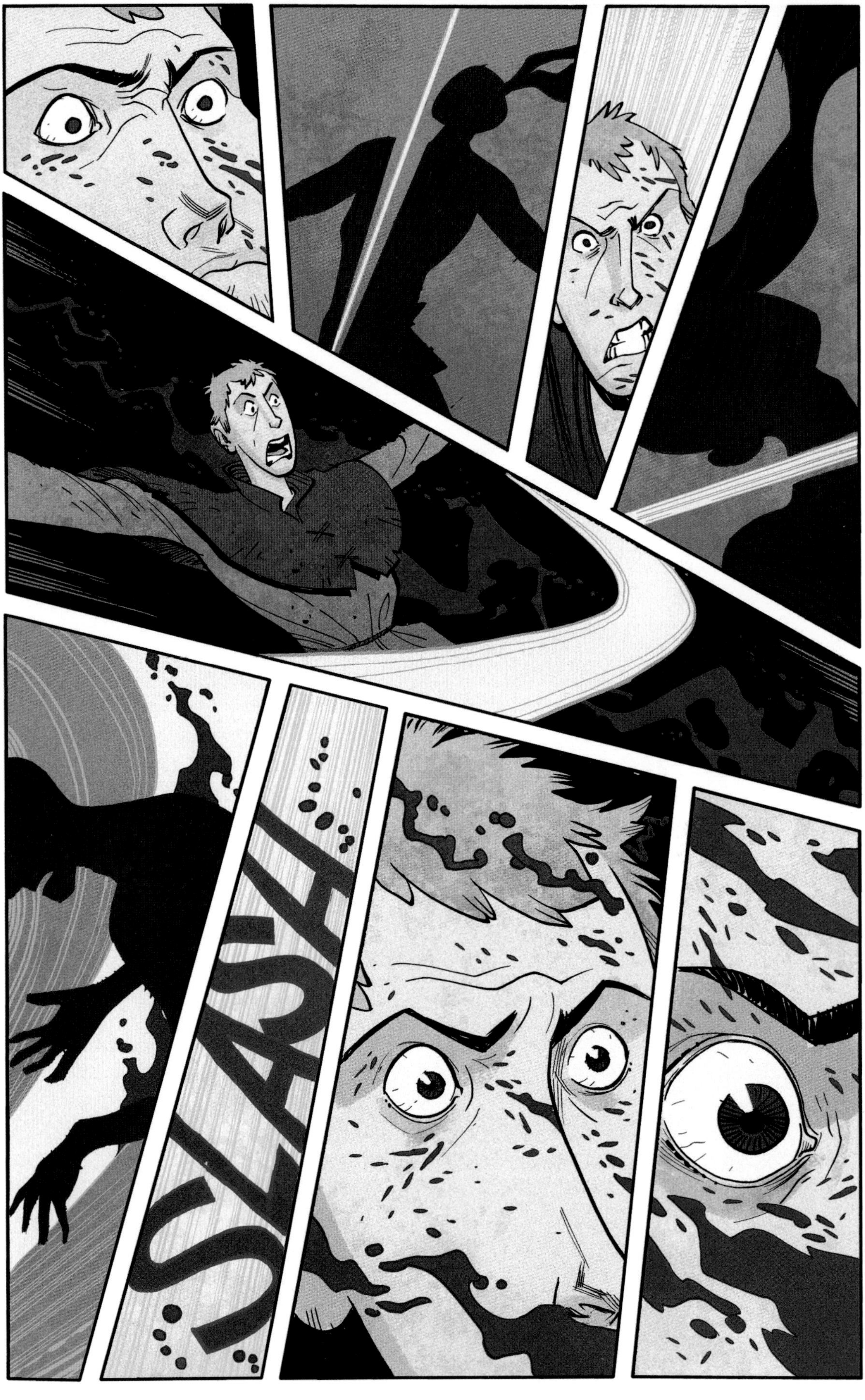
SLASH

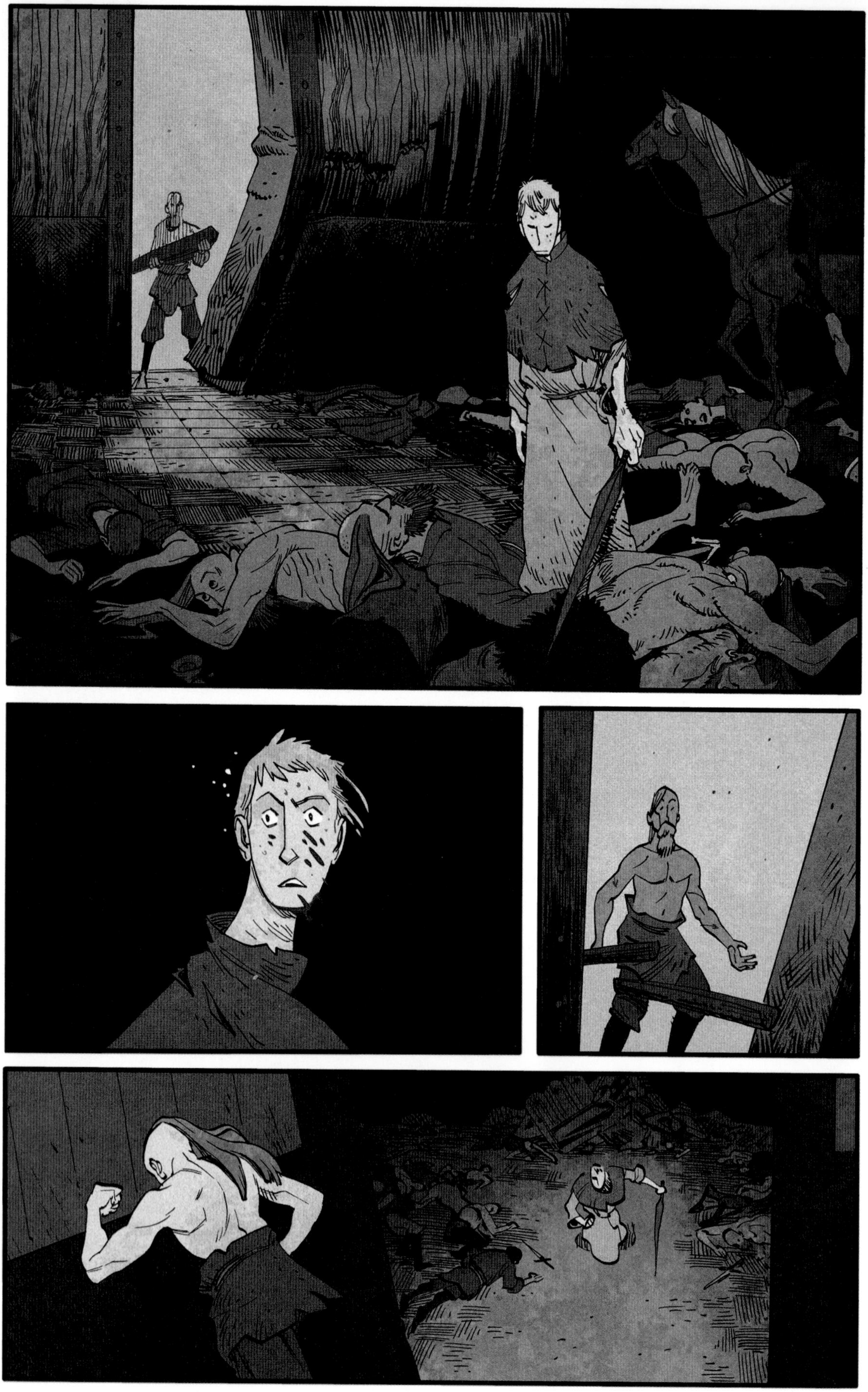

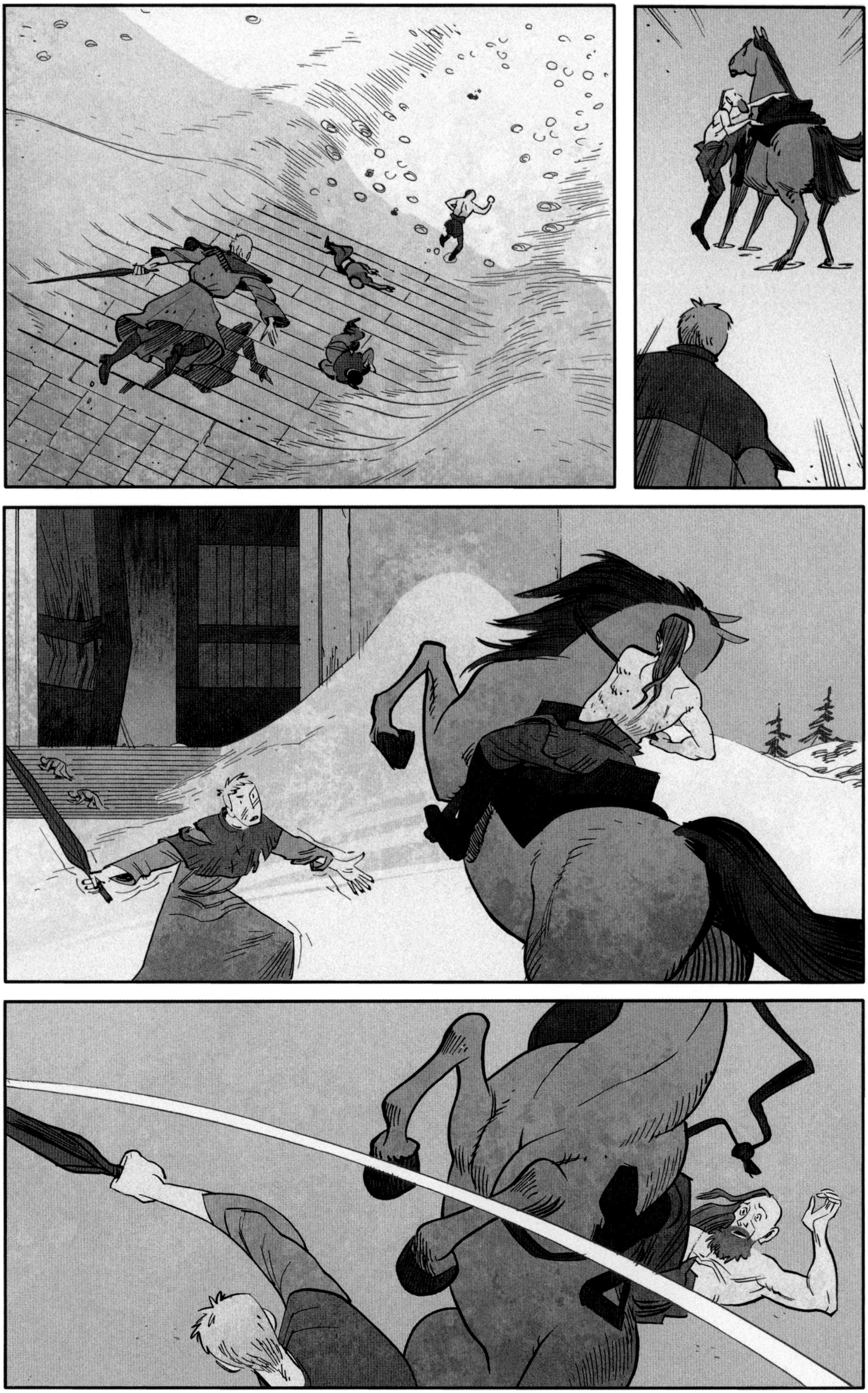

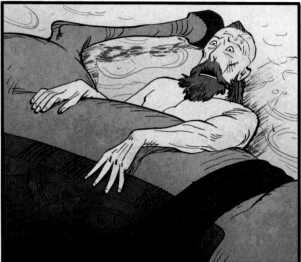

KRAAAK

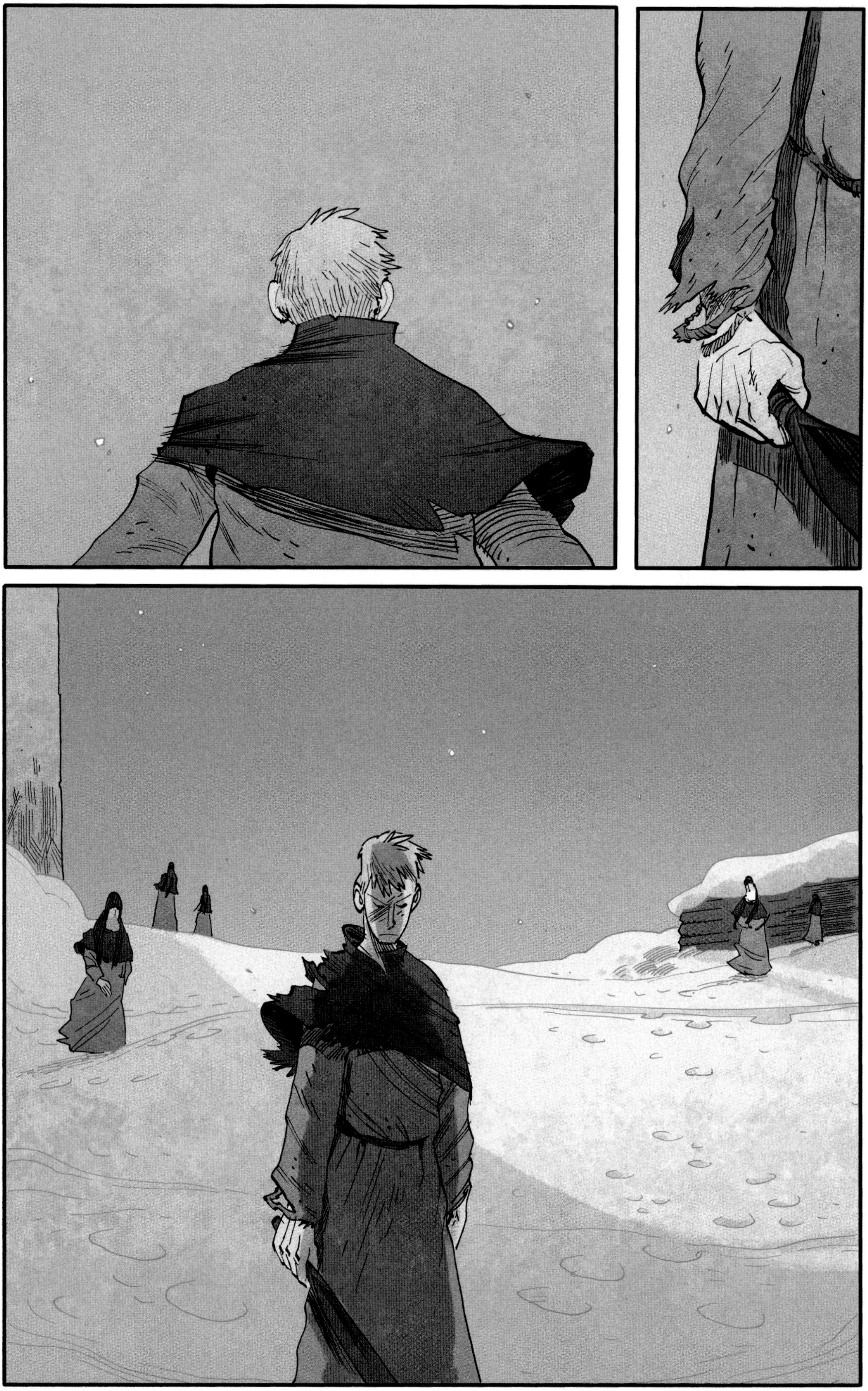

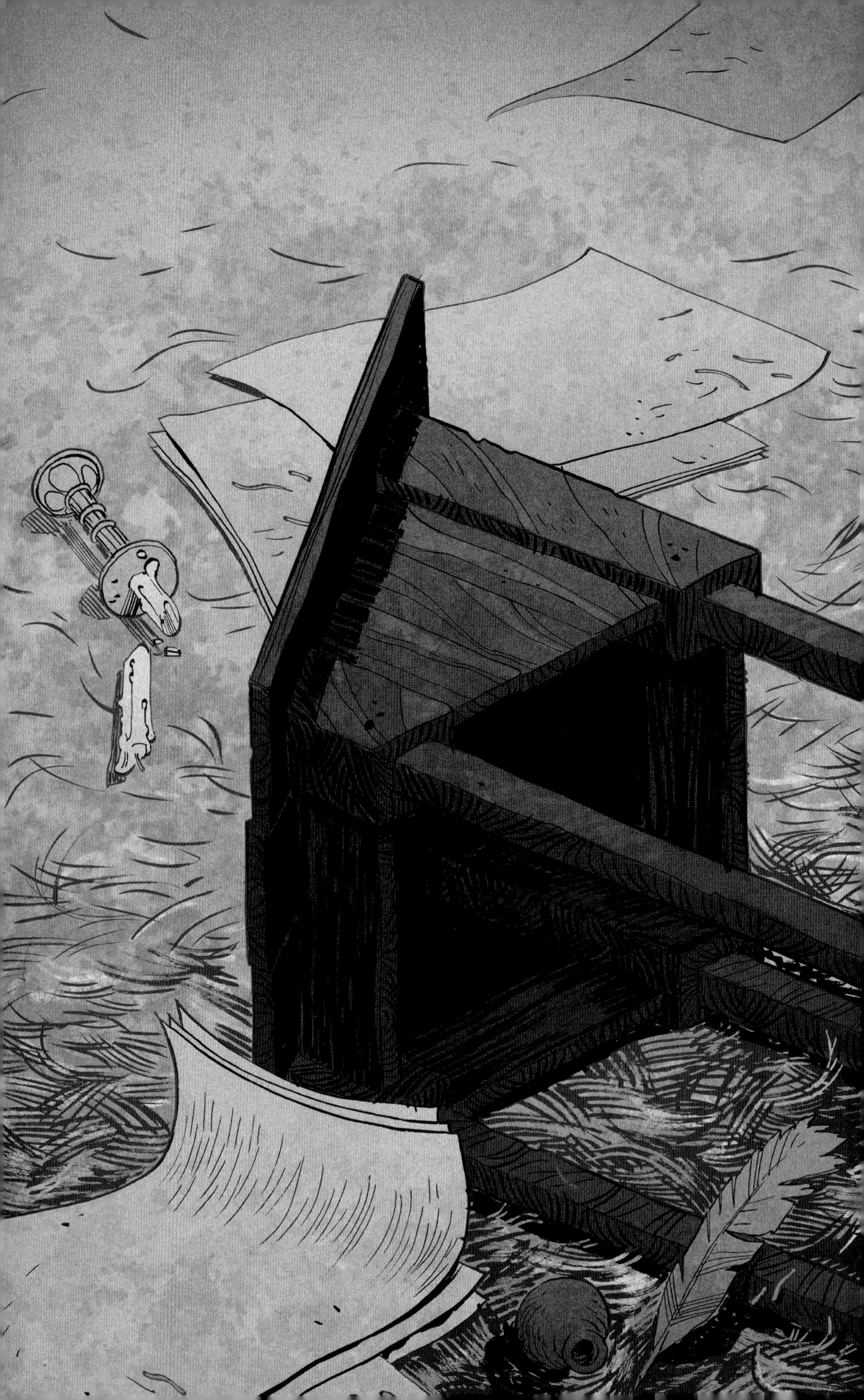

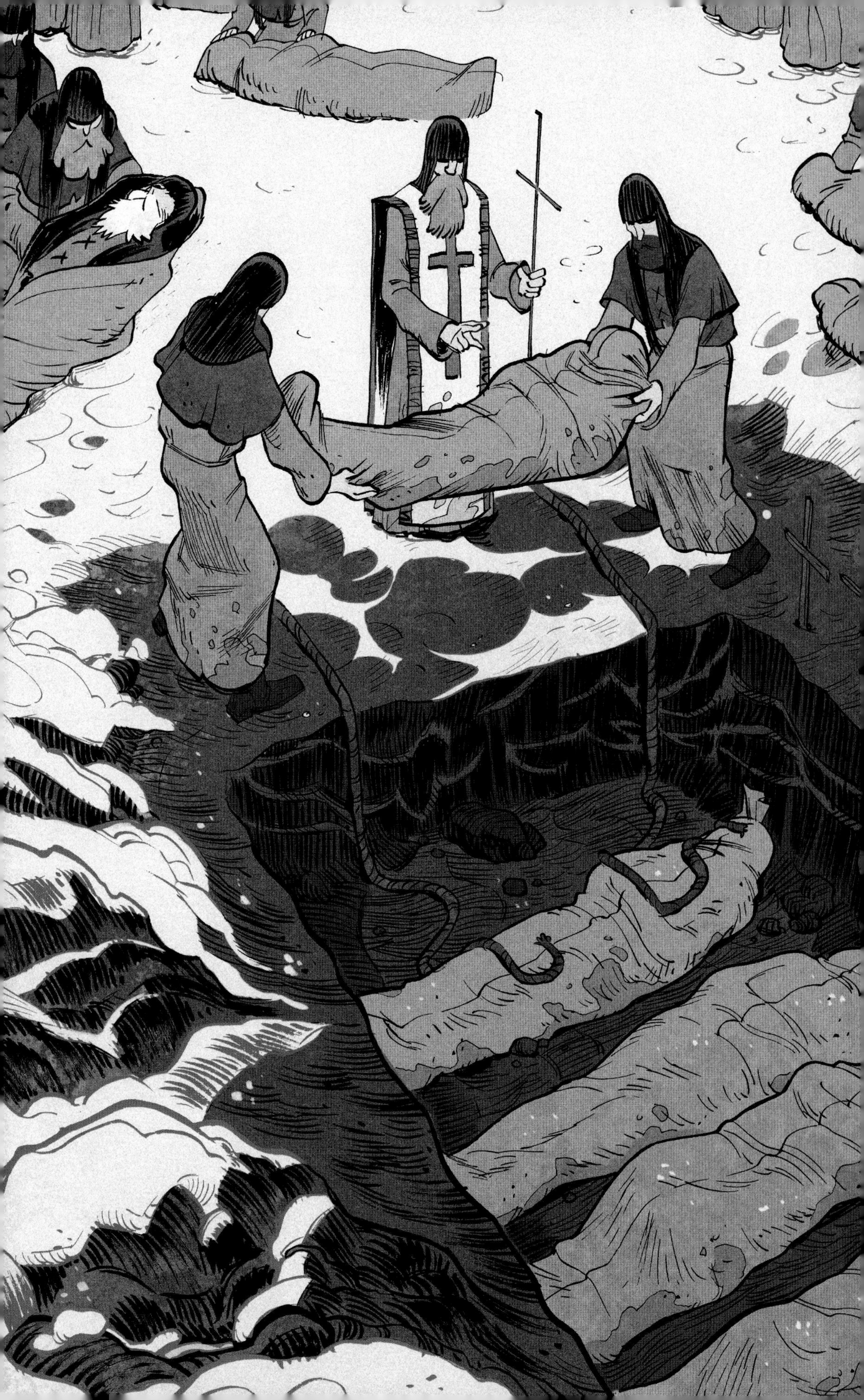

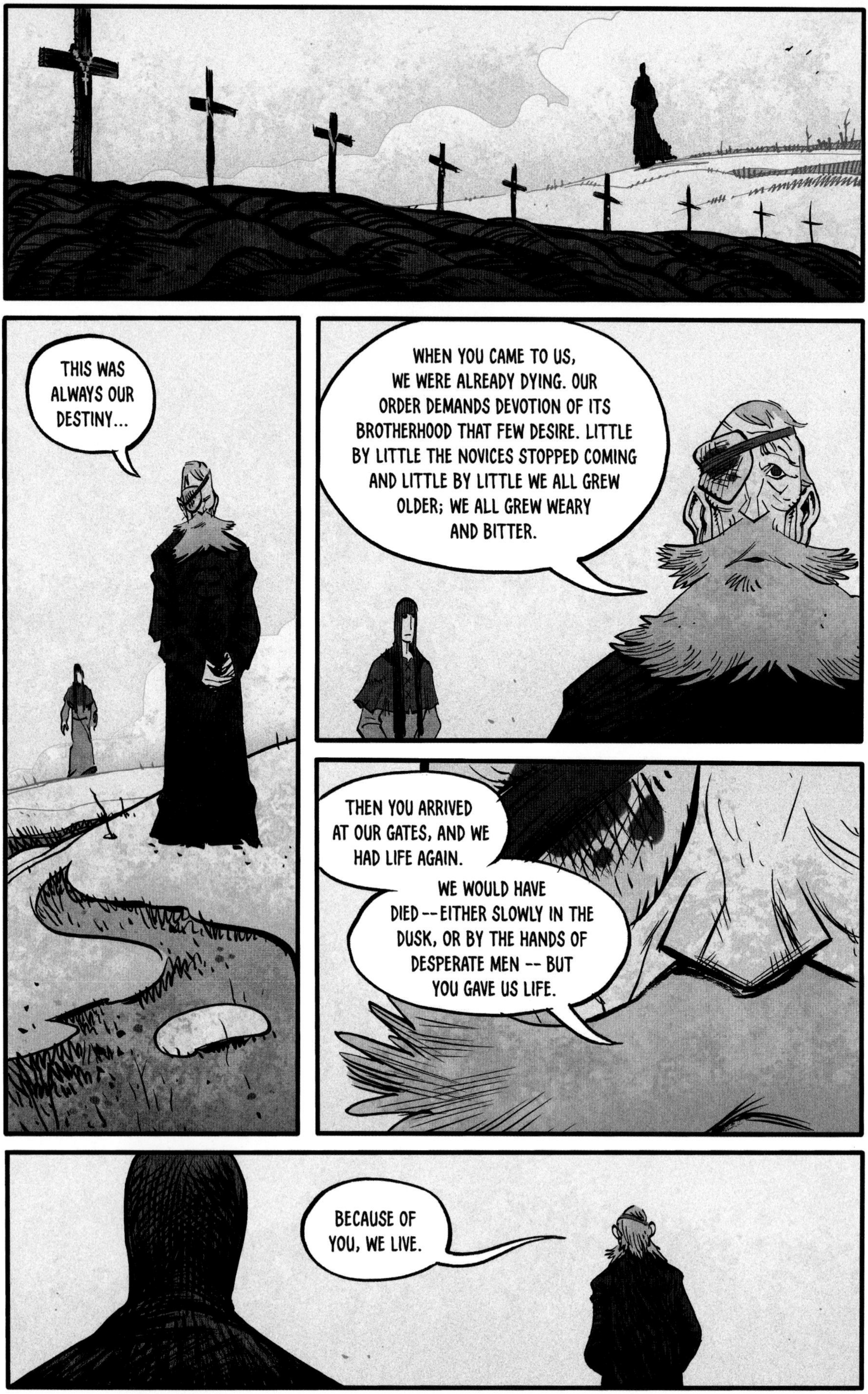
THIS WAS ALWAYS OUR DESTINY...
WHEN YOU CAME TO US, WE WERE ALREADY DYING. OUR ORDER DEMANDS DEVOTION OF ITS BROTHERHOOD THAT FEW DESIRE. LITTLE BY LITTLE THE NOVICES STOPPED COMING AND LITTLE BY LITTLE WE ALL GREW OLDER; WE ALL GREW WEARY AND BITTER.
THEN YOU ARRIVED AT OUR GATES, AND WE HAD LIFE AGAIN.
WE WOULD HAVE DIED -- EITHER SLOWLY IN THE DUSK, OR BY THE HANDS OF DESPERATE MEN -- BUT YOU GAVE US LIFE.
BECAUSE OF YOU, WE LIVE.

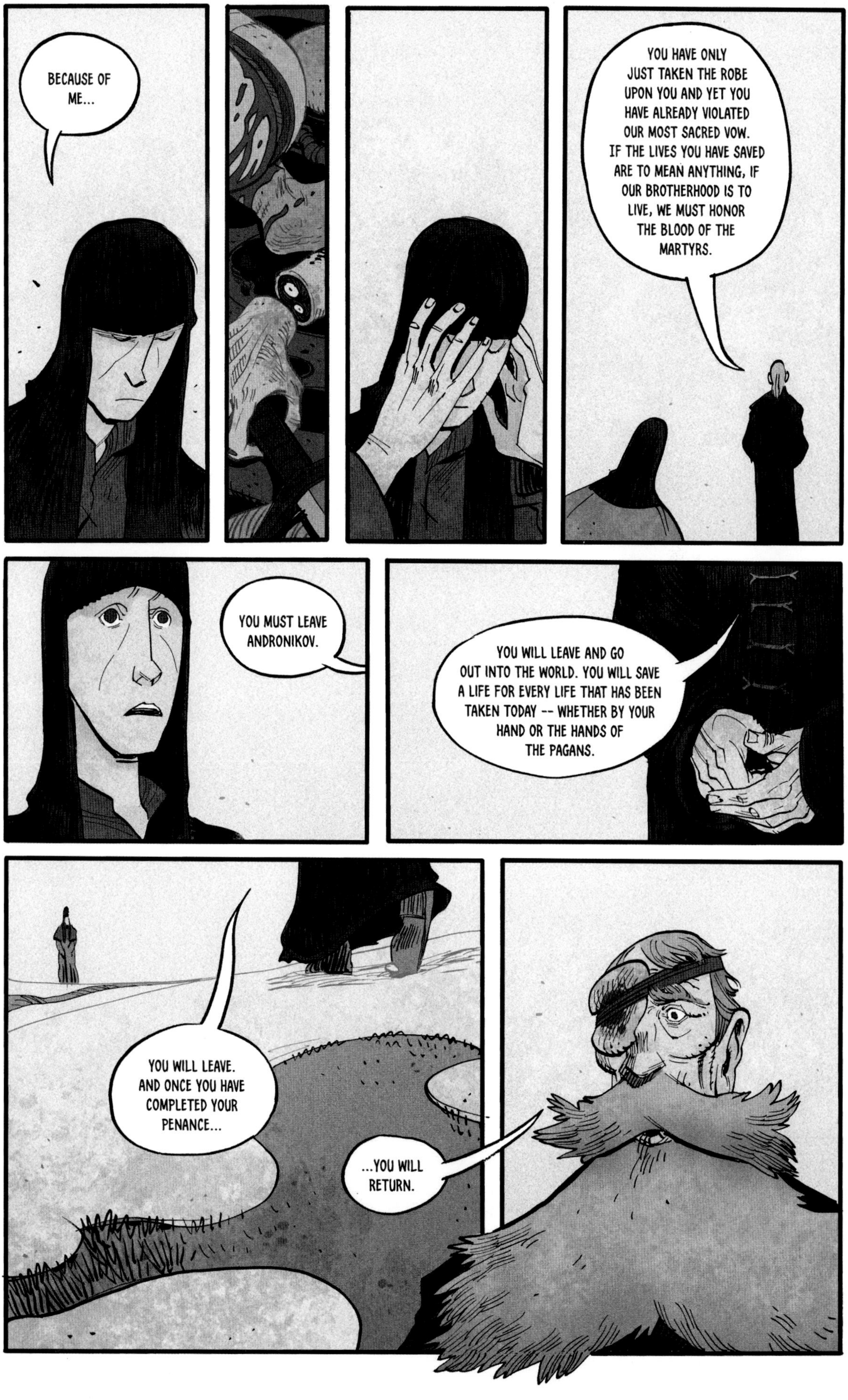
BECAUSE OF ME...
YOU HAVE ONLY JUST TAKEN THE ROBE UPON YOU AND YET YOU HAVE ALREADY VIOLATED OUR MOST SACRED VOW. IF THE LIVES YOU HAVE SAVED ARE TO MEAN ANYTHING, IF OUR BROTHERHOOD IS TO LIVE, WE MUST HONOR THE BLOOD OF THE MARTYRS.
YOU MUST LEAVE ANDRONIKOV.
YOU WILL LEAVE AND GO OUT INTO THE WORLD. YOU WILL SAVE A LIFE FOR EVERY LIFE THAT HAS BEEN TAKEN TODAY -- WHETHER BY YOUR HAND OR THE HANDS OF THE PAGANS.
YOU WILL LEAVE. AND ONCE YOU HAVE COMPLETED YOUR PENANCE...
...YOU WILL RETURN.

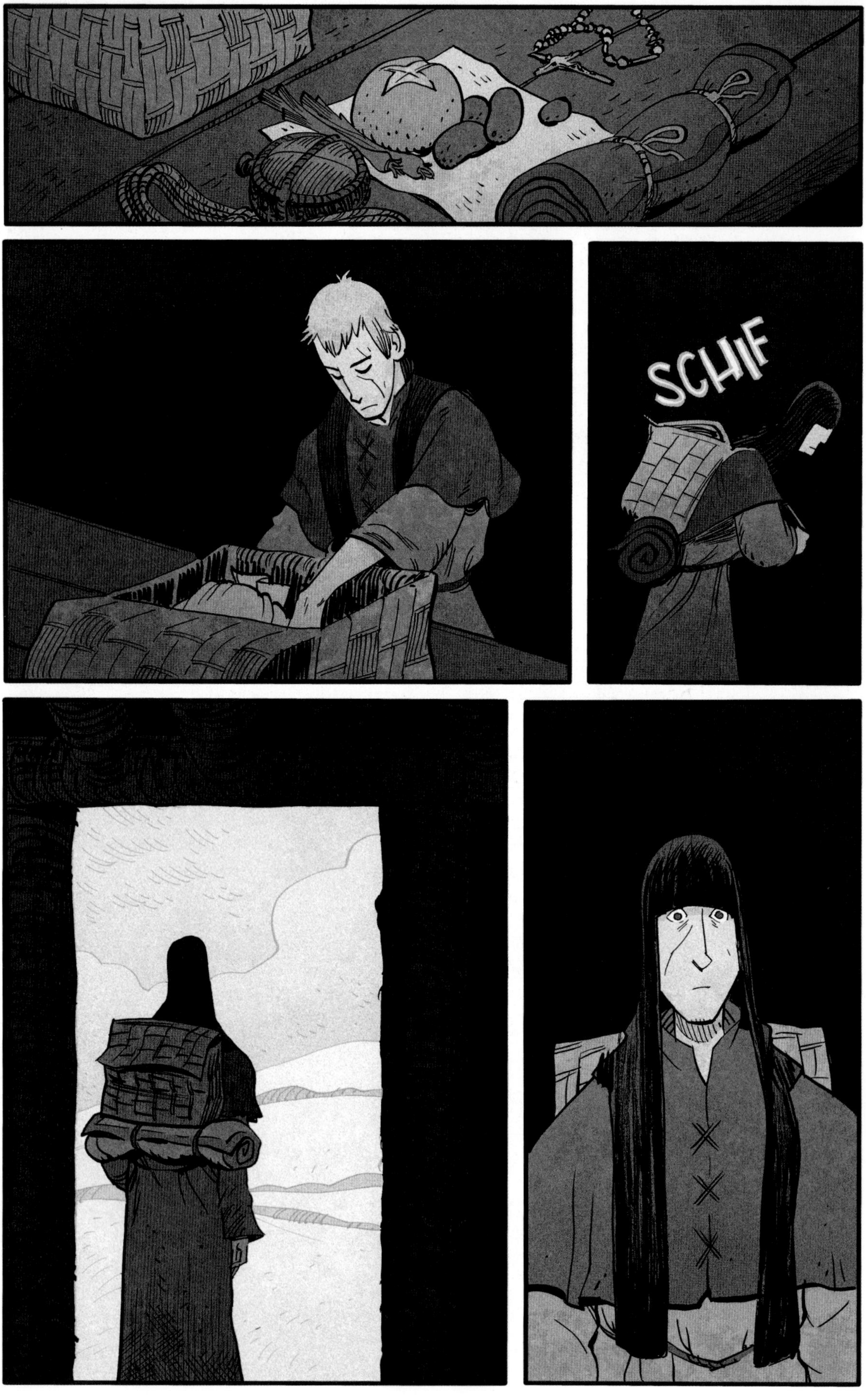
SCHIF

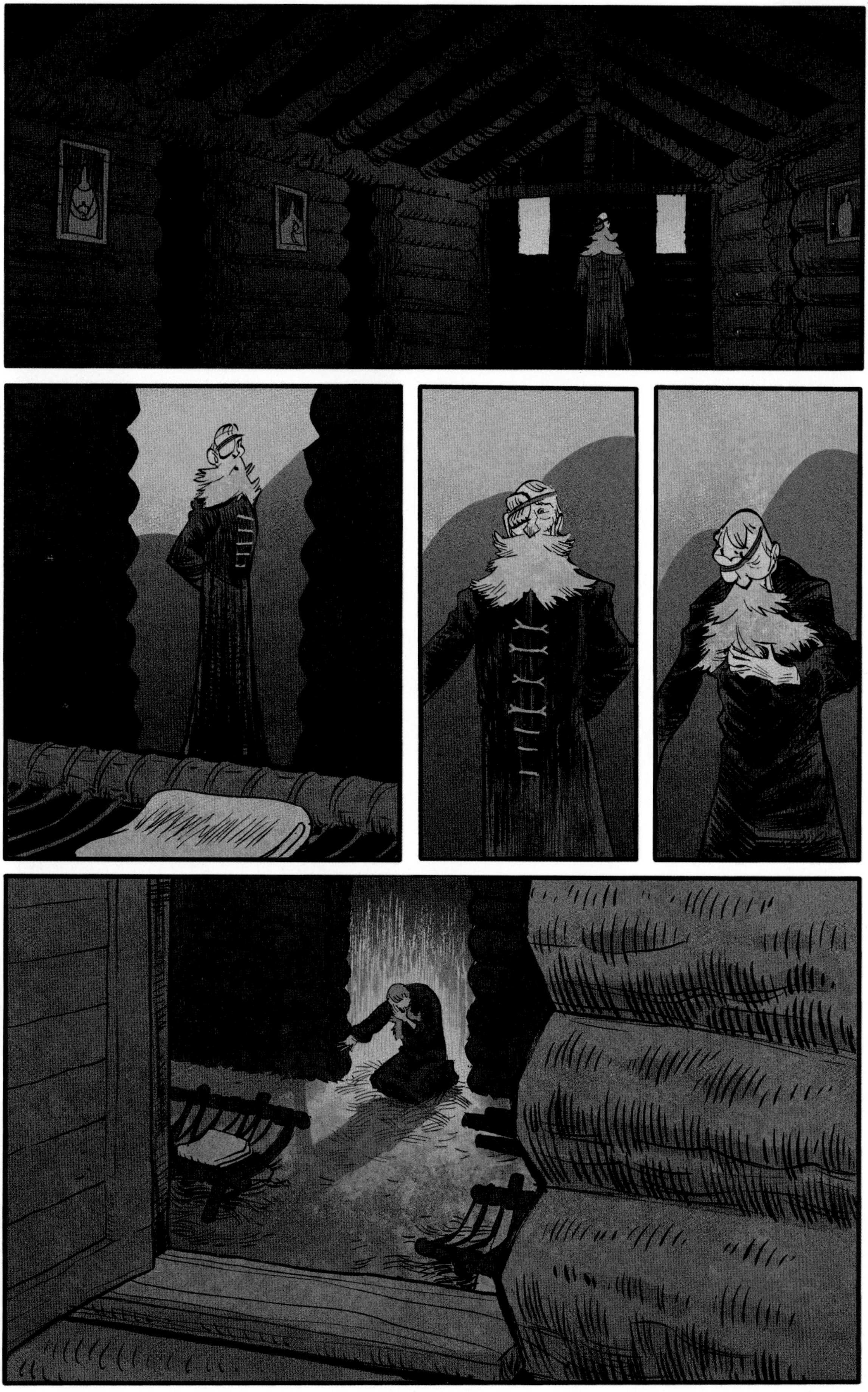

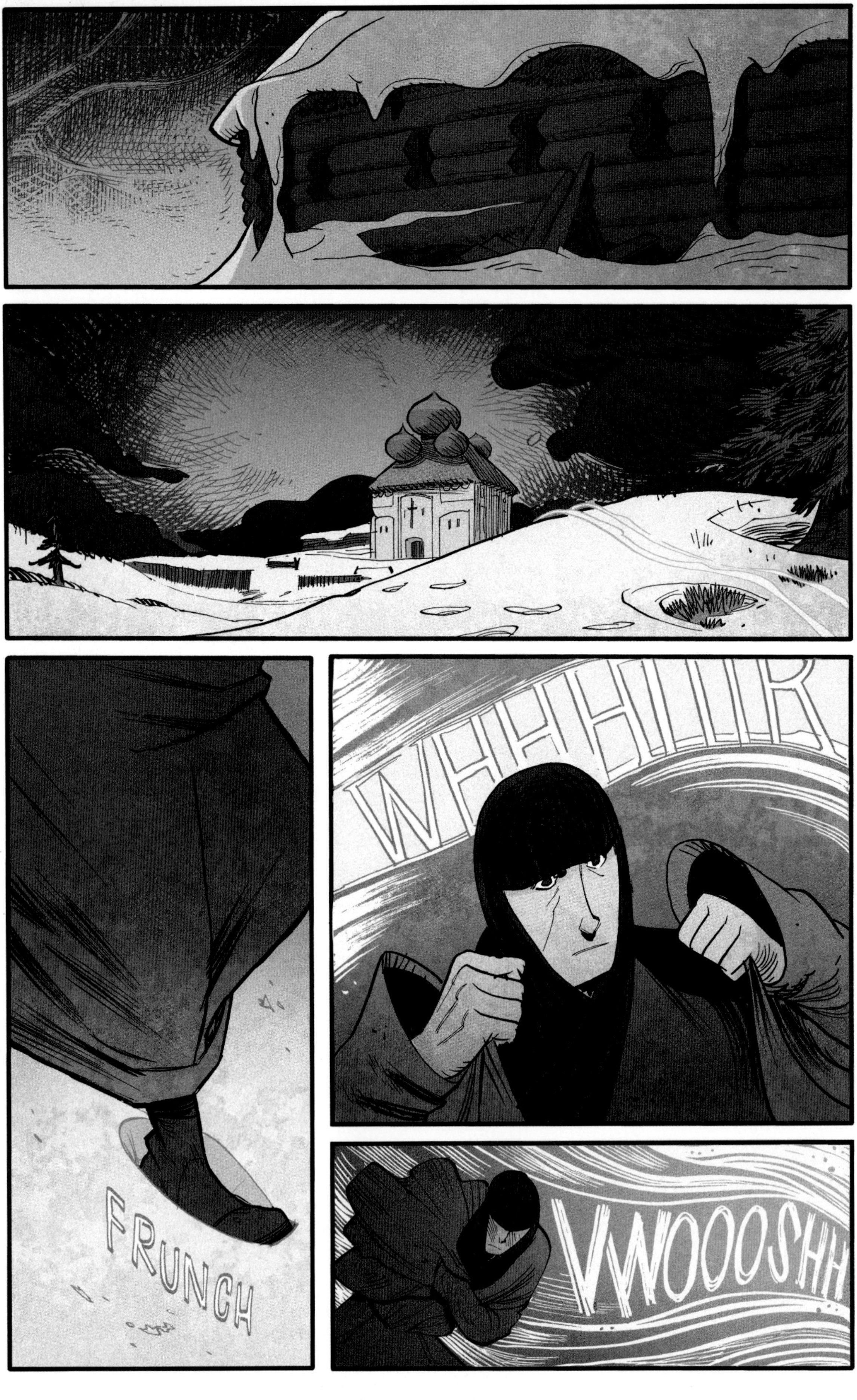
FRUNCH
WHHHUUR
VWOOOSHH

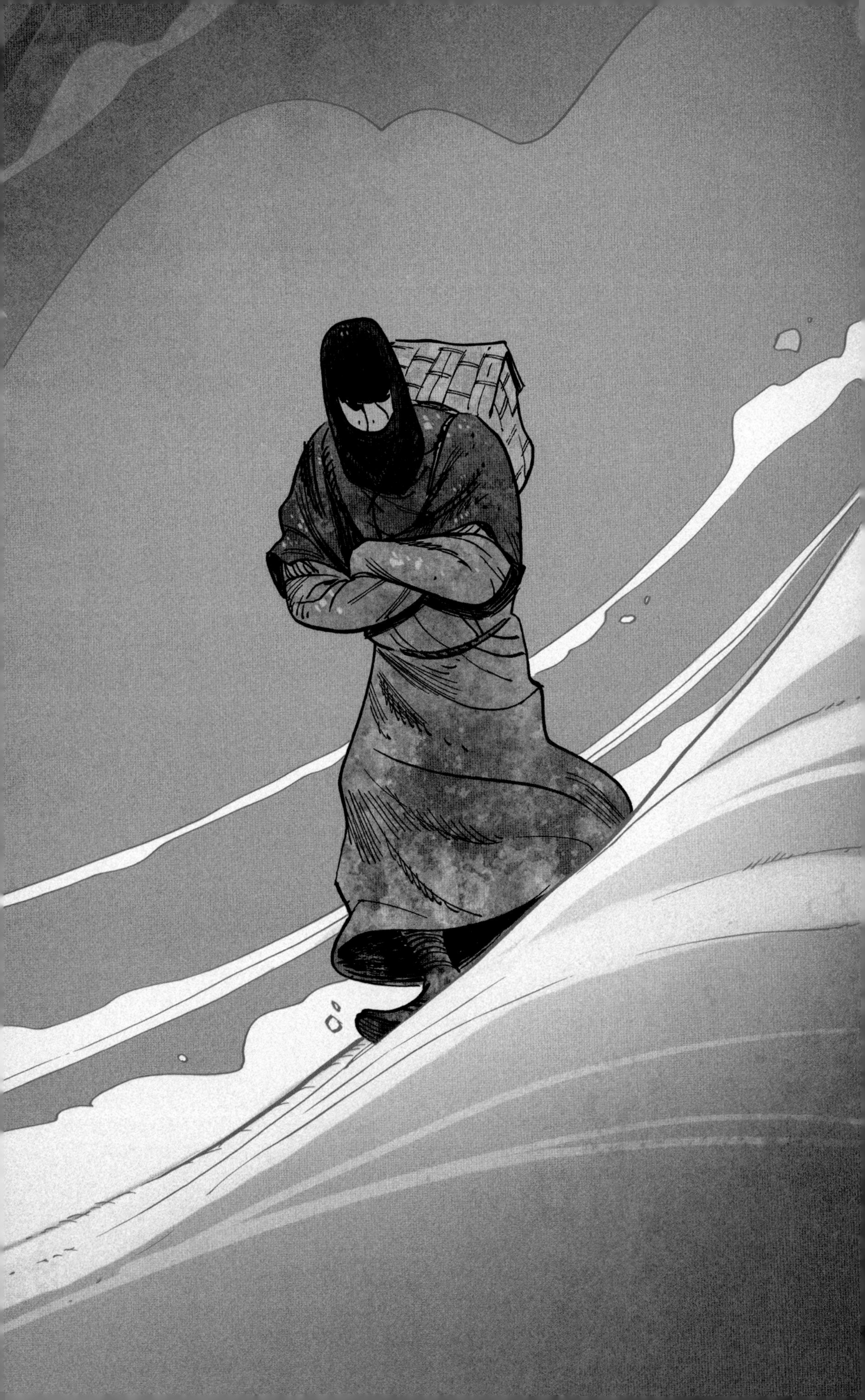

SPECIAL THANKS TO

RYAN OTTLEY AND JERZY DROZD, TWO FRIENDS THAT
HAVE ALSO BEEN MY COMIC BOOK MENTORS, ALAN TEW
FOR CONVINCING ME TO TELL THIS STORY, AND THE
REST OF THE DRAW NIGHT CREW FOR MAKING COMICS
WITH ME FOR THE PAST TEN YEARS, NOBROW AND BLUE
COPPER COFFEE FOR MAKING THE BEST COFFEE THAT I
CAN'T DRINK AND FOR BEING MY FAVORITE PLACE TO
MAKE COMICS, THE BROTHERS, MOM AND DAD, ERIC
STEPHENSON AND ALL THE STAFF AT IMAGE COMICS,

AND OF COURSE...

ANNIE.